Praise for Kristan Higgins's debut novel

Fools Rush In

"Where has Kristan Higgins been all my life?
Fools Rush In is a spectacular debut."
—*USA TODAY* bestselling author Elizabeth Bevarly

"Higgins reached deep into every woman's soul and
showed some heavy truths in a fantastically funny
and touching tale. This book is on my keeper shelf
and will remain there for eternity. It will be re-read
and loved for years to come."
—*Dee & dee Dish…About Books*

"A fresh intelligent voice—
Kristan Higgins is too much fun!"
—Cindy Gerard, *USA TODAY* bestselling author
of *To the Limit*

"Higgins is a talented writer
[who] will make you want to search high and low
for anything that she has written."
—*Chicklit Romance Writers*

"Outstanding! This is a story well worth reading."
—*Coffee Time Romance*

KRISTAN HIGGINS

Catch of the Day

HQN™

ISBN-13: 978-0-373-77224-7
ISBN-10:   0-373-77224-6

CATCH OF THE DAY

This edition published by arrangement with Harlequin Books S.A.

® and TM are trademarks of the publisher. Trademarks indicated with ® are registered in the United States Patent and Trademark Office, the Canadian Trade Marks Office and in other countries.

www.HQNBooks.com

Printed in U.S.A.

This book is dedicated to my sisters,
Hilary Murray and Jacqueline Decker.
You are my dearest friends,
and I love you more than I can say.

ACKNOWLEDGMENTS

Terence Keenan, my brave and handsome husband, is patient, tolerant, funny and oh, heck, just wonderful. Flannery and Declan Keenan are my favorite people in the world, and every day I'm quite thrilled to be their mommy.

Thanks to my mom, brother, smart and talented sisters, my lovely grandparents who always let me have two desserts, and the rest of my sprawling, boisterous family. On the business side, thanks to the world's best agent, Maria Carvainis, who is so wise and gentle with this middle child. Thanks to Abby Zidle for her excellent input and to Tracy Farrell and Keyren Gerlach for putting the final shine on the copy. Thanks also to Cris Jaw, Virginia MacDonald and Gigi Lau for my fantastic covers.

As ever, I am indebted to writer Rose Morris, my great friend from the Pine Tree State, whose input greatly improves everything I write. Brad and Mary Wilkinson helped me fall in love with Maine by taking me to Eggemoggin Reach for two summers, and I will ever be grateful that I got to share their home and their kids on that lovely, rocky shore. When I was seven, my beloved dad brought me to Ogunquit and talked a lobsterman into letting us check pots with him. The boat was called the *Ugly Anne.*

Catch of the Day

PROLOGUE

FALLING IN LOVE with a Catholic priest was not my smartest move.

Obviously, I'm well aware of the whole vow-of-chastity, married-to-the-church thing. I realize that yearning for a priest doesn't exactly further the cause of meeting my future husband. And in case I might have overlooked those little facts, I have an entire town pointing them out to me.

The problem is, even when someone is clearly wrong for you, he might seem…well, perfect. And aside from that one hulking detail, Father Tim O'Halloran is everything I've ever let myself dream of in a man. Kind, funny, charming, intelligent, hardworking. He likes the same movies I do. He loves my cooking. He compliments me often and laughs at my jokes. He cares about the people of my hometown, listens intently to their problems, offers gentle guidance when asked. And he's from Ireland, the icing on the cake, because ever since I was sixteen years old and first saw U2 in concert, I've had a thing for Irish guys. So even though Father Tim has never said or done anything vaguely improper, I can't help dreaming about what a great husband he'd make. I'm not really proud of this, but there it is.

My romantic problems predated Father Tim, though

he's probably the most colorful chapter in the joke book that makes up my love life. First off, it's not easy being a single woman in Gideon's Cove, Maine, population 1,407. Ostensibly there are enough males for females, but statistics can be misleading. Our town is in Washington County, the northernmost coastal county in our great state. We're too far from Bar Harbor to attract many tourists, although we do live in what is undeniably one of the most beautiful areas of America. Gray-shingled houses hug the harbor, and the air snaps with the smell of pine and salt. We're a pretty old-fashioned town—most people make their living either by fishing, lobstering or working in the blueberry industry. It's a lovely place, but it's remote, a good three hundred miles north of Boston. Five hundred from New York City. Meeting new people is difficult.

I try. I've always tried. There have been a few boyfriends, sure. I cheerfully accept fix-ups and blind dates when they're thrown my way, I do. I own and operate Joe's Diner, the only restaurant in town, so I have plenty of chances to meet people. And I volunteer—I volunteer my ass off, to be frank. I deliver meals to the infirm. I cook for the soup kitchen on Tuesday nights and bring whatever leftovers I have on an almost daily basis. I provide dinner at the fire department's monthly meeting. I organize clothing drives and fund-raisers and offer to cater just about any event for a minimal profit, as long as it's for a good cause. I am a pillar of society, and truthfully, I wouldn't have it any other way.

But in the back of my mind, there's a selfish motive. I can't help hoping that my good works and cheerful attitude will be noticed by someone…perhaps some rich and handsome grandson of the elderly man whose dinner I delivered, or some new-to-town volunteer fireman who just happens to be, oh I don't know, a board member of Oxfam and a brain surgeon, too.

However, the charitable neurosurgeon has proved elusive, and as of one year ago, when I was thirty-one years old, I remained single with no credible prospects on the horizon. That's when I met Father Tim.

I had gone for a bike ride out to Quoddy State Park. We were having a warm snap, for March, anyway—the temperature reached forty degrees, the snow had softened, the breeze was quiet. I'd spent most of the day cooped up inside, and a bike ride seemed like just the thing to do. Clad in layers of fleece and microfiber, I rode further than usual in the brisk air and fading sunlight of the afternoon. Then, with classic New England unpredictability, a drenching, icy rainstorm blew in from the west. I was a good ten miles from town when my bike wheel slid on some ice. I went ass over teakettle down an embankment, right into a wet patch of snow that concealed eight inches of mud and ice. Not only was I filthy, freezing and wet, I had also managed to cut my knee and tear my pants.

Feeling very sorry for myself, I hauled my bike up the bank at the exact moment a car went by. "Help! Stop!" I yelled, but whoever it was didn't hear me. Or heard me and was afraid, as I resembled an escaped lunatic at that moment. I watched the taillights of the blue Honda disappear in the distance, noting that the sky was suddenly much darker.

Well, I didn't have a choice. I started walking, gimping along on my cut leg, until a pickup pulled over. Before I could even tell who it was, the driver grabbed my bike and popped it in the bed of the truck. Squinting through the rain, I saw it was Malone, a silent, slightly scary lobsterman who moored next to my brother. He may have spoken—the words "Get in" ring a bell—so I gingerly crawled into the cab of his truck. In my mind, I could hear an imaginary narrator... *Maggie Beaumont was last seen riding her bike one dark and stormy afternoon. Her body was never found.*

To allay my nervousness, I talked maniacally until we reached Joe's Diner, reminding Malone that Jonah was my brother, that I was out for a bike ride (though that was rather obvious), that I should have listened to the forecast, that I fell (again, obvious), that I was sorry to make his truck dirty, et cetera, et cetera.

"Thank you very much, Malone, this was so nice of you," I babbled when he lifted down my bike. "You should come in and have a piece of pie sometime. It's good pie. Cup of coffee, too. On the house, okay? I owe you. Thanks again. This was great. Thanks. Bye now." Malone did not deign to speak, simply lifted his hand and drove away.

As I watched the taillights blur in the rain, I said a prayer. "God, I don't mean to complain, but I think I've been pretty patient here. All I want is a decent man who will stand by me and be a good father to our kids. What do You say?"

I remember all this because the very next day—*the very next day*—I came out of the kitchen of Joe's Diner, and there he was, sitting in the farthest booth, the most incredibly appealing man I'd ever seen. Medium height, light brown hair, green eyes, broad shoulders, beautiful hands. He wore a gorgeous Irish fisherman's sweater and jeans. When he smiled, my knees buckled at the glory of those straight, white teeth. A leaping thrill of attraction and hope shuddered through my entire body.

"Hi, I'm Maggie," I said, giving myself a quick, mental once-over. New jeans, that was good. Blue sweater, not bad. Hair, clean.

"Tim O'Halloran. A pleasure it is to meet you," he answered, and I nearly swooned. A brogue! How Liam Neeson! How Colin Farrell! How *Bono!*

"Would you like some coffee?" I asked, proud that my voice still worked.

"I'd love a spot. Can't think of anything nicer." He smiled right into my eyes. Blushing with pleasure, I looked out into the parking lot and saw the blue Honda. Dear God, it was the man who'd passed me!

"You know, I think I saw you last night!" I exclaimed. "Were you on Route 1A, heading for town around five? I fell off my bike, and I was trying to flag you down."

"I was," he answered, a concerned frown wrinkling his forehead. "How could I have missed you? Oh, dear, forgive me!"

Done. "Oh, gosh, don't worry." His eyes were beautiful, green and golden, like a bed of moss in the sunshine. Lust engulfed me like a thick fog. "Really. It's—don't—it's fine. So. What, um…what would you like for breakfast?"

"What do you recommend, Maggie?" he asked, and it sounded so damn sexy, that accent combined with what seemed to be a mischievous smile and flirting eyes…

"I recommend that you eat here often," I said. "I made the muffins myself, and they're just out of the oven. And our pancakes are the best in town." And the only in town, but hey.

"The pancakes it is, then, thanks." He smiled up at

me again, obviously in no hurry for me to leave. "So you work here, do you?"

"Actually, I own the place," I said, pleased to be able to impart this nugget. Not just a waitress, but the boss. The owner.

"Do you, now! Brilliant! A classic, isn't it?"

'Tis, I almost said. "Yes. Thank you. It's a family business. My grandfather, the *Joe* in Joe's Diner, started it up in 1933."

"Ah, that's lovely."

"So, Tim, what are you doing in Gideon's Cove?" I asked, then realized he might be hungry. "Wait, I'm sorry, let me just get your order in. Sorry. Be right back!"

I raced to the kitchen and called the order to Octavio, my short-order cook, then practically slid across the diner to Tim's table, ignoring three customers who were waiting at the counter with varying degrees of impatience.

"Sorry. You might actually want to eat, of course," I said.

"Well, now, there are some things that are nicer than eating, and talking to you is one of them."

Dear God, You're the best! Thanks for listening! "So, sorry, I was asking you what you were doing in town. Work related?"

"You might say that, Maggie. I'm—"

It was at this moment that the fatal event occurred. Georgie Culpepper, my dishwasher, burst into the diner. "Hi, Maggie!" he shouted. "Hi! How are you, Maggie! It's nice out today, isn't it, Maggie? I saw snowdrops this morning! You want me to wash dishes now, Maggie?" He wrapped his arms around me and hugged me.

Now, Georgie's hugs are usually very pleasant. I've been getting them since kindergarten. Georgie has Down syndrome, is wicked affectionate and endlessly cheerful, one of the nicest, happiest people I've ever met. But right at this moment, I didn't want his burr-like head welded to my breast. As I tried to extricate myself and as Georgie continued to tell me about the wonders of spring, Tim answered my question. I didn't hear him.

Finally, I pried Georgie off me and patted his shoulder. "Hello, Georgie. Tim, this is Georgie Culpepper, and he works here. Our bubble boy, right, buddy?" Georgie nodded proudly. "Georgie, this is Tim."

Georgie treated Tim to a hug, which was returned warmly. Lucky Georgie. "Hi, Tim! Nice to meet you, Tim! How are you, Tim?"

"I'm excellent, thank you, my friend."

I smiled even more…could there be a better character reference than someone who knew just how to treat Georgie Culpepper? I immediately added it to the already impressive mental list I had going on Tim O'Halloran: handsome, employed, charming, Irish, comfortable around disabled people.

"I bet Octavio will make you scrambled eggs," I told Georgie.

"Scrambled eggs! All right!" Though Georgie eats scrambled eggs every day of his life, the thrill has yet to fade. He scuttled to the kitchen and I remained, staring down at Tim. "Well. So. That sounds interesting," I said, hoping he'd reiterate what it was he did for a living. He didn't. The ding of the kitchen bell went off, and I excused myself, got Tim's pancakes and brought them over.

"Can I get you anything else?" The scowls of my regulars were starting to register.

"No, no, thank you ever so much, Maggie. It was a real pleasure meeting you."

Fearful that this was the last I'd ever see of him, I blurted, "Maybe I'll see you again sometime?" *Please, please don't say you're married.*

"I'm going back to Bangor, but on Saturday, I'll be here for good. Do you happen to belong to St. Mary's?" he asked, stabbing a huge forkful of golden pancakes.

"Yes!" I yelped. Any connection, no matter how thin…

"Then I'll see you Sunday." He smiled and took a bite, then closed his eyes in pleasure.

"Wonderful." My heart thumping, I went back to the counter and apologized to two of my regulars, Rolly and Ben.

Okay, so it was a little…devout…to mention where he went to church, but that was okay, I quickly assured myself. Perhaps the Irish were just more religious. But I was Catholic, technically anyway, and St. Mary's was indeed my home parish. The last time I'd been there was two years ago, when my sister Christy got married, but my lapsed state didn't matter. Tim O'Halloran was going to Mass, and so was I.

I called my sister the moment he left. "I think I've met someone," I whispered, massaging cocoa butter into my hands. As Christy's squeals of excitement pierced my ear, I told her all about Tim O'Halloran, how sweet he was, what a connection we had, how easily we'd chatted. I detailed every aspect of his physical appearance from his sparkling eyes to his beautiful hands, reiterated every word he spoke. "There was such chemistry," I finally sighed.

"Oh, Maggie. This is so exciting," my sister sighed back. "I'm thrilled for you."

"Listen, don't say anything to anyone yet, okay? Except Will."

"Of course not! No, no. It's just so wonderful!"

But Christy wasn't the one who blabbed all over town. No, no, I did that myself.

I didn't mean to, of course…it's just that I see a lot of people. Not only the regulars at the diner, not just the people I work with.

Mrs. Kandinsky, my tiny, frail tenant, whose toenails I trim each week, asked me if anything was new. "Well, not really. But I think I met someone," I found myself saying.

"Oh, *wonderful,* dear!" she chirped.

"He's so handsome, Mrs. K. Brown hair, green eyes…and he's Irish. He has a *brogue.*"

"I've always *loved* a man with a brogue," she agreed.

And then I told my mom's best friend, Carol.

"Do you think you'll ever meet someone?" she asked in her forthright way when she came in for pie.

"I may have already," I said with a mysterious smile. She blinked expectantly, and I was happy to gush.

And on it went.

On Saturday night, I went to Dewey's Pub, the only other restaurant in town, if you can call it that. Paul Dewey and I are pals, and occasionally I'll bring some food over, which he offers as daily specials and we split the profit. Otherwise, it's a bag of chips if you're looking for sustenance. But Dewey's does a booming business as the only alcohol-serving institution in town, unless you count the firehouse.

I was meeting my friend…well, a person I hang out

with sometimes. Chantal is close to forty and also single. Unlike me, she's quite happy to stay single, relishing her role as Gideon's Cove's sex symbol, a red-headed siren of lush curves and pouting lips. She enjoys the fact that every man under the age of ninety-seven finds her damn near irresistible, as opposed to me, who's everyone's surrogate daughter. Even though Chantal never lacks for male companionship, we occasionally get together to lament the dearth of really good men in town.

Having met someone so incredibly appropriate as Tim O'Halloran, I was bursting to tell her, and, I admit, to stake my claim. It certainly wouldn't do to have Chantal making a go for my future husband. "Chantal, I met someone," I announced firmly as we sipped our beers in the corner booth. "His name is Tim O'Hallo-ran, and he is so… Oh, my God, he's so yummy! We really hit it off."

As I spoke, my eyes scanned the bar. Tim had said he'd be back on Saturday, and here it was Saturday night, eight o'clock. The bar was moderately full. Jonah, my brother, stood at the bar with a couple of his pals—Stevie, Pete and Sam, all around Jonah's age (which is to say, far too young for me). There was Mickey Tatum, the fire chief, famous for terrifying the schoolchildren with stories of self-immolation (he shows pictures), and Peter Duchamps, the butcher, a married alcoholic thought to be having an affair with the new part-time librarian.

Also present was Malone, his face as cheerful as an open grave, who glared at me when he walked in as if daring me to mention the ride he'd given me. I dared not. Instead, I lifted my hand weakly, but his back was already turned. No wonder we all called him Maloner the Loner.

That was it. Gideon's Cove's offerings to a single girl. Obviously, I was beyond thrilled at meeting Tim.

Jonah, who never missed a chance to flirt with Chantal, drifted over. "Hey, girls," he said to Chantal's breasts, earning a smile from their owner. "What's cooking?"

"Your sister was just telling me about this hot guy she's met," Chantal said, dipping a finger into her beer and sucking on it. My brother, then aged twenty-five, was hypnotized. I sighed with irritation.

"What guy?" he managed to mumble.

So I told Jonah, too, my irritation vanishing with the chance to discuss the new man in my life.

We sat there till closing, but Tim never showed. Still, I was optimistic. He had said he'd see me in church, and see me he would.

The next morning, I spent an hour and a half getting ready. Because I'd told my parents, sister and brother about This Guy I'd Met, they were all coming to church, an activity our family usually saved for Christmas Eve (if we weren't too tired) and the occasional Easter weekend. In we went, Mom, Dad, Jonah, Will, Christy, then pregnant, and myself. Looking around, I noticed that the church was pretty full, more so than usual. Was it a holy day? I wasn't sure, never having cemented those in my mind. Oh, yes, I remembered hearing something at the diner…apparently, Father Morris retired and some new guy was filling in. Whatever.

I tried to scan casually for Tim, looking over my shoulder, pretending to fix the strap of my pocketbook, getting a tissue, adjusting my mom's collar. Any chance to glance back. Then the windy old organ started, and I fumbled for the hymnbook. So busy was I studying the pews that I ignored the priest as he walked past. "Do you see him?" I whispered to Christy.

"Yes," she whispered, her face a frozen mask of horror.

At that moment, the music ended, the church fell silent, and I reluctantly turned to face the priest.

"Before we start our celebration today," said a voice already imprinted on my brain, "I'd like to introduce myself. My name is Father Tim O'Halloran, and I'm very pleased to have been assigned to your lovely parish."

Roughly seventy-five faces swung around to look at me. I stared straight ahead, my heart pumping so hard I could hear the blood rushing through my veins. My face burned hot enough to fry an egg. I didn't look at anyone, just stared at Father Tim O'Halloran's chest area, and pretended to be fascinated and unsurprised. Tricky combination.

"I'm from Ireland, as you might be able to tell, the youngest of seven children. I'm looking forward to getting to know you all, and I hope I'll see you all at coffee hour after Mass. And now we begin today's celebration as we begin all things, in the name of the Father, and of the Son—"

"For God's sake," I muttered.

I didn't hear a word during the next hour. I do know that Christy slipped her hand into mine, and that my father was shushed repeatedly by my mother. Jonah, furthest from me, was laughing that awful, unstoppable church laugh full of wheezes and the occasional squeak, and if he'd been closer to me, maybe I would have laughed, too.

Or perhaps disemboweled him with my car keys. As it was, I pretended to listen, mouthed nonsensical words to songs I couldn't read and stood when everyone else stood. I stayed in the pew during communion.

And when at last Mass was over, we filed out with the others. Christy, my sister, my best friend, the person I loved more than anyone on earth, whispered in my ear. "I'm going to pretend we're talking about something really interesting, okay? And this way no one is going to talk to you. So smile and pretend we're having a conversation, and we'll get the hell out of here. Sound like a plan?"

"Christy, I'm so…" My voice broke.

"No, no, it's fine, just keep going. Too bad they're rebricking the side entrance. Shitty, shitty luck. Okay, we're getting close…can you smile?"

I bared my teeth weakly.

"Maggie!" Father Tim exclaimed. "It's so good to see you. I was hoping you'd be here." He shook my hand warmly, his grip strong and welcoming. "And you've a twin! Isn't that marvelous! I'm Father Tim, so nice to meet you."

Father Tim. The sound of it was like acid on an open wound.

"Hi, I'm Christy," my sister said. "I'm sorry, I'm not feeling well. Maggie, would you take me home?"

We almost escaped until my idiot brother, whom I heretofore loved, asked, "How could you miss the fact that he was a priest?"

My mother grabbed his arm. "Jonah, honey—"

"What's that, now?" Father Tim asked, his eyebrows raised.

"Why didn't you tell Maggie you were a priest?"

Father Tim glanced at me in confusion. "Of course I did. We had that lovely chat at the diner."

"Of course we chatted," I blurted. "Of course I knew! Sure! Yes! I knew you were a priest! Absolutely. Yup."

"But you said you met some hot Irish guy—"

"That was someone else," I ground out, ready to smite my little brother. "Not Father Tim! Jeez! He's a priest, Jonah! He's not—I didn't mean—he's…"

But the damage was done. Father Tim's expression fell. "Oh, dear," he said.

"Maggie? I need to go," Christy said. She grabbed my arm and pulled me away to the safety of her car.

But it was too late. Father Tim knew. Everyone knew.

FATHER TIM CAME TO the diner the next day and apologized, and I apologized, and we laughed about it. I found that there was no use in trying to pretend. I just had to admit that I made a mistake. *Ha, ha, pretty funny, isn't it? I can't believe I missed* that *little piece of information! Ho, ho!* Then he asked if I'd be on one of his committees, and I found myself unable to say no.

In the year that's passed, the sting of being the butt of a joke has faded. Truthfully, Father Tim is a great friend to me. Though I can't quite bring myself to go to Mass and see him in action, I somehow joined just about every committee St. Mary's has—bereavement, altar decoration, Christmas craft sale, community outreach, building maintenance, fellowship, the works.

I know it's wrong to nurse a crush on a priest. I know I shouldn't be doing all that church stuff just to be near a Catholic priest who looks like Aidan Quinn's younger brother. I know that my heart shouldn't squeeze every time I see him, that adrenaline shouldn't spurt into my veins when I pick up the phone and hear that gentle voice. I just can't seem to help it. What I really need to do is simply meet someone else, and this foolish longing in my heart will fade. Someday, I'll meet a really great guy, someone just as nice as Tim O'Halloran, and everything will be just lovely.

There are definitely days when I believe this.

CHAPTER ONE

"GOOD MORNIN', MAGGIE," Father Tim says, sliding into his usual booth. "Lovely out, isn't it?" He smiles pleasantly, and my insides clench.

"Good morning, Father Tim. What can I get for you today?"

"I think I'll be tryin' your French toast, shall I? Brilliant idea, the almond glaze."

That brogue is just not fair. "Thanks. I'll get that right in." *I've had sinful thoughts about you. Again.* I wrack my brain for something to say. "How was Mass this morning?"

He nods. "Ah, the celebration of the Eucharist always nurtures the spirit," he murmurs. "You're welcome to come and see for yourself, Maggie. I'd love to hear your thoughts on my homily any time."

Father Tim often urges me to drop by. Something stops me. Guilt, no doubt. I might be a lapsed Catholic, but I draw the line at having lustful thoughts about priests in church. "Well. Sure. One of these days. You bet."

"Mass can give a person a chance for some insight. Sometimes we tend to overlook what's important in life, Maggie. It's easy to lose perspective, if you take my meaning."

Oh, I do. Losing perspective is something at which I excel. Case in point—still in love with the priest. He looks ridiculously appealing in black, though granted, the white collar takes away some of the zing. Rolling my eyes at my own ridiculous thoughts, I turn away, fill a few coffee cups and slip into the kitchen, where Octavio is deftly flipping pancakes. "French toast for Father Tim," I tell him, grabbing an order of eggs on unbuttered toast. Returning to the counter area, I slide the plate in front of Stuart, one of my regulars. "Chicks on a raft, high and dry," I say. He nods appreciatively, a big fan of diner slang.

"Anything else for you, Mrs. Jensen?" I ask the seventy-year-old woman in the first booth. She frowns and shakes her head, and I leave her check on the table. Mrs. Jensen has come from church. She goes to confession every week. She's in Bible study and on the altar decoration committee. It seems I'm not the only one smitten with Father Tim.

Without meaning to, I look once again at the impossible ideal. He's reading the paper. Profiled against the window, his beauty sends a rolling warmth through me. *If only you were a regular guy....*

"He'll catch you looking," Rolly whispers, another regular fixture at my counter.

"That's okay," I admit. "It's not like it's a secret. Make sure you fill out a ballot, okay?" I tell Rolly, dragging my gaze off the object of my desire. "You, too, Stuart. I need all the votes I can get."

"Ayuh. Best coffee in the state," Rolly announces.

"Best breakfast, Rolly." I smile and pat his shoulder.

For the last two years, Joe's Diner has placed fourth in *Maine Living*'s Best Breakfast contest, and I'm determined to win the county title this year. The magazine holds a lot of sway with tourists, and we could use a little more of the summer nuisance. Last year, we were creamed by Blackstone Bed & Breakfast in Calais (even though they make their pancakes from a box mix).

"We'll win, boss," Octavio calls through the window that links the counter area with the kitchen. "We do have the best breakfast."

I smile back at him. "True enough, but being the best-kept secret on coastal Maine isn't doing us much good financially."

"We'll be fine," he assures me. Easy for him to say. He makes more than I do, and he doesn't have to balance the books every month.

"Hey, Maggie, as long as you're up, can I get a refill?" asks Judy, my waitress. I oblige, then bring Father Tim his breakfast, sneak a glance at his smooth, elegant hands and scurry off to clear a table.

For the last eight years, I've run Joe's Diner, taking it over from Jonah Gray, my grandfather, after he had a heart attack. The diner is one of the larger employers in our tiny town, having four people on the payroll. Octavio is the most irreplaceable, running the kitchen with tireless efficiency. Judy came with the diner. She's somewhere between sixty and one hundred and twenty, gifted at not working, though when pressed, she can handle a full diner, not that we get that a lot. Georgie gets some help in the summer, when we hire a high school kid to deal with the light tourist business that makes it this far north.

And there's me, of course. I cook the daily specials, do all the baking, wait tables, balance the books, maintain the inventory and keep the place clean. Our final, though unofficial, employee is Colonel. My dog. My buddy. My precious boy. "Who's your mommy?" I ask him. "Huh, Colonel McKissy? Who loves you, pretty boy?" His tail thumps at my idiot talk, but he knows not to leave his place behind the register. A Golden Retriever takes up a lot of room, but most people don't even see Colonel, who has nicer manners than the queen of England. At thirteen, he's mellow, but he's always been incredibly well-behaved. I give him a piece of bacon and get back to work.

Father Tim rises to settle his check. "Hello, Gwen, love, how are you today? Don't you look smart in that lovely shade of yellow," he says to Mrs. Jensen, who simpers in pleasure. He smiles at me, and my knees soften. "I'll see you both tonight, won't I?"

"That's right," I answer. I may not be able to bring myself to Mass, but Father Tim has worn me down for Bible study. I stifle the urge to shake my head at myself. Bible study. My social plans for the week. Well, it's not like I'm turning away dozens of suitors. Sadly, Father Tim is closer to a boyfriend than anything I've had in some time.

"Nancy Ringley's bringing the snack?" Father Tim frowns.

"No," I smile. "I am. Her daughter's under the weather, so she called me."

His face lights up. "Ah, wonderful! About the snack, at any rate. Not her dear little daughter. I'll see you later, then, Maggie." He pats my shoulder with avuncular affection, causing lust and exhilaration to flow down my arm, and turns for the door. *I love you,* I mouth. I can't help myself.

Did he hear me? My face flushes in mortification as

Father Tim glances back at me with a smile and a wink before going out into the cold. He waves as he crosses the street, ever kind where I'm concerned. Mrs. Jensen, who is not so tolerant, glares at me. I narrow my eyes in return. She doesn't fool me. We suffer from the same disease—I'm just a little more obvious.

It's a frigid March day, the wind howling off the water, slicing through the thickest wool hats and microfiber gloves. Only a few brave souls venture out, and the day drags. We don't get more than a handful of people at lunch. I wait for Judy to finish her crossword puzzle before sending her home, as she's really only here for show, anyway. Octavio takes off his apron as I scrape the grill.

"Tavy, take the rest of the pie, okay? Your kids will like it," I tell him. He has five children.

"They will if they get to taste it. I already had two pieces." Octavio grins his engaging gap-tooth smile.

I grin back. "Did Judy get any more ballots?"

"I think she gave out a few."

"Great." I've been relentless in asking my patrons to fill them out. Last year we lost by two hundred votes, so I need every one who crosses the threshold to pitch in. "Have a nice afternoon, Octavio," I say.

"You, too, boss."

"Here, take these cookies, too." My cook grins his thanks, then goes out the back door.

Colonel knows what time it is. He gets up from his spot and comes over to me for a little pat, pushing his big head against my thighs. I stroke his white cheeks. "You're such a good boy, aren't you?" He wags in agreement, then returns to his spot, knowing I'll be a while yet.

I flip the Open sign to Closed and wipe down the last table. This is one of my favorite times of day… three o'clock. We're done for the day. Joe's opens at six, though I usually don't roll in until seven (the joys of ownership), but I make up my time by doing all the baking each afternoon. I'm proud to say that Joe's desserts are locally famous, especially the pies and coconut macaroons.

Joe's is a Jerry Mahoney design. Red-and-cream porcelain with stainless steel siding on the outside, red vinyl seats, cream-colored walls and a black-and-white tile floor on the inside. Ten swivel stools are bolted to the floor at the counter. At one end is the requisite pastry display case where my sweets tempt the patrons. There are seven booths with nice deep backs and seats that are just bouncy enough. At some point, my grandfather had those little jukeboxes installed and, as kids, we loved flipping through to see what the new selections were. The kitchen is through a swinging door with a porthole, and there's a tiny supply room and unisex bathroom. In the corner window, a neon sign blinks those timeless words, Eat at Joe's.

For the next half hour, I add up the receipts, check the inventory, print out more ballots and mop the floor. I play the jukeboxes as I work, singing along with Aretha and the Boss. Finally, I go back into the kitchen and start baking the desserts for tomorrow. And the snack for tonight.

Since Father Tim's face brightened when he heard I was on snack duty, I decide to do something special. In the tiny kitchen, I take out the necessary ingredients and set about making apricot squares, one of his favorites. Once those are in the oven, I roll out a few pie crusts and throw together a couple of blueberry pies.

Colonel's tail starts thumping, and I hear him scramble to get up off the tile floor. I reduce the heat on the pies and move them to a higher shelf so the bottom crusts won't burn. Without checking, I know my sister is about to come in.

I'm right, as I usually am about Christy. She's just pulling the baby stroller in through the door. We haven't seen each other for three entire days, which is a long spell when it comes to us. "Hey, Christy," I smile, holding the door for her.

"Hey, Mags," she answers. She glances at me, then does a double take. "Oh, for God's sake." She wrestles the carriage the rest of the way in, Violet sleeping undisturbed, and pulls off her hat. "Me, too."

My mouth drops open. "Christy!" We start laughing simultaneously, reaching for each other's hands at the same moment.

Christy and I are identical twins. And we are quite identical still, though Christy had a baby eight months ago. We weigh exactly the same, have the same bra size, shoe size, pants size. We each have a mole on our left cheeks. We both have a slightly crooked pinky on our right hands. Though Christy dresses a little better than I do, most people can't tell us apart. In fact, only Will, Christy's husband, has never once confused us. Even our parents goof once in a while, and, Jonah, who is younger by eight years, doesn't try awfully hard to distinguish us.

We often call each other only to get a busy signal because the other had the same thought at the same moment. Sometimes we get each other the same birthday card or pick out the same sweater from the L.L. Bean catalog. If I buy tulips for my kitchen table, it's a good bet that Christy has done the same thing.

But once in a while, in order to create some sense of individuality, one of us will get the urge to try something new. And so, on Monday when the diner was closed, I went to Jonesport and got my hair layered a little, had a few highlights put in. Apparently Christy had the same thought. Once more, we are identical.

"When did you get yours done?" I ask.

"Yesterday. You?" She smiles as she reaches out to touch my new 'do.

"Monday, so the haircut is really mine." I grin as I say it. I don't mind. In fact, I've always kind of liked being mistaken for Christy. "I wear mine in a ponytail most of the time, anyway," I say. "Plus, you have better clothes."

"Unstained, anyway," she smiles, sitting at the counter. She takes off her coat and drapes it over the next stool. I go over to the stroller, which is one of those complicated Swedish affairs with everything from a wind guard to a cappuccino maker, and twist my head inside. Stretching my lips, I can just about kiss my sleeping niece. "Hello, angel," I whisper, worshiping her perfect skin and feathery eyelashes. "God, Christy, she gets more beautiful every day."

"I know," Christy answers smugly. "So what's new?"

"Oh, not much. Father Tim was in. I think he may have heard me tell him I love him."

"Oh, Maggie." Christy chuckles sympathetically. She knows better than to spout the platitudes that everyone else does… *Why are you wasting your time on a priest? Can't you find somebody else? You really should meet someone, Maggie. Have you tried the Internet/volunteering/church/dating services/speed dating/singles clubs/singles nights/singles cruises/pros-*

titution? (This last one was suggested by my brother's friend Stevie, who has been hitting on me since he was twelve years old.)

I've tried volunteering. And church, of course, contains the root of my problem. But singles nights and those speed dating things…well, first of all, we don't have much of that in rural Maine. The nearest big city is Bar Harbor, and that's at least an hour and a half south, if the weather is clear. As for the Internet, those services smack of deceit. A person could say anything, after all. What better way to lie about yourself? How many stories have I heard about a person being sorely disappointed by his or her Internet date? So, while there may be merit in that venue, I've never tried it.

Christy knows. She's suffered with me as much as a happily married person can suffer. She had no problem meeting Will, her lovely, nice-looking and yes, doctor husband. They live in a restored Victorian that was built by a sea captain. They have a beautiful view of the water. They go out to dinner in Machias once a week, and I babysit (for free, of course). And while I don't begrudge Christy all the nice things she's got, it does seem a little unfair. After all, we are genetically identical. She has hit Lotto in life; I've got a crush on the priest.

"Want to come for dinner tonight, see if we can fool Will?" she says, toying with the ends of her newly cut hair.

"Sure," I say. "The pies will be out pretty soon. Want me to bring one?"

"No, that's okay. We'll cook for you, hon. Oh, and I picked this up for you when I was in Machias." She fishes a little bottle from her purse. "Got it at a little shop that sells all sorts of neat stuff, earrings and scarves and little soaps. It's got beeswax in it."

One of the byproducts of living in northern coastal Maine and owning a diner—and hence, having my hands in water or near hot oil all the time—is that my hands are horribly chapped. Thickened from work, nails cut short, rough cuticles and red patches of eczema, my hands are my worst feature. I wage a constant quest to find a hand cream that will really help them look and feel nicer, sampling every product under the sun with little or no effect.

"Thanks, Christy." I try some. "It smells lovely. Is that lavender?" I can already tell that it's too light-weight for me.

"Mmm-hmm. Hope it helps."

An hour later, we're at Christy's. A roast is in the oven, and I'm entertaining Violet by dangling some measuring spoons in front of her face. She bats at them, cooing and drooling, and I kiss her hair. "Can you say spoons, Violet?" I ask. "Spoons?"

"Bwee," she answers.

"Very good!" Christy and I chorus. The baby smiles, flashing her two teeth, and another waterfall of drool pours out of her rosebud mouth onto my lap.

We hear Will's car pull into the garage. "Oh, he's home," Christy says. "Quick, give me the baby. I'll go in the living room and you stand at the stove. Here, put on my apron." Giggling, she flings it to me, grabs the baby and scampers off.

For a brief second, I stand at the stove and let myself imagine that it's my home, my husband, my baby, my roast. That a man who loves me is hurrying in to kiss me, that the beautiful baby will call me Mommy. That this warm and lovely kitchen is a place I've decorated, the place where my family feels closest, laughs the most.

Will opens the door that joins the kitchen with the garage. My back is to him. "Hey, Maggie. Your hair looks pretty, too." Laughing, he kisses my cheek. "Still trying to fool me?"

Christy appears, her cheeks bright. "We had to try," she says. "Hi, babe." They kiss, and Violet reaches a chubby hand to caress her father's face. I stir the gravy, smiling. I can envy my sister and rejoice for her, too. The two aren't mutually exclusive.

"So how was work, Doctor?" I ask. Will is one of two town doctors and sees just about everyone in Gideon's Cove. He hired my mother as his part-time secretary, cementing the idea that Will Jones is a saint.

"It was great," he says, taking his daughter from Christy. "Daddy was just saving lives, healing wounded bodies, soothing broken spirits, the usual."

"Does that mean no one barfed on you today?" my sister quips.

"How about you, Maggie?" Will asks. "Anything new?"

How I hate that question, second in loathing only to *Seeing anyone?* "No, not really," I say. "Not that I can think of, anyway. But everything is great. Just fine. Thanks, Will."

"Hey, hon," Christy says, "remember you mentioned that guy at the hospital? You said you'd try to fix Maggie up with him?"

Will opens the fridge and pulls out three beers. "Right. Yeah. Roger Martin. Nice guy, Mags. He's a nurse. What do you say? Want to be fixed up?"

"Sure," I say, taking a long pull on my beer to cover my embarrassment. It still bothers me that I must rely on the kindness of others to get a date. However, I'm thirty-two years old. Time's a-wastin'. "But, you know, only if he is interested. And if he's nice. Is he nice?"

"Of course he's nice!" Christy exclaims, not that she's met him. "You said he was kind of cute, right, Will?"

"Yeah, I guess. But you know, I'm straight, so I couldn't really say, Mrs. Jones." He breaks into the song they danced to at their wedding two years ago. "'Mrs… Mrs…Mrs…Mrs. Jo-ones. We've got a thing going on….'"

"Please stop, you're scaring the baby," Christy says, her cheeks rosy with pleasure.

I love my sister with all my heart. Violet is the joy of my life, and Will is one of the best people I've ever met, one of the few who might deserve my twin. But tonight, it's hard to be with them, as much as Christy and Will genuinely welcome me into their home. The fact remains that I'm a visitor, and I want what they have. The inside jokes, the unconscious affection, the nick-names.

Christy senses this. After the dinner dishes are done, she walks me to the door. "You want a ride?" she asks.

"No, no. That's—it's great out. Great night for a walk." *Great* in March on the northern coast of Maine is a bit of a stretch, but I could do with a walk. I wrap my scarf around my neck, pull my hat over my ears and call to Colonel, who has been enjoying the bone Will sneaked him.

"You'll find someone," my sister whispers, hugging me. "You will."

"Sure! I know. Just a matter of time. Or maybe we could clone Will." I smile and hug her back. "Thanks for dinner, Christy. Love you." I walk down the steps, holding Colonel's collar so he won't fall. His hips are a little arthritic, and stairs can be tricky for him.

"Love you, too," she calls.

I have just enough time to go home, help Colonel up my own stairs, get him settled, go back to the diner, pick up the apricot squares and walk to the rectory. There are five other people there already, all women, all half in love with Father Tim, though not to the degree or with the public scrutiny that I myself suffer.

"Maggie!" Father Tim exclaims. He walks over to me, and I can smell the soap he uses. His radiant smile makes my cheeks burn. "There you are! And what have we here? Ah, now, Maggie, you'd tempt a saint." Mrs. Plutarski, St. Mary's gorgon secretary, frowns. Of course, Father Tim is talking about my baking, not my feminine charms. Crooning softly over the dessert, he puts the tray on a sideboard. His ass is a work of art. *These sinful thoughts are getting you nowhere, Maggie,* I inform myself sternly. But yes, it *is* a work of art.

"Now, then, ladies, I believe we were going to discuss this lovely passage from the Book of Wisdom, weren't we? Mabel, love, why don't you get us started and read verses five through eleven?"

For the next hour, I stare at Father Tim, drinking in his expressive eyes, compassionate and perfect smile, his lilting accent. My feelings flit between lust for him and annoyance with myself. *If only I could meet someone else. If only I could get over Father Tim. Better yet, if only he were Episcopalian! Then we could get married and live here in this cozy home with our beau-*

tiful, green-eyed children. Liam, maybe, and Colleen. A new baby is on the way. We're considering Conor for a boy, Fiona for a girl.

"Maggie, what do you think? Do you agree with Louise?" Father Tim asks expectantly.

"Yes! Yes, I do. Mmm-hmm. Good point, Louise." I have no idea what she just said. I vaguely remember something about light…but no, there's nothing there. Mrs. Plutarski snorts.

Father Tim winks at me. He knows. I feel my cheeks grow warm. Again.

When Bible study is over—not that I've become educated, enriched or spiritually moved, mind you—I feel the uncharacteristic desire to leave. The others have already congregated around the sideboard, pouring coffee and falling onto my pretty squares.

"I've got to go, folks," I say, waving. "Sorry. Enjoy the snack."

"Thanks, Maggie," Father Tim says around a mouthful. "I'll just drop the tray off at the diner, shall I?"

"That would be great."

He waves as he reaches for another square, and I smile fondly, happy to have pleased him. Then I head home, glad that Colonel, at least, is waiting for me.

CHAPTER TWO

ON FRIDAY AFTERNOON, I leave the diner, all the goodies ready for baking tomorrow, and head for home. There's a bounce in my step. Will, best brother-in-law in the world, has come through. I have a date.

It's been a long time. Quite a while. I wrack my brain, trying to remember the last actual date I had, and come up empty. Before Father Tim came to town, that's for sure.

Oh, well, it doesn't matter. I pat Colonel for reassurance and pull my coat a little closer. Tonight I have a date, and I'm going to enjoy it. A nice dinner and some company, the buzz of potential. I turn at my street and make my way to the small house I bought a few years ago. On the first floor lives Mrs. Kandinsky, my tenant. She is ninety-one years old, a lovely, tiny bird of a woman who knits me sweaters and hats with amazing speed, given that her hands curl in on themselves with arthritis.

I knock on Mrs. K.'s door and wait. It takes her a while to get up sometimes. Finally, the door opens a suspicious crack. Then she sees that it's just me. "Hello, dear!" she chirps.

"Hello, Mrs. K.!" I chirp back, leaning down a foot or so to kiss her silky, wrinkled cheek. "I brought you some meat loaf. All the fixings, too."

"Oh, Maggie, how *nice!* I didn't know *what* I was going to cook for dinner! And now I don't *have* to! You're an angel, you *are.* Come in, come *in.*" Her emphatic way of talking makes it sound a bit like she's singing, and I find myself unconsciously imitating her after a few minutes in her company.

Although I don't have to leave for a couple of hours, I want to go upstairs and enjoy the rare feeling of date anticipation. But Mrs. K. is so sweet, and many days, I'm the only person she sees. Her aging children live out of state, and most of her friends are long gone. I usually bring her a meal from the diner for both unselfish and selfish reasons—I don't want her burning my house down, trying to cook. So she gets plenty of blueberry scones and muffins and pot roast, or cheddar mac and cheese or whatever else I've made that day.

We go into her living room, which is crowded with overstuffed furniture, magazines and a small television. She's tapped into my satellite dish and is currently watching a soccer match between Italy and Russia. The smell of old person, close and medicinal and oddly comforting, tickles my throat.

"I can't stay, Mrs. K.," I tell her. "I actually have a date tonight." There I go again, blurting out my news. At least this time I know the guy isn't a priest.

"How *lovely,* dear! I *remember* when Mr. Kandinsky *courted* me. My father didn't *approve,* you know," she said.

I do know. I've heard this story dozens of times. To remind her of this fact, I say, "Right. He used to show Mr. K. his *gun* collection, didn't he?"

"My *father* used to show Walter his *gun* collection while he *waited* for me! Can you *imagine!*" Her wizened face wrinkles even more as she laughs, a lovely, tinkling sound.

"Well, Mr. K. must have loved you very much, if he stood for that," I tell her, smiling.

"Oh, yes. He *did*. Would you like me to *warm up* some meat loaf for you, *too,* Maggie dear?"

I lean down again and kiss her cheek. "No, I have a date, remember? But I'll warm it up for you." I tuck the dish into the microwave and press the buttons. Mrs. K. often forgets how to use the microwave, though I sometimes smell popcorn late at night. I guess she figures it out for important things. On the counter is a bottle of Eucerin Dry Skin Therapy Plus Intensive Repair Hand Crème. "Mrs. K., is it all right if I try your hand cream?" I ask.

"Of *course!* My mother always *said,* you can judge a *lady* by her *hands.*"

"I hope not," I mutter, attacking a cracked spot near my thumb.

Ten minutes later, I go upstairs to my apartment. Colonel seems stiffer than usual, and I have to boost him up the last few steps. "Here you go, big guy," I tell him, fixing his supper. I press a glucosamine pill and some doggy anti-inflammatories into a spoonful of peanut butter and turn to him. "Peanut butter blob!" I announce. He wags happily as he laps his medicine off the spoon. "Good boy. And here's your supper, Mr. Handsome." Given the state of his hips, I don't make him sit first.

Responsibilities finished, I take a minute to flop into my chair and relax. My apartment is small—a minute kitchen, living room, tiny bedroom and fairy-sized bathroom that barely has enough room for me to stand. But I love it. A seaman's chest, filled with afghans from

Mrs. Kandinsky, serves as a coffee table. Pictures of Violet decorate the fridge, and some African violets, in honor of my niece, blossom on the windowsill. Little collections of matchstick boxes and animal-shaped salt and pepper shakers line a shelf that my father and I put up a few years ago. Some old tin pie plates hang on the wall, and instead of hooks, I use old porcelain or glass doorknobs to hang my coats. Six or seven decorative birdhouses hang on the wall, gifts from my dad, who makes them almost as fast as Mrs. K. crochets afghans.

Well. Time to get ready for my date! I've already planned what to wear—black pants, red sweater and a nice pair of suede shoes to slip on at the restaurant. The ice, salt and mud between my apartment and my car would ruin anything other than my faithful L. L. Bean boots in a matter of one step. I shower, dry my hair and take care of my face, then take a look in the mirror, pleased. I don't often wear my hair down, but it looks pretty and soft, thanks to the new cut and color. My gray eyes look bigger with makeup, and the blush I applied does wonders for my pale skin. I put on a necklace, give my dog a rawhide chew stick and leave.

Roger Martin, the nurse with whom I am having dinner, called me three days ago at Will's urging. He sounded pleasant, though we didn't talk too much. We agreed to meet at The Loon, a nice restaurant in Machias that Christy and Will frequent. Why he needs to be fixed up is a bit of a mystery—but then again, *I* need to be fixed up, so I try to reserve judgment.

It takes a while to get to the restaurant from Gideon's Cove, as the roads are narrow and twisting out of our little peninsula. I don't mind; I hum along with the one radio station I pick up as I drive. I don't leave town too often, to tell the truth, and I usually walk around town or ride my bike. My car, a Subaru station wagon, is good for loading up at the Wal-Mart in Calais when I need stuff for the diner—gallons of Windex and bleach, trash bags, flour—but for day-to-day, I prefer human-powered transportation.

I pass the University of Maine campus and continue through town. The restaurant is a cheerful, timber-beam place with fairy lights strewn on the bushes outside. It's lovely inside as well, wide-planked floors, candles twinkling, white tablecloths, a piano in one corner. I ask the maître d' if Roger is here and am led to a table. Sure enough, there he is, studying the menu. The unfamiliar, nervous thrill of meeting someone new washes over me.

"Hi, Maggie, I'm Roger," he says, standing to shake my hand. He is somewhat average-looking; neither handsome nor homely, medium height, just a little chubby. His eyes are blue, his hair brown and receding.

"Hi. Hi there. I'm Maggie. How are you? This is a nice place, isn't it? It's very cute. My sister says they have great food." I cringe inwardly, blushing. Really should get that babbling tendency looked at.

Roger smiles. "Have a seat."

I sit and settle my bag at my feet, then fiddle with the silverware. "So," I say. "This is nice. Thank you for coming, too. I mean, for, well…oh, shit, I'm sorry." I laugh nervously. "I don't go out much." *Stop talking. Stop. Talking.* "On blind dates, I mean. I'm a little nervous, I guess. But you seem nice. And you have a good job, nothing scary, just nursing. So, you know. So far, so good."

Jesus, listen to me. I sound like a chimpanzee on

speed. Roger looks on. "Uh, would you like a drink?" he asks.

Alcohol exacerbates my tendency to blather, so I should definitely refuse. "I'll have a glass of chardonnay," I tell the waiter. Clamping my lips shut, I force myself to wait for Roger to speak.

"Will is married to your sister, right?" he asks.

"Yes." *Good job, Maggie!*

"And am I correct in thinking that you guys are twins?"

"Yes."

"Identical, right?"

"Yes."

His eyebrows rise slightly. Perhaps now is not the time to shut up, after all. "Yes, uh-huh. We're twins. Identical twins, you're right. She's older by two minutes, but I like to say that Mom loves me best because I weighed less. Christy was nine pounds. Came out of Mom like a bullet. Caused some pretty nasty tearing."

No wonder I'm still single.

"I see," says Roger. His smile has faded.

I turn my burning face to the menu. *Relax,* I tell myself. *This is not a game show. You have nothing to lose. He likes you or he doesn't. You like him or you don't. Calm yourself.*

The waiter comes and we order dinner. I'm careful to choose a dish that's neither the cheapest nor the most expensive. I take another sip of wine. "So, Roger, do you like being a nurse?" I ask. *That's more like it, Mags.*

"Yeah, I sure do." He tells me a little about his work, the hospital. And here's the thing. He's not right for me. He's a little dull…instead of talking about the patients and doctors and that sort of human interest thing, he's off on a tangent about overtime and benefits and his 401K. *Give him a chance,* I can hear my sister saying. I try.

Our dinners come. Unlike me, Roger has had no compunction about ordering the most expensive item on the menu. The waiter puts down an enormous lobster, red and steaming, and proceeds to tie a bib around Roger's neck, making him look like a giant toddler. The lobster must weigh four or five pounds, making it a sumo wrestler among its peers. Roger rips off a claw with gladiator-esque machismo and vanquishes it with the provided nutcracker.

"So you're a chef, Maggie?" he asks. He twists his fork into the claw and wrestles out a huge piece of meat, dunks it in butter and shoves it in his mouth. Butter and lobster juice run down his chin, but he takes his time wiping. The odds that I will love this man for the rest of my life are rapidly waning.

"Oh, no, no. Not a chef. I own Joe's Diner in Gideon's Cove. I cook, but I'm not a chef. Big difference." I can't take my eyes off his greasy, glistening mouth.

"What's the difference?" he asks. Crack. Peel. Another crack. It's like watching Vlad the Impaler conduct an autopsy.

"Um…well, a chef is…has more…uh, training, I guess…" Rip. Dunk. Chew. Slobber. "Um, here, you have some butter on your chin." I smile weakly and gesture with my own napkin.

"There'll be more before dinner is through." He smiles, and I can see the creamy pink lobster meat bulging in his cheek. My own baked scrod sits cooling before me. Unable to look away from my dinner companion, I watch as he rips off a smaller leg and chews it in horrifyingly delicate nibbles, working the lobster meat up with his teeth, sucking, slurping. A sudden vision of sex with Roger deals my appetite the death blow.

"Don't you like your dinner?" he asks, drowning another lobster chunk. "Hey, can I have some more butter, please?" he asks a passing busboy.

"Oh, it's good. No, no. Good. Yummy. I like it." I take a forkful and chew listlessly. Perhaps I'll become a vegetarian.

I am at a loss for words—a rarity, I assure you—but Roger, drunk with the hedonistic devouring of the poor crustacean, doesn't notice. And it's not just the lobster that is laid waste by this locust horde of a man. He smacks and groans his way through mashed potatoes, stuffing overly long green beans into his mouth, then turns his attention to my plate. "You gonna eat that?" he asks, and I shake my head, fascinated and horrified, as he devours my rice pilaf and vegetable medley. Finally, he spears up my barely touched fish, which he dips in the last of his drawn butter, and swallows it joyfully, an orca whale finishing off the hapless seal pup.

Finally, he pushes away the pillaged lobster shell and wipes his mouth, then takes the little wet nap and cleans his hands. "Well, that was fantastic," he pronounces, leaning back. His girth is noticeably bigger. "Do you want dessert? I could go for some cheesecake."

"Wow! Are you kidding?" I ask. He frowns. "Oh, I'm...I'm sorry. It's just...wow! That was a big lobster!

Boy! You can eat!" *Okay, enough, Maggie.* "So, Roger, do you have any interesting hobbies?" I ask. It would be really nice to think of something other than food at this point, and it's a good date question. Not that there's any chance of us getting together. The thought of kissing that rampaging mouth...I shudder visibly.

"You cold?" he asks.

"No, no. Tell me about your hobbies," I order.

"Well," he says, "actually, I'm glad you asked. I love being a nurse, of course, but what I find really fascinating, what I think might be my true calling, is animal communication." He looks at me expectantly.

"Oh! That sounds neat," I say. I'm not really sure what it is, but anything is better than watching him eat. "So is that like, um, animal training?" Our waiter is glancing our way, and I try to wave him off discreetly. Any more food, and Roger's belt will slice him in half.

"No. It's not training at all, Maggie. I'd think a smart girl like yourself would know that."

I yearn for Colonel. Was I complaining about being single? Foolish me.

"An animal communicator reads the thoughts of animals," he lectures.

"Oh." I pause. "Do they speak English?"

"Who?"

"The animals. I mean, if you can read their thoughts, wouldn't it be in cat language or dog or goat or whatever?"

Roger frowns, clearly displeased. "No, Maggie. It's no joke, either. Don't you watch *Pet Psychic* on Animal Planet?"

"You know, I've missed that one. But, hmm. Well. Interesting. So you, what, try to read their thoughts and,

I don't know, tell if they're hurt or if they've been abused or something?"

He smiles condescendingly, and my desire to be home, fasting and watching TV, grows. "Some people do that, yes. But I have a more specialized talent, Maggie. I communicate with animals who have passed."

"Wow. That's so…gee."

He must see the disbelief on my face, because he sits forward suddenly, staring at me intently. "Did you ever have a pet when you were a kid, Maggie?" he asks.

"Yes, we did," I answer. "A nice—"

"Don't tell me!" I jump, startled. "Sorry," he amends. "Just think of this pet. Picture him…or *her*…remember him…or *her*…and all the good times you had with him."

"Or her," I add.

"Whatever. Just picture."

A tickle of laughter wriggles in my stomach. I picture him…or *her*…actually, it's a him. Dicky, our childhood dog, a lovely chocolate Lab as solid and wide as a barrel. Christy and I used to hold little Jonah on his back and Dicky would walk proudly and slowly around the house, flanked on either side by us girls. Our parents' photo albums hold many images of this happy pastime.

"Okay, okay," Roger says. "I'm getting something. Was this pet…a mammal?"

Amazing. "Bingo," I answer.

"Good, Maggie, and please just answer with yes or no." He closes his eyes and I take the opportunity to drain my wineglass.

"Maggie, was this animal…a cat?"

"No."

Roger frowns slightly but doesn't open his eyes. "Are you sure?"

"Yes."

"Not a cat? You're sure."

"Yes." My voice is tight with the effort of not laughing.

"A dog?"

"Yes."

"Great!" Roger exclaims. He opens his eyes and frowns at me. "Are you sure you're picturing the animal?"

Dicky, Dicky, come to me, Dicky... I press my napkin against my mouth to suppress a laugh. "Yes, I'm really picturing him," I manage to say.

"You weren't supposed to tell me it was a him! Come on, Maggie, do you want this reading or not?"

"I really don't—"

Roger clamps his eyes shut again. "Okay, okay, he's back. Right...this is a black and white dog. A Dalmatian. Yes."

"No." A little snort escapes through my nose. Roger's trance is not disturbed.

"Okay, right, right...is this dog black?"

"Nope."

"An Irish setter?"

"No," I squeak.

"Are you *sure* it's not a cat?"

My laughter can't be contained any longer. "Okay, Roger, thank you. Listen, I really should get going. It was nice meeting you, but I just don't think we're right for each other," I say as kindly as I can.

"No kidding. I could tell that the minute you walked

in." He whips out his wallet, throws some bills on the table and stalks off. Can't say I'm sorry to see him go. I wonder if the hospital knows about his special gift.

"Is everything all right, miss?" the waiter asks.

"Oh, sure. It was fine. Thank you. Can I have the check, please?"

I'm not surprised to see that Roger has left only enough to cover his lobster. He didn't even leave enough for his wine. Oh, well. I make up the difference and leave a huge tip for the waiter.

When I get home, there's a message waiting on my machine—Father Tim asking a question about the spaghetti dinner next week. Perfect. It's too late to call my sister and tell her about the date, and Father Tim has just given me a great excuse to call him. He keeps late hours, something he's mentioned in the past and which I stored in the Father Tim encyclopedia I keep in my brain. Besides, I just drove past the rectory and couldn't miss the fact that the lights were still on.

"Maggie, how are you?" he says warmly.

"Oh, I just had the funniest date," I say. By the time I'm finished filling him in on Roger Martin, enemy of lobsters and animal communicator, he's laughing so hard he's just wheezing.

"Maggie, you're a special one," he says when he's regained control. "I must say, I was in need of a good laugh, and you came along and answered my prayers."

I smile and scratch Colonel's tummy. "Glad to be of service, Father Tim," I say. "I have to tell you, though, I'm a little...I don't know. Disappointed. I don't meet a lot of new people."

"I know, I do, Maggie," he says. "But you'll meet that special someone one day soon, mark my words.

You're a jewel, Maggie Beaumont." As to *how* the special someone and I will meet is something Father Tim doesn't address.

"Well. Thanks. You're sweet to say so." I pause.

He goes on to tell me about the date change for the spaghetti dinner. As usual, my schedule is free.

"Wonderful!" he exclaims. "I don't know what St. Mary's would do without you. One of these days, you'll join us properly, not just as a volunteer, mind you, and won't that be a happy day! God bless you, Maggie."

I never know what to say to that. Amen? Thank you? "God bless you, too," I say, wincing as he chuckles. "I mean, good night, Father Tim."

"Good night, Maggie."

I hang up the phone very gently, then lie back against my pillows and indulge in just one quick fantasy. That it was Father Tim with me at dinner tonight, only he wasn't a Father. That we were just two people in love, on a date, eager to talk and laugh and share the details of our day. That he played with my hands, which are smooth and lovely in this fantasy, and that his eyes crinkled when he laughed. That he insisted that I order dessert, because he knows how I love dessert.

Colonel groans.

"I know, I know," I say. "Waste of time." It's wrong, dreaming about dating the priest. Unfair to the good father and all that. I'm sick of reminding myself that it's pointless and stupid…and yet…and yet somehow it's so easy to see. Tim and Maggie. Maggie and Tim. With a sigh, I glance at my copy of *The Thornbirds,* given to me by my brother the day after I learned what the hot guy I'd met did for a living.

Colonel's eyes are full of reproach. "Sorry, pooch," I tell him. "You're right. I'll stop now."

I pat his head, hug my pillow and try to go to sleep.

CHAPTER THREE

IT WASN'T ALWAYS SO, my state of solitude. Once, I thought I was going to get married. Once, I was pre-engaged (not that that's an official title or anything, but I do have a cheap little pearl ring to prove it). Once, I had a steady boyfriend whom I loved and who, I thought, loved me.

Skip Parkinson was a high school god—handsome, reasonably smart, from a well-off family and, most importantly, gifted at sports. Baseball, in particular. And when I say gifted, I mean fantastic. Because of Skip, our school made states each year. Because of Skip, we won three of those four years. Because of Skip, newspapers and college scouts visited Gideon's Cove, sniffing around, eating at the diner, coming to games.

Skip (somehow short for Henry) played shortstop, the sexiest position of all. He batted .345 freshman year, .395 sophomore, .420 junior and an astonishing .463 our senior year. Stanford called and Skip answered, hoping to join the ranks of the university's famous alumni: David McCarty of Boston fame, or, less impressive to a son of Red Sox Nation, Mike Mussina of the New York Yankees.

We dated from sophomore year on. I was the chosen one and not a bad match for Skip; I was smart, too, smarter than he was, honestly. It was because he needed to pass trig that we fell in love. I was his tutor, and one day as I attempted to explain the joys of angle conversion capabilities, he suddenly said, "Maggie, I can't think. You smell too good." We kissed, and it was magical.

Skip was my first real boyfriend, though I had held hands with Ricky Conway on the bus in fourth grade, danced twice with Christopher Beggins in eighth grade and kissed Mark Robideaux after a football game freshman year. But with Skip, Mom would have to pry the phone out of my sweaty adolescent hand each night and order me to go to bed; Skip would take me to the movies and we'd kiss during the coming attractions, then watch the show in squirming, wonderful discomfort. I loved him with all the intensity that only adolescents can feel, to the point where Christy actually felt jealous.

Skip and I lost our virginities to each other on the bunk of his parents' sailboat on Fourth of July weekend, a grave event unlightened by any laughter or humor. I considered going to college in California to be near him, but I ended up at Colby instead, unable to venture further from home or Christy than that. All through college, Skip and I stayed together, calling each other, writing, e-mailing, reuniting on those happy holidays where we flew into each other's arms and stayed there till the final call for his plane. His parents, both lawyers, didn't quite approve of him having a townie girlfriend while the fruits of Stanford were ripe for the picking, but hey. We loved each other.

When Stanford went to the national finals our senior year, Skip was talking to coaches, scouts and reporters.

The Minnesota Twins picked him in the draft, and he went to New Britain, Connecticut, to their farm team. That summer, I made the ten-hour drive down four times, cheering and screaming maniacally when my boyfriend—my boyfriend!—came up to the plate. But it was hard. If we managed a night together, it was rare. He was so busy, you see. Traveling so much. I understood completely.

When Minnesota called him up, Gideon's Cove went wild. A Major League Baseball player…from Gideon's Cove! It was a miracle. People couldn't stop talking about it. My family subscribed to the *Minneapolis Star Tribune,* as did about half the people in town, and we pored over it each morning. When Skip's name was mentioned, the article would be enlarged on the town hall photocopier and hung in the diner, "Skip Parkinson, rookie shortstop" highlighted in yellow so all could see. He would make it, we all said. Our Skip! Little Skip from Overlook Street! He was so good, so talented, so special.

Except in the world of professional baseball, he wasn't. It's a lot easier to hit off a twenty-year-old college kid than a forty-year-old veteran who can throw every kind of strike imaginable at ninety-five miles an hour. Skip's numbers dwindled from an acceptable .294 in New Britain to a dismal .198 in Minnesota. In the field, balls were hit harder, took more vicious bounces. Runners slid into base with damaging accuracy, knowing just how to intimidate a rookie so he'd miss his throw or bobble the ball.

I wrote upbeat letters, called him after every game to try to bolster his spirits. I'd talk about the mechanics of the pitcher, the dive that had been *this close* to being a double play, the unfair call from the second base ump. Relentlessly optimistic, I spent hours that year cajoling Skip into a better mood.

When his first season was over, and when I was helping out at the diner while Granddad had his heart valves replaced, Skip announced that he was coming back to Maine. He'd "reassess" his baseball career, see "what other options" were out there. The town fathers decided that we'd show our support for young Skip, local hero. A big welcome-home parade. Why not? We could use a little boost at this time of year, the brief tourism season over, another long winter ahead of us.

So Skip's parents picked him up at the airport and drove him into town where the high school band waited, where the cheerleaders stood shivering in their tiny skirts, where dozens of little kids in Little League T-shirts and caps clutched Skip's rookie card or a baseball they hoped he'd sign. Just about everyone in town gathered to welcome home Gideon's Cove's most famous citizen.

And I waited, too, of course, right in the front of the crowd. Skip had been very busy over the past few weeks, and we'd only talked once or twice. I had called his parents and offered to go to the airport with them to pick Skip up, but they didn't return my call.

My heart leaped when his parents' car pulled up to the town green, and we the worshipful began to cheer. I couldn't wait to see him, to run into his arms and give him a kiss, blush as the crowd would no doubt whistle and yell for Skip and his high school sweetheart. College was over, I didn't have a real job yet, was just working in the diner, and now Skip was back. Were we too young to get engaged? I thought not.

Yes, I knew it was rare for high school sweethearts to marry…but it certainly happened. Some of the happiest couples out there met in high school. As I scraped the grill or mopped the floors with bleach, took abuse from the summer nuisance and treated grease burns on my hands, I thought of the nice house Skip and I would have. Winter Harbor, maybe. Bar Harbor, even. If he did get re-signed, I'd just travel around with him, be the loving arms he came home to each night, whether he felt discouraged or triumphant. I'd make a great baseball wife.

So Skip got out of the Lexus. And then he turned and gave his hand to someone else. He always was courtly, Skip.

She was a beautiful, elegant girl—woman, I guess—blood-red knit suit, blond hair in a French twist. The mayor and high school baseball coach and head of the Little League waited up on the little gazebo, and Skip and his parents and the blond girl went up and took their seats. There were four chairs waiting for them, I noted, and that fourth chair was not for me.

That was the first time my heart was broken in public.

There were probably murmurs as I pushed my way through the crowd, away from the gazebo. I didn't hear them. Probably, I was sobbing. I know I was covering my face, because I stumbled a couple of times, my rubbery knees buckling. My parents saw and followed, and it was the most humiliating, painful moment of my life bar none, even counting Father Tim's first Mass in Gideon's Cove.

People must have said, "Oh, no, poor Maggie… Gosh, Skip's moved on and she didn't even…poor thing." And while Skip had done an awful, unkind thing, he was nonetheless a star, and it was understandable, wasn't it? I mean, why stick with your little townie girl-friend if the daughter of a Texas oil baron will have you?

He called me, not right away, but later that weekend. "This thing with Annabelle just happened so fast…I tried to tell you… Things with us were winding down anyway… It's not like we were exclusive."

Silly me. I thought we were.

Skip and Annabelle left Gideon's Cove the next week. That same week my father gave me a two-year-old Golden Retriever and hugged me wordlessly, and Christy had me visit her at grad school. Then my grand-father died suddenly, and I had other things to think about. I was a business owner now. I had a dog to train. A little brother who needed help with homework. Lots to do.

It was with deep satisfaction that I saw Skip sent back to the AA league after an abysmal start with Min-nesota. But it didn't stop him from marrying Annabelle later that same year, and they moved to Bar Harbor, to a house on the water purchased, no doubt, with her daddy's money.

Skip is now a salesman for a high-end car company, and when they come back to Gideon's Cove, which is rare, it's always in some much-admired, sexy sports car or an environment-raping SUV. He never comes to Joe's Diner, thank God. I haven't spoken to him since he dumped me.

So if my love life is a source of amusement to the town, it's understandable. First Skip, now the priest. I try to take it well. For the most part, I'm very happy with my life. I love the diner, and I love my little apartment. I love the old folks I feed and I certainly love my family.

But sometimes at night, when I'm folding laundry or watching TV or planning the diner's menu for the week, I pretend I'm married. "What do you think? Will people eat butternut squash bisque in this town?" Or, watching the Fan Cam during a Red Sox game, "Look at that guy. Do you think he could chew with his mouth shut?" Or even, when I just want to test it out, I might say "How was your day, honey?"

Colonel wags his beautiful tail when he hears me speaking to my imaginary hubby. Sometimes he comes over and pushes his big white head against me until I smile. That dog licked away a lot of tears during our first few weeks together, and he's been my emotional barometer ever since. If he could take on human form, I'd marry him instantly. But since that won't happen, and since Father Tim is not going to leave the priesthood and marry me, I'm a bit helpless when loneliness decides to shove its way so rudely to the front of the line.

CHAPTER FOUR

"HELLO, BABY BOY," I call to my brother. I'm at the diner, which Jonah visits daily. "How are the traps?"

"Not bad," he answers. "Got any French toast today, Maggot?"

Much to my parents' dismay, Jonah is a lobsterman. Having lived in Gideon's Cove their entire lives, our folks know what a hard life it is. Dad's a retired teacher, and my mom recently left the hospital, where she was head secretary of the OB/GYN unit. In fact, she was the one who introduced Christy and Will.

Mom and Dad didn't really want their kids to go blue collar. They themselves are both college grads, which is rare around here, and my dad's master's degree is even more special. But despite my graduating from college, and Jonah having been given the same chance, Mom and Dad ended up with a diner owner and a lobsterman. Only Christy has done what they hoped—she graduated from college and even went on to get her master's in social work. She loved her career with the Department of Children and Families, then became a stay-at-home mom when Violet was born.

But last year, Jonah went in on a boat with another guy and has been making ends meet since. It's back-breaking work and means getting out of bed as early as

3:00 a.m., depending on how many traps you have. Most lobstermen do other kinds of fishing, too— flounder, cod, mackerel, halibut, sea bass, so when the lobstering season finishes, the boats keep running. Occasionally, a tourist will want a charter, and Jonah, who is handsome and good-natured, gets hired quite a bit during the brief Maine summer. But regulations and decreasing sea life and a million other things have turned lobstering into an even more difficult job.

Jonah lives in a little house with two other guys, a place so filthy and infested with nasty socks, moldy leftovers and dirty underwear that Human Services should shut it down. It's no wonder that he comes into the diner every day. The fact that I feed him for free is an added allure.

"Heard you had a crappy date the other night," Jonah says as I set his plate down in front of him. Judy reads the paper and ignores my brother…he never leaves a tip, so she never waits on him. The morning rush, as it were, has subsided, and only a few lobstermen, back from checking their lines, come in this late.

"Yes, it was kind of bad," I admit, wiping down the counter. "Want more coffee?"

"Thanks, sissy." He lets me fill his cup, dumps some cream into it and takes a slurp. "Well, speaking of dates, Christy called me yesterday. Wants me to keep an eye out for you."

As if summoned, our sister appears in the doorway, pink-cheeked from the wind. "Mmm," she says, inhaling appreciatively. "It smells so good in here. Can I have some coffee, too, please?"

"Cuppa joe, coming up," I tell her. I ring up Bob Castellano while Christy takes off her coat and sits next to

Jonah. "Thanks for coming in, Bob," I say, handing him his change. "Did you fill out a ballot?"

"Ayuh. And don't worry, sweetheart. You'll meet someone. Have a good day, now, hear?"

"Thank you, Bob," I answer, mortified. I take off my apron, bend down to scratch Colonel, then sit with my siblings. "And I don't know, maybe we could not talk about my love life in front of my customers, how would that be?"

"Why? You want them to think you're still stuck on Father Tim?" Jonah asks.

I scowl, then sigh. "I *am* still stuck on Father Tim, that's the whole problem."

"Well, that's kinda dumb, isn't it?" Jonah asks needlessly.

"Yes, Jonah, it is. Which is why I asked you to be on the lookout," Christy answers.

"Christy, Jonah is eight years younger than we are," I point out. "And in addition to being mere children, his friends are also idiots."

"Good point," Jonah murmurs.

"Well, he might run into someone new," Christy says, staring thoughtfully into her cup. "A new fireman or something. A new boat at the dock. Something like that."

"Mmm. Unlikely," I say. "But I like your optimism."

"So, yeah, I'll be looking out for you, Mags. Wanted…boyfriend for my sister. Must be…well, what are you looking for, Maggie?"

"Someone who's not married to Holy Mother Church," I say. "Let's start with the basics. No priests, no married men, no alcoholics, drug addicts or prison inmates."

Jonah laughs. "Well, shit, Maggot, that rules out everyone I know."

"What about Malone, Joe?" Christy asks, suddenly sitting up straight. "The guy who moors next to you?"

"Malone?" Jonah says. "Yeah, sure. Mags, how about Malone?"

"Maloner the Loner?" I say. "Come on! He's a mute hermit." I take a sip from my coffee, remembering my agonizing ride last year from Maloner the Loner. "No hermits."

"He's not a bad guy," Jonah says.

"He's scary, Jonah," I answer. "But thanks."

LATER THAT NIGHT, Chantal and I meet at Dewey's Pub. She's at our usual table, facing the bar, flirting with Paul Dewey by tying a maraschino cherry stem in a knot. With her *tongue.* Paul sits in front of her, slack-jawed, as Chantal's ripe mouth works seductively. Then her tongue pops out, and voila! There's the stem, tied in a near-perfect circle.

"Thee?" she lisps. "Ten buckth, pleathe."

"Jeezum crow," Dewey mutters, fishing out his wallet. "Hey, Maggie."

"Hey, Dewey. How did the casserole go over?" I say.

"Sold out already," he says, dragging his eyes to me. "Twenty bucks for you."

"Great. Hey, Chantal. Up to your usual tricks, I see." I force a smile.

I'll be honest. Chantal is one of those friends of necessity. She has some nice qualities, but it's probably fair to say that aside from our single status and the fact that we both live and grew up in this town, we don't have a lot in common. She has the kind of 1940s glamour of Rita Hayworth, the curves of Marilyn Monroe and the ethics of Tony Soprano…at least when it comes to men. Use 'em and lose 'em is her motto.

However, she's also lively and funny, and a pretty good listener to boot. Like me, she is available, single and looking for a good man (so she says, though it seems like she'll sleep with just about anyone). And because Christy shouldn't be the only female friend I have, I try to ignore the fact that Chantal is every man's fantasy come true.

"How was your date?" she asks. Small town, nothing to talk about except my embarrassing love life, I guess.

"Well…it was freakish." I get a beer and tell her about Roger, the ruination of the lobster, the attempt to contact Dicky in the great beyond. Like Father Tim, she is crying with laughter by the end of it. I sit back and take a pull of my beer, satisfied that, if I can't find a good man, I can tell a good story.

"Jesus, what a…God, I don't even know what to call it," Chantal says, wiping her eyes. She snorts again, then scans the bar. "We should move," she muses. "Alaska has a lot of men, doesn't it? Plenty to screw in Alaska."

"The last frontier," I murmur. "Of course, we won't move. Well, I won't. Would you?"

"Nah. You know…too much effort, I guess. Plus, I have a good job and all."

"Right." Chantal works in the town hall as a secretary, one of four employees there. She knows everyone's business and is free with her gossip.

"Hey, I went to church this morning," Chantal says with a sly smile. Like a lot of local women under the age of one hundred and four, she's going to church again. "And guess what?" Chantal continued. "I joined the bereavement group."

I close my eyes and sigh. "Chantal…"

"For widows and widowers, you know. There was an announcement in the bulletin." Chantal adjusts her shirt so that more of her impressive cleavage shows. Conversation at the bar stops briefly as the men admire the show. Another inch and they'd be able to nurse.

"And how long have you been a widow?" I ask.

"Oh, gosh…twenty years, I guess. I was eighteen when we got married, nineteen when he died."

Chantal mentioned once, when we first starting hanging out, that she was widowed ages ago. It's strange to think that Chantal was married; she's only six years older than I am but has been a widow more than half her life. "What was his name, your husband?" I ask.

"Chris. Cute guy."

"That must have been really hard," I say.

"It sucked," she answers. "At least we didn't have kids."

"Did you want to?"

"Oh, shit, no. No, Maggie, I'm not the motherly type." She laughs and takes a swig of her drink, emptying the glass.

"So you're suddenly seeking the solace of a grief group?" I ask, raising an eyebrow.

"Well, I guess I'd rather sit there and have Father Tim comfort me than sit at home, scratching my ass," she says cheerfully. "He gives great hugs. He must lift weights or something."

I am simultaneously jealous and irritated with my own hypocrisy. Chantal has joined a church group in order to be near Father Tim. Sounds familiar. I picture

Father Tim patting my hand, looking sorrowfully and deeply into my eyes as I detail the terrible loss. "Bereavement group. You're so lucky," I say without thinking, then blush. "Sorry, Chantal. That didn't come out right."

"Well, I'm pretty lucky," she says, shrugging. "Hey, Paul, can we get another round?"

Dewey nearly soils himself in his haste to get close to Chantal again. "Sorry, what did you say?" he says, staring down her blouse. Chantal smiles and arches her back. I roll my eyes, feeling very flat-chested indeed, my plain little 34-Bs nothing compared to the bounty that Chantal is offering. Dewey licks his lips. My teeth clench.

"Another round, honey. Maybe on the house, what do you say? For your favorite girls?" Chantal tucks a finger into her shirt and pulls it just a fraction lower.

"Sure," Dewey whispers.

"Chantal! Stop," I say. I'm blushing, even if she's not. Paul walks in a trance back to the bar. "I'll have a Grey Goose martini, Paul," she says, as if he carries that high-end stuff.

"Burnett's okay?" he calls back.

"Sure, baby." Preening, she turns her attention back to me.

"Nice floor show," I comment.

"We're drinking for free, aren't we?" she says smugly. "What were we talking about? Oh, yeah, my husband."

Jonah comes in and does a double take when he sees Chantal. She smiles back at him. In order to distract Chantal from undressing my baby brother with her eyes, I ask, "So, did you love him?"

"Who? Oh, Chris? Sure. I guess. I mean, we were teenagers. Screwed our brains out, I'll say that."

"God, that's so romantic," I say, unable to suppress a smile. "I think Hallmark has a line of cards like that. 'I miss screwing your brains out, my darling departed husband.'"

Chantal laughs her big, rolling laugh. "'Baby, no one did me like you.' There's probably a market for that. Should look into it." She excuses herself to go to the bathroom, and I go up to the bar to say hi to Jonah, despite the fact that it's been mere hours since we last saw each other.

"Hi," I say. "What's up?"

"Hey, Mags. Nothing. How about you?" he says amiably.

"Hanging out."

"Is it okay if I come over to watch TV tomorrow night?" Jonah asks. "There's that crabbing show on Discovery. Looked cool."

"Sure." I own one of the few satellite dishes in town. The cable service frequently goes out way up here, and as a single woman, well, let's face it. I watch a lot of TV.

Chantal returns. "Jonah! My, how you've grown," she purrs.

My earlier amusement at her antics evaporates. Even though Jonah is a grown man (officially, anyway), I don't want him decimated by a man-eater like Chantal. "Chantal, stop. Not my brother. Leave Jonah alone."

"No, no, no. Chantal, stay. Don't leave Jonah alone," Jonah says, grinning. "Hey, Chantal, you know anyone Maggie here could date? We're trawling for men who will go out with her."

"Thanks so much, Joe," I say, pinching him. "A little louder, please? I don't think they heard you in Jonesport."

"Hell, I don't know," Chantal says. "The pickings are certainly slim. Present company excluded." She edges closer to Jonah.

I get up and wedge myself between them. "If you sleep with my brother, I will be very mad at you, Chantal," I say firmly. "Jonah, Chantal is a diseased woman. Crabs, chlamydia, gonorrhea, herpes, syphilis…"

"Don't believe her, Jonah. Underneath all this, there's a heart of gold." She gestures to her chest.

"Is there?" Jonah asks. "Can I see?"

"Stop, Joe!" I smack my brother on the back of his head.

Chantal smiles. "Back to your problem, Maggie. How about Malone?"

"God, you're the second person today who's said that!" I exclaim, jarred out of my irritation. "First Christy, now you."

"Why not?" Chantal says. "He's kind of cute."

"This from the woman who said Dick Cheney had that 'sexy bald thing' going on."

Chantal shrugs. "Well, I can't help it if it's true."

I stare at her. "Chantal, please. Maybe, I don't know, Andre Agassi or Montel Williams. But not Dick Cheney. Dick Cheney will never have a sexy anything going on."

"Well, Malone's got that Clive Owen thing going on," she continues, taking a sip of her martini.

"Clive Owen after being beaten and left for dead, maybe."

"More importantly, he's single. Right, Jonah?"

My brother nods sagely at Chantal's breasts. "Ayuh."

"Malone is surly, scary and ugly," I say. "So I'm gonna pass on him, if you don't mind."

"I don't know," Chantal says. She looks past me. "What do you say, Malone? Want to go out with Maggie?"

Crap. Crappety crap crap. I close my eyes and let the mortification wash over me. Big Mouth strikes again. And Chantal led me right into it.

I open my eyes and glance past my brother. There he is, surly, scary and ugly. "Hi. Sorry."

As nothing brings my brother as much joy as his sister's humiliation, Jonah is slapping the bar in mirth. "You know Maggie, right, Malone?" he chortles gleefully.

Malone stares at me, unsmiling, and he *is* a little scary. But I never noticed, on the rare occasion that I've been this close to him, that his eyes are actually quite nice, light blue contrasting with thick black eyelashes. Short, curly black hair, heavy eyebrows, sharp cheekbones. Deep lines run between his eyebrows, out from his eyes, alongside his mouth, and let me assure you, they're not laugh lines. It occurs to me that I've never really looked Malone straight in the face before. Actually, I can kind of see what Chantal means…a little. He's definitely masculine and—

"So, what do you think, Malone?" Chantal asks. "You want to go out with Maggie?"

By now, the whole bar is listening. Though I should be used to public embarrassment, my cheeks are burning. Malone drops his gaze to my chest, looks for a minute, then looks up at my face again. He shakes his head. The bar erupts in laughter. Chantal and Jonah clutch each other, shrieking, Stevie and Dewey high-five each other at Malone's insult, and I just sit there and nod my head.

"Right," I say over the hysteria. "Well, I deserved that. Sorry, Malone. That was a crummy thing to say."

He gives a slight nod, then turns to the beer that Dewey presents him.

"Okay, I've embarrassed myself enough tonight," I say to my brother and Chantal. "I'm going home. Good night."

"Bye, Maggot! Thanks for the laughs," Jonah says, sliding his arm around Chantal's shoulders. She blows me a kiss, then turns to say something to Jonah. My jaw clenches momentarily.

I get my coat from the table and head out. At Malone's stool, I pause. "Sorry again," I murmur.

He nods without looking at me.

"I still owe you that pie," I remind him. He doesn't respond.

Although I catch a glimpse of Malone once in a while at Dewey's or at the dock, I haven't spoken with him since he drove me to Joe's in the rain. He did a kind thing for me last spring, and tonight I insulted him.

As I walk home through the quiet town, an unpleasant sense of shame keeps good pace beside me.

CHAPTER FIVE

A FEW DAYS LATER, whatever shame I felt has faded to a distant prickle. Once again, the presence of Father Tim melts away all bad feelings, his beautiful smile simultaneously reassuring and thrilling.

Last night, my parents had summoned their offspring to a family dinner, something they insist on about once a month or so, and much to my delight, Father Tim was invited, as well. As I showed Colonel to his doggie bed in my old bedroom, I could hear Father Tim laughing downstairs, the rumbling voice of my dad, Violet's happy, ear-splitting shrieks. It seemed so natural.

We had a very nice dinner and a lemon cake that I'd baked in honor of the occasion. Father Tim had two pieces. "Maggie, you're a genius, you are, my girl," he said, finally pushing back from the table. I smiled sappily, heart fluttering.

Talk turned to the inevitable—my failure at finding a boyfriend. "Will, dear, can't you find anyone for Maggie?" Mom asked.

"Apparently not," Christy intoned, nudging her husband, who looked rightfully chagrined.

"It's not funny, Christy," Mom said sharply. "She's never going to meet anyone behind that counter. Think of how you're going to end up, Maggie! A spinster waitress like Judy."

"I like Judy," I answered weakly. Mom likes to go right for the kill.

"Now, Lena," Dad said meekly. I knew it was no use. There was no stopping my mother on this subject. No daughter of hers was going to be unmarried. Not if she had a breath left in her body!

"Well, I just don't understand why it's so difficult," Mom said to Father Tim. "She's perfectly nice! Look at Christy! Did Christy have trouble finding a nice husband? No! So why can't Maggie do the same thing? Maggie, if only you'd get a real job, some place where you could meet some eligible men. Like Christy—"

This comparison theme song, which I have mentally entitled "Christy is Better," is one Mom's sung many times. "Do you have to be so perfect?" I asked my sister.

"Sorry," she sang, wiping mashed-up carrots from Violet's eyelid. "I really can't help it. It just happens."

"—in my day, people wanted to get married," my mother was saying. "Now, of course, everyone's out there, doing all sorts of things. Why buy the milk when you can just rent the cow for free?"

Jonah shot me a quizzical look—Mom's never been good with clichés—then mooed softly at Violet, who banged her spoon on the highchair tray in approval. Jonah mooed again, this time in my direction.

"I have a great idea," I said. "Let's pick on Jonah! Jonah, why haven't you given Mom any grandchildren yet? What's the matter with you? Don't you have unprotected sex anymore? Don't you care about your own mother?"

"Maggie!" Mom admonished. "There's a priest in

the room! Father Tim, I don't know where she gets this trashy talk."

But Father Tim was laughing, as I knew he would be. "I've no doubt that Jonah conducts himself like a gentleman," he said. "Furthermore, Jonah, my man, I trust that you've given thought to—"

"Actually, Maggot, thanks for reminding me," Jonah interrupted blithely. "I've got a date. Thanks for dinner, Ma."

"Wait, honey, I have some leftovers for you," Mom said, pressing a huge plate into his hands.

"Goodbye, you spoiled little prince," I said, allowing him to kiss my cheek.

"Goodbye, you dried-up old hag," he returned fondly. He turned to Christy. "Goodbye, beautiful, nice sister. Goodbye, filthy little baby."

"You put me in mind of my own family," Father Tim said. He looked a little sad, and I took the opportunity to pat his hand.

"You must miss them so much," I commented.

"I do, Maggie. I do." He patted back, and a shameful heat flowed up my arm to my heart.

After Violet was tucked into her portable crib, my parents broke out the Trivial Pursuit. "Three teams," Dad announced. "The Mrs. and I are undefeated, Father Tim, so we don't want to break our streak. Will, you can be with your lovely bride there, and Maggie, you won't mind showing Father Tim the ropes, will you, sweetheart?"

Christy grinned wickedly. "I think we all know the answer to that," she murmured so that only I could hear.

"Have you gained a few pounds?" I asked. "They look good on you."

And so the rest of the night was spent quipping and insulting and laughing. Really, how could I not imagine Father Tim and me together? Maggie O'Halloran. What a great-sounding name!

The next day, I'm sitting in the rectory living room, having dodged the Gorgon Plutarski, who guards Father Tim like a pit bull protecting a steak. I stare at Father Tim's beautifully shaped mouth and idly rub a patch of eczema on my knuckle. Tonight is the big spaghetti supper to raise money for a new roof on the western side of the church, which started leaking after a nor'easter last winter.

"The final count is closer to sixty people," Father Tim says. He leans forward, clasping his hands together loosely. The scent of his soap drifts to me, and I try not to swoon. *For God's sake, Maggie. Literally. For God's sake. He's a man of the cloth*— "Do you have enough? I hate to be putting this on you on such short notice, but apparently we had a few last-minute reservations."

"Oh, no problem," I say. It's so cozy in this small living room, Father Tim sitting just across from me. I swear, I could look into those eyes for the rest of my life….

"Can you do the bread, as well, Maggie? I'm sorry it's so late, my asking, but it completely slipped my mind."

"Hmm? Oh, the bread? Sure. No problem."

"Ah, thank heaven for you, dear girl," he says, though he is only a year older. "You're a treasure."

A jewel, a treasure, darlin'… I know he calls everyone by those pet names, but still. We were so natural together last night, playing couples' Trivial Pursuit, sharing huddled discussions over whether the answer was Eisenhower or Nixon, David Bowie or Iggy Pop…

I stand up, trying to shake myself mentally. *Get over him, Maggie,* I instruct myself. I need to stop. I really do. I want to. I'm going to. I sound like a drug addict. Perhaps there's a twelve-step program for me. Priest Lovers Anonymous.

In the rectory office, Mrs. Plutarski pauses in her phone conversation to shoot me a suspicious glare. I ignore her and walk out into the frigid rain.

Sighing, I glance down the street. The familiar weight of loneliness presses down on me. The spaghetti dinner is hours away, the diner is closed. If only I had that nice guy I've imagined…the sweet, hardworking one with the easy laugh and dancing eyes. It's a great day for cuddling, and while Colonel is excellent at cuddling, he's not exactly the same thing as a hubby. No, Colonel could lie in front of a warm, snapping fire as my husband and I sat cuddled up on the couch, reading, drinking coffee…

My thoughts are cut off as a Hummer growls down the street, plowing through an enormous puddle. A sheet of muddy, icy water slaps down on me, drenching and punishing. "Hey!" I yelp. The vehicle slows at the library, pulling into a parking space near the front door.

"Asshole," I mutter. Fully intending to march down the street and tell them they're idiots, I find myself slowing down. A woman, dressed in a cheerful red raincoat and matching hat, gets out of the passenger's side. She opens the back door and out pop three blond children wearing colorful raincoats and brightly colored boots. The mother extends both hands, and the smaller children each take one, the oldest kid running ahead to hold the door for his mother and sisters. Even from a half a block away, I can hear their laughter.

I guess I won't tell them off. They're not idiots, after all. As a matter of fact, they look like an ad for clean American living, aside from the earth-defiling vehicle they drive. They look like the kind of family I'd like to have someday. The woman seems like the kind of mother I'd want to be, laughing, well-dressed, unconsciously affectionate, automatically protective.

Then the driver's door opens and out gets Skip Parkinson.

His presence is like a punch to the stomach, so silent and stunning that I actually bend over. I haven't seen him since the day he dumped me, that awful day when he brought his fiancée back home.

Skip glances down the block, and though I knew him immediately, it's clear he doesn't have that same instinct for me, despite having just soaked me through to the skin. My teeth begin to chatter, but I don't move, just watch as Skip casually jogs into the library, still full of easy, athletic grace.

Skip must be visiting his parents. No doubt the lovely, adorably dressed children got antsy being stuck inside, so Skip and Mrs. Skip took them to the library to get a book or a movie that would occupy them for the rest of the day. No doubt Skip and Mrs. Skip will return to the Parkinsons' lovely home on Overlook Street and cuddle and read on the couch, the fire crackling, their legs entangled.

That could have been me in the bright red raincoat, being driven through the cold rainy afternoon by Skip, my husband. Those cheerful, hand-holding kids might have been mine.

Turning around, the cold rain slicing my face, I race home. It's only three blocks, but I run as fast as I can, and by the time I get there, I'm gasping. I pound up the stairs, hoping that Mrs. K. doesn't decide she wants a chat or a pedicure, and burst inside. The only sound is of my rasping breath and the rain drumming on the roof.

Colonel hauls himself out of his dog bed and woofs softly. I kneel down and hug him, burying my face in his beautiful fur. "Oh, buddy, I'm so glad to see you," I say. "I love you, Colonel."

When an eighty-five pound mammal licks your tears away, then tries to sit on your lap, it's hard to feel sad. I give my dog some chicken breast to reward him for his love, then go to the bathroom and stare at myself in the mirror. Bad idea. Bedraggled, wet hair sticks to my face, which is blotchy with cold. My mouth is grim.

I slam my way out of the bathroom and go to the cupboard above the fridge—the rarely-used liquor cupboard—and take out the unopened Irish whiskey given to me by a nice old man who died about five years ago. I used to bring him dinner on Wednesday nights. Mr. Williams. Nice guy. I slosh about six ounces into a glass and raise it. "Here's to you, Mr. Williams," I say, drinking. Yuck. I grimace hugely, shudder, then take another swallow.

Grabbing the phone, I call the bakery in Machias and order eighteen loaves of Italian bread, then call Will, who is at the hospital up there today, on his cell.

"Will, can you do me a favor?" I ask abruptly.

"Sure, Maggie, sure. You okay?" he asks.

I tell him about the bakery order, remind him to come to the spaghetti supper. He is happy to pick up the bread. Great guy, that Will. I drink to him, too. "And here's to you, Colonel Love Pup," I say, raising my glass to my dog. He wags his tail and rests his head on my foot.

I look at the clock. 3:09. Octavio closed today, and is probably already home with his wife and five kids. I hope he remembers to bring the two huge pots of homemade sauce and twelve dozen meatballs I left on the diner's stove. That's how I spent my morning, from 4:00 a.m. until seven. Cooking for a church event, even though I don't go to church. That's our Maggie, anything for Father Tim. Nothing else to do, right? It's not like anyone's home waiting for her.

By the time I leave my apartment, I'm feeling a bit more cheerful. I trip off the curb and step into a frigid puddle up to my ankle, but it's okay. Weaving over to the church, I flip on the lights in the echoing basement and get out the big pasta pots. "You are the sunshine of my life," I sing, glad that Stevie Wonder can't hear me. "That's why I'll always stay around, oooh, oooh, yeah, yeah…"

Over the past year, I've become well-acquainted with this kitchen. I've cooked corned beef on St. Patrick's Day, mulled cider for the carol sing, boiled eggs for the Easter egg hunt. Here I make huge pans of lasagna for after-funeral gatherings, throw together blueberry cakes and cookies for bake sales. Coffee hour? No problem… I donate the scones, set up the beverages, fill the creamers. My home away from home, this kitchen. "You're such a loser," I tell myself. My voice echoes through the basement.

I fill the huge pots with hot water, throw in some salt and turn on the gas. Then, feeling a little bit dizzy, I decide to lie on the floor and wait for the water to boil. It's nice on the floor. Cool and smooth. My back aches a little, and I stretch, then close my eyes. A brief nap, perhaps, before everyone comes.

"Hey, boss." The voice floats to me over the counter. Octavio and his wife come in, each carrying a giant vat of sauce, followed by their many children.

"Oh, hi!" I say. "Hello! How are you? It's nice to see you, Patty. Hello, Mookie. Hello, Lucia. Hi, other kids! Hi!"

"You okay, boss?" Octavio asks, giving me a questioning look.

"Yes. Yes, I am. I am A-okay. Thank you," I answer. Perhaps I should get up? I do, groping for a handhold on the counter and hauling myself unsteadily to my feet. "And you? How are you lovely people?"

"We're fine." He and his wife exchange a look, then set the sauce down and go back to the van for the meatballs. The kids start running around, playing hide and seek. I turn the sauce on low and notice the bottles of wine under the counter. That's right—this is a wine event. How nice! Not just another boring spaghetti supper—a nice wine dinner. That's nice. It's nice to have wine. "You kids are nice," I announce to the Santos children as I uncap a bottle.

The oldest girl, Marie, who is seven, stops running. "Thanks, Maggie," she says, smiling shyly. "You're nice, too."

"I know," I say. I wrinkle my nose and smile at her. What a nice girl.

An hour later, the place is full and conversation bounces around the basement like a hundred ping-pong balls. I must not think about that, or it will make me woozy. And I'm already very busy trying to conceal the fact that I might be a little tipsy. Every movement must be carefully planned, every phrase prethought. My parents come over, looking the nice part of the nice parents they are.

"Hello, Maggie. This looks very pretty," Mom says. She glances at the tables we set up, the little fake flower centerpieces. In order to avoid that prison-cafeteria feel that so many church events have, we've turned on only the recessed lighting, not the fluorescents.

"Thank you, Mom. You are so nice to say so," I say. "Hi, Dad. It does look nice. Not like prison. Like a nice place. Like a church."

Luckily, Mom is scanning the room for someone for me to marry. "Maggie, are you…have you been drinking?" Dad asks quietly.

"A little," I admit. It's hard to keep both eyes focused right now…the left eye seems to be wandering. I squint it shut so it will stop bothering me.

"Have you had anything to eat today?" Dad asks.

"Hmm. Yes. I had a sour cream cranberry muffin this morning, and let me tell you, Daddy, it was freaking fantastic."

"Okay, baby, let's get you fed." Dad, good old Dad, steers me to a table and pushes me into a seat.

"Can't I sit with Octavio?" I ask. "I love that guy!"

"Stay here," Dad says. "I'll be right back."

It's nice, staying here. I'm glad I have to. But the room is spinning just a little, so I put my head on the table. It's like being on a carnival ride…I can feel the movement, but with my eyes closed, I don't have to see.

Someone sits next to me. "Hello," I say without lifting my head. "Welcome to the dinner."

"Are you drunk?" It's my sister.

"Mmm-hmm. Daddy's getting me some food." I lift my head. Oops. I'm drooling. There's a wet spot on the table. I grab the flowers and place them on the splotch, then turn to face Christy. "Hi."

"Whoa," she says. "What happened?"

It doesn't seem prudent to mention the whiskey I drank earlier. "Oh, I don't know…I think I had a glass of wine on an empty stomach. Thash all. Jushta li'l wine." I smile to cover the fact that I'm slurring.

Dad returns with some salad, bread, a glass of water and a bowl of pasta that could feed a family of four. "Eat, sweetie," he instructs. "And Christy, can you run interference with your mother? She's over there talking to Carol."

"Sure," she answers. She stands up and pats me on the shoulder.

"I love you!" I call, waving to her. "You are so sweet, Christy."

I eat the food—it's delicious, I have to say—and begin to feel drowsy. Christy, Violet and Will come over with plates, and after a little while, Mom, too. Another family dinner. My eyelids droop, but Dad has me on the far end, away from Mom so she won't know her spinster daughter is now also the town lush. *Maybe I can go lie down on the coat pile,* I think. It looks so cozy. People mill around, going up for seconds. "Great food, Maggie," several people call, and I wave sloppily in response.

Then I see Father Tim. He's chatting up Mr. and Mrs. Rubricht, laughing, clapping Mr. on the back. Mrs. Plutarski, his self-appointed bodyguard, preens in her proximity to the priest. Preening proximity to the priest. I chuckle. "Preening," I say out loud. Dad turns to me, concerned, but I can't take my eyes off Father Tim.

He's so *nice,* Father Tim. We had so much fun the other night, didn't we? That man is a great guy. He's no asshole, not like Skip. Nope, Father Tim is my best friend. I love him.

When everyone is just about finished and eying the dessert table with unabashed greed, Father Tim takes the microphone and clicks it on. His beautiful Irish lilt fills my ears.

"It warms my heart to see so many people here tonight, in spite of the nasty weather," he says, smiling at his flock. "And what a lovely dinner we've all been enjoying! Thank you, Maggie and Octavio, for putting together such a fine feast, as always."

People clap and turn toward me. I stand up, stagger back a little, but decide that no one really noticed. "You're welcome!" I call out.

"And thanks in advance to the hospitality commit-tee, too, who'll be doing all the hard work of cleaning up afterwards," Father Tim continues. "I'm happy to say that we've raised more than—"

"Can I just say something?" I call out, waving to dear, kind Father Tim.

"Oh, stop her, Daddy," Christy murmurs, her voice urgent.

No! They will not stop me! I scoot with surprising agility around our table, only bumping into six or ten chairs as I make my way to the front of the room, where Father Tim stands smiling with a little uncertainty.

"Can I have the mike?" I ask him. I am not so drunk that I miss Mrs. Plutarski's mouth purse in jealousy. Yeah. That's right. Because I'm Father Tim's friend. She's not the only one who adores him.

"Ah…sure, Maggie," he says, handing it over to me.

I've never spoken into a microphone before. It's kind of neat, holding it. I feel a little like Ellen DeGeneres, like I have my own show. I wriggle onto the edge of the stage where last year's confirmation class butchered *Godspell* and blow into the mike. The rushing sound reassures me that it's on.

"Thank you so much, Father Tim," I say, proud not to slur. "Oh, that's funny! I sound like Christy!"

Everyone laughs. I'm a hit!

"So, I guess I just wanted to say how grateful we all are to be here, on this beautiful planet, in this great little town. It's so nice, isn't it?"

My mother is staring at me, her face a mixture of disapproval and horror. I think she might be mad at me. "Hi, Mom!" I say, waving. "Anyway, I also want to say thanks to Father Tim. We are so lucky to have him in our parish, aren't we? I mean, remember Father What's-His-Name, that weird little fat guy? The guy at Christy's wedding? He was no fun, no fun. Uh-uh. Not funny, that guy. And now we have Father Tim! He's so good, right? I mean, he's like a holy man, don't you think?"

"Thanks, Maggie. I'll just be taking that microphone back, shall I?" Father Tim says, making a move toward me.

"No! No, no. No." I scoot back further, then stand, so that if Father Tim wants to get me, he has to come and get me. Ha! I point to him as he stands frozen, and waggle my index finger. "This is good. You should hear this, holy man. Because we all love you. Really. Don't we?" I ask the assembled guests. They are certainly paying excellent attention. "Everyone here loves you, Father Tim. Me, too. I just…you're such a…and we all just… I love you, Father Tim."

I keep talking, but now I can hardly hear myself, the place has gotten so loud. Will is suddenly standing next to me, clever lad, and he takes the mike from me.

"I wasn't done," I protest.

"Oh, you're done, honey," he says. "Come on, I'll take you home."

CHAPTER SIX

FRAGMENTS OF LAST NIGHT WHIZ around in my brain like ice being crushed in a blender. Snatches of conversation, images, a deep concern that yes, I really did say that.

It's three-twenty in the morning. I'm not really sure what time Will and my father tucked me in. My brain grinds against my skull, and my right eye apparently has an ice pick in it. My teeth have sprouted fur, and my mouth feels like something reptilian and evil died in there.

I stagger into the bathroom and swallow two Motrin and two Tylenol at the sink. I know this isn't good to take these on an empty stomach, but I don't care. The thought of drinking milk causes ugly things to happen in my digestive tract. I take a shower and feel that I've advanced an inch toward normal humanity.

My apartment feels stuffy and close, and I certainly don't want to be around food right now, so the diner is out. I pull on my coat, my wool hat, mittens, and grab a flashlight.

"Colonel," I say, and my brain recoils from the awful noise. "Come, boy," I whisper.

Colonel has never needed a leash; he just follows me everywhere with breathtaking devotion. We head out into the pitch-black morning.

The town is quiet; there is only the gentle sound of water shushing against the rocky shore. The wind is still at this hour, and the moon long gone, making the stars glitter in the inky black sky. I walk down dark streets, past sleeping houses, until I get to a little path that will take me up to Douglas Point. It's not a nature preserve precisely, but it's close. There's just one house up there, owned by a wealthy Microsoft executive, and he only visits it once or twice a year. He's quite nice about letting us locals use the grounds for hiking and fishing.

The smell of pine and sea makes my roiling stomach feel better, and the breeze seems to blow all thought from my head. I know what I did last night, but at this moment, my mind is empty. It's just Colonel and me right now.

I go along the sea to a large outcropping of rock that sits directly over the water. In fact, it's called Bowsprit Rock, as it resembles that particular part of a boat. Rising behind me like a specter is the granite memorial to fishermen who died at sea. Carved on it are the names of eighteen men Gideon's Cove has lost to the ravenous ocean. Eighteen men so far, that is.

The wind is a little stronger here, and still quite cold, though it is almost April. The rock is like ice under my bottom, but it feels good, cleansing and solid. I switch off the flashlight and let my eyes adjust. Colonel lies down next to me, contentedly chewing a stick, and I put my arm around his neck and look east. Dawn is far away, but the stars are brilliant enough tonight that I can see whitecaps here and there. The water slaps against the rocky shore, shushing and whispering.

With a sigh, I lie back and look into the Milky Way. It's so beautiful, so cold and pure and distant, hypnotic.

Colonel snuggles against my side, and I idly stroke his thick fur, just looking into the heavens. How long I stay like this, I don't know, as I've forgotten my watch, but the sound of a motor causes me to sit up. There goes a lobster boat, out to check the pots. The lights of the boat seem warm and welcoming compared with the distant ice of the stars. It might be Jonah, though he's on the lazy side of lobstermen. I squint, but I can't make out who it is. Malone, maybe. Jonah's mentioned that he's usually the first one out, the last one back.

Last year, the story goes, Malone and his cousin, Trevor, a man as sunny as Malone is dark, went in on a new boat. Real pretty, the local gossip sources said. Eighty-five thou, maybe more. They were going to do some more commercial work, perhaps even start a few scallop beds. But Trevor, who often came into Joe's Diner and flirted equally with Judy and me, disappeared one day. Apparently, he sold the boat out from under Malone and took off with the money, leaving Malone with the payments. Trevor was never seen again. Rumors flew—Mafia, drugs, homosexuality, murder— but Malone remained, silently working his traps himself, using the boat he'd had for the past ten years.

Well. I'd heard about it—you don't own the only restaurant in town and not hear these things—but I don't really know Malone. He was five or six years ahead of me in school. As he's barely spoken to me, ever, I don't really know what his situation is, a rare event in Gideon's Cove.

The grinding in my head has subsided to the pulsating of a wounded jellyfish. My ass is numb, my cheeks stiff with cold. With a sigh, I stand up. "Let's go, big boy," I say to the dog. We turn and head for the diner as the sky lightens almost imperceptibly on the eastern horizon.

I put on coffee and start pulling together some muffins. Cranberry lemon today, and raisin bran for Bob Castellano, who needs his fiber. Mrs. K. likes them, too.

Soon the diner will start to fill up with people who will want to hear about my little speech last night. Or people who witnessed it and want to relive it. Once again, I've embarrassed myself. At least no one can say I'm not entertaining.

By the time the second batch of muffins comes out, I've started the potatoes for Octavio's rightfully famous hash browns. As if summoned, he clatters through the back door, and I wince at the noise. "Hi, boss," he says cheerfully.

"Hi." I wait for the questions, but none comes.

Instead, Octavio busies himself at the stove, checks the muffins. "How about some coffee, boss?" He doesn't wait for the answer, just pours me a cup and hands it to me, then starts cracking eggs into a large bowl. His big hands can handle two eggs at a time, and he's ambidextrous, at least when it comes to egg cracking. Smack! Four eggs. Smack! Eight. Smack! A dozen eggs lay waiting innocently in their bowl, not realizing they're about to be whisked without mercy. He glances at me, his face open and friendly.

"Would you like a raise?" I ask.

"It's okay, boss."

"You deserve one."

"Maybe in the summer, then." He smiles. There's a space between his two front teeth that I find very appealing.

"So I really told Father Tim I love him, didn't I?" I ask.

"Yeah, boss. Sorry." He winks at me and continues frying the hash browns.

"Any questions?"

"Nope."

"You're getting a raise this week."

"Whatever you say, boss," he agrees.

Octavio is excellent at getting raises. Last year he got a whopper by not talking about *that guy I'd met,* and now he'll get one for just being kind. "I wish I were as cool as you, Octavio," I say.

"Keep trying," he answers encouragingly.

At eight-thirty, Father Tim comes in and slides into his usual booth. I take a deep breath and close my eyes. "Good morning, Maggie," he says gently. Rolly and Ben halt their conversation shamelessly, and the board of education members in the corner drop their discussion on cutting the art program. It's to be expected— I'm the best show in town.

"Oh, Father Tim," I sigh. "I'm so sorry. I don't know what to say. I hope I didn't embarrass you, though I certainly embarrassed myself."

He smiles ruefully. "Not to worry, Maggie, not to worry." He allows me to pour him a cup of coffee. "Maggie, sit with me a moment, won't you, dear?"

I obey. He smells like damp wool and grass, the smell of Ireland, though he's been in America for six years now. His hands are elegant and smooth, and I hide my own hands in my lap, conscious as always that they're rough and red, the hands of a much older woman.

"Maggie, I've been thinking about our little problem

here," he says in a low voice. His eyes are kind, and my heart squeezes with painful, hopeless love. "This…this crush on me, it's getting in the way of things, isn't it?"

I nod, feeling the blush creep down my neck. "I'm sorry," I whisper.

"I've given it some thought, Maggie, dear, and I wondered if I might help you in some way." He takes a sip of coffee, then cocks his head. "What would you think if I set you up with some proper men?"

My mouth drops open. "Uh…well…um… Excuse me?"

"Well, Maggie, I think it might help you, ah, move on, shall we say, if you'd a nice man in your life, don't you think?"

Humiliation sloshes through my limbs. The priest is trying to fix me up. Oh, God. "Um…I…"

"Proper men, as I said. Believe or not, I know a few."

"Okay, um, well, what exactly do you mean by proper men?"

Tim leans back in the booth, takes a sip of coffee. "Well, Catholic would be the best place to start, of course."

"How optimistic you are," I say. "Single Catholic men in Gideon's Cove. I can think of one, Father Tim, and he's eighty years old and a double amputee. Plus, he's already proposed, and I turned him down."

Father Tim chuckles. "Ah, Maggie, ye of little faith." He pauses and glances toward the counter. "Would you mind if I grabbed one of those muffins? I haven't had breakfast yet."

A pang of guilt makes a direct hit. Here he is, hungry and unfed, trying to solve my problems. "Sure, Father

Tim! Of course! Whatever you want. Would you rather have pancakes? Or an omelet? I can have Octavio make you something more substantial than a muffin."

"Well, now, that would be lovely. If it's no trouble, that is." He tells me what he wants and I call the order to Octavio.

"Judy," I ask. "Would you bring this out to Father Tim when it's ready?"

Judy sighs hugely, then nods, undeterred from reading the paper. "Can I have some more coffee?" Rolly asks.

"Why don't you just help yourself?" she answers, gesturing in the direction of the coffeepot. I hop up and refill his cup, then return to Father Tim.

"All right then," Father Tim says. "Now, bear with me, Maggie, because I know that when it comes to dating, you haven't had much luck. But you're also a bit on the fussy side, aren't you?"

"Well, I don't really think so," I answer. Am I? Granted, I'm not Chantal, whose male friends require only a beating heart, but I don't think I'm really fussy, either....

"I think it's better if you keep an open mind. I'll have the gentlemen give you a call, and you can arrange a meeting and have a chat. How's that, dear?"

After Gifted Roger, I think I'd rather feed myself to sharks than go on another blind date. "Yeah…no," I say.

"Maggie," Father Tim says, frowning slightly. "Let me be blunt." I wince, but he continues. "You're a lovely girl, but I think you need a little help when it comes to dating."

From a priest? I yelp in my head.

"We can't have you embarrassing yourself every time we run into each other, now, can we?" Father Tim whispers, smiling sweetly.

I slide lower in the booth. My fists are clenched so hard in mortification that the skin over my knuckle cracks. My knee bumps Father Tim's, and I jolt upright in my seat.

"Think of it as your penance, Maggie," he says, eyes twinkling. "For overindulging last night."

"What about forgive and forget?" I mutter. "Turn the other cheek? Go and sin no more?"

"Save it, lass, you're with a professional. I won't take no for an answer."

I sigh. Rolly spins on his stool toward me. "I think you should try it, sweetheart," he offers.

"Thanks, Rolly." I close my eyes. "Okay, Father Tim. But you have to promise that they'll be good, okay? Real possibilities." I think for a minute. "Hey, what about Martin Broulier? He's single, isn't he?" Martin works out of town, a seemingly nice guy in his forties, maybe, not bad-looking. His wife and he divorced about a year ago.

Father Tim's face brightens as Judy trudges over with his plate. "Thank you, Judy, darlin', thank you. That's lovely." He takes a bite and closes his eyes in pleasure. "About Martin, no. He's divorced."

I frown. "Can't we be Vatican II about this?"

"Well, Maggie, you couldn't get married in the church, and we wouldn't want that, would we? It wouldn't be a true marriage. Unless he can get an annulment, that is."

Maybe I'll check Martin out on my own, outside the auspices of the papal police here. Father Tim continues.

"No, I've a few ideas. I spoke with Father Bruce at St. Pius, and we're sure we'll come up with something."

Great. Two priests plotting my love life. Sadly, they'll probably be better at it than I am. I have nothing to lose, I suppose, having tossed away my dignity many times before. In fact, maybe this will work better. Having your friends pick out someone for you isn't a bad way to meet a man. Father Tim knows me, he likes me—surely he'll pick someone decent.

"Yeah. Okay," I say, my enthusiasm rising. "Thank you, Father Tim. I mean, after last night, I can't believe you're even talking to me, let alone fixing me up on a date. God, I was such a jerk! I'm so sorry. Again."

"Water under the bridge, Maggie," he says around a mouthful. "Georgie! How are you, lad?"

"Hi! Hi, Maggie! Hi, Tim! It's a beautiful day, isn't it, Maggie? It smells so nice in here! I love the smell in here, don't you, Tim?" Georgie slides in next to me and buries his face against my breast. "Hi, Maggie!"

"Hi, Georgie," I say. "How's my best buddy?"

Father Tim and I exchange fond smiles over his breakfast, and for the first time in a while, I feel some real hope.

THE FIRST DATE is less than pleasing for both parties involved.

I've agreed to meet Oliver Wachterski at a bowling alley outside Jonesport. This way, I think, we'll have something to do in case we hate each other.

I get to the ratty little building, which is packed. Once inside, I realize that I've neglected to ask Oliver what he looks like or tell him what I look like. Instead, we've just agreed to meet somewhere at Snicker's Alley.

The pleasing crash of bowling pins thunders around me, and I wander around a little, being a few minutes early. I walk past the game room, music and gunfire twisting together in a rather interesting cacophony. I don't see any men by themselves; instead, there are fathers and team members and buddies.

I stroll the length of the alley again, pretending to look simultaneously amused and nonchalant. *Ah, the bathrooms. Fascinating.* I stop at the end of the alley, where a cute little family is ensconced. The older kids, both girls, watch as their little brother heaves the ball onto the lane with both hands. He must be only four or five, a small kid, and the ball rolls with hypnotic slowness toward the pins. It hits the left bumper, then drifts back to the center.

"Won't be long now, pal," calls the dad. "Getting closer!"

"I think you might get a strike, Jamie," says the younger sister.

The parents are sitting at the scoring table, holding hands. The woman looks at her husband, smiling, and he gives her a quick kiss.

"No!" the little boy cries out. His ball has stopped in the center of the lane. "No!" He bursts into tears.

Immediately, the older girl picks him up. "Don't worry, buddy! That's really special when that happens! Hardly anyone can do that, right, Melody?"

"That's right, Jamie. You get extra points for that!" The girls exchange a conspiratorial big-girl smile over Jamie's head.

The alley attendant comes over and ventures out to retrieve the ball. He has a sticker for the boy, which cheers him up immensely. "I won a sticker, Mommy!" he shouts.

I smile. What a wonderful family, I think, studying the parents. They seem to be perfectly ordinary people, neither handsome nor ugly, fat nor thin. And yet they obviously love each other and have tenderhearted kids. How is something so simple so hard to get?

Someone taps my shoulder. "Maggie?"

I turn. "Oh! Oliver?"

He nods. "Nice to meet you." He's nice-looking, even features, lovely brown eyes that hint at smiling. My heart rises with hope.

"Hi. Yes, I'm Maggie Beaumont. It's really nice to meet you, too. I was just watching this cute family. The boy's ball didn't make it to the pins, and the sisters picked him up and they were all…" I realize I'm in danger of entering the city of Babble-On. "Well. They were very nice."

"Want to get some shoes?" Oliver asks. He's smiling.

"Sure."

We rent our shoes and find our lane, number thirteen. I forget if thirteen is lucky or unlucky, so I decide that it is indeed lucky. We're between a group of serious league bowlers and another family with young kids.

"So you own a diner?" Oliver asks.

"Yes, I own Joe's in Gideon's Cove."

"I've never been there," he says. "But now I have a reason to come." He has dimples when he smiles, and I blush in pleasure.

"Why don't you go first?" he asks.

The first few rounds are fine. We cheer for each other and chat easily. It's when I mention Christy that the first warning shot across the bow is fired.

"You're an identical twin?" he asks.

"Yup." My smile fades at the speculative look on his

face…slightly lecherous, eyebrows raised, smirk on his lips. The boys in high school used to make the same face.

But he says nothing, and when we sit together for a moment, he casually puts his arm around my shoulders.

"This is fun," he says. His hand brushes my neck, and my skin breaks out in gooseflesh. Not the good kind. He leans in for a kiss. I don't stop him, but I don't really want…ew. Very wet. Very spitty. Tongue already? Okay, enough. I jerk back.

"Yes. It's fun. Bowling…well, I've always liked bowling. Okay! Your turn! Tie-breaker, so put on your game face! You're the Red Sox, I'm the Yankees. Actually, I want to be the Red Sox. Okay? So watch out! Give it your best shot."

Finally, I manage to wrestle my mouth into submission. I stare at my hands and wish I hadn't bothered using my ultra-expensive rose oil/lanolin/honey cream this evening.

Oliver gives me an odd look and gets up, and I take a quick swipe at my mouth. He picks up his ball from the little conveyor belt and goes into his windup. Just as the ball flies from his hands, he falls to the floor, writhing.

"Ow! Shit! Ow!"

I rush to his side, and the people from lanes twelve and fourteen stop what they're doing.

"Are you okay?" I ask. "What happened?"

"My groin! I popped my hernia. Damn it!"

"You *what?*" I wince. His face is bright red, and he's clutching himself rather graphically with both hands. Several people gather around us.

"I popped a hernia, okay? Just push on it, and I should be able to stand." Though his face is red, his eyes are…calm. Hmm.

"Do you need any help?" the mother from lane fourteen asks.

"No," Oliver snaps. "Just push on it, Maggie."

My hands instinctively grasp each other. "Well... why don't *you* push on it?"

"Because I can't! You need leverage! Just do it, Maggie!"

"Push on where, exactly?" I ask. A prickle of mistrust crawls up my neck.

"My groin. Right there. Jesus, Maggie, I'm in pain here!"

Is he? Or is he faking? Would he do this just for some weird sexual thrill? I barely know this guy. I don't want to push on his groin! Blech!

"Come on, Maggie!" he says.

"Right. Right, okay...it's just that I never...you know...hernias? I don't know anything about hernias. Maybe we should wait for a medic. I'll call 911."

"No! This happens all the time. For God's sake, Maggie, just push." His teeth are gritted now, and I can't tell if it's from pain or frustration that I'm not feeling him up. He certainly looks pissed off.

"Um, okay, so where exactly?" I say, biting my lip.

"Here." He grabs my hand and shoves it on his... well, you know. His male place. The family next to us hustles their kids away.

"Go ahead, honey," one of the male league players says. "Push."

Grimacing, I look away and give a tentative push against his, um, flesh.

"Harder, Maggie! Harder!" Is that pain or sexual frenzy? I just can't tell. "Push harder!"

Oh, crap, is this for real? He certainly isn't good

with pain, and that doesn't make me like him any better. I push a little harder.

"Will you stop fucking around and do it?" Oliver snarls.

Years of lifting giant bags of potatoes and onions, wrestling economy-size sacks of rice and flour, endless bike riding and walking, have made me quite strong. It's something I'm rather proud of, my strength. I look down at Oliver's speculative eyes, and push with all my might.

His scream rips through the air, soaring over the clatter and smash of pins. Every single person in the place turns to look, reducing the racket of the bowling alley to the silence of an empty church, except for Ollie's shriek. Then his voice breaks out of the range of human hearing, and all is perfectly quiet.

"Better?" I ask.

Twenty minutes later, Oliver is carried out by the ambulance people. "Good luck," I call as he is trundled past.

"Bitch," he chokes. His face has returned to bright red from the purple my great strength induced. I feel no guilt whatsoever. Harder he said, and harder he got.

"Well, if he didn't have a hernia, I hope you gave him one, sweetie," says a woman leaguer kindly. "I thought he was kind of a prick."

I smile at her. "Me, too."

I make a mental note on the drive home: thirteen is definitely bad luck.

CHAPTER SEVEN

ANOTHER GREAT STORY of the horrors of dating. I entertain half the town with Oliver's Groin, the latest in a series of laugh-out-loud jokes that comprises my love life. Soon I'll have enough for a daily calendar.

My second date from Father Tim's list of eligible bachelors is Albert Mikrete. We meet at a steakhouse on Route 1, Al and I. And while he is a good-looking man, financially secure, considerate and pleasant, and while we agree that Maggie Mikrete would be an excellent name, and while he was apparently quite brave during his colonoscopy last month *and* his cataract surgery in January, we decide at the end of our meal that perhaps we aren't quite right for each other.

"You're a lovely girl," Al says as he pays the check (at least there's that). He puts away the pictures of his grandchildren and smiles. "And you've been so kind to an old man like myself, sitting here all night, listening to me go on."

"I'll probably kick myself for letting you go," I say, horrified to realize that Al's been my best date in years.

"Well, I can't wait to tell my bridge club that I went on a date with a sweet young thing. Imagine! Me, dating a woman forty-six years younger!"

We laugh and hug and part as friends, and he drives

with painstaking care out of the parking lot, another senior citizen fallen to my charms. When I get home, there's a wheezing, laughing message on my machine from Father Tim. "Oh, shite, Maggie," he says, and I smile at the rare curse. "You've already gone, then. Well, by the time you get home tonight, you'll find that wires got a wee bit crossed…" He dissolves into more gales of laughter. "Ring me when you get in."

I pick up the phone and hit number three on speed dial. "You're speaking to the future Mrs. Albert Mikrete," I say when he answers.

"Oh, Maggie!" he says. "I'm so sorry. It seems that Father Bruce was thinking of the wrong person…tell me it wasn't awful."

"It wasn't, actually. He has beautiful grandchildren."

This causes another shower of laughter, and I lie back on my bed and listen happily.

That Sunday as I field the after-church brunch crowd, I'm surprised to see Al come in. He waves vigorously as I serve the Tabors their pancakes.

"Thought I'd stop by and see you, sweetheart," he announces loudly, adjusting his hearing aid. The diner becomes quiet. "I wanted to tell you again what a wonderful time I had on our date."

I smile. "Me, too, Al." At least this time, I'm not embarrassed. Or drunk.

"WHAT ABOUT KEVIN MICHALSKI?" Father Tim asks the next week, taking his usual seat at the diner.

"I used to babysit him," I answer, gazing out at April. Sadly, it doesn't look different from muddy March, though the air is a bit gentler. There may be a slight fuzz of red on the distant oaks, but I can't really tell.

"Ah. And that puts him out of the running, does it?"

"He must be twelve or thirteen years younger than I am, Father Tim. He's nineteen years old. I'd like someone who can buy a six-pack."

"All right, then," says Father Tim. He seems to have really gotten a tickle out of arranging my dates and consults his list with a serious expression. "I've one last man to try, and if that doesn't work, I'm giving up on the world of dating."

"You realize how that sounds, don't you?" I ask him.

"This one's a winner, mind you," he says. "I've been saving the best for last."

"Crafty of you," I murmur.

He grins. "You'll thank me for this one, Maggie. You will."

"Good," I say. "Because this is your last chance. If he doesn't work out, I'm putting myself on eBay."

The breakfast crowd is now finished. Octavio is singing in the kitchen, Georgie is packing up leftovers for me to take to the soup kitchen, and Judy is painting her nails in the corner booth. I've already baked five dozen chocolate chip cookies for the fire department tonight, and later this afternoon, I'll do my Meals on Wheels route. Mrs. K. and I have plans to watch a movie together...*The Cave,* I think she said. She likes a good scare. It's a typical day, busy, full, tiring. Not a bad day at all.

But loneliness gnaws at me, and filling my time with pleasant tasks ain't cutting it. While watching a gory movie with Mrs. K. holds its charms, it's not what I really want. I want to watch a movie with my husband while our kids sleep upstairs. He'll ask me if I want some ice cream as I go upstairs to check that the covers haven't slipped off the baby. Then he'll say, "Hey, move over," so he can sit next to me and play with my hair. "I love you," I'll say, and he'll answer, "Thank God for that."

AFTER MRS. K. HAS fallen asleep on our movie, I creep up to the apartment, satisfied that Colonel, even if he isn't young, would at least alert me to the presence of evil. Then, I supposed, he would watch me be slaughtered by the creature that he barked at, and eventually he'd probably curl up and gnaw one of my bones for the rest of the night.

"You wouldn't eat me, would you, boy?" I ask, getting him a chew stick just in case. He takes the treat delicately from me and lies down gingerly. His hips must hurt. "You're the best, Colonel." He glances at me and thumps his tail in agreement.

I go to my little desk in the corner and glance out the window. From here I can see the harbor and the few lights that twinkle sweetly there. I turn on my computer and go on the Internet. I usually don't surf unless I have a reason, but tonight, that loneliness is waiting to pounce. I'll just look. No one will ever know.

Last night I babysat for Violet. I love my niece so much, marvel at her perfect dimpled hands, her sweet breath, silky dark hair, her fascinating, pulsating soft spot. After Christy and Will left, I did what I usually do—pretended she was mine. Do I covet her? Absolutely. I cooked her some carrots and oatmeal, ground up some chicken and gave her a mashed banana for dessert. Then I bathed her and let her dump water out of a cup for a half hour, nearly becoming drunk on the smell of Johnson's baby shampoo. Holding her on my lap, I read *The Big Red Barn* seven or eight times. Violet never failed to be charmed at my animal imitations, and every time I said, "Cocka-doodle doo! Moo, Moo!" she would turn to me, eyes dancing, her little pearl teeth gleaming with saliva.

When I could keep her awake no longer, I sat in the rocking chair in her room and settled her against my chest, humming tunelessly until she fell asleep, holding her until my arms trembled from not moving. Laying her in the crib, I pulled up her tiny down comforter just so, arranged her bunny and her moose to be close to her head but not too close, and watched her sleep, pink as a new rosebud, her eyelashes a sooty smudge on her cheeks.

"I love you so much," I whispered. I rather hoped she would wake up and fuss so I could comfort her, but she slept deeply, not moving as I stroked her cheek with my pinky, the least rough of all my fingers.

Right. So. Can't have a baby if I don't have a mate.

I type in a few terms for Google, then click on the first Web site that comes up without giving myself time to chicken out. Before I am allowed to see who is ripe for the picking in northern Maine, I must first answer some questions. *Are you a woman seeking a man?* I most certainly am. Then I enter in my approximate date of birth and zip code. *Pick a user name,* I am ordered. Okay, I think. Something nauseating and memorable. "Booboobear." *Sorry, that name is already taken. Please choose again.* "Reallyniceperson." *Sorry, that name is already taken. Please choose again.* I glance at my dog. "Colonel McKissy." *Sorry, that name—*

"Oh, for heaven's sake," I mutter. I type in some gib-berish and finally get through. The next few questions are easy…my body type, hair color, eye color. For these, I'm truthful. Body type, average. Eyes gray, hair… hmm. Am I light brown or dark blond? Dark blond sounds more alluring, so dark blond I am. Then we get to the interesting stuff. Body Art. Does double piercing my ears count? Apparently not. The choices include things like *inked all over, fanged* and *branded.* Branded? Do people get branded these days? Should I invest in a brand, perhaps?

"See?" I tell Colonel. "This is why I don't do Internet dating."

Still, it's interesting. I skip the body art section and move onto best feature. Hmm. I guess everyone would say their eyes…so I'll say smile. I have a nice smile, a ready smile. My teeth are straight and even… Smile it is. But smile is not on the list. Calves are on the list, and forearms, nipples and navel, but not smile.

Tell us about yourself, the computer form urges. Will do.

"Hometown girl, love my family, love my dog. Want to make a nice life with someone loyal, funny and kind-hearted. I love to bake, feed people and ride my bike. Nice-looking and once or twice a year, I can even pull off beautiful." Yes, if I spend a few hours fussing with my hair, using a pore-minimizing mud mask, soaking my hands and spending a half hour on makeup, that is. Not that I *do,* mind you, but I *can.*

"I'm good-natured and don't mind laughing at myself, either." As I've demonstrated far too often, I think. "Enjoy reading, scary movies and baseball. Want to settle down and have kids." Why be coy, right?

After numerous other sections, such as religious preferences, turn-ons (fangs are among the choices listed) and my idea of the perfect first date, I am finally allowed to see the eligible men within 75 miles of my zip code. There are two.

Looking for goddess to rain with me as we conquer the universe and all it's mysteries, explore the depths of our sensual natures and experament on the laws of love. You are big-breasted, young, stunning, adventurous, sexually daring and don't mind being submissive when your god commands it. So much can be learned from exploring each other physically... why wait is what I say. Come with me and bend to my desires, o goddess, and you will not be sorry.

I'm sorry already, actually. The misspellings are enough to put me off, let alone the gist of the message. I click on the second.

Single father of two, abandoned by whore of a wife and left to deal with everything alone. She cleaned out the bank accounts, took the good car and left me with nothing, and this after fifteen years of sucking my soul dry in the first place. Let alone talk about what it's doing to the kids. Your mother's a bitch, I tell them. Sorry kids, but that's the way it is. So anyways, I'm looking for someone who loves kids and doesn't mind watching mine. Preferably someone who doesn't have kids of their own, because you know how fucked up that can be. I work long hours and won't be home much, so you should love taking care of the house, too. I'm extremely good-looking and have a great sense of humor.

"I don't care if you're Jude Law," I say. "You need some serious counseling." Colonel shares my disbelief and rises to put his head on my lap. I stroke his ears, and he burps softly in response, tail wagging. The phone rings.

"Maggie, I've got you set up for a phone date," Father Tim announces.

"Bless you, Father," I answer. "I think you're my last hope. Not that I've forgotten Oliver and his groin, mind you."

"I'm asking for your forgiveness on that one, Maggie," he says. "That was a fluke. This time I've a fine fellow by the name of Doug Andrews."

"What does he do?" I ask.

"I believe he's a fisherman."

"Okay." Plenty of men around here are. "Anything else?"

"Well now, I've not met him myself, nor has Father Bruce. He's from Ellsworth, a member of the church down there, and Father Bruce was kind enough to speak to his pastor. But from the account I've heard, our Mr. Andrews is a good-looking man in his thirties."

"Mmm-hmm. And why does he need to be fixed up by a priest?" I ask. Even though I myself require this service, I'm suspicious of others who also need it.

"He's a widower," Father Tim answers. "Lost his wife a couple of years ago."

"Great!" I answer, then immediately correct myself. "I mean, of course, *not* great. That's awful. So sad." I roll my eyes. "What I mean is, at least he was normal enough to meet someone once. It's better than just being a weirdo who never was able to get married in the first place." I pause. "Like me."

"Maggie, you're not a weirdo. Granted, you talk a bit too much, and you've a way of sticking your foot in your mouth, but you're a jewel. And if a girl as wonderful as you needs a bit of help in finding someone, doesn't it stand to reason that there's a wonderful man out there who does, as well?"

"Um…I guess so." Did Father Tim just insult me or compliment me? A little of both, it seems. "Well, is he going to call me?"

"He is, yes. Tomorrow night. Nine o'clock. I assume you'll be in?"

"Yup." I hop up and make the note on my blackboard. "Father Tim, I really hope something turns out with this guy," I say. "I'm so tired of first dates. I just don't know why it's so hard to meet someone."

He sighs in my ear. "Nor do I, Maggie. As I said, you're a fine person. And you will find someone. The Lord works in mysterious ways."

"A priest finding me a boyfriend *is* on the mysterious side, Father Tim." His laughter warms my heart.

CHAPTER EIGHT

DOUG ANDREWS DOES INDEED sound very nice. We spoke for almost an hour and agreed to meet at a restaurant between Ellsport and Gideon's Cove. There aren't that many restaurants open year round up here, but Jason's Taverne is, which makes it a fairly popular place. It's a squat, unremarkable structure sitting at the edge of Route 187, easy to get to, clearly visible from both directions. Half of the place is the bar area, which has a big-screen TV permanently set to the New England Sports Channel. Because of this, and because it's open twelve months a year, the bar is always busy. The restaurant section is quieter, and the food is simple and good.

This afternoon, Christy came over and helped me pick out what to wear, even lent me a beaded necklace and hair clip to "bling" me up a little. It was fun, like high school, almost, when Christy, who didn't have a boyfriend until senior year, would help me get ready for a Saturday night with Skip. The end result is that I look pretty nice, in my own opinion. My hair style is elegant but casual, the streaks that I got a few weeks ago going a long way to turn me from light brown to dark blond. I'm wearing a black shirt with a pretty, curving neckline and velvety black pants. I even put on makeup.

Although I caution myself not to get excited, I can't help it. Doug and I talked easily. He sounded so reassuringly normal, talking about work (he's a manager at a fisheries plant), sailing, even a little about his wife, who died in a small plane accident. There were no warning bells, no awkward pauses. He seemed interested in me, wanted to hear about Joe's Diner, asked nice questions about Christy and Colonel, my two favorite people.

I get to the restaurant early, go inside and ask the hostess if Doug has arrived. At the bar are a couple of men engrossed in the Red Sox pregame show, and although I can only see their backs, I know Doug isn't among them. He told me he is prematurely gray, and the guys there are dark-haired.

The hostess shows me to a table near the gas-fueled fireplace. I sit facing the door, my back to the bar and the giant TV, so that I can see Doug when he comes in.

"Would you like a drink?" the hostess asks.

"Well, maybe I should wait for my friend. Actually, no. I'll have a, um…I don't know. Glass of wine? How about a pinot grigio? Do you have that by the glass?"

"Santa Margarita?" she asks.

"Sounds great," I say.

Trying to look comfortable when you're waiting for someone in a restaurant is difficult. I study the few other diners. An older couple eats in silence two tables away, and a young woman and a much older woman chat animatedly in the corner. Grandmother and granddaughter, I'd guess. Aside from them and the guys at the bar, the restaurant is fairly deserted.

I glance over at the door. The hostess is reading a book. I should have brought one, too. I hate waiting. I turn in my seat and glance at the game. The Sox are trying out a rookie pitcher. If I were home tonight, I'd be watching. It's nice to have somewhere else to be.

A waitress comes over with my wine. "Would you like to see a menu?" she asks.

"No, no, I'm sure my friend will be along soon. But thanks," I say. I glance at my watch. It's ten after seven, and we agreed to meet at seven. I take a sip of wine to take the edge off my nervousness. *He'll come,* I tell myself. He sounded so promising. And eager to meet me. He'd even said how nice I sounded.

Please, God, I pray silently, straightening out the salt and pepper shakers. *Don't let this turn out to be a disaster, because I don't think I can take another one. I hate to bother you when I'm not dying or lost at sea or a soldier or whatever, but if you have just a sec, can you please, please send me a good guy this time? I don't need much...just a decent, goodhearted man. Please. Sorry to bug you. Over and out.*

The table now looks quite tidy. Nothing left to straighten. I take another sip of wine, then check my cell phone. No missed messages. I sneak another look at the door. We did say we'd meet in the restaurant, didn't we? Yes, I'm sure we did. *Let's meet in the restaurant so we can talk,* Doug had said. *The bar is pretty noisy.* That's right. He's been here before. So he's not lost. Just a little late. Well, not so little any more. Sixteen minutes.

The waitress brings the older couple their food, then glides over to me. "Would you like to order an appetizer?" she asks.

"No, no! I'm fine. My friend is just a little late," I tell her.

"Sure," she says. Is that pity in her gaze? "Just flag me down if you change your mind."

Just then the door opens. This has got to be him, I think, willing it to be Doug.

It's not. Feeling like I've just been slapped, I drop my gaze to my lap, away from the people who just came in. *Please, no.* It seems my bones have just evaporated, and my heart begins to pound. *Don't let them see me. Shit, shit, shit. Don't let them see me.*

"Maggie? Oh, my God! It *is* you!"

I look up with a firm smile. "Skip. Hello."

Mr. and Mrs. Skip Parkinson stand at my table. I stand up, too, trying to wrap my brain around the fact that I've seen Skip twice in one month after a decade of reprieve.

"Wow!" Skip announces. "You look just the same! It's so great to see you! You remember Annabelle, don't you? Annie, this is Maggie, a girl I went to school with."

A girl you slept with, too. The first one. The one whose heart you broke in public. "Hello. I don't think we've met."

I didn't get a look at her face in the rain a few weeks ago, but now I see that her features are small and delicate and girlish. Her makeup is perfect, subtle, invisible except for her deep red lipstick, which looks daring and provocative on her. We shake hands, and I can't help wince as my peasantlike paw envelops her satiny, manicured hand.

"Hello, Maggie," she says, and she has a soft drawl. "It's so lovely to meet any old friend of Skip's."

"Uh, thank you." I can't bring myself to look Skip directly in the face, and the three of us stand there awkwardly. Finally I say, "Well, um, would you like to sit down?" and instantly regret my foolish offer.

"Oh, well, now, we don't want to intrude," Annabelle says politely.

"Meeting someone, Maggie?" Skip asks, glancing at the empty place across from me.

"Well, yes. I'm meeting a friend, and I got here a little early, and, um, well, please join me." I sit down heavily and swallow. They sit on either side of me, flanking me. I can't help it anymore—I look at Skip.

He is still wonderfully handsome. His boyish face has improved with age, crinkles and lines giving him character that was lacking before. A neatly trimmed goatee hides his soft chin—he used to hate those profile shots when he was at bat. His suit looks expensive, a soft, dove gray with a dark blue tie.

"So how've you been, Maggie?" he asks, and instead of awkwardness or shame in his voice, there's a touch of arrogance.

"Fine, fine, great," I babble. "And you? How are things?"

"Couldn't be better," Skip answers. "Right, Annie?"

She gives a cute little smile and rolls her eyes, as if to say, "Isn't he a nut?"

"Still working at the diner, Maggie?" Skip wants to know.

I take a long pull of my wine and glance hopefully at the door. *If you came in now, Doug, I'd kiss you. Hell, I'd have sex with you right on this table.* "Yes. Um, I own it now." What is usually a source of pride to me now sounds slightly embarrassing. *A diner owner. Never left Gideon's Cove after you dumped me. Couldn't even find a different job.*

"That's very interesting," Annabelle says. I wonder if he's ever told her about me. If so, she must have ice water in her veins, because she looks calm and relaxed. She smiles pleasantly.

"Do you work, Annabelle?" I ask. It's easier to look at her than at Skip.

"Well, not any more," she admits. "Not since Henry was born. Our oldest. I do a little pro bono work on the side."

"She's a lawyer," Skip announces loudly.

"Well, now, honey, that's sweet," she says affectionately. "Maggie, I *was* a lawyer before having the children, but now, between them and trying to take care of the house and all, I just don't have the time."

Lawyer, wife, mother. "So are you visiting your parents, Skip?" I manage to ask. My heart is thudding in my temples, and I try to keep my hands on my lap so they won't see that they're shaking.

"Exactly. We left the kids with them, thought we'd go out and grab a bite."

"It's our anniversary," Annabelle says with another doe-like look at Skip.

"That's great," I say. Much to my disgust, I feel tears prick at my eyes. I clear my throat and say, "Well, don't let me keep you from your romantic dinner. It was nice seeing you—"

"Oh, not at all," Annabelle interrupts. "This is wonderful, two old friends getting the chance to catch up. We can surely spare a few moments."

Southern hospitality at its finest. I keep my eyes on the tablecloth.

"You're not married, are you, Maggie?" Skip asks. His voice is like a knife. He must know that I'm not. His parents still live in town. They even come to the diner once in a great while.

"No," I answer.

"Any kids?" he asks, his eyes boring into me. I wonder why he's being so cruel.

"Nope. No kids." I force a smile as I say it.

"And you're meeting friends tonight?" Annabelle says.

"Yup! Just one, actually."

"Anyone I know?" Skip asks.

"So you have a couple kids?" I ask Annabelle. I can't think of anything else to say.

"Yes, we do. Three, actually." She shoots Skip a mysterious little smile.

"And another on the way," Skip announces. *See what a colossal stud I am?*

"Oh, that's nice," I say. "Wow. Four kids. That's nice."

Skip always wanted four children. He said so once, when we were enjoying a post-coital cuddle. "Let's have four," he said, and the memory is so vivid I can practically smell his sweat. "Two boys for me, two girls for you." I thought it sounded wonderful.

"Would you like to see a picture?" Skip doesn't wait, just fishes out his wallet and shoves it across the table to me. There they are, the Skip Parkinsons and their progeny.

"That's Henry, Henry the fourth, actually," Annabelle says, pointing with her lovely fingernail. "Here's Savannah, and here's Jocelyn." The girls' blond hair is neatly braided, their plaid dresses matching. The little boy is the image of Skip.

No doubt the new baby will be also be a boy. Skip always got what he wanted. I nod and blink, hoping the candlelight will hide the tears in my eyes.

"Hey."

Someone thumps into the chair across from me. I look up. It's Malone. Maloner the Loner, surly, scary Malone. My mouth drops open.

"I was at the bar. Didn't see you," he says, and his blue eyes stare into mine.

"I—um—"

"Sorry you had to wait," he says. His voice is like a growl, rough from lack of use, no doubt, and it takes me a minute to realize what he's doing. My eyes pop open a little, and the lines around his mouth move slightly. It might be a grin.

"Um, well. Hi. Hi, Malone. Uh, this is Skip Parkinson. Do you know each other?" Skip extends his hand, but Malone keeps staring at me. Then, as if reluctant to do so, he slides his gaze from me to Skip and gives a brief nod. He doesn't shake Skip's hand.

"And this is Annabelle, Skip's wife," I say. Malone takes her hand briefly and nods again. Then he looks back at me. I smile tentatively.

"Well, Skip, why don't we leave these two to their dinner?" Annabelle suggests. "It was wonderful meeting you, Maggie. Hope to see you all again."

"Good luck," I tell her, then look at Skip. "Bye."

"See you, Maggie," he says. As they walk away, Skip glances at Malone, then leans down to whisper loudly into Annabelle's ear. I catch the words "poor white trash." The shithead.

I look back at Malone. "I can't say I've ever been so glad to see someone in my life," I tell him honestly.

He raises an eyebrow.

"That's my old boyfriend," I confide. "He dumped me for her. I'm supposed to be on a blind date, but apparently, I'm being stood up, and they came in and whipped out pictures of their perfect kids and I was just about to lose it."

Malone keeps looking at me, and I realize he knows all this. He came to my rescue.

"Thanks for pretending to be my date," I say.

"Want some more wine?" he asks after a minute.

"God, yes," I answer.

From over at their table, I hear Mr. and Mrs. Parkinson laughing merrily. I try not to look.

"Malone, how did you know I was…you know… being stood up, trapped, whatever? And what are you doing here?"

The waitress comes over. "Here you are!" she cries merrily to Malone. "What can I get you?" Malone orders a beer and another wine for me, and the waitress bustles off.

Malone looks at me for another minute before answering my question. "You're pretty obvious," he says.

"I am? How? I mean—"

"You kept looking at the door, then your watch. Then that arrogant asshole came in and you looked like you wanted to crawl under the table. Good enough?"

Jeez. Surly guy. "So you just dropped by for a beer?" I ask.

He doesn't bother to answer, just looks over at Skip. Over in the bar, there's a cheer as the Red Sox do something great. Skip doesn't look. Too many painful memories, no doubt.

The waitress brings our drinks, and I clink my glass against Malone's. "To you, Malone. Thanks. Another piece of pie awaits you, courtesy of Joe's Diner."

He rolls his eyes. I gather we won't be talking much.

"So you don't have to stay or anything, Malone. Maybe I'll just head out."

"You hungry?" he asks. It's like talking to a bear, just a series of low growls and grunts that I must translate into words.

"I'm starving, actually."

"Let's eat, then."

And so begins one of the strangest dinners I've ever had. My emotions roll and collide...distress at seeing Skip, gratitude toward Malone—who knew he'd do something so nice?—irritation with Malone, because he's about as friendly as a hungover troll. Still, I try to make conversation.

"So, Malone, you have a kid, don't you?" Attempt number one.

He nods once in response.

"Boy or girl?"

His blue eyes, which would be beautiful on someone else—someone who smiled, say—just stare back at me. "Girl," he says after a minute.

"Does she live around here?" I ask.

"No." He stares at me as if daring me to go on, but I lose my nerve. Belatedly, I remember the story of his wife and child moving across country.

I make attempt number two a little lighter. "So, Malone is your last name, isn't it?" He nods. "What's your first name?"

I get the death stare and silence, then, "I don't use it."

I sigh and drink some more wine. We order dinner— hamburgers for both of us—and the silence stretches on.

Skip and Annabelle seem to have no such problems. Lots of laughs from over there. Twinkling giggles from her, low chuckles from him. At one point during our meal, one of the guys at the bar goes over to Skip and asks, "Didn't you used to play baseball?" and Skip says with false lightness, "Oh, hell, a long time ago when I was a kid," as if he gave it up for something more meaningful...like selling cars.

"I really think I hate him," I whisper to Malone. He nods.

The Parkinsons are not finished. Apparently (I have forbidden myself to look at them), a gift is given, because Annabelle cries, "Oh, Skip! Oh, sugar, you shouldn't have!"

Malone doesn't look over. Neither do I. We look at each other instead, united in this odd, uncomfortable way. I've now had enough wine that it's starting not to bother me.

"You don't talk much, do you, Malone?" I ask.

He doesn't answer.

"Want to have a staring contest?" I ask. Bingo! The lines around his eyes deepen and the corners of his mouth move upward a fraction. "I think you may have just smiled," I inform him. "How did it feel? You okay?"

As usual, he doesn't answer, but there's something a little different. It takes me a minute to realize it, but Malone is kind of...appealing. Those lashes are so long they're actually tangled in the corners. His hair is thick, curling a little around his ears and neck. And while his face is slashed with harsh lines, and while I have yet to see a real smile, his mouth is full and slightly pouting and rather sexy, actually. Life has left its mark on Malone's face with a heavy hand, but it's an interesting face, scruffy and rugged and gloomy. His cheekbones are sharp and angular, carved by the wind, almost, and it's this phrase that makes me realize I shouldn't have ordered that second glass of wine.

I clear my throat and look away. The waitress brings our check, and I fish around in my purse for my wallet. Malone takes out his first and withdraws a few bills.

"No, no, let me," I say, taking his money and holding it out to him. "This is definitely on me."

He scowls, making his face a little scary again. He doesn't take the money. I put it back down and stand up.

"Okay. Thank you for a lovely dinner and everything else," I say. He follows me across the restaurant.

"Bye, now. So nice meeting you," Annabelle calls out.

"Ditto," I say. Malone offers nothing, and neither does Skip.

In the parking lot, I pause. "Thanks again, Malone," I say.

"Ayuh." He walks to his truck, pleasantries complete.

I get into my car and turn the key. The engine doesn't start. This is not an uncommon problem for me, and I sigh, pop the hood and get out. Malone is still there, sitting in his truck, watching me.

"It's fine," I call. "Happens all the time."

But it's dark, and I have to fumble in my purse for the screwdriver I carry at all times. If I can just find it, I'll open the hood, stick the screwdriver in the air filter, and the car should start. But I can't find it, because I failed to transfer it from my everyday pocketbook to the smaller one I'm carrying now. Nor can I find anything else that would work, like a pen.

Sighing, I walk over to Malone's truck. "Do you

have a screwdriver?" Surely he must. He's a man, isn't he?

"No."

I close my eyes. The restaurant door opens, and Skip and Mrs. Skip walk over to their expensive, shining car.

"Good night, now!" Annabelle calls. Skip holds the door for her, then goes to the driver's side. He looks over to me and pauses.

"Malone, how about a ride home?" I ask before Skip can do anything.

"Sure," Malone says. He leans across the seat and opens the passenger door for me, which is unexpectedly polite from a man who has uttered only a handful of words this evening. I climb in. Tomorrow, Jonah or my father will have to drive me back here, but at least I'm safe from Skip's eyes for now. Malone starts the truck and pulls out of the parking lot.

"I really appreciate this," I tell him. He glances at me but doesn't say anything.

We don't talk on the way home—I'm too engrossed in thought to try to lure Malone out of his cave. When we get into town, I break the silence and direct him to my house. He throws the truck into park and hops out. I get out before he can open my door.

"I'll walk you in," he growls.

"No, that's okay, you don't—" But he's already waiting by the porch. I sigh. "I live upstairs," I say. "That's Mrs. K.'s apartment. Mine's up there." Malone waits for me to go first. The stairway is a straight shot to my door, and there's barely enough room for both of us to stand on the tiny landing. I fish out my key and unlock the door, then turn around to thank him.

"Thanks again, Malone. That was really—" My words are cut off, because Malone leans in and kisses me.

At first, I'm too shocked to think a damn thing. Malone! *Kissing* me! Of all the—but then it occurs to me that I'm kissing him right back, and it also occurs to me that Malone knows what he's doing. His mouth is surprisingly soft and warm, and his razor stubble rasps gently against my skin. His hands cup my head, holding me steady, and I realize that my own hands are pressed against his chest. He feels deliciously solid, his heart thudding under my palm. His mouth moves to my jaw, and I breathe in the smell of soap and salt. Then he kisses my mouth again. My knees tingle and grow weak, and I grip his shirt, giving a little sigh. Then Malone pulls back, smooths his thumb across my mouth and looks down at the floor of my porch.

For a moment, I think he's going to say something, but he doesn't. He just gives a terse nod and heads down the stairs.

"Um…good night," I call. He lifts his hand and gets into his still-running truck, then drives off in a most ordinary manner, leaving me dazed and stunned on my little porch. "Right," I say. Perhaps I will wake up in the morning and find that this whole night has been just a bizarre dream. Those wiggly knees of mine are telling me different.

I go inside and kneel down to pet Colonel, who is waiting patiently by the door. "Hey, buddy," I say. "How's my pooch?" He licks my chin, then, satisfied that I am indeed home again, goes back to his doggy bed in the corner and lies down with a groan.

"Malone kissed me tonight," I tell him.

Colonel doesn't understand it, either.

CHAPTER NINE

I GET A CALL on my cell phone the next day while I'm at the diner, and for a brief second, I think it might be Malone. It's not. Of course not, as he doesn't have the number.

"Maggie, hi, it's Doug," says the caller.

Doug? Oh, Doug. "Hi," I say.

"Listen, I'm so, so sorry about last night," he says. There's a pause. I wait to feel bad, but nothing comes. "I just panicked at the last minute," Doug says. His voice is heavy with misery. "Maggie, I guess I'm not really ready to see someone."

"That's okay," I tell him. I ring up Stuart and move the phone away from my cheek. "Everything okay today, Stuart?"

"Wonderful, Maggie." He hands me his filled-out ballot, and I wink at him and resume my conversation. "Don't worry about it, Doug."

"No, it's not okay. I completely chickened out and didn't even call. I feel awful," he says. I think he's crying.

Some high school girls open the door in a cloud of giggles. "Sit wherever you'd like, girls," I tell them. "Doug, hang on a sec." I take the phone into the closet that serves as my office and wedge myself inside. "Hi. Sorry, I'm at the diner. But I can talk now."

"I was all set to meet you," Doug chokes. "I was actually in the car, but I just couldn't do it. You sound like the nicest person—"

"Listen, Doug," I interrupt gently. "It's okay. To tell you the truth, I ran into an old friend and we had a really nice time." A bit of a stretch, but the truth is rather complicated at this moment.

"Really?" Doug asks hopefully.

"Yes," I say. I can hear Georgie making his exuberant entrance, Octavio singing quietly. "It sounds like you're just not ready yet to meet somebody, and that's perfectly fine. When the time is right, you'll know it."

Doug doesn't answer for a minute, and I realize he's crying in earnest. "Do you think so?" he asks thickly, confirming my guess.

"I sure do, Doug." I pause. "From what you said, your wife sounded like a really great person. It'll take some time for you to want to be with someone else."

"I think you're one of the nicest people I've never met," Doug says with a choked laugh.

"If you ever want to get together as friends, I'd like that," I tell him. I wonder if I'd be so generous if Malone hadn't given me something else to think about last night.

Last night, I lay awake in bed for nearly an hour, wondering at the strangeness of humanity. Usually when someone is attracted to someone else, there are signs. Not so with Malone. In fact, I'd have bet my last dollar that he suffered through every minute of our bizarre dinner together. That he didn't like me a bit, especially after I was so catty in the bar with Chantal that night.

Father Tim comes in at 8:30, right after Mass.

"Maggie, I want to hear every detail," he says, rubbing his hands together eagerly. "Oh, and I'll have the eggs benedict today, I think. With regular bacon instead of Canadian, if that's all right?"

"Sure. One Father Tim special coming up." I smile and pour him some coffee, then go into the kitchen to put his order in. When I come out, Chantal is sliding into the seat across from the priest. Any male, no matter his profession, is open season for Chantal.

"Hey, Chantal," I say.

"Hi, Maggie. What's new?" she purrs.

I feel my cheeks grow warm at her question. Chantal hears everything. Did someone see Malone and me together last night? Were there any Gideon's Cove residents at Jason's Taverne? Did someone perhaps see us kissing? I wonder if he'll call me and ask me out. I mean, why would he kiss me—the mere memory of it causes a flutter—if he didn't want to see me again?

"She's blushing," Father Tim observes. "Must have been some date last night."

"Date? What date?" Chantal asks. No, thank God, she doesn't know.

"Well, actually, I'm sorry to say that Doug isn't quite ready for a relationship," I say. I busy myself by refilling the creamers behind the counter. "Still kind of in mourning for his wife."

"I can relate to that," Chantal murmurs. I roll my eyes, but Father Tim is tricked and pats her hand.

"Poor dear," he says, and Chantal sighs hugely, her breasts rising dramatically in her low-cut shirt. Father Tim's compassionate expression doesn't flicker, nor does his gaze drop a millimeter. The man is a saint.

At lunchtime, the bell over the door tinkles and I look up to see my sister, Violet and my parents. "Good morning!" Christy says.

"Fashoo," says Violet, reaching out a plump hand for me to smooch.

"That means 'I love you, Auntie Mags,'" Christy translates, pulling off Violet's pink coat. My parents likewise take off their coats and line up like penguins at the counter. For some reason, no member of the Beaumont family ever sits at a booth.

"How was your date last night?" my mother asks without preamble. "Did you finally meet someone with potential?"

"Oh, it was fine," I answer, feeling that heat creep up my neck again. "Doug is very nice, but he's not ready for a relationship. His wife died about two years ago." There. Nothing I said was untrue. An image of Malone's slight smile causes a sudden cramp in my abdomen.

"Well, he should get out there anyway," Mom says, irritated that a daughter remains single. "A rolling stone gathers no dirt."

"Well said, Mom," Christy says. Our dad smiles into his coffee cup.

"Don't laugh. Maggie's not getting any younger. Before long, Maggie, you'll have problems getting pregnant, and then where will you be?"

I stare at her, stunned that the woman whose womb I began my life in could be so cruel.

"Jeezum, Mom," Christy says.

"It's true," our mother states.

"You'll meet someone when the time is right. Don't worry," my father says in a rare show of defiance to Mom. He pats my hand. My mother snorts.

"Hey, Dad, you know who I ran into last night?" I say, grateful for the chance to change the subject. "You know Malone? The lobsterman?"

Dad looks blank until Christy says, "You know, Dad. His boat is next to Jonah's."

"Oh, yes. Dark-haired fellow? Quiet?"

Pathologically so, yes. "Yeah. Did you have him in school?" Dad taught biology for thirty years and knows just about every person who ever went to school in Gideon's Cove.

"Sure. I think he transferred in midyear. Why, honey?"

"Oh, I just was wondering what his first name was. He wouldn't tell me." I realize I have erred as Christy's left eyebrow lifts. No one else notices.

"Hm. Let's see. Malone. Skinny kid, tall…not a bad student toward the end, but way behind at first. I think there was trouble at home, to tell you the truth. Was it Michael? No, no, not Michael, I'm thinking of the Barone kid. I think it was an Irish name. Liam? No, no, that's not right. Brendan. It was Brendan. Brendan Malone. Or no, that was Brendan Riley. Hmm." Dad thinks for a minute, then shrugs. "Sorry, honey. As I recall, everyone just called him Malone."

"Oh, well. Not important. I was just curious."

Christy looks quite speculative, and I turn away to wait on Ben at the counter, since Judy is doing a crossword puzzle.

Our mother offers to take Violet for the afternoon, claiming that she never gets to see her only grandchild (here with a significant look at me, the daughter who has failed to reproduce). She ignores the fact that she sees Violet almost every day. Once we're alone, Christy pounces.

"So, why the sudden interest in Malone?" she asks, pretending to help me as I pack my car for meal deliveries.

"Oh, I just ran into him last night," I say, feigning nonchalance.

"Mmm-hmm. And?" she prods. Damn this twin thing. She knows far too much.

"Okay. I'll tell you, but you can't tell anyone else." Knowing she won't, I give her the story from last night—Skip, Annabelle, Malone—but for some reason, I don't tell her the ending.

"So he drove me home. Jonah brought me out to get my car this morning and, unlike some siblings, he didn't ask prying questions."

"Well," Christy says. "That was awfully nice, pretending to be your date. Wicked nice."

"Mmm," I murmur. "Listen, I have to go. Do you want to come? It'll be fun. They'll have Colonel *and* you."

"Double the pleasure, double the fun," my sister says. "Sure, I'd love to."

And it is fun. The fourteen people on my route are always overjoyed to see Colonel and me, and when encountered with my mirror image, they nearly wet themselves in delight. We bring in the meals, tidy up at one house, check a prescription at another, chat with the clients, let them pet my gentle dog. I urge Christy to show pictures of Violet, and a lot of old faces break into tender smiles at the sight of my beautiful niece.

"She could be yours," Mrs. Banack says, handing the picture to me.

"True enough," I answer. "I couldn't love her more if she was."

We finish up our route and head for home.

"So still no boyfriend," Christy says as we drive home. I don't comment. "Any ideas?"

"Not really," I say, glancing in my rearview mirror. "I think I'll just give it a rest for a while. I've been on four dates in the last month, and none of them worked out very well."

"You sure? Idle hands are the devil's workhorse, as Mom would say," Christy advises somberly. I laugh, but at the back of my mind is Malone and his gently scraping kiss.

When I get home from dropping Christy off, I zip over to the answering machine, hoping to see the blinking light. No blinking. Malone has not called me.

Nor does he call me that evening. The next day is Sunday, and as I flit between tables, clearing and serving, Malone is on my mind. Why hasn't he called me? Why would he kiss me and then not call me? Should I call him? I shudder at the thought—I wouldn't be able to see him either nod or stare from my apartment, would I? And since that seems to be his main form of communication, it wouldn't be much of a conversation.

It's not that I really like him, I tell myself. Because really, he's a complete stranger. Almost. I liked kissing him, yes. At the thought, my stomach knots and my knees tingle. The after-church crowd takes their time finishing, and when they're done with breakfast, the Sunday lunch crowd comes in. Finally, by about two, all my customers are gone. I wipe down with unusual speed, opting to skip the floor-washing. I'll just wander down to the dock, I think. See how Jonah's doing. Check on the little brother.

Jonah's boat is right against the dock, not moored at its usual spot, which is convenient for me. Inconveniently, Malone's boat is out, so I'll just have to hang out with my little bro for a while. "Hey, Jonah!" I call down. It's low tide, so the dock is a good twenty feet lower than it will be six hours from now. Tides in this part of Maine are dramatic, and the gangplank is pitched quite steeply. The smell of fish and salt and tide greet me as I totter down carefully and walk over to Jonah's boat, which is named *Twin Menace* after his beloved big sisters. My brother is not in sight.

"Hey, Joe!" I yell.

"Maggie," he calls back, climbing out of the hold and shutting the door firmly behind him. "What are you doing here?"

"Oh, nothing. Permission to come aboard, captain?"

"Um, no. Actually, I'm just leaving. Sorry."

Drat. "So, do most people go out on a Sunday?" I ask. I've never really taken note of the patterns of the lobster boats; it's something that's so familiar and constant here that it's like background noise. During the summer, it's against the law to haul traps on a Sunday, that I know, but as for the practices of the off-season, I'm clueless.

"Nah. Most of us stay in, even now, I guess." He glances back at the stern of his boat.

"But some go out?" I prod.

"Ayuh."

"When do they come back?" I glance casually over the railing at a small school of baby stripers.

"Dunno."

I sigh. Malone is rubbing off on Jonah, apparently. Usually, my brother won't stop talking…rather like me, I guess. I give it another try. "So they just come back whenever?"

"Maggie, I just said I don't know. What's it to you?"

"Nothing. Just making conversation."

"Well, I have to tie up, and then I'm going," he says. "See you." When I don't move, he frowns. "Did you want something else?"

"I— No. Sorry. Have a nice day."

He nods and starts the engine, pulling the *Twin Menace* away from the dock out to his mooring, then disappears back into the hold, busy with whatever keeps him there.

Clearly, I have to go. I can't be here when Malone comes in, because that would be too obvious and desperate. *Hi, Malone, I'm just hanging around waiting for you. How was your day? Want to kiss me again?* I wince and wisely decide to go home.

CHAPTER TEN

MONDAY IS MY DAY OFF, and I use it to clean my apartment and Mrs. K.'s. As I vacuum up her popcorn crumbs, she follows me around carefully, pointing with her cane at parts I've missed.

"Right *there,* Maggie, dear. And *gracious!* There, too! I can't get over how *sloppy* I am!" I smile—she says this every week. When I'm done, I check her fridge and make sure she's got enough of the barley soup I brought over yesterday.

"Need anything, Mrs. K.?" I ask.

"Dear, I'm *fine.* But tell me, did you have a *friend* over the other night?"

I freeze momentarily. "No, no. Just, you know, someone, um, gave me a ride home."

"I thought it was a *man,*" she says.

"Well, yes, actually, it was a man. Malone. My brother's friend." I hope she doesn't pick up on my blush.

"Malone? I don't *know* anyone by the name of *Malone.* Is he good people? Should you be driving around late at *night* with strangers?"

"Well, he's not really a *stranger,* Mrs. K., because my brother *knows* him."

But of course he is a stranger. And he still hasn't

called me. I looked up his phone number to make sure he has a phone, and he does. Whether he uses it is another question. Again, I can't imagine why he'd kiss me like that and then just…

"He's certainly a *manly* man, isn't he?" Mrs. K. offers. God, did she have binoculars trained on him?

"Malone? Sure, I guess so." I pause in mopping the floor of the tiny kitchen.

"I've always *liked* the manly ones, you know. Mr. Kandinsky wasn't *like* that, but he was a dear. He never understood why I just *loved* Charles *Bronson*, but I did! I think I've seen every *Death Wish* ever made."

"Well, we'll have to *rent* them, won't we?" I say, giving her a kiss on her soft, wrinkled cheek.

Upstairs in my neat little apartment, I still have no messages. My mail contains only credit card offers and my phone bill. Nothing from Malone to indicate he's interested in me.

By five o'clock, I'm climbing the walls. I've cleaned, baked, dropped in on Chantal at town hall and gone grocery shopping. I've read a little, took Colonel to the beach and then brushed his fur afterward. I decide it's time for a walk.

Colonel pads after me as we leave the center of our little town. Gideon's Cove hugs the rocky shore, as the town was founded for shipbuilding purposes. I can see the turret of Christy and Will's house, the gold-painted cross of St. Mary's. I head in the opposite direction.

The air is soft and damp, and while it will probably drop into the low forties tonight, it's still pretty mild. House lights are on, giving a cozy feel to the neighborhood, and I can smell various meals cooking…the Mastersons are having chicken…something garlicky and delicious at the Ferrises' house…Stokowskis are having cabbage…Colonel licks his chops and lingers at that driveway.

We walk uphill, away from the water. Rolly and his wife are sitting on their porch. "Hello, Christy, dear," calls out Mrs. Rolly.

"Hello," I call back. "It's Maggie, actually."

"Oh, I'm sorry, of course. Christy's the one with the baby. What was I thinking?"

"That's okay," I answer. "Nice night, isn't it?"

"Sure," Rolly answers. "Enjoy it before the black flies hatch out."

"You betcha."

I turn onto Harbor Street, a neighborhood of cottages and bungalows owned mostly by summer people. The street looks down onto the water, and I can see the boats bobbing there on the tide, the white of the hulls almost glowing in the deepening dusk.

Feeling like Harriet the Spy (a book I must have read ten times as a kid), I slip into the yard of one such cottage. I know the owners, the Carrolls, since they're summertime regulars at the diner, and I know they live in Boston. Their house is dark, the curtains drawn. I follow the little walk that goes along the side of the house to the backyard. Shielded by dusk and their row of hedges, I peek at the property that backs up to the Carrolls'. If the listing in the phone book is correct, Malone lives here.

It's an ordinary little yard with an oak tree that's just beginning to bud out. There's a small back entryway with a couple of garbage cans lined up neatly against the outside wall. A light shines in a window. Suddenly, the door opens, and Malone appears with a bag of trash.

He takes the top off the garbage can and drops the bag in, replaces the lid and then goes back into the house. It takes about three seconds.

Though it's dusk now, I feel a rush of guilt and embarrassment. Imagine if he caught me, lurking in his neighbors' yard, stalking him…it's so high school. Still, I wait a few minutes, hoping to see him again, in the window, maybe, or back out with his recycling. Nothing. No one. A crow caws in a tree. The wind blows, and I shiver. Colonel grows bored and flops down under a tree.

"Okay, I'm coming," I tell him. One last peek. Nothing. I turn around to leave.

A man is standing an inch from my face. I scream and leap back, my hands fluttering around like a pair of frightened birds. "Jesus, Malone! You scared me! God, I didn't even hear you! Sneaking up on a person like that. Jeez." I press my hand against my heart, which is thundering like a racehorse on speed. Malone looks at me, and the deepening creases of his face may indicate amusement. Or irritation. Hard to tell. "You are one quiet guy, Malone."

"Wanna come in?" he asks, a trace of humor in his gruff voice.

"Um…" Now that I no longer fear for my life, it occurs to me that I've been busted. "Right. Well. I was, you know, walking. Going for a walk. With Colonel here. And, um, well…here we are. Spying on you."

"Try knocking next time," he says, heading into his yard. After a pause, I follow.

He holds the door open for me, reaching down to pat Colonel's head. My dog apparently has a good vibe, because he walks in without pause and begins sniffing.

I come in a bit less bravely, and Malone closes the door behind me. I am trapped in his lair.

We're in a small kitchen with a little counter along one side. The floor is green linoleum, the counter green Formica, the worst of the 1970s. I try to see everything without being obvious, but I miss the boat, ignoring Malone's outstretched hand for a second or two too long. I look at it. Does he want to shake hands? Take me somewhere?

"Your coat?" he says. It takes me a minute to decipher his rumble as human words.

"Right! Here. Thank you. That's great. Okay."

His eyebrows rise slightly, but he says nothing, just hangs my coat on a hook near the door and takes off his own.

"So," I say to fill what I consider to be a gaping silence. "You live here?"

His mouth twitches. "Yeah."

Well, of course he does. "I mean, alone? Do you live alone?"

"Ayuh."

"I see. Hmm. And how long have you lived here?"

"About a year."

A year. "So you've lived here since—" Damn it. I probably shouldn't finish that thought—*since your cousin screwed you*—but I can't think of anything else to fill the space. "Since a year ago?"

Malone just stares eerily back at me, and I look around for Colonel, wanting to know that a friendly face is nearby. Malone finally breaks his vow of silence (and I have to admit, I'm grateful).

"Want a beer?" he asks.

"Oh, no thanks." What am I thinking? "Actually, yes,

please. That would be nice." My palms are sweating with nerves, and I really hate the fact that I can't seem to say anything even moderately intelligent. Malone opens the fridge and hands me a Sam Adams.

"Thank you."

At the sound of refrigerator action, Colonel comes in, wagging hopefully. Malone squats down and pets him. At last, a character reference—he likes my dog.

"Hey, pal," he says, scratching Colonel's head. Wow. A two-word sentence. Colonel moans in pleasure, then licks Malone's hand and walks into the living room. Malone stands up and fixes me with that unwavering blue gaze. Apparently, I am quite fascinating.

"Is that your daughter?" I ask, pointing to the fridge. There are a couple of photos there, one of a chubby-cheeked toddler eating an apple, another more recent shot of a girl around ten or twelve sitting on a boat, shading her eyes from the sun.

"Yup."

Back to the one-worders. My frustration and nervousness get the better of me, and I finally blurt, "Malone, let me ask you a question, okay?"

He nods, a brief jerk of his head.

"Why did you kiss me the other night?" There. Said it. And if my cheeks are now flaming, so what? At least he has to answer.

"The usual reasons," he says, but the lines around his eyes are deeper. He takes a sip of beer, still looking at me.

"The usual reasons. Well, that's funny. Because most times you can tell if someone, you know, likes you. Or is attracted to you. And I never really picked up on that before. With you, I mean."

He doesn't answer. A clock on the wall announces the inevitable passage of time…tick…tick…tick. Finally, I'm about ready to jump out of my skin. "Can I look around?" I ask.

"Sure."

The living room holds a battered old upright piano with what looks like a pretty hard song. *Sonata in A major,* it says. Beethoven. Huh. "Who plays the piano?"

"I do," he grunts.

"Really? You can play this?" I ask, impressed.

He comes in and glides a finger over the keys, too softly to make a sound. "Not that well," he answers.

He's standing pretty close to me. Very close. He smells warm, a little like wood smoke. I can see that he must have shaved at some point in the last day or so, because his face doesn't look as scratchy as the night he kissed me. My eyes fall to his mouth, his full lower lip. So soft. I look away abruptly and take a step back. There's not much else to see. A TV in the corner, a woodstove in the fireplace. A couch. Coffee table. I could tap dance, I have so much nervous energy flowing through me.

"You hungry?" Malone asks.

"No. I had a late lunch. Are you? Am I interrupting dinner? I should probably go." My heart is thudding away, my eyes feel hot and tight.

"Don't go."

Malone takes my hand. His is warm and smooth and thickly callused. He rubs his thumb gently across the back of my hand and doesn't say anything more. It seems the nerves in my hand are directly linked to my groin, because things are definitely tingling down there. I swallow and look around. My dog is sleeping in front of the couch.

Then Malone frowns a little and lifts my hand for a closer look. He makes a little tsking sound, and my jaw tightens.

"Yes, well, my hands are in the water all day long, and then with being near the grill and all—"

"Come here," he says, pulling me back into the kitchen. He lets go of my chapped, disgusting claw, opens a cupboard and rummages around. I lean against the counter, miffed. So what? So I have chapped hands. Big deal. A little eczema and everyone gets distraught. Malone takes out a small tin and opens it. Then he scoops out a little bit and rubs it between his palms. I guess my nasty skin has reminded him of the importance of moisturizing.

"I've tried everything," I say, looking over his shoulder. "Beeswax, lanolin, Vaseline, Burt's Bees, Bag Balm…nothing works. I have ugly hands. My cross to bear. Big deal."

"You don't have ugly hands," he chides. It may be the longest sentence I've heard him say yet. He takes my hand in his and starts working in the cream. It's waxy and cool at first, then, after a few seconds, gets pleasantly warm.

He's not gentle. Malone rubs my hands hard, pressing deep into the soft parts around my thumb, my palm, the heel. He works every finger, giving attention to each rough cuticle, each reddened knuckle. His eyes are intent on my hands as he works, and his face loses some of its harshness. Those sooty lashes go a long way toward softening his expression.

"That feels really nice," I say, and my voice is husky. His mouth pulls up at one corner as he glances at me. He gently returns my hand to my side and starts on the other one, and I close my eyes against the lovely pressure. My hand feels boneless and small in his, smooth and warm and cherished. When he's done with the left, he takes both my hands in his, sliding his fingers between mine with a slowness that makes it feel like the most intimate gesture in the world. He gently folds my arms behind my back, making me arch out toward him a little. He waits until I open my eyes.

"So," I say, and he kisses me then, not letting go of my hands. He kisses gently at first, but with such intensity, like it's the most important thing in the world that he kiss me just exactly right. And he does. God! His lips are firm and smooth and warm, and he takes his time, kissing and kissing me until I pull my hands free and grip his thick, wavy hair. Then without his lips leaving mine, he lifts me onto the counter and moves closer. His tongue brushes mine, and electricity jolts through me, weakening my limbs. His arms are around me so tightly I can hardly breathe. It's like being pulled against a granite wall, safe and solid.

When he pulls back a little, I'm literally panting and it's hard to focus. His eyes are heavy-lidded, too, his mouth parted.

"Stay," he rasps.

"Okay," I breathe.

Then he kisses me again, lifts me off the counter and carries me into his bedroom.

CHAPTER ELEVEN

I WAKE UP ALONE, roughly twelve hours after I arrived. It's just starting to get light outside.

"Malone?" I call out softly. There's no answer, but Colonel's head pops up at the side of the bed. "Hey, Colonel," I say, patting him. I get out of bed, pull on my shirt and pants and pad into the kitchen. There's a note on the table, anchored by the little tin of hand cream.

Maggie— Coffee's there if you want it. Take this.

And that's it.

I sigh and flop in the chair. I gather the "this" in his note is the hand cream, and I take a minute to study my hands. They do feel better than usual, and the redness is a little less, but I still feel mildly disappointed. After changing-your-perspective-on-the-world, mind-altering, life-transforming, earth-moving, sky-shattering sex, it would have been nice to see the other party responsible.

I realize I'm smiling. Possibly purring. Then, acknowledging that I have to get home for a shower and change of clothes before I go to the diner, I get up to find my socks.

All that morning, I'm in a great mood. Every now and then, a bit of last night will flash through my head, and I feel quite steamy. A little smile stays on my lips as I flip home fries and pancakes, crack eggs and pour coffee. Malone, I assume, is out checking his traps. Soon he'll come back. Maybe, for the first time, he'll come into the diner. Maybe he'll finally cash in on that piece of pie. Maybe he'll stare at me as I try to act normal. He might even smile as he drinks his coffee.

I didn't see him smile last night, not really. It was dark. But boy, it was—

"Maggie, love, could I get a spot of coffee?"

"Hey, Father Tim," I call. Now the blush on my cheeks is from guilt.

"Don't you look rosy this morning! I rang you last night but got your machine." Tim holds up his cup for me to pour, the move of a regular.

"Oh, well, you know, I think I just felt like going to bed early," I stammer. It's not a lie. "You know, sometimes you just get…and you just…have to go to…bed." Or get carried to bed, as the case may be, by the incredibly sexy guy who lifts you like you're a bit of milkweed seed and kisses you like it's his last act on earth…which, I'm happy to say, it wasn't.

Father Tim notices my daze. "Are you all together, Maggie? You seem distracted."

I glance around the diner. The morning rush is past, Judy is checking lottery numbers and Georgie is whistling in back. I decide that I owe my pal here a little time and sit down. "Sorry, Father Tim. How are you?"

He leans back in his seat. "Well, now, I'm just fine, Maggie," Father Tim says, and proceeds to tell me about the choir's latest endeavor. "It would've required divine intervention for them to pull off that Beethoven piece, and it seems that our Lord was busy with other things," he chuckles.

Beethoven. Malone plays Beethoven. My cheeks warm, but I force my thoughts back to Father Tim.

Maybe it's because I'm not a proper parishioner, maybe it's because we're roughly the same age, but I know Father Tim and I have a different relationship. A true friendship. He's told me all about his family, his childhood, and I've reciprocated. I like to think he's not just a priest with me, but a regular guy, if priests are allowed to be regular guys. Of course, that's the kind of thinking that leads me into trouble, but even a priest must need to relax around someone once in a while.

Half an hour later, he leaves the diner. And while I'm always happy for his friendship, it's something of a revelation that I suddenly have someone else to think of. Even if it's Malone who barely speaks…at least it's something. In the space of a night, Father Tim isn't the only man in town. *About time you left My boy alone,* I imagine God saying. "Sorry," I whisper.

I glance at my watch. Jonah usually takes only a couple of hours to check his traps, but I know that Malone is more serious than my brother. He has a lot more traps, too, and further offshore, as well. Still, I hope Malone will make it in today. If he doesn't, maybe he'll call.

By three o'clock, I'm irritated with myself. By five, disgusted. By eight-thirty, I'm mad at Malone, and by ten, I hate him.

He didn't drop by the diner. Or my apartment. And he hasn't called me. I throw myself onto my couch with punishing force.

It seems I've made the mistake of far too many women…assuming that last night meant something. Something more than a physical sensation, that is.

Colonel comes over and nudges my feet until I move them, then climbs carefully onto the couch. "Naughty boy," I tell him automatically, sitting up a little to give him more room.

What do I really know about Malone? I search my memory, sifting through the reams of gossip that I've heard in ten years of diner work.

Malone was a few years ahead of me in school…four or five, maybe. I can't remember us being in high school at the same time, and as my father pointed out, he moved to town at some point during his teenage years. Maybe from Jonesport or Lubec, somewhere north of here. I know he married young, maybe just out of high school. I can't remember his wife's name, but I do remember the buzz when she left him.

I had just taken over the diner, was struggling through a crash course in restaurant management, dealing with things like inventory and ordering and how not to burn people's food, so I don't have a clear memory of it. But it was quite a little scandal in our town, and people gossiped about it fiercely. She left while he was away, as I recall. He came home to an empty house, found out that his wife had taken their daughter to Oregon or Washington with another man. There were rumors that Malone had knocked her around, that he couldn't get joint custody because of it, rumors that she was a lesbian, rumors that she joined a cult. The usual nonsense from a small town.

Aside from that, I haven't heard much about dark, silent Malone. He works hard, that's widely known; first one out, last one back. His haul is usually the largest of the year, despite the fact that he only hires a sternman to help him during the summer and does the rest of the season alone. He is or has been president of the lobstermen's association around here. Once in a while, the local paper will mention him speaking out against over-regulation and fishing rights, but again, I haven't paid too much attention. Malone never meant anything to me, other than being the slightly scary guy who gave me a ride last year.

"We know he's great in the sack," I tell Colonel. "And that he doesn't know how to use a telephone."

As irritated with myself as I am with Malone, I pace around the apartment. I put the TV on, then turn it off. *Maybe I'll paint my toenails,* I think, then immediately dismiss the idea, as it takes patience and I have none. Time for Christy. I snatch up the phone and hit speed dial. "Hi, it's me," I say. "Hey, I was just, you know, reading this book about a woman who's sleeping with this guy, and the sex is really good and she thinks it means something, but he never calls her. What do you think?"

"Ah…do you mean about the plot or…"

I choke. "Shit! Father Tim! I'm sorry! I thought I hit the button for my sister…"

He laughs. "Not to worry, Maggie, not to worry." He pauses. "It sounds like your book makes another strong case for marriage first, don't you think?"

I flush with guilt. "Oh, I guess. It's just that that hardly happens anymore. Waiting for marriage."

"And no doubt that explains why the divorce rate is so terribly high. More people should be like you, Maggie. Willing to wait to get to know someone before rushing into a purely physical relationship."

I grimace, so very, very glad that Father Tim can't see my face. "Sometimes," I say, trying to get it through my thick head, "you feel such a strong attraction to someone that you think it must be a sign."

He pauses. "I...I really wouldn't know." His voice is gentle.

"Of course not! I'm sorry... It's just that some-times...you know what? Forget it. I was just thinking of someone—well, this person in the book." I stop talking, picturing Father Tim at home, maybe in his bedroom (not that I've ever seen it), his kind and laughing eyes, his ready smile. "Father Tim," I ask ten-tatively, "do you ever wonder if you made the right choice? You must get so lonely sometimes."

Father Tim is quiet for a moment. "Well, sure, of course. Don't we all? Of course I sometimes think about what life would have held had I not been called to the priesthood."

I sit up straighter. "Really?"

"Sure, now." His voice is wistful. "It's a common enough complaint in my vocation, loneliness is. Every once in a while, I find myself picturing what it would be like to have a wife, a few children..." His voice trails off.

"Uh-huh," I breathe, afraid that saying more will break the intimacy of the moment, simultaneously thrilled and horrified to get this glimpse behind the curtain, as it were. To see the great Oz revealed.

"But those thoughts are fleeting," he says, his voice stronger. "For me, it's like dreaming you're the presi-dent or an astronaut. I love the life I have as a priest, and those daydreams are just that...bits of fluff that pass right out of my head."

Moment over. "I guess it's only human to wonder," I say. "And you know, Father Tim, even if you don't have, you know, a family…well, we all love you here in Gideon's Cove. You're a wonderful priest."

"Thank you, Maggie," he says gently. "You have a gift of making people feel very special. You know that, I hope."

I smile, feel a warm squeeze in my chest. "Thanks, Father Tim," I half whisper.

After we hang up, I go into the bathroom and look at myself in the mirror. I like my face. It's not beautiful, not really, but it's nice enough. Pretty. A pleasing, friendly face. And to hear Father Tim confide in me, tell me I have a gift…well. I like my face even more. Of course, Christy's face is exactly like mine, but that's a minor detail.

There's a knock at the door, and I jump.

It's Malone, his face as cheerful as the angel of death. Irritation, nervousness and attraction flutter around in my chest as I open the door. "Hi," I say. "Hey. How are you, Malone? Oh, what a nice night, isn't it? I thought maybe it was raining."

He stands there, looking at me as if assessing my babble, then deigns to speak. "Hi."

"Hi," I echo in full idiot mode. "So. Want to come in?"

He steps inside, immediately making my apartment seem even smaller than it is. Colonel slips off the couch and comes over to greet my guest, wagging gently. "Hey, boy," Malone says, bending down to pet Colonel's head. Colonel licks his hand and goes to his doggy bed in the corner and begins his nightly ritual—five turns in a tight circle, followed by intensive sniffing, followed by the actual lying down. I watch him intently so as not to have to look at Malone, who is staring at me. *Don't say anything, Maggie. Let him go first. Keep your mouth shut.*

"Can I get you a beer or some coffee or something, Malone?" I ask. My inner self rolls her eyes at me.

"No, thanks," Malone says.

"Okay, well, um, do you want to take off your coat?"

He takes it off and hangs it on a hook. The silence stretches on.

"So, Malone, what are you doing here?" I ask. "I mean, it's a little late. Almost eleven."

"I wanted to see you," he says, and there's a softening around his mouth. My stomach squeezes gently in response. God, I'm such a slut.

"Well, you know, Malone, I do have a phone. And I am in the book. Maybe you could call next time." My prissy tone doesn't fool me; even now, I'm kind of hoping he'll take me on the kitchen table. He steps closer, and my heart rate kicks up. *Oh, yes, the table…*

"Line was busy," he murmurs, his scraping voice sending tremors to my joints.

"What? Oh. Yes. Yes. That's right. I was…on the…you know…the phone."

He takes my hands in his and pulls me closer, studying my mouth. I can feel the heat from his body, smell his soap and laundry detergent and a faint, salty smell. Resisting a strong urge to lick his neck, I swallow. "Who were you talking to?" he asks, just when I want him to kiss me the way he did last night. He raises an eyebrow, waiting.

"What? Excuse me, I mean?" My voice is tight.

"Who were you talking to?"

"Um…I—well, I think it was Father Tim."

Malone's eyes meet mine.

"Yeah, you know, I'm on all these committees and stuff. At church. Church committees."

His eyes return to my mouth, his tangled lashes lowering. Lashes like that are just not fair. "That's nice," he mutters.

"Malone," I whisper hoarsely, then clear my throat. "You think you could drop the chitchat and kiss me?"

CHAPTER TWELVE

So WHEN I wake up in the morning, alone again, I really have no one to blame but myself. I'm as clueless as I was yesterday. Perhaps I should make a list and mail it to him, because that man does something to my brain. *Things to Ask Malone. 1. Are we seeing each other or just sleeping together? 2. Do you like me at all, or is this just a physical thing?* (Unfortunately, I suspect the latter…at least on my part.) *3. Can you tell me about yourself so I don't feel like you're a total stranger? 4. Why don't you ever come into the diner?*

Oddly enough, it's the last thing that bothers me the most. The diner is a surprising little treasure in Gideon's Cove. For the first few years that I ran it, I worked a second job over at the hospital, filing medical records from four until ten each night so that I could sink some money into the diner. It took me almost four years to completely restore it. I pulled up the linoleum that Granddad put down over the tile floors, painstakingly retiling the areas that needed it, scouring the grout with bleach until my hands were raw. Reupholstering the seats in their original red vinyl took some money, and I had to buy the bigger oven so that I could bake all the homemade goodies that we're now known

for. I'd like Malone to see it, to have that pie that I
promised him.

Chantal comes in for lunch, something she does
every Thursday, and because Judy is in a rare mood and
actually working, I sit down and have lunch with the
resident expert on the men of Gideon's Cove.

"These fries are the best in town," she says, popping
another curly, spiced delicacy into her mouth.

"The only fries in town," I correct her with a smile.
When Chantal's not busy seducing some man (or any
man), she can be quite pleasant.

"You want to go to Dewey's tonight?" she asks. "I
could use a drink."

"Um…well, no, I'd better not. I have stuff to do." It's
true. Laundry. Bills. Possibly Malone. And speaking of
tall, dark and not exactly handsome, I risk a question.

"Chantal, remember how you were telling me I
should check out Malone?" I blush and take a bite of
my cheeseburger to cover.

"Oh, Christ, I wasn't serious," she says. "He's all
wrong for you. Not husband material at all, if you know
what I mean."

"No, no. I know that." I don't, actually, but for some
reason, I don't want to admit to my…whatever it is that
Malone and I are doing together. "No, I was just wondering if you ever…you know. Hooked up with him," I
ask, dreading the answer.

Chantal sucks up some milkshake through her straw,
managing to look quite pornographic as she does, something I'm sure she practices. "Nope. I haven't. Not yet,
I should say, and not for lack of trying, mind you," she
says easily.

My shoulders drop in relief and, I admit, pleasure.

"He turned you down?" I ask, surprised—Chantal could fill the bleacher seats at Fenway with the men she's entertained.

"Well, sort of. I mean, I flirt with him, because he really is pretty hot in that ugly guy way, but he just kind of smiles and drinks his beer. I think he's gay."

Doubt that. "He smiles?" I ask.

"Well, maybe not. But there was this thing once, long time ago now, back when we were still in school…" She stops and drops her eyes, her thickly mascaraed lashes shielding her expression.

"What?" I ask, leaning forward.

"Well, it was nothing. I gave him a ride. Someone had roughed him up…this must've been when I was a senior, because I was driving my dad's Camaro, I remember, and Malone was out walking by the blueberry plant, and I pulled over and drove him home."

"Really?" This little nugget of history fascinates me, picturing Malone as a youth. "Did he say what happened or anything? Did you guys talk?"

"Not that I remember," Chantal answers, chewing thoughtfully on a fry. "I just gave him some tissues for his lip, because it was bleeding. For a while, I thought he might have had a crush on me…you know, we had this little secret between us, and he was a year or so behind me in school, but nothing ever came of it." She drains the last of her milkshake. "Still, that brooding thing he's got going on is pretty steamy. Don't you think? Or, no, I forgot. You like them all sunshine and light and goodness. And speaking of, there goes Father What-a-Waste." Chantal's voice drops to an unmistakable purr as Father Tim walks past, throwing us a wave and a smile as he goes about his business. "God, he's delicious."

"Now, now. You know he doesn't like us to talk like that," I say primly.

"Mmm. But he is, isn't he?" she purrs, smiling widely.

I laugh, unable to resist. "Yes. He is."

"I SLEPT WITH Malone," I tell my sister later that day.

"What?" she shrieks, dropping the baby's plastic bottle. "Jesus, Maggie! Give a person a little warning here!"

Being the one with the news packs a certain wallop. It's definitely been Christy's life that has grabbed the most headlines, aside from my own embarrassing forays into the Catholic church. And so dropping this choice little nugget is, I admit, incredibly satisfying.

It's showering outside, a gentle, nourishing rain that patters in the gutters and against the lead-paned windows of Christy's house, deepening the three inches of mud that already blankets the great outdoors. Violet is sleeping, Christy is tidying, I'm lounging.

Christy sits down across from me and takes a sip of her now-cold tea. "Let me warm this up," she says, sticking her mug in the microwave and pressing some buttons. "I want to hear every detail. And Violet better not wake up, because she's going to have to wait."

I tell her, starting with the kiss when he drove me home and ending with waking up alone this morning.

"Wow," she sighs. "This is…wow. And I have to say, I told you so. Remember?"

"Yes, I do. Well done." I salute her with my mug.

"So…Malone. He's really…well, what's he like? What do you guys talk about?"

I blush. "That's a good question. Of course, it's only been a couple of days. We haven't talked much."

"Oh, really?" Christy purrs. "So. Okay. He's sexy, we knew that. I love the scruffy ones."

"You do?" I ask. Will is quite tidy and clean-shaven.

"You always want what you don't have," she tells me with a wink. "More about Malone, please. What else?"

"Okay, well, we covered the great in bed part. Incredible kisser. Doesn't talk much. That's all I know." I sigh. "He really hardly talks at all, Christy." I frown and trace the rim of my cup. "To tell you the truth. I'm sleeping with a guy I really don't know very well. It's a little slutty."

"Is that how he makes you feel?" Christy asks, mirroring my frown with one of her own.

I think about that. "No. He makes me feel...beautiful."

Christy's frown morphs into a smile. "Oh...that's nice," she sighs. "Beautiful is good."

I smile, too. "Yes, it is. I just wish..."

"What?"

"Well, I just wish he was more...talkative. More like..." I wince but tell my sister the truth. "More like Father Tim."

"Well, I for one am glad he's not," Christy chides. "Father Tim is a—"

"I know, I know. Save it. What I meant was, I wish Malone would just...open up a little."

"He will, Mags, he will," Christy assures me, not that she has any authority over Malone. "You know how they grew up, the Malone kids," she adds.

"Actually, I don't," I say. First Chantal had something on him, now my own sister. Does everyone know more about Malone than I do?

"Oh, no? Well, it—" she pauses, considering. "It wasn't good."

"How do you know?" I ask.

"His sister was in our class, dummy," Christy informs me. "Allie Malone. Don't you remember? She was shy, black hair like Malone's…pretty quiet."

I wrack my brain for some recall. "Oh, okay, okay. God, I hardly remember her."

"Too wrapped up in Skip."

"Yeah. True. So tell me what you know," I prod.

Christy takes another sip of her tea. "Well, I never went over there or anything," she says. "And I don't exactly remember how much she told me and how much was just what the kids said. But we were lab partners junior year, and we were kind of friendly."

She stiffens as Violet rolls over, the rustling clearly audible over the monitor, but when no coo or cry follows, she goes on. "I guess the father was abusive. I don't think sexually, thank God. But there was definitely some bad stuff. The police came once, I remember Allie talking about that. She was crying in the bathroom one day and told me that her brother and father both spent the night in jail…"

"Yikes," I murmur.

"So, anyway, I really don't know more than that. She went away to Boston and we never really kept in touch."

"Did you ever hear that Malone hit his wife?"

Christy frowns. "No. I never did. He's not—you know, rough or anything, is he, Maggie?"

"Oh, no. No, no." My cheeks grow hot. "Not rough at all…just…intense."

"I wish you could see your face right now," my sister says, laughing.

"Listen, don't tell anyone about this, okay? About Malone and me. It's not like we're actually seeing each other…we're just…I don't know…."

"Fuck buddies?" Christy laughs.

"Christy! No! Oh, hell, maybe." I can't help laughing, too.

"Can you imagine what Mom would say?"

"I really don't want to think about that," I answer truthfully. Mother is not one to be sympathetic to hormonal urges. *Young people today are so trashy,* she's fond of saying. *Don't they have any self-respect?* Even if Malone and I had a real relationship, he's not exactly what Mom has in mind for me. *Why can't you meet a doctor, Maggie? Or a lawyer? Or maybe that Microsoft executive on Douglas Point? If you'd just clean yourself up a little, you'd be quite presentable, you know. You need to stop lighting your fire under a bushel.*

At this moment, my niece lets out a coo over the monitor, signaling the end of her nap. Christy gets up and goes upstairs, and I sit at the table, mulling over what she's told me.

I stay to play with Violet, rolling on the floor with her, encouraging her to grab the little moose puppet Jonah gave her at birth. She finally does, and Christy and I cheer as the genius baby stuffs an antler into her drooling mouth and chews on it. Christy convinces me to stay for supper, and I do, drinking in their domesticity and happiness.

On my way home, I try to imagine Malone acting like Will, laughing, pulling me onto his lap the way Will does to Christy, kissing his baby and practically leaping at the chance to change her diaper. I can't. Malone doesn't inspire thoughts of husband and father.

So what are you doing with him, Maggie? Mom's voice asks in my head. *Killing time until the real thing comes along? Or just scratching an itch?*

I'm pretty sure I don't want to answer those questions, but I have a long time to think about them. Malone doesn't come over that night. He doesn't call, either. And I don't call him.

CHAPTER THIRTEEN

"So, Maggie, how's the quest going?" Father Tim asks me as I pour him some coffee.

"The man quest?" I ask.

"Are you on any other kind?" he quips, raising his eyebrows with mock sincerity.

"Oh, how cutting! And you a priest. Tsk, tsk." I glance around the diner—pretty full, since it's raining hard outside, and people love to go out for breakfast when it's raining. "The quest is on hold at the moment, Father Tim," I answer. "When the time is right, yadda yadda. What can I get you this morning?"

"I guess I'll have the special, Maggie. Sounds lovely."

The special is French toast made with homemade sweet almond bread and soaked in a peach glaze. It is lovely, and an original recipe, and if I could get a restaurant critic out here, I'm sure he or she would love it. "You got it," I tell him. "Bacon with that?"

"You know me well," he smiles.

"Mmm, yes, and I know you'd better get your cholesterol checked."

"You're a wonderful friend," he says, and unexpectedly, he takes my hand and pats it, looking up at me. And though I have a coffeepot in my other hand and he's

wearing his priest clothes, there's something very…
marriage proposal about our little tableau. For one
second, that sense of longing and rightness I always get
around Father Tim hits home, and I feel my face grow
hot.

"Well," I say. "Right back at you." To hide my discomfort, I glance out the window and freeze. Malone
is standing in front of the diner, and with him is a
woman. A *beautiful* woman. A young, gorgeous, wow
kind of woman. She's laughing, and he's smiling. He's
smiling! A baseball cap shields his face against the rain
so his expression isn't completely clear, but yes, that is
a smile, ladies and gentlemen.

Father Tim releases my hand, and I smile automatically
at him. When I glance up, Malone's smile is gone, and
he's looking at me. The lines that slash down his face are
emphasized from the lights in the diner. Is he angry? He
says something to Miss Universe, and without so much
as a wave, they continue on their way, away from Joe's.

"What the hell is his problem?" I mutter. My face is
burning. Suddenly I feel quite grimy in my worn jeans
and the sweater with the coffee stain on the left wrist.
Who cares? I ask myself, but my heart feels tight.

"Ah, Louise, love," Father Tim calls, "come and keep
a lonely priest company." Louise, a middle-aged widow,
wrestles her umbrella inside the door.

"Back in a flash, Father Tim," I say as the kitchen
bell dings. I get to work, bringing Father Tim and
Louise breakfast, chatting up Georgie, exchanging
diner slang with Stuart, bussing tables and wiping up
spills. But my thoughts stay with Malone. Who was that
woman? I've never seen her before…and truthfully, I
never want to again.

I can't say I've ever seen Malone with a woman, though surely he hasn't been without female company since his wife left him all those years ago. But still. Smiling with that young, beautiful creature… It stings. It's been three days since I last saw him. During that time, he hasn't called me or stopped by once. Not once. So I'm forced to think that yes, indeed, any connection we have is purely physical.

I'll admit, I've been feeling a bit conflicted. It seems wrong, somehow, to have these intense physical reactions to Malone when I don't even know his first name. My mother's voice keeps floating through my head— *When are you going to find someone decent to marry? Why can't you settle down with someone like Will?*

My protestations to my mother that I'm *trying* fall on deaf ears. I'm not succeeding, and as she so ruthlessly points out, the years are passing. Of course I'd love to settle down with someone like Will. Someone who found me delightful and couldn't wait to come home to me, someone who loved children and wanted a couple.

Malone is not that guy. After all, there he is out with Maine's answer to Catherine Zeta-Jones. If he finds *me* delightful, it's only in the sack. The only time we've spent when we weren't all over each other like black flies on tourists was the evening he rescued me from the Skipmonster. There was no joy in Mudville that day, that's for sure. No happy exchange of information took place there, no laughter, nothing other than some primal attraction. It's not enough. Especially if he's primally attracted to more than one woman at a time, damn it.

Father Tim is right—people shouldn't jump into bed with people they don't know well. Because this is what happens. You make a fool of yourself with someone who doesn't even care about you, and then you still have to live in the same town.

It's not enough, I repeat to myself as I refill coffee mugs and bring out breakfasts. *I want more.*

CHANTAL CALLS ME a day or so later. We're both suffering from varying degrees of cabin fever induced by three days of rain. Malone hasn't called me. Bastard. I remind myself that I don't want him to call. "Sure, I'd love to go out," I tell her. We agree to meet at Dewey's for a few drinks. Knowing my low alcohol tolerance, I opt to walk, even though it's still raining steadily.

I've decided that Malone is an indiscretion created by too many months unrelieved by human contact from a nonfamily member. Aside from Georgie and Colonel, Malone is the only male who's touched me outside of Dad, Jonah and Will. I probably would have humped the eighty-year-old double amputee if I'd gone much longer.

"Hey, Dewey," I call as I hang up my slicker.

"Hi, Maggie," he calls. Without my asking, he pours me a glass of wine and brings it over to the booth where Chantal and I usually sit. "That nice Chantal joining you?" he asks.

"She's not nice, Dewey," I say, taking the glass. "She's a wicked, wicked woman."

"Don't I know it," he sighs. My laugh lands somewhere between irritation and amusement. Does every man in town under the age of one hundred and two have to be so damn smitten with Chantal? Do I have to be everyone's surrogate daughter?

The red-haired temptress comes in, hips swaying,

blouse revealing, lest anyone forget just how stacked she is. "Hi, Paul," she sighs, rubbing past him as if we were trapped on a crowded subway car instead of in a nearly empty bar. "Paul, sweetie, could you bring me a martini, hon? Make it a cosmo, okay? My friend and I haven't seen each other in ages."

"You sure have a gift with men," I observe dryly as Paul hurtles to the bar to do her bidding.

"Oh, it's nothing," she says, batting her eyelashes. "Man, this rain! I'm climbing the walls! Tell me what's new with you."

I wrack my brain for something I wish to tell her and come up empty. "Not much. What about you?"

"Well, *I* had the most incredible sex the other night," she purrs.

Me too, I almost say, then chide myself. *That was just a fling, Maggie! Stop thinking about him.* "Oh. Well. That's very nice. Good for you."

"Guess with who?" She leans forward, her beautiful dark eyes mischievous.

There's a strange sinking feeling in my chest, like I swallowed a rock. "I—I don't know, Chantal. Who?"

"Take a guess."

"Malone?" I say, my throat tight.

She leans back in the booth. "Malone? No. Not Malone."

Oh, thank God. I let out a deep breath. "Um… Dewey?"

She laughs. "No, not Dewey. That was just once, a couple of years ago, before he put on all that weight." She drums her fingers on the table. "Any more guesses?" she asks.

"It better not be Jonah," I warn.

"No, no, not your precious baby brother," she answers. "You suck at guessing, so I'll just have to tell you. Mickey Tatum."

"The fire chief?" I blurt.

"Mmm-hmm. You know what they say about firemen," she smiles. "And it's true."

I look away. "Actually, Chantal, I don't know what they say."

"Guess."

"Can we not do this twenty questions thing? I don't know."

"Come on!" she implores. "Guess."

Paul brings Chantal her drink, peeks down her low-cut, lacy blouse, squeezes her shoulder and leaves. She looks at me expectantly, smiling.

"Firemen do it hotter?" I guess resignedly.

"No, honey."

"Um…firemen have longer hoses?"

"No. But that does seem to be the case." She takes a sip of her pink drink. "Guess again."

"I really don't know, Chantal. Please stop making me guess."

"They still know how to use a split lay." Chantal laughs merrily.

"I don't…I don't know what that means," I say, laughing in spite of myself. "And please don't tell me."

"Well, okay. But I joined the fire department, so say hello to the newest member of Gideon's Cove's bravest."

Chantal launches into far too much detail about Mickey Tatum, who must be sixty if he's a day. As he was my CCD teacher the year I made my confirmation, I'm not really comfortable hearing this. But Chantal is entertaining, that's for sure. The bar grows fuller. Jonah comes in and waves, but he's with a pretty young woman and can't be bothered with his sister tonight. Some of his pals are there, Stevie, and Ray, who co-owns the boat with Jonah. The regulars.

Chantal and I are discussing a movie we both want to see when Malone walks in, alone. No Zeta-Jones tonight. Good. He hangs up his coat, then glances around, sees me, and gives a little jerk of his chin. My smile turns to stone. That's it? A chin jerk?

"Oh, Malone just came in," Chantal says. She's been documenting the arrival of every man here. "Let's make him sit with us." She slides out of her seat.

"No, no! You know what? Let's not. Let's just have, you know, girls night. Okay? No guys. Chantal?" But she's already gone up to the bar. She slides her hand across Malone's back and says something. I pretend to fumble in my purse for something, hoping he doesn't think I sent her over. Damn. Malone smiles at her, a little, anyway, and I'm embarrassed at a sudden longing to have him smile at *me,* then immediately disgusted with myself for feeling that way. *This is the guy who slept with you and ignored you, Maggie. The guy who may also be sleeping with someone prettier and younger than you. Ignore him back. Say nothing. I mean it.*

"Okay if Malone joins us?" Chantal asks, slipping back into the booth, graceful and lithe as a snake. Malone sits down next to her, his face grim and lined— normal, in other words.

"Sure. I don't care," I say. "Sit wherever you like. You can sit anywhere, right? Free country."

"Malone," Chantal says in her man-seduction voice, a lower, sexier tone that she saves for the X-Y chromo-somers. "Maggie and I were just talking about you the other day." Damn her. She turns to him to offer him a view of her breasts, but he's staring at me. My jaw grows tight and I take a slug of wine. Malone tips his head to the side slightly, and there might be a little upward movement to one corner of his mouth. His knee brushes mine under the table, and a prickle of lust creeps up my thigh.

Chantal puts her hand on Malone's bicep, and I can just about feel it, too, that solid, bulging, rock-hard—"Maggie was wondering if you're gay," she purrs.

"Jesus! Chantal! I was not!" I look at Malone. The hint of smile is gone. "I wasn't."

"So are you, Malone? You don't seem to like girls. I mean, if you've passed over me *and* Maggie…"

I try to come up with an expression that will hide my embarrassment and advertise my indignation. I fail miserably.

"So, Malone, are you?"

Malone finally decides to speak, a decision not reached lightly. "No."

"But you don't like women?" Chantal persists. I psychically—and ineffectually—order her to shut the hell up. "Are you just sort of asexual, Malone?"

An image of Malone on top of me flashes through my head. I believe the fading hickey just below my collarbone can prove he's not exactly asexual. At the thought, my knees start with that watery, wiggly feeling. I gulp down some wine.

"I like some women," he says, still looking at me. I believe my name has just been removed from his list, judging from the ice in his eyes. My cheeks are on fire, much to my disgust. Chantal, at least, is too busy thrusting her prowlike bosom into Malone's arm to notice my discomfort.

"Well, too bad Maggie and I aren't your type," she pouts.

"Too bad," he agrees, then turns to look at her, dropping his gaze to her obvious charms.

You know, I kind of hate him at that moment. Make that both of them. Actually, there's no "kind of" about it. I drain my wine and look away. If he wants to make me feel inadequate, he's doing a great job.

At that moment, a cry goes up from the bar, and a most welcome cry at that. "Father Tim!"

The cavalry has arrived. He shakes hands, claps a few backs, then sees me, and bless his dear Irish heart, his face lights up. As he makes his way across the now-packed bar, I can't help the wave of pride I feel. Out of everyone here, he picks me as a seat mate.

"Maggie, how are you, love?" he asks happily. "And Chantal, too, what a treat." He's wearing civvies—a beautiful knit sweater, made by his sainted mother, no doubt, and jeans. Yes, jeans. The look is Catholic Rugged, and nicely done. I smile widely and scooch over to make just enough room for him to sit down. I hope Malone notices. I shoot him a glance. Yup. He does, giving the words *thunderous expression* new clarity. My smile grows even more.

"Hello, there," Father Tim says to Malone. "I don't think I've had the pleasure. Tim O'Halloran. *Father* Tim, in case you missed that." He winks at me and extends his hand.

"Malone." Tall, Dark and Scowling shakes Father Sunshine's hand.

"Ah, a fine Irish name! Is that your first name or your

last?" Father Tim asks. *See, Malone?* I think. *This is how people talk.*

"Last," Malone grunts.

"And your first name? Sorry, I didn't catch it."

Chantal intervenes. "He doesn't use it, Father Tim. It's a local legend. He's just listed on the tax registers as plain old M. Malone."

"Well, that's all right. Are you Irish, Malone?"

"No."

For heaven's sake! To break the awkward pause, I jump in. "How are you, Father Tim?" I ask. "Would you like a beer?" Paul Dewey appears at our side.

"I think the weather calls for something a bit stiffer," Father Tim says. Chantal raises her eyebrows at me. *Stiffer,* she mouths. My jaw clenches. Luckily, Father Tim doesn't see her. "How about an Irish whiskey, Dewey, my fine man?"

Malone is staring at the table, which somehow avoids turning into a puddle of black tar. He lifts his gaze suddenly to mine, and I turn instantly to Father Tim.

"So how did the funeral go in Milbridge?"

"It was a sad affair, Maggie, quite sad. Thanks for asking. You're very kind."

I nod compassionately and give Malone a satisfied glance.

"You were such a comfort to me the other night, Father Tim," Chantal says, widening her doelike eyes. "At bereavement group," she explains to me. Malone shoots her a look. "I lost my husband some time ago," she reminds him. "And dear Father Tim has been very helpful."

"I'm so glad to hear it, Chantal," Father Tim murmurs.

I bite my lip. Helpful, my ass. I know—and Chantal knows I know—that she's there for voyeuristic purposes only. She gives me a look and smirks. Meanwhile, Dewey brings the whiskey, and Father Tim takes a deep sip.

"That's the thing for a night like tonight," he says appreciatively, taking another. "So, Malone, is it? Malone, what do you do for a living?" Father Tim grins his beautiful smile, and I find myself smiling sappily back at him.

"Lobsterman," Malone says tersely.

"Ah, a fine profession indeed. And have you got a wife and children?"

"A daughter."

"Are you married, then?" Father Tim asks, looking around the room.

"Divorced."

"That's such a shame, isn't it?" Father Tim leans back in the booth, his arm pressed against mine. "A terrible shame for the children. It ruins their world, doesn't it now?"

Malone's mouth is rapidly disappearing in a tight line, and his jaw looks ready to pop. He doesn't answer.

"Maggie, tell me, how did that seafood lasagna go over yesterday?" Father Tim asks, and again, I glance at Malone, hoping to impress upon him that there are people out there interested in more than my girl parts.

"It was really good, Father Tim. Thank you so much for asking. I had some left over, but I brought it to Mrs. Kandinsky. I'll be sure to save you some next time."

"Oh, you're a generous girl." He smiles at me, that irascible lock of hair dropping over his forehead. It's all I can do not to smooth it back. "So how do you know Malone here, Maggie?" he asks.

I look at Malone a long minute. *I know him biblically, Father,* I answer silently. "He moors next to Jonah," I say out loud. Malone stares back.

"And does he know about your little situation?" the priest murmurs.

"Which situation?" I ask.

"How you're looking for a nice man to marry?"

Shit! Hopefully, Malone didn't catch that. His scowl tells me otherwise. Ears like a bat, that Malone. Chantal speaks up. "Father Tim, honey, I was wondering how a poor widow like myself, or a nice girl like Maggie, should meet some new people. Because just between the two of us—well, the four of us," she amends, leaning forward, her cleavage clamoring for release, "we women have certain needs. Desires. And it's so hard to meet anyone really decent. I mean, a roll in the hay is one thing, but finding a husband is another. Right, Maggie?"

"I think I'll go say hello to Jonah," I blurt, ignoring the terror in Father Tim's eyes. "Didn't see him today. I'll just go check in with him. See how he's doing. If he needs anything."

I practically fly across the room to my brother, but it's no use. Malone is right behind me.

"Maggie," he says. "Listen." His voice is very quiet, just a bare rumble of distant thunder, and I can barely hear him. He pauses. "My daughter's been visiting," he finally says.

"Hey, no problem," I answer. "You can do whatever you want. See whoever you—what did you say?"

He frowns. "My daughter. Emory. She was visiting for April break."

"That—that was your daughter?" The woman I saw

him with had to be twenty-three, twenty-four at least. Didn't she?

"Ayuh."

"How old is she?" I demand. Bob Castellano pushes past me with an apologetic pat on the shoulder.

"Seventeen," Malone answers, a black eyebrow rising.

"She's seventeen? Your daughter is seventeen?"

He scowl deepens. "Why, Maggie?"

"Well, how old are you, Malone?" My face burns painfully.

"Thirty-six."

I do the math…so he was nineteen when his kid was born. Huh. Okay. I guess that fits, given the little I know about Malone.

"Who'd you think she was?"

It takes me a second to realize I've been busted. I risk a look at Malone's face and wish I hadn't. "You know what?" I babble. "There's Jonah! I think I'll go say hi to Jonah." I gesture to my brother, who is making out with the pretty woman from before. "Actually, I guess I'll hit the loo." And I flee.

In the safety of the bathroom, I lean against the sink and take a few cleansing breaths. God, what a stew of emotions out there! No wonder my hands are shaking. I'm mad, frustrated, horny (let's be honest), guilt-ridden and irritated. I look at my reflection in the mirror. My face is flushed, my hair lank from the humidity. Why does Chantal look like a dew-kissed apricot when I look like a drowned rat? I wet some paper towels and press them against my cheeks.

Malone could have saved me a little trouble with a phone call, couldn't he? I ask myself. *Hey, my daughter's in town, and I'll be a little busy.* But no. We don't have that kind of relationship. We don't have any relationship. He can't even pick up the phone to tell me something simple like Catherine Zeta-Jones is his *child.* For heaven's sake.

A little voice in my head wonders if he's telling the truth. During the brief time I was at his house, I didn't see any pictures of a beautiful young woman, did I? No, there were just pictures of a little girl. No seventeen-year-olds. And frankly, the woman I saw last week looked older than that to me.

Well. If he says she's his daughter, she probably is…after all, in a small town like Gideon's Cove, that would be a pretty big lie to pull off. The thing is, it doesn't matter, does it? Emory—cool name, if I cared to think about it—doesn't have anything to do with the lack of communication between her dear old dad and me. I'm a roll in the hay as far as Malone is concerned.

I wish I could meld Father Tim and Malone into one. Malone's sex appeal and single status, Father Tim's everything else. Well, maybe a few more things from Malone. He's hardworking, not that Father Tim isn't, but Malone is the kind of guy who can get things done. Fix-your-car-type things. Father Tim's helpless at that. And Malone is…well, shoot, I don't really know what he is, do I? I know he has a certain effect on me. That's it.

When I come out, our little party appears to be breaking up. Chantal wriggles from her seat, making sure everyone sees her lush behind as she smooths her tight jeans. Malone hands Chantal her coat.

"Thank you, Malone, sweetie. Maggie, Father Tim's giving me a ride home," Chantal says. "I think I've had too much to drink," she pretends to confide.

"I see," I sigh. She could drink a roomful of firemen under the table.

"Would you like a ride, as well, Maggie? The rain's punishing out there. I'd be happy to drop you off." Father Tim pleads. His eyes are begging…I'm sure there are rules against priests driving loose women home, and even a *castrati* would need a chaperone when alone with Chantal.

I glance out the window, which is too steamy to give me an actual view. Will Malone offer me the olive branch of a ride? To apologize for not calling, for not telling me his daughter was occupying his time for the past week?

He doesn't, just stands there looking at me, and who the hell knows what he's thinking.

"I'd love one, Father Tim. You're so nice. That's very thoughtful. Thank you." In case Malone doesn't get the point, I turn to him. "Always lovely to see you, Malone."

"Maggie," he says, giving me the nod. Then he goes back to the bar from whence he came.

Four minutes later, I'm home, watching Father Tim pull away from the curb toward Chantal's house. Lucky Chantal. She lives twenty minutes outside of town. Twenty extra minutes with Father Tim, chatting, laughing, driving through the pouring rain. Poor Father Tim…well. I'm sure they teach priests how to handle this kind of thing in the seminary.

Loneliness twangs its familiar discordant note. Though it's a reasonable hour to go to bed, it feels that the night stretches in front of me, endless. I feel it so sharply I even wish—briefly—that Malone would call me.

"Screw it," I say, filling Colonel's water bowl. "You just can't win sometimes, can you, boy?" My dog doesn't answer.

CHAPTER FOURTEEN

I MAKE THE MISTAKE of going to see my parents a few days later.

"Hi, Mom," I say. She's still in her little uniform from Will's office—she wears scrubs with bright patterns on them, dogs and cats, flowers, happy faces— although why, we don't know. She hates sick people and never gets near them if possible, preferring to spend her day fighting with insurance companies instead, usually emerging from her headset in grim victory.

"Oh, Maggie," she says, slamming a cupboard. "What's the matter now?"

My mouth drops open. "Um, nothing. Just thought I'd come by."

"Do you have to bring that dog with you everywhere you go? Honestly, he's like the security blanket you had when you were three."

I stare at my mother and stroke Colonel's head. "Right. Is Dad around?"

"Why? Do you need something?"

"No, he's just my father, and I love him," I answer.

"Fine. He's in the cellar."

Dad has a little corner in the basement, where he often hides from Mom, pretending to do something constructive. He likes to make birdhouses, and the yard outside is full of tiny creations in every style and color imaginable—Victorian, log cabin, gourd, southwestern, apartment building. His corner has stacks of tiny pieces of wood, a shelf of tools and six or seven birdhouse books. He also has a stash of Robert Ludlum novels and a tiny radio. Dad's bomb shelter, we call it.

"Hi, Daddy," I say.

"Go talk to your mother," he orders, giving me a kiss. "She says you only come here to see me."

"I'm scared of her today. She's in quite a mood."

"Tell me about it. Go."

"Coward," I tell him fondly. Obediently, I go upstairs.

"Mom, would you like some tea?" I ask, putting the kettle on.

"When are you going to stop wasting your time at the diner?" she demands, yanking out a chair and slamming herself into it.

Okay. So it's going to be one of those days. A "Christy Good, Maggie Bad" day.

"I don't think I'm wasting my time, Mom," I say resignedly. "I really love it, you know."

"We didn't send you to college to be a waitress," she snaps. "Christy managed to find a decent career. Why can't you?"

"Right." I sit down. "I do *own* the diner, too. And run it. And cook."

"Well, it's not as if you bought it. You just took it over from my father. And it's just a diner, Margaret." The use of my Christian name indicates that I've done something quite heinous. If she calls me Margaret Christine, I'm dead.

"It's not like you went to cooking school," Mom

continues, her voice brittle and sharp as broken glass. "You just crack eggs and sling hash and fry bacon. Look at your hands, Maggie! Don't you know people judge you by your hands? Hands make the man, they say."

Do they, I wonder? "It's actually clothes, Mom. 'Clothes make the man. Naked people have little or no influence on society.'"

"What? What are you babbling about?"

"It's a Mark Twain quote." She looks blank. "And I might not have gone to culinary school," I continue, "but the food at Joe's is great. You know that."

"So what? Are you going to spend the rest of your life in that greasy little diner?"

"It's not greasy!"

"That's your opinion," she snaps.

"Why are you on my case today, Mom?" I ask through clenched teeth. "Have I done something wrong? I just came to see you and Dad, and you're all over me."

"You'd better do something about your life, young lady. And fast. If you want to have a family and do something meaningful with your life, you'd better stop hiding out at the diner."

I study her. These are the kinds of lectures I've heard all my life. In high school, it was *Don't Become Obsessed with That Boy* (unfortunately, she was right). In college, it was *Study Something That Will Help You Find a Job* (again, right on the money…while being an English major at least allows me to quote the classics better than Mummy here, it hasn't done much to further my career). We've since moved on to *That Diner is a Dead End* and my personal favorite, *Your Ovaries Are Shriveling.*

These lectures tend to bounce off me like hailstones bouncing on the roof of a car…tiny pings, but no real damage. Doesn't mean I like them, of course. But today, she seems more worked up than usual.

"Why do you hate the diner, Mom?" I ask. "It was your dad's."

"Exactly," she snaps.

"So? Now it's a family business. It's a nice place. I might even win best breakfast in Washington County. I'd think you'd be kind of happy about that."

"Oh, that silly contest is pointless. And yes, it was my father's. He worked there seven days a week so I could go to college, make something of myself. Not so my own child would go back there, like some high school dropout. You pay that cook of yours more than you make yourself! Why, Maggie?"

"Because he has five kids, Mom," I tell her patiently.

"So? If he doesn't have the sense to use birth control—"

"Okay. That's enough. I'm leaving. Love you, even though I'm not sure why." I get up and open the cellar door. "Daddy, stay down there. It's not safe up here. Love you, you big chicken."

"Love you, too, baby."

"I only want what you want, Maggie," my mother says, her voice a little gentler. "I want you to meet—"

"—someone like Will." I say the words along with her. "I know, Mom. He's a great guy. But Christy got him, okay? In fact, you're the one who picked Christy for him. You didn't pick me." I shrug into my coat, my movements quick and angry. "And yes, I want to marry someone nice and have kids, but if it doesn't happen, it's not the end of the world, right? I'll be that helpful spinster daughter everyone dreams of, bringing you a bedpan, changing your sheets, spooning gruel into your mouth. I'll even give you that nice morphine overdose when the time comes, okay? In fact, I'm tempted to give it to you now. Gotta go."

I tell myself that I don't mind, but my hands clench the handlebars of my bike in a death grip. I pedal slowly and carefully so my dog can keep pace. I realize my eyes are tearing. It might be the wind.

Back at Joe's, Colonel flops down into the bed behind the register and yawns. I squat down to give him a hug, kissing his beautiful white cheeks repeatedly. "I love you, puppy," I tell him. "I love you, best boy." He licks me gently, enjoying the salt deposits on my cheeks.

"Hey, boss," Octavio calls. "Beautiful day, isn't it?"

Judy approaches me. "Four more ballots, Maggie," she says, fishing some papers out of her apron. "I think we're gonna win this year." Judy showing optimism is a near-biblical event, so my mood must be written clearly over my face.

As I'm doing the last bit of cleanup, I decide to drop in on Christy. Before the thought is fully formed, she sticks her head in the diner door, and I can glimpse Violet's stroller just behind her on the sidewalk. "Maggie? Want to run some errands with me?" my sister asks.

"Sure," I say. "Just let me finish scraping the grill."

I finish my chores and wash my hands, grimacing at the grease under my fingernails. But my hands are a little better. The painful cracks that appear at my fingernail line are healing. I'll have to find out where Malone got that cream.

Christy is waiting on the sidewalk. "I heard you're wasting your life, slaving away for nothing," she says.

"It's always been a dream of mine," I tell her. "Can I push Violet?"

"Sure."

The thrill of having identical twins in town has never left the good folk of Gideon's Cove. Colonel walks beside us like a guard, and we make a bit of a parade (or freak show, depending on how you look at it). School is getting out, and several kids beeline for my dog, one pretty young girl cooing at the sleeping Violet. Two ladies from church stop to admire the baby and advise Christy to bundle her up a little more. "Thanks, I will," Christy tells them as we continue. "She's wearing a onesie, tights, a turtleneck, a wool sweater, corduroys, socks and a coat," Christy mutters to me. "I may be cooking her as it is."

The barber comes out to greet us and give Colonel a cookie. From inside his shop, Christy and I hear a roar of laughter…there's the usual gang of older men—Bob Castellano, Rolly, Ben—and, strangely enough, our dad. Apparently, Dad left the bomb shelter and is hanging out with the guys.

"Your father sure is funny," Mike, the barber, tells us fondly. "What a riot that guy is!"

Christy and I exchange a glance. *Riot* is not the usual word that leaps to mind when thinking of our henpecked, quiet dad. Mike goes back inside, but Christy and I linger a minute in silence. Dad waves, smiling, and continues regaling the other men.

"That's kind of nice, seeing Dad with some friends," Christy comments.

"Sure," I agree. Odd, but nice.

We go into the little pharmacy to get some diapers. Colonel waits outside, patient and trusty as a statue. As I am separated from my dog and pushing the carriage, a few people call me Christy, and I answer as if I were. Christy smiles and pretends not to hear as she peruses the aisles for shampoo and chocolate.

"Tell Will I said hello," says Mrs. Grunion.

"I sure will," I answer.

We leave the store, and Christy takes over pushing. Violet starts to stir, and I peep in at her. "Hi, sugar plum," I say. She rewards me with a smile and a yawn, her cheeks rosy. "Who's your auntie, hmm? Can you say hi to Auntie Mags?"

"Ah-nu," she says cheerfully.

"I think that was hello," I tell my sister.

She grins. "So what's going on with you and Malone?"

"Nothing," I tell her. "We're not really...I don't know. Nothing. Just a fling. It's over."

"Really?" She looks disappointed. "He doesn't seem like the type for a fling."

"Ask him. There he is." I feign nonchalance as Malone comes out of the liquor store, a six-pack under his arm. He lurches to a stop at the sight of us.

"Hi, Malone," Christy calls out pleasantly.

"Hi," I echo.

"Hey, Christy," he says. His eyes flick to mine. "Maggie."

It's almost strange to see him during daylight hours. He has the looks for a vampire, that dark hair and grim face. He's wearing a black wool coat and faded black jeans, rubber-soled boots. But the lines around his face are less harsh, and the wind ruffles his hair teasingly.

He bends down for a look at Violet. "Hey, there," he says to her.

Violet stuffs a corner of her blanket in her mouth and chews, staring at him solemnly. The lines around Malone's eyes deepen. I look away, embarrassed by the softening of my wicked heart. "Sweet baby," he tells Christy.

"Thank you," she smiles.

"Good to see you, Maggie," Malone says. He turns and walks away from us.

When he's a safe distance, Christy hisses, "See? He still likes you."

"Jeezum. You sound so eighth grade."

"Well?" she huffs indignantly.

"Well, nothing, Christy. He said a handful of words and left. Where you come up with your theories is beyond me. We haven't spoken since we slept together. Well, hardly."

"Mmm-hmm. But I can just tell." She looks at me. "It's true. I can."

"Okay, Great Swami. Thanks for the input." I smile and pat her arm. How patient I am today! First with Mom, now with my sister. Clearly I deserve some Ben & Jerry's tonight while I watch the Sox game. Perhaps the entire pint.

"Do you like him, Mags?" my sister says, irritating as a greenhead at the beach. My patience evaporates.

"I like him in bed, Christy. Okay? In bed, he's awesome. Otherwise, we barely speak. So. Any other questions? Would you like to know if he has any identifying marks or deviant tendencies?" I realize I'm barking.

Christy shoots me a grin. "Well, actually…"

"A tattoo. On his arm. A Celtic band, right around his bicep."

"I'm more interested in the deviant tendencies." She widens her eyes expectantly, and I can't help laughing.

CHAPTER FIFTEEN

IT TURNS OUT she's a little bit right.

That night, I'm at home as usual, already dressed in my pjs at eight-thirty, a huge basket of laundry on my coffee table. Ever since my Skip days, I've been a baseball fan, and, because it's a Maine state law, I am a devotee of the Boston Red Sox. I watch with smug satisfaction as the designated hitter clips a double into right field, then decide I deserve that Ben & Jerry's. While I rummage in the freezer, there's a knock on my door.

"Sissy, it's me, your favorite brother," Jonah calls.

"Dmitri?" I call.

"Wicked funny," he says.

"Come on in," I say.

"TV's out at the firehouse. Can we watch the Sox game with you?"

"Sure. It's already on." The freezer is crammed with foil-wrapped leftovers from the diner and I can't find the damn ice cream. Shoot. "Um, who's we?"

Jonah sticks his head in the kitchen door. "Just me and Stevie. Malone, too."

I jerk my head out of the freezer. "Malone?"

"Ayuh," Jonah says, turning his head to see the TV. "Saw him at the dock, asked him if he wanted to come."

He seems unaware of the import of his actions, but then again, Jonah is unaware of much in life. He blinks owlishly at me.

"Right, Malone," I say. "Okay. Sure. Yeah. That's fine."

A sudden image of my laundry causes me to lunge into the living room. I'm too late. Underwear of varying ages litters the coffee table. "You need some new stuff, Mags," Stevie says, snatching up a pair of once-white panties.

I reach for them, feeling my face go nuclear-hot. "Out on parole, I see, Stevie."

"Maybe some thongs. I like a woman in a thong," he says.

"Not that you've ever seen one," I say, snatching the panties back. I stuff them, along with my faded bras and T-shirts, deep into the laundry basket. "Hi, Malone," I say, hoping my voice sounds casual.

"Maggie," Malone says.

He makes the boys look like just that—boys. He's not smiling exactly, but he's not glaring, either, and he doesn't look away. It seems very small in my apartment; of course, it *is* a very small apartment, and three full-grown males make it microscopic.

"Got any beer, Maggie?" Jonah asks. "Maybe a snack?"

I yank a sweatshirt over the tank top I'm wearing. "Sure, hang on. Don't move him, Stevie, he's old," I say as my brother's friend, who must weigh close to three hundred pounds, tries to wedge himself in next to Colonel. "Sit on the floor."

"Me or him?" Stevie asks.

"You, dummy. Want a beer?"

"Yes, ma'am." He bats his eyes at me and lies on my floor, taking up approximately half of it.

I speed back into the kitchen and open the freezer again, letting the frosty air cool my face. *Calm down, Maggie,* I urge myself. *Nothing to worry about. Malone's here, it's no big deal. Just think of him as another one of Jonah's annoying friends.*

"Need some help?"

Malone leans in the doorway between the kitchen and living room. His coat is off, and he's wearing a faded blue work shirt. The color matches that of his eyes, and he's so attractive, tall and angular and so damn *male* that I feel slightly dizzy.

"Sorry, what did you say?" I ask, pretending to look in the freezer for something.

"Need any help?"

In the other room, Stevie and Jonah give a yell and high-five each other. "No, I'm fine," I tell my other guest. "So, Malone, what a surprise. Are you a big Sox fan? I mean, you probably are, I guess we all are, right, living here in Red Sox Nation and all th—"

"Not really," Malone says, stepping closer to the fridge, where I continue to stare. "Your brother asked if I wanted to come over and watch the game here, and I said yes."

"Really. Uh-huh. And, um…why is that?" I ask, leaning a little deeper into the freezer.

"I wanted to see you."

"Oh." I risk a glance at his face, and the little smile he's wearing causes a tug of desire to pull at my insides. "I do have a phone, you know," I whisper. Without thinking, I take an ice cube from the bin and press it against my forehead.

"I don't like talking on the phone," Malone says softly, and his voice scrapes a soft place in me.

"Really? What a surprise," I manage. He reaches out and smoothes the little hairs at the back of my neck, and my knees practically buckle.

"Maggie! How 'bout that beer, hon?" Stevie calls from the living room.

"So is it okay?" Malone asks.

"Is what okay?" I ask, tossing the ice cube in the sink.

"Is it okay if I stay?"

I look him full in the face. It's a face I'm really starting to like, I realize. "Sure," I say, smiling. He grins back, and my heart squeezes hard, because his front tooth has the tiniest chip in it, and that imperfect smile makes him suddenly the most delicious, appealing man I've ever seen, and without even being fully aware of what I'm doing, I've wrapped my arms around his neck and am kissing him greedily, relishing the scrape of his five-o'clock shadow, clutching his hair, practically wrapping my legs around him.

Malone's hands slide under my shirt, and his hands are so hot after the cold air from the freezer, his mouth hard and soft at the same time—

"Maggot! The beer!" my brother yells. "Come on, you're missing a great game."

With a shaky laugh, I untangle myself from Malone. His eyes are smoky. "Listen," I say, swallowing, glancing toward the living room, "I'd rather that Jonah…um…well, not know about this…you know, this thing of ours. Okay?"

Malone opens the fridge and takes out a couple beers. His face is back in its usual lines. "Sure."

For the next hour, Stevie and Jonah ignore me, except to ask for snacks, which I bring to them obligingly, glad for the excuse to distract myself from the lust that writhes around in the pit of my stomach. Malone deigns to drink a beer, but he doesn't eat anything. Stevie takes up most of my floor space, and Jonah has the club chair that I got three years ago at a going-out-of-business sale in Bangor. Malone and Colonel sit on the couch, the dog's head in Malone's lap. Malone's hand rests on the dog's shoulder, and Colonel sighs contentedly once in a while.

I fold my laundry discreetly, putting my shirts and jeans on top of anything I don't want the guys to see. I sneak a look at Malone every once in a while, and each time I do, he seems to know. Blushing becomes my permanent facial state. I pretend to watch the game, though the Sox could have all been murdered and left disemboweled on the field for all the attention I truly pay.

It's Stevie, good old Stevie whom I've known since he was in kindergarten, who livens things up.

"Hey, Maggie," he says idly, eyes fixed on the TV, "I heard you told Father Tim you were in love with him the other night. At the spaghetti supper."

I choke on the beer I'm nursing, the fizzy burn surging up my nose. Stevie and Jonah roar with laughter. Malone, I note through tearing eyes, does not.

"Yeah, so what's going on, Mags? You dating Father Tim?" Stevie continues.

"No!" I rasp. "No! Of course not! Jeez! I'm not—God!" Malone isn't moving, just staring/glaring at me, his eyes like chips of ice.

"That's not what I heard!" Stevie singsongs. "Have you kissed him yet, Mags? Father Tim and Maggie, up in a tree, K-I-S-S-I-N-G…"

"Jesus, Stevie, you're such an ass," I say, getting better control of my voice. "I wasn't…there's nothing… he's a priest! Come on! Kissing! Jeez."

"'Cause, Maggie, if you're that desperate, I could help you out, babe. Show you a good time, if you know what I mean."

"Jonah! Can you beat him up or something? That's your sister he's talking about," I remind my brother, shooting another nervous glance at Malone.

"Shut up, Stevie," Jonah says automatically, stuffing a fistful of popcorn into his mouth.

"I'm not dating Father Tim," I say emphatically, my eyes darting between Malone and Stevie. "He's a priest! Of course I'm not…you know. Oh, look, another run." *Thank God,* I think, as the Red Sox divert Stevie's tenuous attention.

It doesn't divert Malone's. He continues to look at me, the lines that run between his eyebrows and slash alongside his mouth harsher. I shrug as if to say, *Stevie, what an ass,* but I'm betting my face gives me away. Goddamned fair skin.

At the next commercial break, Malone extricates himself from Colonel and the couch. "Thanks, Maggie. Guys. I'm gonna go."

"The game's not over!" Stevie protests.

"Gotta get up early," Malone says. "See you." He grabs his coat and opens the door. I start to go after him, then stop.

"Okay, bye, Malone. Nice to see you," I call out idiotically. He gives a curt nod and walks out, his feet thumping down the stairs.

"There's an odd one," Stevie says, glancing at the door.

"He's not bad," Jonah says mildly. "Hey, Maggot, got any more beer?"

Because my luck is pretty bad these days, the Devil Rays (the Devil Rays!) somehow catch up with the Red Sox, and the game goes into extra innings. It's after eleven by the time the boys finally leave, full of popcorn, beer and woe. The minute they're gone, I throw on my coat, stuff my feet into my wool clogs and call to Colonel. It only takes me a few minutes to get to Malone's house.

There are no lights on inside, and the house is quiet. I knock softly, then wait. No answer. I knock again, a bit more loudly this time. After a minute, I hear Malone's footsteps. Colonel wags as he opens the door.

"Hi," I say.

"It's late, Maggie," he answers, looking over my head.

"Right. I'll just be a minute. Can I come in? It's kind of important. Plus, it's cold. Got really chilly, didn't it?"

I clamp my mouth shut against the automatic babble that pours out of me when I'm nervous and slip past Malone, who looks wicked sexy, if less than welcoming. He's wearing a pair of jeans and a white T-shirt, and his feet are bare. Even so, he's a good six inches taller than I am.

Colonel is panting after our walk, and without a word, Malone goes into the kitchen, takes a bowl down from the cupboard and fills it with water. He sets it on the floor, kneeling down to scratch Colonel's ears as my dog drinks. "You're a good crittah," Malone says, our Maine designation for anything four-legged. Colonel wags in agreement, then goes under the table to lie down. Malone stands up and leans against the counter, folding his arms across his chest. "So what do you want, Maggie?"

I take a deep breath, distracted by the sight of his thickly muscled arms. How I ever felt Malone was unattractive is a mystery. I remind myself to focus, but before I can, I start talking. "Well, I just…I guess…" I guess I should have planned what to say, that's what. "I just wanted to say, you know…Stevie, what Stevie said about me telling Father Tim that, um, you know…well, of course I'm not dating Father Tim. Of course. I mean, he's a priest, right? So of course not."

Malone purses his lips as if deciding whether to believe me or not, and the words continue to rush out of my mouth.

"We're friends, Father Tim and I. He's actually one of my best friends. We hang out sometimes. Well, I mean, he comes into the diner every morning for breakfast. Sometimes we go to a movie. Once in a while. Actually, it was maybe twice. There was a group of us, not just us two, of course… And I do a lot for the church, you know? Committees and stuff like that. But no dating. Obviously. Since he's a priest."

Malone looks at the floor, and I force my mouth shut and wait for him to speak. He sighs, running a hand through his hair. "Look, Maggie," he says quietly. "I live in this town, too. I hear things." He looks back at me.

My nervous energy drains into the floor. "Right." The clock over the fridge ticks loudly, reminding me that it's almost midnight and Malone and I both have to get up early. "Well, the thing is, I did have a thing for Father Tim. And I did actually—" I swallow "—I did say that I loved him. While I was under the influence, I might add."

Malone says nothing.

"So. There you have it." I fiddle with the zipper of my coat, wondering if I just severed things completely with Mr. Happy here. As the silence stretches on, I feel a stir of irritation. "You know, Malone, I've heard things about you, too," I say, a defensive note creeping into my voice. "And just because that's the gossip doesn't mean I believe it."

His face darkens, but I continue anyway. "There was that thing about your cousin last year, right? I mean, people had a whole lot to say about that. But I didn't jump to any conclusions or anything."

Still no reaction from Malone, which I find slightly ominous. But, true to character, I keep going. "Let alone what they say about your wife."

Oh, shit. Now I've gone too far, and even I realize it. My heart starts thumping erratically against my rib cage. Though Malone hasn't moved or changed expression, I'm suddenly a little afraid.

"And what do they say about my wife?" he asks very, very quietly.

"Oh, well, you know…I don't know. People talk about all sorts of—"

"What, Maggie?"

I swallow. "That you hit her. That she was scared of you and that's why she moved across country."

His face looks so hard now it could be carved from granite. "And do you believe that?" he asks in that scraping, quiet voice.

"I wouldn't be here if I did, Malone."

He stares at me and I force myself not to look away. Finally, his gaze flicks somewhere past me. "When?" he growls.

"When what?"

"When did you make your little announcement?"

"Oh! Well, that was a while ago. You know, a couple, three weeks ago? A month, maybe. But before you and I…um…hooked up." Colonel's tail starts thumping in his sleep. Malone exhibits no such happiness, just continues glaring at me, the creases between his eyebrows unrelenting.

"Okay, well, I wanted you to know that," I say, peeved at his lack of reaction to both my confession and my trust. "Whatever. I'm sorry I woke you up, if I woke you up. I just thought you should—I don't know. I didn't want you thinking anything—"

"Do you still have a thing for him?" Malone interrupts. There's a note in his voice I haven't heard before, and it gives me pause.

For once, I don't immediately answer. Instead, I stare back at Malone a minute, then decide to take a chance. "No," I say softly. "It seems like I have a thing for you."

He looks back at me, not smiling, then covers the space between us, takes my hand and leads me to bed.

CHAPTER SIXTEEN

AT LEAST I DIDN'T wake up alone, I think the next day as I slice onions for potato soup. Malone was already dressed, granted, and it was still dark out, but he kissed me gently and said the tender words, "Gotta go." And he did.

But he kissed me, he woke me up…that must be a step forward, I think. Last night marks the third time we've spent the night together. This must be a relationship, right? The fact that I still don't know much about him rankles, though. What we really need to do is go out and not just go to bed. This idea holds a good bit of appeal in theory, until I remember the night we spent staring at each other at the restaurant. Maybe I should go ahead with that list and just hand it to him. *Please fill in the answers to the following questions. What is your first name? Do you have any hobbies? Are you going to introduce me to your daughter? Am I your girlfriend?*

The sun is shining brightly today, the air cool and clean, and business is slow. A few people come in to pick up an order, but that's about it for the lunch crowd. It's Octavio's day off. Since we're so slow, and since she's reading a novel anyway, I send Judy home at noon and handle the few customers who actually come in to eat.

After I close, I take Colonel home and swing by the soup kitchen with the vat of soup and a few dozen biscotti. Then I spend an hour or two writing letters to tourism writers and restaurant critics, hoping to lure someone to Joe's Diner. But my mother is probably right. Even if Joe's wins best breakfast in our county, or even in the whole state, it wouldn't change much. Gideon's Cove is just too far from anywhere to be popular.

I take a walk to the harbor. My brother's boat is in, but Malone's, the *Ugly Anne,* is not. I wonder how he picked the name, who Anne is. Another question for the list, I suppose. I walk back home, oddly deflated.

Having cooked all day, the last thing I want to do is make myself some dinner. On a whim, I get into my car, which is caked with dried mud, drive twenty minutes to the next town, which has a car wash. I've always loved the car wash, that feeling of surrender to the conveyor belt, the ease with which the car is suddenly sparkling clean. As I'm feeding quarters into the vacuum machine, another car pulls up next to me.

"Maggie, how are you?" says Father Tim, getting out. "Great minds think alike, don't they?"

"Hi, Father Tim! How are you?" I haven't spoken to him in several days, and that mere fact gives me pause. He hasn't come into the diner since…heck, a few days. And I haven't really noticed.

"We missed you at Bible study last night," he chides gently, fishing around in his pockets for quarters of his own.

"Right. Shoot. I'm sorry. I guess I had some things to take care of," I say. My face and other parts grow warm at the thought of just what those things were, but I cover by vacuuming the back seat.

When Father Tim is finished, he straightens up and glances down the street. "Would you care to grab a cup of coffee, Maggie?" he asks. "I thought I saw signs of life at Able's."

"Sure! That would be nice."

Able's Tables is a tiny little café down the street, and they are indeed open, though business is light at this time. A sign promises open mike night beginning at eight, but I don't expect Father Tim and I will be around for that. We order coffees—and Father Tim gets a brownie the size of Rhode Island—and sit at a table near the window.

"Imagine, us meeting," Father Tim says. "There I was, feeling a bit lonely, and who should I run into but you. A happy coincidence. God knows our hearts and hears our prayers, sure enough."

"Why were you feeling alone, Father Tim? I'd think you'd love a little solitude, away from all your fans." I smile, taking a sip of my cappuccino.

He laughs morosely. "Sure enough, that's true sometimes. God speaks to us in the silences, after all. You're right. But today, I think I'm merely in need of a little companionship, Maggie," he tells me. "Sometimes, even when a person's surrounded by others, he can feel a bit on the lonely side of things."

"Sure," I murmur sympathetically.

"Ah, yes. You know just what I'm speaking about, don't you, Maggie?" He gazes at me thoughtfully, his eyes soft and kind on mine. "It must be hard for you, having Christy being married with a baby and all."

I sit up straighter. "No, it's not hard," I say, frowning. "I love Will. And Violet…well, don't get me started. It's not hard. I'm very happy for my sister."

"Good for you, then, Maggie, good for you." He pauses. "I'm terribly sorry my efforts at finding you a decent man haven't panned out."

I shake my head. "No, no, don't worry about it. Not at all. Thanks for trying."

"A lovely girl like you should have someone," he continues almost sadly.

I don't answer for a moment, just look out at the street. "Well, actually, I might be seeing someone," I venture.

"Is that right?" Father Tim exclaims. I nod. "Is he good enough for you, Maggie?"

I blush. "Sure."

"Wonderful, then," he says. "It's funny, I was thinking about you the other day and that person we met at Dewey's, the fisherman. Dark hair?"

"Malone?" I say, my face going from blush to inferno.

"That's it. Malone. I wouldn't want you with someone like that, now. Such a churlish fellow, barely speaking. He was hardly civil the whole time we were there. Couldn't take his eyes off Chantal, either."

"Actually—" I attempt.

"So I'm glad you've found a man with potential, Maggie. I'd hate to see you settling for someone who wasn't blessed with the same good heart that you have."

My mouth opens and closes a couple of times before the words come out. "Actually, Malone is the person I'm…seeing."

Father Tim's mouth falls open with comical surprise. "Is that—is he? Oh, dear. I'm terribly sorry, Maggie." He looks away, wincing.

"He's not really that churlish," I manage. *Great job,*

Maggie. Talk about damning with faint praise. "Let's change the subject."

The waitress comes by with a free refill for Father Tim. "Here you go, Father," she croons. She ignores my now-empty cup.

"Ah, thank you, that's lovely," he says, smiling up at her. Her cheeks grow pink.

Is that how *I* am? Oh, God, it is, isn't it? Gross. I'm mortified. Poor Father Tim, to have us waitresses fawning over him all the time! The woman finally fills my cup and goes back behind the counter, her eyes still on my companion.

"Is it hard being a priest, Father Tim? Always having to be so, um, well-behaved?" I ask.

He laughs, long and hard. "No, Maggie, it's not hard. It's a beautiful calling, a privilege, really."

"But you're always a little—" I stop, fearful that I'm once again about to put my foot in my mouth.

"A little what?" he asks. He really is just pointlessly good-looking, those soft green eyes, the gorgeous hands.

"A little apart from everyone else," I venture.

His smile drops. "Mmm. Well, yes, you've a point, don't you, Maggie?" He sets his cup down. "The price we pay to serve the Lord." He forces a smile and takes another sip of coffee. "Maggie," he continues, more quietly, "did you know Father Shea when you were growing up?"

I gasp, unfortunately just at the moment I'm sipping my cappuccino, and burning foam drips into my lungs. "I…yup," I rasp.

Father Shea was our priest when I was probably ten or eleven. He was handsome, somewhere in his forties or fifties (who can tell when you're little, right?), a jovial, teasing priest who shamelessly bribed us kids to be good in church by giving us Hershey's Kisses after Mass.

Then Annette Fournier's husband dropped dead of a heart attack when he was out for a run one day. Father Shea was a great comfort to the tragic young widow and her three kids. Such a comfort that he left the priesthood and married her a year later. I believe they had one or two more kids themselves, making Father Shea go from Father to plain old Dad.

"Yeah, I remember Father Shea," I say, still coughing a little. "He was…well, he was pretty nice. But he…you know. Left. Why do you ask?"

Father Tim shakes his head a little, his eyes distant. "No reason. Well, no reason I should be discussing, at any rate, Maggie. Sorry to bring it up. He's just…never mind. On my mind lately. Enough said."

I stare out the window, my face hot. Guilt flashes like heat lightning—how many times have I wished Father Tim wasn't a priest? In truth, I don't really…he's a very good priest, from all accounts, anyway, and I'd hate for him to scandalize the town as did Father Shea. Leave the priesthood. Break his vows.

"Well, I'd best be getting back," Father Tim announces, putting down a dollar for the waitress. "Thanks, Maggie, for the nice chat. You're a lovely friend." He squeezes my shoulder. "The church's doors are always open to you, you know. God is waiting, and His patience never wears thin." He grins and winks, ever campaigning.

"Okay. Thanks. Nice to see you, Father Tim," I say, slipping another couple bucks for the waitress, glad that he's back to his normal, chipper, priestly self. I get into my newly clean car and head for home, but the trickle of discomfort remains. Why would he ask about Father Shea? Why would he ask *me,* in particular? Surely the dragon Plutarski would give him every salacious detail at the merest flicker of interest.

By the time I get back to Gideon's Cove, the sky glitters with stars overhead, the air so clear that I can see the Milky Way swirling above me. Standing on my front porch, I take a deep breath. The smell of wood smoke from the many fireplaces and stoves mingles with the faint smell of pine and sea, and to me, it's the best smell there is. I suck in another breath, then jump at the sound of the door behind me.

"Maggie, dear!"

"Oh, hi, Mrs. K. You startled me," I laugh.

"Dear *me,* I'm terribly *sorry.*" She motions for me to come in, and I obey. "There was a *man* here earlier," she says. "That *dark* man who came over the other day. The tall one."

I am simultaneously thrilled and nervous, which seems to be the hallmark combination of emotion Malone evokes. "Malone? He was here? When was that?"

"About an *hour* ago, dear." She shuffles over to her chair and lowers herself carefully into it. "Maggie, would you find the remote control? There's *nothing* on tonight, nothing! Three hundred *channels* and nothing worth seeing!"

The remote sits in plain sight on the coffee table. I hand it to her. "So, um, did you talk to the…to Malone?"

"Well, I must say, I *tried.* He didn't say much in

return, Maggie. He seemed quite *angry,* if you ask me."
Mrs. K. flips through the channels.

"Angry? Are you sure? I mean, I can't think of why
he'd be mad."

Mrs. Kandinsky stops on a station. Linda Blair's
head rotates around as Father Damian looks on in
horror. "Oh, look, Maggie! *The Exorcist* is on! Damn
it all to *hell,* I've missed the first *part!*"

"Mrs. K.," I say, trying to steer her back to our conversation, "did Malone say anything?"

"Hmm? Oh, the angry man? Malone, you say his
name is? Well, *yes,* I told him I didn't know where you
were, and he said he'd see you soon."

"That doesn't sound *angry,*" I say.

"Oh, my! Isn't she *hideous,*" Mrs. K. croons appreciatively. "My *word.*"

"Okay, well, this one is too *scary* for me." The priest,
however, is quite good-looking, but I have enough
good-looking priests in my life. "I'm gonna go, Mrs. K.
Enjoy the movie." She doesn't acknowledge me as I kiss
her goodbye, too engrossed in the terror on the telly. I
head up to my apartment.

There's no note or phone message from Malone. I
pick up the phone book, look up his number and call.
The line is busy. Fifteen minutes later, I try again. Still
busy. The idea that Malone can speak for this long is
somewhat surprising. Certainly, he never speaks to me
that much. No, we seem to have other things to do than
speak.

Well. He said he'd see me soon. Maybe he wasn't
angry. What does he have to be angry about, anyway?
It's not like I was out with my boyfriend… Father Tim
is a friend, and I don't have to feel guilty about having

a cuppa joe with him. Besides, he needed me. He was lonely. We spent an hour talking. Just talking. Nothing to feel guilty about at all.

Out of curiosity, I check the Internet dating site I visited last time. The messages haven't changed. The god is still seeking his goddess, the angry husband is still angry.

"Come on, Colonel," I say to my dog. "Let's go to bed."

I take the phone into the bedroom with me, but Malone doesn't call.

CHAPTER SEVENTEEN

"Foosh," Violet says, patting Colonel. "Mubba."

"That's close, honey," I tell her. "It's doggy. Can you say doggy?"

She opts to kiss Colonel instead, leaving him with a large wet spot on his side and her with a mouthful of fur. Colonel wags his beautiful tail as Christy swoops in with a tissue, smiling and grimacing at the same time.

"You love Colonel, don't you, Violet?" she asks. "He's a nice dog."

"Maggie, for heaven's sake, don't let the baby lick that dirty animal," my mother says.

"Colonel is not dirty," I snap. "He's immaculate. Look at that coat. People stop us in the street to tell me how beautiful he is. I brush him every—"

"Christy, there's still a hair on her lip. There you go. Come here, Violet." My mother appropriates the baby, taking her off to an area free from germs and dog hair. We've gathered for our command family dinner, and while my mother is a fine cook, I feel as welcome as a cockroach in a salad. Dad is in the den, reading and hiding, and Will, Christy and I sit in the living room, waiting for our summons to the table.

"She's really on my case these days," I tell Christy.

"I'll say," Will agrees. "That's all we hear about at work."

"Are you kidding me?" I ask. "She talks about me at your office?"

Christy shoots Will the "shut up" glare, and he pretends he doesn't hear me and reads the paper instead.

At that moment, my brother bursts through the door. "You'll never guess what happened today," he blurts.

"Three women came to your doorstep, announcing that you're the father of their babies," I guess.

"No. Stop joking around, it's serious." He flops down into a chair. "Malone went overboard."

"What?" Christy and I bark simultaneously. Panic floods my limbs, and it feels like my heart drops to my knees.

"He was pulling up a pot, and this Masshole came by in a speed boat, tangled the line, and bam. Malone went right over."

"So what happened? Is he okay?" I ask my brother. Adrenaline makes my joints feel too loose and electrified.

"Masshole?" Will murmurs. He's from away, having only moved to Maine during his residency.

"Massachusetts tourist," Christy tells him.

"Jonah, is he all right?" I repeat. My palms are slick with sweat.

"He's all right," Jonah says. "He wasn't caught in the line, thank God, but he was in the water for about twenty minutes, half an hour. Got wicked cold."

The water in the Gulf of Maine is cold enough to cause death if you're in it long enough. Every few years, it seems, a lobsterman drowns when he goes overboard, tangled in the line that connects his pot to the buoy.

Even if they don't get pulled under, an arm caught in the line can be torn right off. Or sometimes they simply can't climb back aboard. A lot of lobstermen work alone, especially in the off season.

"Was he wearing a survival suit?" I manage weakly.

"No," Jonah says grimly. "Just his coveralls. Must be colder than a witch's tit."

"But he's okay?" I insist.

"Yeah, yeah. He's fine. Still out there, though," Jonah said. "Fuckin' foolish if you ask me. Said he still had to check his traps. At least he had a change of clothes."

Christy turns to look at me.

"Mom, I gotta go," I call, standing up. My knees are weak and sick-feeling, and I stagger a little, knocking into the coffee table.

"Maggie, God, you are still the gawmiest girl," she says from the kitchen. "What do you mean, you're leaving? I've already set the table."

"Gawmy is clumsy, right?" Will asks.

"Right," my father tells him, emerging from the den. "And you're not, sweetheart." He pats my head as I shove my arms into my coat.

It's nearly dark by the time I reach the harbor. Malone's boat isn't back yet, and the adrenaline continues to zing through my joints. As I stand on the boardwalk, looking down at the many berths, Billy Bottoms come along. He's a fifth-generation lobsterman and looks the part—white hair, chiseled, leathery face, crisp, snowy beard. In the summer, tourists often ask to take his picture, and his accent puts the rest of us Mainahs to shame.

"Hello theah, Maggie."

"Hey, Billy," I answer. "Listen, did you hear what happened today?"

"About Malone? Ayuh. He's not back yet."

"So what happened?" I ask.

"Some flatlandah was flyin' by in a sweet little corker. Buoys so thick you could walk home, but this guy don't care. Seems Malone was haulin' a pot when his line got picked up by the out-a-townah and he got pulled in. Flatlandah didn't even stop. Your brother saw the boat circlin', came over to see what was what. Said Malone was madder than a bucketful a' snakes."

"Shit," I whisper. "He could have died."

"Well, now, Maggie, most of us go ovah at one time or anothah. Malone's fine, I'm sure." He pats my shoulder. "You have a good night, now, Maggie, deah."

The images in my head are too terrifying. Malone being towed to the bottom of the ocean by his weighty trap. Malone trying helplessly to climb back aboard the *Ugly Anne* until his strength is sapped away by the cold. His head slipping under, his body floating—

I can't bear those thoughts. Before I've fully decided what to do, I'm running to the diner, Colonel loping happily at my side, and burst in through the kitchen door. Among the items in the freezer are a quart of potato soup and an apple pie. I grab them, add a block of cheddar and a loaf of pumpernickel and bag them up, then head for Malone's.

That will be just the thing, I think as I climb the hill. A house filled with the smell of hot apple pie, a hearty soup simmering on the stove, a sympathetic woman and an excellent dog. What could be a nicer homecoming? Certainly, it's what I'd want after a shitty day. Aside from the woman thing, of course.

His house is locked, which presents a problem. I put the food on the porch and walk around, wondering if there's a spare key hidden in an obvious place, like under a doormat or in a pot, under a rock near the porch. No such luck. But in the back, the window is cracked, and without too much struggle, I lift the window and manage to boost myself in, flopping onto the floor with the grace of a dying haddock. But I'm in.

After I bring in the food, preheat the oven and find a pot, I take a look around. I've only been here twice, I realize, and I haven't seen much of the house. Not that there's much to see. It's a bungalow, three rooms downstairs, a bedroom and bathroom upstairs. It's a bit sloppier than last time; there are dishes in the sink, a cup and plate in the living room. It's chilly, too. After a dip in the frigid Atlantic, Malone shouldn't have to come home to a cold house.

Because I'm a Maine native, I have no problem starting a fire in the woodstove. I tidy up the pile of newspapers in the woodbin and refold the afghan and drape it over the couch.

There are a few photos here and there; snapshots of a younger Malone and the little girl who grew into such a beauty. I study the photos, unable to see Catherine Zeta-Jones in the chubby-faced child. Well. People change. I touch Malone's image, his chipped tooth smile makes my chest tighten. A few books are scattered around the living room, and I stack them neatly on the coffee table. *The Perfect Storm.* Cheerful little ditty, that. *In the Heart of the Sea,* which apparently tells about cannibalism after a whaling accident. Jeezum. No wonder Malone scowls all the time.

Still restless, I walk past the piano, which has a light

coat of dust on the top. I push a few keys. The Beethoven sheet music I saw the first time I was here is gone, replaced by a Debussy piece. It looks hard, but I never was any good at reading music, despite four years of clarinet lessons in school, so everything looks hard to me.

Malone can play the piano. So I do know something about him, I realize. He likes classical piano music. It's a nice little fact.

Colonel is snoring quietly in the kitchen. The oven has reached four hundred and twenty-five degrees, so I brush the top of the pie with some milk, sprinkle it with sugar and pop it in. I look at the clock. It's seven-thirty, and the temperature is dropping outside. It'll probably be in the thirties tonight. I hope Malone gets home soon.

The dishes beckon, and as I'm still filled with nervous energy, I wash them, then figure out where they go through a process of elimination. For the most part, Malone is pretty neat. His bed isn't made, though, and the sheets are tangled and twisted. I open a closet in the hall and find some clean flannel sheets and remake the bed.

There. I turn down the heat on the pie, set the timer, check the soup. What a nice little place this could be with a few personal touches here and there, a few more prints, maybe some better furniture…

I sit on the sofa and wrap up in the afghan. Leaning my head back, I close my eyes. Colonel comes over and sits next to me, putting his big head in my lap. Worn out from worry, I find myself getting drowsy. Poor Malone, I think. But lucky, too, because God knows he was spared today. And I'll be waiting for him when he comes home from this terrible day, offering both comfort and company. I can't wait to see him, to make sure he's okay.

Some point later, I jerk awake at the sound of the door and scramble off the couch. The smell of apple pie is rich in the air. Relief and joy have me leaping off the couch. "Hi, Malone!" I call. "How are you? Are you okay?"

He stands in the doorway, his orange coveralls balled up beside him, a length of line coiled on top. He looks thinner, gaunt instead of lean, and utterly exhausted, the lines on his face seemingly carved by a heavy knife today. I'm already in the middle of the kitchen, headed straight for him, when his voice, scratchy and hoarse, cuts me off.

"What are you doing here?"

I lurch to a stop. "Well, um, I heard about your day…um, Jonah came by and told me you went in the drink." Suddenly the idea of giving him a hug or kiss or even patting him on the shoulder seems out of the question. "I thought I'd bring you some—"

"I did *not* ask for this," he grates out. There are streaks of salt deposits on his sweater, and his hands are shaking with fatigue.

My mouth falls open. "Well, I know. I just thought you might want a hot—"

"Jesus, Maggie! This is the last thing I wanted! You here playing house, for Christ's sake!" he barks. Colonel comes from the living room at the sound of his voice, wagging gently, but Malone ignores him. The dog takes the hint, flopping down in front of the oven.

"Look, Malone," I begin, more than a bit confused. "I just brought over some soup and…"

He peers into the living room. "Oh, for God's sake, did you clean up, too? Damn it, Maggie!" Slamming over to the counter, he bangs his hands down. Colonel startles at the noise.

Okay, now he's pissing me off. Taking a deep breath, I say calmly, "Excuse me, but what the hell is your problem? I did something nice for you. No big deal. For God's sake, Malone, you were submerged in the Atlantic Ocean today! I thought you could use a little—" I stop myself from saying "TLC"— "food. That's all."

"I'm not one of your little church projects, all right?" he barks. "This is—oh, for Chrissake, you did the goddamn dishes."

"Okay, Malone. I guess I should have just left you alone to snarl and brood and do whatever else the hell you do. Take the pie out when the timer goes off. Enjoy it, you surly bastard. Come on, Colonel."

"You don't get it, do you, Maggie?" Malone growls, and his glare could cut glass. "I don't want your pie and your soup and whatever the hell else you've got in your little picnic basket. Okay? Save it for your priest and your little old ladies and whoever else you've got on your list. Not me."

My temper snaps. "I can't believe you're mad at me! How can you be mad? I'm just trying to help!"

"That's the whole point, Maggie! I don't want your help. I don't want you doing anything for me!"

"Fine. I'll send you a bill. And I don't have a picnic basket." With that, I snap my fingers at my dog, who lumbers to his feet and follows me. I stomp off the porch and down the street. When I'm safely at the intersection, I sit down on the curb, the cold seeping through my jeans immediately. My breath fogs the air in front of me, but we don't have any street lights, so I know Malone can't see me. My legs are shaking.

Colonel nuzzles my hair, and I automatically put my arm around him. My throat is tight with tears and anger, but I don't cry. "Screw him," I say. "Ungrateful bastard."

So, fine. Malone doesn't want anything from me. Fine. Just fine. He's made things clear, at least. No, I'm not his girlfriend. Just a roll in the hay now and then. Well, too bad. I want more than that.

"When people care about each other, they show it," I tell my dog. He licks his chops thoughtfully. "There's nothing wrong with that. That's the way things are supposed to be." The image of Malone rubbing lotion into my long-suffering hands flashes through my brain. Well. That was just a seduction move, and it worked brilliantly. "I don't think Malone is a very nice person, do you? You don't, either? Well, you've always been smart about these things." Colonel lies down next to me, but the pavement is too cold for his old bones. I stand up, and my dog does the same. "At least we got that out of the way," I say. My dog wags reassuringly. Still, my throat stays tight, like there's a piece of glass wedged there.

CHAPTER EIGHTEEN

FOR SOME REASON, Joe's Diner is hopping the next day. It always seems to be the case—something in the tides or the moon causing a mass hysteria for breakfast out. People are actually waiting for tables, which usually only happens on Thanksgiving weekend or during both good weekends of summer. Octavio whips orders out, and both Judy and I are working at top speed, smiling (well, I am, at least), sliding orders to the hungry of Gideon's Cove, passing out ballots and pens for the best breakfast rating, trying to ring people up before a line forms at the register. Jonah comes in, but I don't have time to do more than shove a plate of French toast in front of him—as he eats for free, he gets what I give him.

"Thanks, sissy," he calls as I fly into the kitchen.

My parents, also succumbing to breakfast fever, make a rare appearance. Mom frowns as she surveys noisy crowd. "Well, I guess we'll have to wait," she says. When she comes in and things are slow, she tells me I'll never make a living. If I'm busy, she's put out. And today, I'm just not in the mood.

"Business looks good today, Maggie," my dad says.

"It sure is, Dad. Hi, Rolly. How was everything?" I ask.

"Cracklin'," he says. I take this as a compliment.

"You filled out your ballot, right?" I ask.

"Every day, Maggie, every day."

Finally, a booth is free for Mom and Dad, since the counter is jammed. "What would you like, Mom?" I ask.

"Oh, I don't know. I should have eaten a bowl of bran flakes, really."

"How about pancakes, Maggie, hon?" Dad asks.

"Pancakes it is." Having been a waitress for half my life, I don't need to write down orders. "And you, Mom?"

My mother sighs. "Well, I just don't know. I guess I'll start with orange juice, only don't fill the glass. It's too much. Your glasses are too big. Fill it about three quarters full. Can you do that? Because otherwise, I won't be able to drink it all."

"Squeeze one, three quarters. Got it."

Georgie comes in and attaches himself to my side, his head only reaching my collarbone. "Hi, Maggie! How are you, Maggie?"

I put my arm around him and kiss his crew cut. Mom assumes her lemon-sucking expression. "Hey, buddy," I say to Georgie. "Someone spilled juice under the last stool. Can you take care of it?"

"Sure, Maggie!" He gives me a squeeze and goes to the back room to get the mop. I glance back to the counter, where people are in various stages of eating and ordering, then do a double take.

Malone's here.

He's sitting next to Jonah, talking to him, and his presence causes my face to go hot. He looks my way, his face as blank as a blackboard in July. No sheepish grin. No apologetic shrug, just the penetrating blue stare and the slashing lines of his perpetual scowl. I turn back to my parents.

"Mom?"

"I don't know, Maggie! There's too much to choose from."

"Fine. You get nothing." I snatch the menu from her hand and fly back into the kitchen, ignoring Malone, ignoring my mother's squawks of indignation. I grab an order of the spinach omelet special, some pumpkin bread French toast and a plate of silver dollar pancakes. "Another stack for my dad, Tavy," I tell Octavio.

"Ayuh," he answers.

I serve the family at the fourth booth, then grab the coffeepot and head for the counter, overhearing Jonah saying, "Oh, shit, it was nothing. You'd do the same for me."

So. Malone came here to see Jonah. To thank him. Not to see me, or, God forbid, thank *me*.

"Good morning, Malone," I say briskly. "Coffee? Let me guess. Black, murky and bitter. Maybe you'd just like to suck on the grounds?"

Malone turns his clear blue eyes to me. "Maggie," he mutters.

"Hope you slept well," I snap. Jonah's eyes widen, but he wisely refrains from comment. Malone's eyes don't flicker from mine. I slosh some coffee into his cup, spilling some, and smack the pot down on the counter. Without looking away, Malone deliberately takes the creamer and dumps about half of it into his cup, then shakes four sugar packets, tears them open and pours them in as well.

"All done, Maggie!" Georgie calls cheerfully.

"Thanks, Georgie. Don't know what I'd do without you," I call back, not looking away from Heathcliff of the moors here.

"What a lovely day it is outside. Hello, Mabel, love, how are you this fine morning?" Father Tim is here, but still I don't look away from Malone's somber face.

"Have you got something to say to me, Malone?" I say.

"Oh, I've got a lot to say to you, Maggie," he answers grimly. Jonah slips away to join our parents.

"I'm waiting," I say.

"Excuse me, can we get some ketchup over here?" calls Helen Robideaux from the corner.

"Hello, Maggie dear. How nice you look today." Father Tim comes behind the counter—he's a regular, after all—and grabs a mug. Finally, I break the staring contest between Malone and me and turn to greet my friend. My happy, cheerful, dependable friend.

"Father Tim! How nice to see you! And what a great mood you're in today. You really brighten a place up, you know that?" I believe I hear Malone growl.

"Ah, Maggie, you're too kind. I'll just grab some coffee, shall I, and let you get back to work." He opens the kitchen door a crack and sticks his head in. "Good morning, Octavio, my fine man. Can I throw myself at your mercy and get an order of the pumpkin French toast?"

I have work to do. Malone can go to hell and play with his compatriots there. Stepping around Colonel, I ring up a young couple who's been waiting patiently, ask about their kindergartner and bring the ketchup to Mrs. Robideaux. Malone sits at the counter, staring straight ahead.

The bell over the door tinkles, and I sigh. Another customer, a man about my age with silvery hair. He looks around uncertainly.

"Be with you in a sec," I call. Judy has disappeared. Must be time for her ciggie break.

"Maggie, for heaven's sake, can I please have a fried egg?" my mother asks.

"Fine." I've heard about how, in some fancy New York restaurants, the wait staff spits on the orders of bitchy customers. I'm tempted to give it a whirl. "Hi, Stuart. You want the usual?"

"That'd be great, Maggie," he says, sitting next to Malone.

"Adam and Eve on a raft, burn the British," I call to Octavio, slang for two poached eggs on a toasted English muffin.

"Side of hash, too?" Stuart asks.

"Sweep the kitchen!" I call, hearing Octavio grumble; he's quite proud of his hash and doesn't like that particular moniker. Stuart, however, laughs.

"Sweep the kitchen," he repeats to Malone, chuckling. Malone doesn't chuckle back.

"Hi," I say to the gray-haired stranger. "Sorry, we're a little swamped today. Just one?"

"Are you Maggie?" he asks.

"That's right."

"I'm Doug," he says, holding out his hand. "The guy who stood you up," he adds at my look of incomprehension.

"Oh! Hi!" I shake his hand and look over my shoulder. "Here, why don't you sit with Father Tim? He kind of fixed us up, right, Tim? This is Doug…oh, sorry, I forgot your last name."

"Andrews," he says. He's a nice-looking man, kind brown eyes with shadows under them.

"Listen, I'd love to sit and chat, but I've got to take care of those people. Be right back."

Malone is gone. There's a five-dollar bill tucked under his cup. I note that he hasn't drunk any of the overly sweetened coffee. Should've stuck with the grounds.

I clear and wipe and take orders and serve and pour coffee. I don't have a chance to talk to Doug, who is deep in conversation with Father Tim. Occasionally, I catch a snatch of their conversation…"not for us to understand the reason"…"comfort of knowing she was deeply loved"…and my heart warms at Father Tim's kind, gentle words. Finally, Doug comes to the register to pay his bill.

"Maggie," he says, "I just wanted to apologize in person for not meeting you that night."

"Not at all," I answer. "I'm sorry I didn't have a chance to talk to you this morning. The joint's been jumping since six."

"That's okay. I really enjoyed talking with Father Tim," he says. "And I wanted to say again that I'm really grateful for how nice you were about everything. Under different circumstances…" His eyes tear up.

"Well, listen, now, don't cry. You're welcome," I say. "You're a nice guy, Doug. Take care."

By the time I turn off the Eat at Joe's sign in the far window, my feet are throbbing, my face is oily, my hands are raw and my back hurts. Needless to say, I'm in a bit of a mood. Because I would hate to snap at Georgie, I send him home early (Judy's long gone), and Octavio and I clean up in silence.

"Everything okay, boss?" he asks as he shrugs into his jacket.

"How long have you been married, Octavio?" I ask, wringing out the dishrag.

"Eight years," he smiles.

"You and Patty seem really happy," I say.

"Oh, we are."

"I have a feeling I'm never going to find someone," I say, and suddenly that tight-throated feeling is back.

Octavio gives me a thoughtful look. "What?" I ask him.

"Malone came in today," he says. "Never seen him here before."

I snort. "Yeah. He came in to thank my brother. Jonah gave him a hand yesterday."

"Hmm." Octavio is a man of few words. "Well. Good night, boss."

"Bye, big guy." And it's only four o'clock.

It's beautiful out, finally, fifty degrees or so. The trees have the soft fuzz of buds on them, the palest green imaginable, and the wind is salty and gentle. Unfortunately, I'm too busy today to take a bike ride or even a decent walk. Instead, I bake some brownies for tomorrow's dessert offering. Then I load up the car and head over to the firehouse.

I get paid to cook their monthly dinner, and though it's not much, it's one of those fees that helps, especially during the off-season. While I'm able to pay all my bills each month, there's usually not a lot left over. Mornings like today's are few and far between. I know I should have a cushion in case something goes wrong, but I'm tapped out. Winning the best breakfast title would help, even if it was just to get people from neighboring towns to take a drive in on the weekends.

Colonel settles himself down in the corner of the firehouse kitchen while I unload the car. The soft April air beckons, and I wish again that I could take a bike ride, but by the time I'm finished, it will be getting dark. Plus, Colonel needs to get home. He seems stiff today, quieter than usual.

"You okay, pup?" I ask him. He looks at me with his beautiful eyes, but his tail doesn't wag. "Who's my pretty boy?" I croon, kneeling to stroke his head. There. His tail swishes. I give him a piece of roast beef and get to work.

What's Malone doing tonight? I wonder, then immediately purge the thought from my head. Malone is a callous user, and I'm no better. My behavior toward him has been embarrassingly slutty, says a chastising inner voice sounding exactly like my mom. *Fools rush in where angels fear to bed,* she'd say. And in this case, she'd be correct. I snap on the radio to drown out my self-condemnation.

The boys—sorry, firefighters—start filing in around five-thirty, Jonah among them. He waves to me but is engrossed in a conversation with the head of the truck committee…the firefighters are convinced that Gideon's Cove needs a ladder truck, though we'd also need a new structure to house it, which would be just fine with the boys—sorry, firefighters.

I set up the Sterno burners and bring out the trays of food, basic, hearty fare—roast beef, horseradish mashed potatoes, green beans, pesto chicken, pasta and sauce. Twenty or so guys usually show up. Chantal pokes her head in the kitchen.

"Hey, girlfriend," she says.

"Hey, Chantal," I answer. "I forgot you're a member here." I grin as I say it.

"Best thing I ever did," she sighs dramatically. "Community service and all that crap. Not to mention the best-looking guys in town."

"I didn't realize sleeping with the fire department was community service," I retort, pouring the sauce over the ziti.

"Oh, it is, it is. Don't let her talk you out of it, Chantal," Jonah says, coming in and putting an arm around my laughing friend. "And here's a fireman who needs your special skills."

"You're disgusting," I tell him. Chantal purrs.

"Wanna test some hose?" Jonah murmurs, ignoring me.

"Jonah, leave us," I command, and for once, my little brother obeys. "You want to go out later on, grab a beer or something?" I ask Chantal. Her eyes are still on my baby brother. His *ass,* to be precise. "Chantal!"

She jumps. "Oh, sorry, Mags," she says. "I've got plans." Her voice changes. "Hi there, Chief," she coos, her voice dropping into a sultry croon.

"How's my little recruit?" Chief Tatum croons back. "Practice any search and rescue lately?"

"Okay, I can't take anymore," I say, sounding quite peeved even to my own ears. "Come on, Colonel. I don't want you hearing this kind of talk, anyway." Chantal and the fire chief don't seem to notice.

I bring some ziti to Mrs. K. and heat it up for her. Then I help her find her comfortable slippers, "not those *horrible* ones that make my bunions *ache.*" But I'm edgy and irritable tonight and make my visit quick.

Faced with my long flight of stairs, Colonel turns to me, and I boost him all the way up.

Adding insult to injury, the soup, bread, cheese and pie that I made for Malone are sitting in front of my door. I let Colonel inside and then go back and grab the food, slamming the pot on the counter. Frickin' Malone. Let him starve, then. Who cares?

Colonel doesn't seem interested in dinner tonight. I give him some EtoGesic and glucosamine and fluff up his doggy bed, then write a note on the blackboard to call the vet and see if there's anything else I can do.

Maybe my mother is right, I think as I dump the soup down the drain. Maybe the diner is a dead end. It was something I fell into. Granddad put us to work at a young age, washing dishes, clearing tables, working our way up to waiting tables. But is it something that I really want to do for the rest of my life?

I stare out the window toward the harbor, thinking.

The answer is yes.

Maybe it's not the most illustrious career in the world, but what Joe's Diner does—what *I* do—is give a center to our town. A meeting place. Anyone can come in, even if they just want a cup of coffee, and spend the morning catching up on news, seeing their neighbors. There's Dewey's, of course, but that's only open at night, and it has a different attitude. People go there with more of an agenda—meet someone, have a few drinks, and if you're hardcore, get drunk. But Joe's is a social center in a town that desperately needs one. And the fact that it's an authentic Mahoney design doesn't hurt. I wonder if I could get it listed on a national register or something.

But my mother's constant nagging has dented my

armor lately. When I picture growing old at the diner, I picture a husband and kids coming in and out, or me going home to them. I don't picture me alone, soaking my swollen feet in Epsom salts every night with only a series of increasingly smelly dogs for company.

I throw a pizza into the oven, wait for it to heat, then eat listlessly. How many dates have I gone on in the past month or so? Four? Five? And let's not forget Malone, not that we dated, of course. Just sex. Best sex of my life, in fact.

Time to call Christy, I think when the self-pity disgusts even me. I punch number one on the speed dial.

"Hey, it's me," I say when Will answers.

"Hi, Maggie. How are you?"

"Okay, I guess. You guys still going out tomorrow? Same time as usual?" I ask. Thursday is my babysitting night.

"Actually, I'm not sure. Christy's not feeling great. There's a stomach bug going around, and I think she caught it."

"Oh, dear. Well, if you need anything, let me know. Tell her I said I hope she feels better fast."

"Thanks, honey. Will do."

When Christy met Will, it was instantly clear to both of them that they'd met their soul mate. Six months later, Will, then a resident in Orono, took a rare night off and asked me out for dinner. Alone. He took me to a nice restaurant, and though he was exhausted from a long shift, he was nonetheless funny and charming. While we were eating dinner, he took out a velvet box and handed it across the table to me.

"Um, I think you might have the wrong twin," I said, wincing.

"I know who you are," Will smiled.

"So is this a test run or something?" I asked.

"Listen, Maggie," he said, his face growing serious. "I want to marry your sister. I've never met someone as wonderful as she is. Every day I wake up feeling like I'm in a dream because I get to call her or see her or hold her hand."

"That's so nice," I said, my eyes growing misty. At the time, I was quite sure I would soon find someone just as wonderful as Will.

"But I know how close you are, and I know I'm asking…well, not exactly to come between you, because I know I could never do that, and I never want to. But I'm asking you to share Christy with me. I need your blessing, Maggie." His eyes were teary.

In the box was a beautiful garnet ring, Christy's and my birthstone.

Of course I gave him my blessing. The thought of my sister spending her life with a man who adored her…well. Who could say no?

I haven't met anyone like Will. There may be no one like Will in the whole world. The best I've come up with is a tearful widower, a sullen lobsterman and a priest. "Well, crap," I say. I offer the crust of my pizza to Colonel, who eats it delicately. "You feeling better, pal?" I ask him. He puts his head on my lap.

The Red Sox have a travel day, which is just as well. They've been playing with all the skill of blind, one-legged five-year-olds lately. I click around aimlessly until nine-thirty or so, then decide to just call it a night. It's not lost on me that going to bed with my dog is the best thing that's happened all day.

CHAPTER NINETEEN

COLONEL WON'T GET off the bed in the morning. He wags his tail listlessly but doesn't even raise his head when I ask if he wants to go out. I check the clock; it's too early to call the vet.

After yesterday's rush, the diner is back to normal—my regulars sit at the counter, Ben, Bob and Rolly. Stuart is at his booth at the window, reading the paper. But I'm worried about Colonel, and as soon as the clock hits eight, I make the call. They tell me to come in tomorrow.

"He's probably just feeling his age," the nice tech tells me. "He's in great shape for an old guy. How old is he now, fourteen?"

"Thirteen," I say.

"That's pretty good for a big dog like him."

"I know. But he's just not himself."

For the rest of the day, I hop back and forth between the diner and my apartment. I manage to coax Colonel off the bed and outside so he can pee, but he laboriously climbs the steps as soon as he's done. I help him back onto my bed and give him some water. "What's the matter, boy?" I ask, stroking his head. "We'll go see Dr. Kellar tomorrow, okay? He'll help you out, Colonel."

I have to throw together a couple of lasagnas for a

funeral and bake a few dozen cookies, but all day, I'm itching to get home to my dog. It's the awful plight of a pet owner: knowing something is wrong with your loyal companion, unable to figure out what. Could he have eaten something that's made him sick? Did he get hurt somehow? Does he have cancer?

I get home for good around four, finally done for the day, then call Christy to see if she might come over and keep me company while I watch Colonel. But she's still under the weather, and after hearing a description of her all-nighter with the toilet, I feel uncomfortable telling her about my dog's listlessness. I'm lonely enough that I find myself calling Father Tim.

"Maggie, I'm terribly sorry, I've got to run," he says. "I'm having dinner with the Guarinos tonight. Thanks for the lasagnas, by the way. They were wonderful."

I manage a smile—Father Tim is the only man I know who can eat lasagna at four and go out to dinner at six. "Well, that's okay," I say. "I'm just a little worried about Colonel. He's kind of quiet today. Not himself."

"Don't you worry," he answers. "I'm sure he'll be just fine. Tell you what, I'll ring you later, shall I?"

"Sure." I hang up and stretch out on the bed next to my dog. I stroke his ears and run my fingers through his silky ruff. He nestles closer and groans in contentment.

My father gave me Colonel just after Skip dumped me. I was staring out the window a week or two after Skip's triumphant return to Gideon's Cove, and my father walked in with Colonel, a blue ribbon tied around his neck. Rescued from one of those breeding mills down south, Colonel was then an overly large, rambunctious two-year old. It was love at first sight. That first night, he climbed, paw by paw, cautious as a jewel thief, onto my bed. Perhaps he thought if he went slowly, I wouldn't notice the extra eighty pounds wedged into my twin bed. I was still living at home, and my mom had had a fit when she saw us the next morning, Colonel's head on my pillow, my arm around his shaggy tummy.

"For heaven's sake, Maggie! It's an animal! Get it off! It might have fleas or lice or something."

The next week, I moved out, into the very apartment I still live in, and Colonel and I began the next phase of our life together. When the humiliation and grief over Skip threatened to overwhelm me, Colonel would come over and nudge my hand with his nose until I petted him. Or he'd drop a ratty tennis ball at my feet, and if I ignored him, he'd repeat this ten or twelve times until I got the hint. He slept on my bed each night, his big head resting on my stomach as I fought off loneliness and tried to come up with a plan for my adult life.

Colonel only needed a little training, and I soon became known as "the one with the dog" to distinguish me from Christy. I never used a leash; Colonel just followed me cheerfully, always able to keep pace with my bike or walking beside me, his plumey tail waving like a flag. I'd go into a store, and he'd lie down on the sidewalk outside, patiently waiting for me to emerge. He took to the diner like a veteran waitress, never bothering the customers, just lying behind the register, watching people come and go until it was our turn to leave. Sure, it was against the health code, but no one ever found a dog hair in the food, and no one ever complained.

When my mother mused out loud that I'd never meet anyone, or when another date went wrong, when I came home from babysitting Violet, filled with yearning for a baby of my own, all I had to do was turn to his golden face and ask for a kiss. He never told me I was wasting my life—he thought my life was the best thing that ever happened to him. He never thought I talked too much; instead, his eyes would follow my every move, his ears pricked and alert when I spoke. He accepted every tummy scratch, every head pat, every evening on the couch as if it were a gift from God Himself, when really, it was just a drop in the bucket compared to the devotion he gave me.

"You're my best bud," I tell him. His tail thumps reassuringly. Cuddled together, we fall asleep.

I WAKE UP around three in the morning, knowing immediately that Colonel has died.

His body is still warm under my hand, but there's just something missing. Tears flood my eyes, but I keep petting him, his beautiful soft golden fur. I stroke his white cheeks, feeling the wiry whiskers, the soft jowls of his throat. I don't turn on the light—it would be sacrilegious somehow, because then I'd have to see that my dog of the past eleven years is dead. Instead, I just move closer to him, wrap both arms around his neck, bury my face in his fur and cry.

"I'm sorry, Colonel," I choke out. Sorry that I didn't rush him to the vet to see if there was anything wrong, sorry that I didn't take the day off to be with him. "I'm so sorry, boy."

I cry until the sheet beneath my face is soaked, until the sky goes from black to blue velvet to pink. When I can't avoid it any longer, I sit up and look at him, his noble, gentle white face, the silky feathers of his belly and legs.

"Thanks for everything," I whisper, my words piti-fully inadequate.

The phone rings, and I know it's Christy before I hear her voice. We know when the other is hurting.

"Is everything okay?" she whispers. It's only five in the morning.

"Colonel died," I tell her.

"Oh, no! Oh, Maggie!" she cries, and I start crying again, too. "Maggie, I'm so sorry, honey. Did he—did you have to—"

"He just died in his sleep, right on my bed," I whisper.

"Oh, Colonel," she murmurs, sniffing. I hear Will's voice in the background, and Christy tells him my sad news.

"Can we do anything?" she asks.

"No, no," I say. "I'm calling Jonah. He'll give me a hand. How are you guys doing? Still sick?"

Christy sighs. "I'm still pretty whipped, and Violet's got it now. She threw up all night, after she ate three helpings of ground-up spaghetti and meatballs for supper. We've barely slept."

I notice that I'm still petting Colonel's soft fur. "I hope you feel better," I tell her.

I call my brother and ask if he'll help me bring my dog to the vet for cremation when they open. Then I call Octavio and ask him to cover for me.

When Jonah comes over at quarter to eight, he thumps up my stairs and hugs me tight, tears in his eyes.

"Shit, Maggie. This just sucks," he says, looking at the floor. "Maybe he's with Dicky now or something. They were both awesome dogs."

We go into the bedroom, and I kiss Colonel's head

once more as Jonah wipes his eyes on his sleeve. Then we wrap him in a blanket and carry him down to Jonah's truck. Mrs. K. comes out to see what's going on.

"Colonel died last night, Mrs. K.," I tell her, and the old woman, who has buried a husband, three sisters and two of her four children, bursts into tears.

"Oh, *Maggie,*" she weeps, and I hug her frail shoulders, crying again myself.

Jonah and I slide Colonel into the back of his pickup, and I climb in beside my dog. "It's gonna be cold back there, Mags," my brother says.

"That's okay," I tell him. I hunker down and put my arm over the blanket so it won't blow off, because that would just be too sad to see.

The people at the vet's are so kind. They help us carry Colonel in through the back entrance and give me a moment to say goodbye.

"I'll wait in the truck," Jonah offers, closing the door softly behind him.

I pull the blanket off Colonel's head and take one long, last look. He seems cozy, wrapped in the red plaid blanket that we used together on chilly nights. "I'll miss you so much, buddy," I whisper, my throat barely able to force the words out. "You were such a good dog. The best."

I kiss his cheek, my tears wetting his fur. And then I leave.

Jonah drives me home so I can shower and strip the bed. I can barely look at my apartment, so lonely and empty, so I trudge to the diner, where Judy and Octavio cry over the news.

"Won't be the same without him," Judy sobs. "Shit. Shit, shit, fuck. I'm going out for a cigarette."

Octavio makes a little sign that says "We regret to tell you of the passing of our great friend, Colonel" and tapes it to the cash register. Rolly shakes his head sadly, Bob Castellano gives me a whiskery kiss. Apparently Jonah or Christy calls my parents, because they come in around ten with Christy, who still looks pale and a bit shaky. She and my dad, who is crying openly, sandwich me in a hug.

"Thanks for coming," I whisper. My own eyes are dry for the moment.

Dad blows his nose, then hugs me tightly. "I'm so sorry, honey," he whispers.

"He was the best," Christy says, her mouth wobbling.

"I know. Thank you."

"Well, Maggie," my mother says, and I brace myself for what comes next. "I'm sorry."

I blink in surprise. She never tried to hide her disapproval, not being a dog lover herself. She barely tolerated Dicky, another of my father's saves.

Judy takes care of the two remaining breakfast patrons, shooting us little glances and pretending not to listen.

"At least you won't have to vacuum up its fur every day," Mom says idly. "And the diner here will certainly be more sanitary without it."

Ah, here she is, my real mother. My swollen eyes narrow.

"Mom!" Christy squeaks. "Jeezum!"

"What?" she says innocently. "It's true. And look at you, Maggie, you're a wreck. You look awful. All over a dog."

"Mom," I say, my voice is pleasingly calm, "Get the hell out of my diner."

"Excuse me?" she asks. Dad steps back in alarm, and Christy puts her hand on his arm protectively.

"Get out, Mom. I loved that dog. He saw me through some of the worst times of my life. I'm sick of you disapproving of me, sick of you telling me that my life is a dead end, sick of you comparing me to Christy and her perfect life. Get out. Come back when you can act like a mother who loves all her children."

My mother's mouth is hanging open, and it's odd, because at that moment, I love her more than I have in a long time. But enough is enough.

"Dad," I say, "you really should stick up for me more."

"I know," he whispers.

"Christy, sorry. Love you." I give her a stiff hug. "Hope you feel better. I'm going in the kitchen. Please be gone when I come out."

Octavio, diplomatic as Switzerland, says nothing as I come in. I open the supply closet and sit down on the floor among the vinegar and canned tomatoes. My breath is ragged, and my hands, I note, are shaking. Tavy gives me five minutes, then opens the door.

"You okay, boss?" he asks.

"Peachy," I say.

"About time you told that woman off," he says, smiling his nice gap-toothed smile.

I give a grim laugh. "Thanks."

I SEND JUDY HOME EARLY, preferring to stay as busy as possible. Word has spread, apparently. Chantal comes in for lunch, hugs me with uncharacteristic sweetness and hands me a bunch of tulips.

"Sorry, pal," she says, sliding into a booth.

"Thanks. What can I get you?"

"Oh, I don't know. Maybe just some coffee today. I'm not feeling great."

"Right. There's a stomach bug going around," I tell her. "Christy and the baby both have it."

"Yuck. Well, if I don't have it, I'd be happy to come over tonight, okay? If you want some company?"

"That's okay. I think I just want to be alone."

Chantal nods. "Hey, has Father Tim been in today?" she asks, checking her lipstick in the chrome of the little jukebox.

"Actually, no. I have to drop by and tell him about Colonel." Suddenly, the idea of seeing Father Tim, being comforted by him, maybe having a cup of tea in the rectory living room, overwhelms me with longing. That's where I'll finally be able to find some comfort.

I call Beth Seymour and ask her to handle my meals on wheels tonight. When she hears about Colonel, she offers to tell my clients, many of whom loved my dog.

"Thanks, Beth. That would be nice," I say. My eyes feel grainy and hard.

When I leave the diner, I automatically hold the door open a second too long before it occurs to me that my dog won't be following me. There's no one to look out for, no one to talk to…shit. Mom's right. I'm pathetic.

Mrs. Plutarski glares at me when I ask if Father Tim is in. "He's quite busy today, you know," she says, pushing up her glasses on her razor-sharp nose. "This might not be the time for a…social visit."

"I've just had a death in the family, Edith," I say, knowing she hates it when I call her by her first name. She waits for a name, but I don't give her one. "Is he in or not?" I demand.

"Maggie? I thought I heard your voice."

There he is. "Hi, Father Tim. Do you have a minute? In private?"

"For you, Maggie, always. Edith, my darlin' girl, would you mind faxing this over to the mother ship? It needs to be there today." He hands her a piece of paper, which she accepts as if it were an engagement ring. "Sorry, Maggie. Official diocese business. Thanks, Edith."

"Don't forget you have that meeting in Machias at six," she says, her eyes on me. *Make it short* is what she's really saying.

"What can I do for you today, Maggie?" Father Tim asks, ushering me into the parlor.

I sit in the chair, ready to be comforted. "Father Tim, Colonel…he died last night."

At first, the news doesn't register. I suddenly remember that Father Tim said he would call me last night and didn't. "Oh, dear," he says, his expectant smile turning to sorrow.

I wait for more. It doesn't come.

"He died in his sleep," I say.

"Well, that's a comfort, then, isn't it? Better than having him put down, I'd imagine." He glances at his watch.

"Do you have to go?" I ask brusquely.

"No, no. I've got a bit." He sits back and folds his hands. "Well. You must be feeling quite sad."

"Yes," I agree.

"I'm sorry, then." He smiles kindly, but for the first time ever, I get the feeling that he's not really listening.

"Father Tim," I say, "do you think animals go to heaven?" The question comes only from my desire to engage him, not from any spiritual need. I know exactly where Colonel is.

"I've been asked that before," he answers thoughtfully. "And while you might say that though God created them, the truth is that they don't have the ability to make a choice. That's a gift God only gave to man, Maggie, free will, don't you know. And so—"

He keeps talking. I stop listening.

Father Tim is not going to comfort me. He's not going to say something that's tender, compassionate and insightful. He's off on some tangent about church teachings, ignoring my sadness, oblivious to my irritation.

"Okay, whatever," I interrupt. "Listen, I have to run."

"Maggie," he says, standing. "I'm terribly sorry." He folds me into a hug. It doesn't do much for me today, but I soften a little. At least he's trying.

"Thanks, Father Tim," I say, extricating myself. "I'll see you tomorrow."

Mrs. Plutarski doesn't acknowledge me as I come out, choosing instead to bustle frantically around the room to show just how busy they are. "Father Tim, you've really got to get going," she calls out for extra measure. I hate her.

I walk home slowly. My eyes automatically check for Colonel at each corner, and I almost expect a nose to bump reassuringly against my hand.

Mrs. K. is lying in wait for me. The second my foot hits the step, she opens her door. "Hello, dear," she says.

"Hi, Mrs. K.," I say. The last thing I want to do is cut her toenails or plunge her toilet. "Everything okay?"

"Well, *yes*, Maggie, for me, at any rate. Here. I *baked*

today. I can't *remember* the last time I baked. These are for you." She hands me a paper plate of peanut butter cookies, the crisscross marks sparkling with sugar. Her wizened, soft face is so kind and sweet that my eyes instantly fill.

"Now, you probably need some time *alone,* so I won't keep you," she says. "But I'm *here* if you need me." She squeezes my arm and closes the door.

I open the door to my apartment and step in, then stand for a minute, facing my loss. I've never come home and not had Colonel either with me or here to greet me. His bowl is still there, still filled with kibbles. His doggy bed, worn on one side where he draped his paw over the side these many years, seems enormously empty.

A COUPLE OF HOURS LATER, I'm in my oldest, most comfortable flannel pajamas. Winged blue coffee cups float over an orange background, a color combination that explains why I got them for three dollars. Two inches of my ankle stick out, and my bosom—or lack thereof— is now coated with peanut butter cookie crumbs. Exhausted but not sleepy, I listlessly watch the Red Sox blow a four-run lead. My mother hates me, my father's disappearing, my sister's perfect, and hey. Let's not forget that my dog is dead. In a word, I'm not feeling too chipper. Of course, that's when someone knocks on the door.

I heave myself off the couch. Probably Jonah, I think. But it's not. It's the last thing I need. Malone.

I open the door. "Malone, it's not the best time for me," I say, looking at his chest.

"I'll just be a minute," he answers, pushing past me.

Why is he here? Do we need to break up? Did we have a relationship that actually requires a breakup scene? "Look," I say, but I'm talking to his back because he's ignoring me and going into the kitchen. Taking off his coat, even. The nerve. And opening a cabinet. Pretty rude, if you ask me. I stay where I am, hands on my hips. If he wants a fight, he's in for it. I am in no mood for shit today, as Mommy Dearest could attest. This has been a piss-poor day, and my throat grows tight with anger.

"Malone, I really don't want you—"

Malone comes back in the living room with two glasses of what looks and smells like scotch. He hands one to me, then clinks his glass against mine. "To Colonel. He was a great dog, Maggie."

Whatever hardness I'm feeling crumbles like a sand castle. I cover my eyes, which have instantly filled with tears. "Malone…" I whisper. He puts his arms around me, kisses my head, and the kindness of the small gesture just destroys me. My fists clench in his shirt, and I sob against his chest.

"Jonah told me," he says, kissing me again. "Here, take a drink. You'll feel better."

It's one of his longer speeches. I obey, wincing as I swallow. Then he leads me to the couch and sits down, pulling me with him, tucking my head against his shoulder. My tears leak out, wetting the wool of his sweater, and I hiccup occasionally. We sit there like that for a long time, watching the Sox lose, not saying anything. I sip the drink, feeling a pleasant warmth grow in my middle. Malone's fingers play idly in my hair, and I'm curled against his side. My eyes begin to burn, my thoughts grow sketchy and jumbled.

I don't remember falling asleep, but when I wake up, I'm in bed, the covers pulled up to my chin. My arm reaches out automatically, and I do touch a warm, solid figure, but it's not Colonel, of course. It's Malone. He's lying on top of the covers, fully dressed. The moonlight that pours through the window allows me to see that he's awake.

"Hi," I whisper.

"Hi," he says.

"Did you carry me to bed?"

He nods once.

"You're pretty strong, then," I say, and he smiles, tugging my heart.

He reaches out and pushes a strand of hair back from my face, his smile fading. "Maggie," he says, his voice as gravelly as the stones at Jasper Beach, "the other night, when you came over…I wasn't exactly at my best."

My goodness. An apology. "I think you're making up for it now," I tell him.

"Can you spend the day with me tomorrow?" he asks, still playing with my hair.

A date, I think. He wants to take me on a date. Octavio and Judy can run the place without me for a day. It's been known to happen. "Sure." My eyes are getting tired again. "Do you want to come under the covers?" I murmur. "It's pretty chilly."

The bed squeaks as he gets off it. I hear his clothes rustle, but I can't keep my eyes open another minute. He slides under the covers with me, minus his sweater, though the jeans and shirt remain. He pulls me against him, and I slip my hand under his shirt against his warm skin. Malone kisses my forehead, and in another minute, I'm asleep.

CHAPTER TWENTY

MALONE WAKES FIRST, sliding out of bed. "Meet me at the dock at seven, okay?" he asks.

"Okay," I say, rubbing my eyes. He leaves, closing the door quietly behind him.

I get up, trying not to look for Colonel in every corner, and take a quick shower, then throw on some jeans and a sweater. I pause for a minute by Colonel's bed, kneeling down to pat the fleecy cushion. "Miss you, buddy," I whisper. Then I call Octavio and tell him I'm taking a day off.

"Sure, boss," he says. "You deserve it."

Now while seven isn't early if you work in a diner, it's downright late if you're a lobsterman. Most of the boats are already out, including the *Twin Menace*. Malone's *Ugly Anne* sits bobbing on its mooring as the tide rushes in. He's waiting for me by his dinghy.

"So are we going lobstering?" I ask.

"Nope," he says, handing me into the little boat.

The smell of herring, the bait lobstermen use for their traps, is musty and thick, but it's a smell I've dealt with most of my life. Still, I breathe through my mouth until we get to the *Ugly Anne,* the waves slapping against the hull of the dinghy, spraying me occasionally. "Charming name," I comment as we approach the boat. Malone's face creases into a smile. "Who's Anne?"

"My grandmother," he says.

"And does she know that you've immortalized her this way?"

"Ayuh." He smiles but offers nothing more, climbing aboard and reaching out his hand to me. "Have a seat," he says.

A lobster boat is all about work, nothing about comfort. There are no chairs, just an area in the middle where you can sit if you're so inclined, which the lobstermen aren't and therefore don't. The pilot house is crammed with equipment—a couple of radios, the GPS equipment, radar. There are barrels for bait and a holding tank for the lobsters. If Malone was going out to check pots, there'd be ten or twelve extra traps stacked on deck and miles of line coiled and waiting, but each night, the lobstermen unload at the dock, and the deck is clear and empty right now. I sit on the gunwale, not wanting to get in the way.

Malone does his preflight check, as it were, and then starts her up and releases the *Ugly Anne* from her mooring. The wind is brisk as we head out to sea. Malone steers us past Douglas Point, dodging Cuthman's Shoal. Colorful buoys illustrate the water, so thick you could walk home, as Billy Bottoms would say, and we work our way as if navigating a maze. It takes us about twenty minutes to hit clear water, and even then the Maine coast is loaded with abrupt shoals, tiny islands, currents and tidal dangers. Once we're out a bit, Malone sets the wheel and glances over at me.

"Are we going to check your traps?" I guess, pulling the hood of my coat on.

"No."

"Where are we going, then?"

He adjusts the controls, then looks over to where I sit on the gunwale, insecure enough that I'm clenching a handhold. "It's a surprise," he says, unscrewing a thermos lid. "Want some coffee?"

He pours me a cup—black—but I don't complain (or mention the fact that I just *knew* he took his coffee black). Then he turns his attention ahead, and I tilt my head back and watch the seagulls and cormorants that follow us, hoping for some bait. Colonel would have loved this, I think. The smells, the fish…maybe he'd roll around in something foul, a pastime he loved above all others.

The sound of the motor is soothing, and the damp breeze is tinged with salt and the slight smell of fish. The sun flirts with the idea of putting in an appearance, then reconsiders, and strands of fog still hug the rocky, pine-dotted shoreline.

I sip my coffee and study the captain, who seems different out here. He's at ease, I realize, something I've rarely seen in Malone. He checks the instrument panel occasionally, makes adjustments to throttle, steers steadily and with confidence. Because the door of the pilot house is open, the wind ruffles his hair and jacket. "You doing okay?" he asks.

"Sure," I answer.

Malone points out a group of puffins, the fat little black-and-white birds toddling on the shore of a small island. I ask him a few questions about the boat, but otherwise we don't talk much. It's actually kind of nice, being quiet. The dark head of a seal pops up about ten yards off the port side. It watches us for a moment, the silky brown fur gleaming, then slips noiselessly beneath the surface. My hair blows around my face until Malone offers me an elastic, one of the thousands he has to slip over the strong claws of the lobsters. The motor is loud and strong, but not strong enough to drown out the cries of the gulls that follow us, or the slapping of the waves as we cross a wake or current.

After an hour or so, we once again encounter a sea of offshore buoys. Malone slows down, navigating carefully through them, and heads to a wooden dock where about a dozen other boats are tied.

"Where are we?" I ask.

"Linden Harbor." He doesn't look at me.

"And what are we doing here?"

He shrugs, looking a little sheepish. "Well, there's a thing here. A lumberjack competition. Thought you might like to see it." He secures a line and steps onto the dock, then reaches a hand back for me.

"A lumberjack competition?" I ask, hopping off the boat.

"Ayuh. You know, tree cutting, axe throwing, the like. There's a little fair, too. Games, craft tent, that sort of thing. Good food, too."

Is he blushing? He turns for the gangplank before I can tell for sure.

"Malone," I call.

"Yeah?"

"This sounds suspiciously like a date, you know." I smile as I say it. "Sounds like you actually planned this."

His eyes narrow at me, but he's smiling. "You want me to win you one of those ugly carny toys or not?"

"Oh, I do, I do," I answer, tucking my arm through

his and continuing up the dock. "The question is, can you?"

"Of course I can, Maggie," he says. "The question really is, how much money will I lose doing it?"

It's almost surreal, being here with gloomy old Malone. Arm in arm, no less. There's a bubble of happiness in me, a strange and lovely new feeling as we head toward the tents on the town green. The smell of fish is drowned out with something deliciously cinnamon.

"Looks like the rod and gun club's selling breakfast," Malone says. "You hungry?"

"God, I'm starving. Your bait fish was starting to look good."

Malone orders me a ham and egg sandwich, a cinnamon roll and a cup of coffee, then the same for himself. We take our food and sit at a table, watching people.

"Can't say I've ever seen you eat much, Malone," I comment around a mouthful of what is surely the best breakfast sandwich ever made.

"Almost every day," he says. "Come on, let's walk around."

For this part of Maine, it's a pretty big event. We're too far south to have driven along the coast…it would have taken us hours, but by boat we were able to go in a fairly straight line. There's a small midway with a few rides. Kids dash from the merry-go-round to the Ferris wheel, tugging their parents' hands, asking for more rides, more food, more games. The happy sound of a fair washes over us in waves, the music from the rides, screams of kids, laughter of parents. Before I think about it, I slip my hand into Malone's. He turns his head to look at me, and as the corner of his mouth pulls up in a smile, my heart pulls, too.

"Win a prize for the lady!" calls a carny. "Shoot the target just three times, win a prize." A row of battered-looking BB guns lines the counter.

"Oh, goody," I say. "Here's your chance, Malone. Prove your manliness and win me, oh, gosh, let's see…how about that blue stuffed rat?"

"You sure? Don't you want that the pink zebra instead?"

"Oh, no. I'm a blue rat kind of girl."

"Blue rat it is, then."

Twelve dollars later, I am the proud owner of the ugliest stuffed animal I've ever laid eyes on. "Thank you, Malone," I say, kissing my prize.

"You're welcome. And I want you to know that gun barrel was bent."

We pass on the rides, as I'm afraid of heights, and aside from the merry-go-round, the rest look like a quick way to die. Instead, we walk over to see the speed-climbing competition, the men scampering up forty-foot wooden posts with the agility of squirrels. When that event is over, we watch a man carve a life-size black bear from a huge block of wood.

"That would look great in front of the diner," I say, half serious. Malone laughs.

There's a crafts tent where quilts and afghans and embroidery hang on display, ribbons fluttering in the breeze. I pore over the baking tables, eyeing the coffee-cakes and cookies, the beautiful pies and cheesecakes. Malone buys me a slice. "I like a woman who can eat," he says, and I punch him in the arm.

"So, Malone," I say as I take a bite of the creamy,

lemony cheesecake. "Are you ever going to tell me your first name?"

"Why do you want to know?" he asks. He doesn't look at me.

"Because…because I just would."

"Mmm-hmm. Well, too bad."

"I could ask Chantal, you know. She has all the public records. I bet your name is listed somewhere. Plus, I won't give you a bite of this cheesecake if you don't, and as you can see, it's disappearing fast. Your chances are dying."

"Another time, maybe."

I sigh. "You realize you don't talk that much, don't you, Malone?" I say, taking the last bite of cheesecake.

"You talk enough for both of us," he says. He takes my hand again.

It's a wonderful day, not painfully cold, not raining, which by our standards means gorgeous. A barbershop quartet sings a corny song from World War II, and apparently some bagpipers will make an appearance later in the day.

By one-thirty, we've exhausted the event, having seen every little corner of it, and we walk down to shore. There's a breakwater made from great slabs of rock, and we walk out on it a way, then sit. The stone is cold, but I don't mind. Malone puts his arm around me.

"Cold?" he asks.

"No," I answer. I lean my head against his shoulder. "So, Malone," I say, "tell me about your family."

He doesn't stiffen so much as go completely still. "What do you want to know?"

Of course, the first thing I want to ask about is his daughter. A teenage daughter…what must that be like for him? And, let's be honest, what would that be like for me? Truthfully, I haven't dared to picture anything with Malone past what we've had thus far, but I want to. Would his daughter approve of her dad having a girlfriend? Would we be friends? Would she hate me, refuse to come visit her dad, stick pins in a Maggie-style voodoo doll? I clear my throat. "Well, you have a daughter, right?"

"Yeah."

"Are the two of you close?"

"Close as you can be when you live on opposite coasts," he says neutrally.

"You must miss her," I say.

"Ayuh."

I stifle a sigh. The subject of his daughter seems closed. "Did you know I went to school with your sister?" I offer.

"Ayuh."

I wait, but more doesn't come. "I seem to remember that you guys didn't have the best childhood," I venture carefully. It's not exactly true—Christy's the one who remembers, not me—but I hope it will open things up a little.

Malone's arm drops from my shoulders, and he turns to face me. "Maggie—" His mouth becomes a tight line. "Look. You're right. It wasn't great. But it was a long time ago, and I took you here so you could have a nice day, all right? Let's not talk about this shit."

"Okay, okay. Fine." The lines between his eyebrows are fierce. *All in good time, Maggie.* I pick up his hand. "I'm sorry. And I am having a nice day. Very nice." The lines soften. "You're being really sweet. In fact, I had no idea you could be such a prince."

At last he smiles, grudgingly. "Okay. Well, it's been half an hour since you ate, so you must be starving. Want some chowder?"

"How about some lobster bisque? I want to support the local industry and all."

He stands up and pulls me to my feet, and we head back for the tents, stopping in front of a sign that says Best Freakin' Lobstah Bisque Evah. And I have to say, it just might be. As I scrape my bowl, I notice Malone's amused gaze.

"I don't really eat that much," I tell him. "It's just that you barely eat at all."

"You mean I don't eat your food," he says.

"I have noticed that, yes. Which is your loss, since my cooking skills are incredible."

He leans in close, his unshaven cheek scratching mine. "I'm more interested in your other skills, Maggie," he whispers. My knees grow weak, and I toss my empty bowl into a nearby trash can, then wrap my arms around his lean waist. He kisses me, that deliberate, wonderfully intense kiss, his lips warm and silky smooth in contrast to his rasping stubble.

"Come on," he mutters. "Let's go back to the boat."

Malone steers the *Ugly Anne* out of the cove to the far side of a tiny island, where he teaches me a few more things about a lobster boat—that you can make love standing up in the pilot house, though there's little room for error. We bang into a few things here and there, and my legs are still shaking when we're finished, my breath coming in gasps.

"Sorry if I was too loud," I whisper. Sure, I'm quiet *now*…two minutes ago, I was—well. Not quiet.

"I thought you sounded just about right," Malone

says, smiling against my neck. A few minutes later, Malone starts the engine once more and steers us out of the maze of lobster buoys.

I zip my jacket and watch Linden Harbor disappear behind us. Some hopeful seagulls follow the *Ugly Anne* for a while, then, realizing we're not going to catch anything, give up and wheel toward land.

"Shit," Malone says from the pilot house.

"What's the matter?" I ask.

"Oh, the fins on the turbo charger are clogged again. Damn it."

I go over to the little doorway. "Can we get home okay?"

"Yeah, we'll be fine for that. I'll just have to clean it later, see what's going on." He glances at me, then stands aside. "Here. Want to be captain for a day?"

We're already away from the buoys and lines that could become entangled in the propellers, so I'm safe enough. Malone stands behind me, gently correcting my course when he needs to, and I lean against him, his chin resting on my head.

"Do you like lobstering?" I ask.

"Sure," he says.

"Tough life, though."

"Great life, too." He smiles at me. "Okay, look out there, Maggie, we've got some porpoises about three o'clock."

"You know what, Malone?" I ask as we watch the silvery-white flashing of the porpoises.

"What's that?" he says.

"This is the best day I've had in a long time." I turn away from the wheel to kiss his cheek.

"Watch out there," he says as the boat veers suddenly.

He reaches around me and adjusts us. "Tide's coming at us pretty strong." He swings us back around. "Me, too, by the way."

When we get back to the dock, it's near dinner time. "Do you want to try out my cooking skills, Malone? Since you've sampled my other skills already?" I smile as he makes the boat fast to the mooring.

He straightens up. "I'm sorry, Maggie," he says. "I need to fix the charger before morning, and it's an ugly job."

"Oh. Okay."

I'm suddenly deflated. Malone climbs into the dinghy and reaches up to help me, and before I know it, we're back at the dock. Billy Bottoms waves to us from the gangplank, heading for home, but aside from him, no one seems to be around.

"Well, okay. Thanks, Malone. It was, um, a very nice day. Thank you so much." I feel my cheeks grow hot as we stand there, looking at each other. The old uncertainty about the two of us has returned.

"See you soon," he says. He pinches my chin. *When?* I want to ask, but I can tell his mind is on his boat.

"Thanks again. Bye." I scurry up the gangplank to solid ground and walk home.

There are four messages waiting for me—Christy, Jonah, Chantal and Father Tim. They all want the same thing—to know how I'm doing, if I want company. But for tonight, I think I want to be alone. The sadness I feel over the loss of my pet is tempered with Malone's surprising sweetness, and I want a night to indulge in both of those feelings. I put a frozen pizza in the oven and then pack up Colonel's things in a box, letting myself have a vigorous cry as I do. Someday I'll get another dog, but there will never be a friend like Colonel. But I do have a new friend—Malone. When I needed it most, he really came through.

CHAPTER TWENTY-ONE

IN A SHOCKING NEW DEVELOPMENT to our relationship, Malone actually picks up the phone and calls me a couple of days after our date, just when I'm starting to grow irritated. Jonah had mentioned that Malone had to go down to Bar Harbor for a part, so I had granted him a grace period, but his time was running out. And I miss him, I realize with a bit of a shock.

When the phone finally rings around five on Thursday night, I am washing my kitchen floor, wondering how it gets so dirty when I am the only one who lives here. I actually expect it to be Father Tim, wanting to hit me up for the upcoming bake sale.

"Maggie," comes the gruff voice.

"Malone! My God! You're using a phone!" I can't help the smile that has burst over my face.

"Very funny," he says. There's a pause, then, "How are you?"

"Fine. How are you?"

"Fine. So. Are you busy tonight?"

"You cut right to the chase, don't you, Malone?" I grin.

"Answer the question," he growls.

"Sorry, pal. I'm busy. I'm babysitting my niece tonight."

"That right?"

"Yup."

He sighs. "All right, then. What about tomorrow?"

My grin fades a bit. "Well, actually, tomorrow I'm supposed to have dinner with, um, a friend. With Father Tim. A bunch of us, actually. Church people. You know." It's an appreciation dinner Father Tim hosts for the five or six of us who do everything he asks. "How about Saturday?"

He doesn't answer for a minute. "Sure. Saturday's fine. Seven?"

"Seven o'clock. Um, do you want me to cook you dinner?"

"No, Maggie," he says, his voice dropping to a scraping bottom note. "Don't cook for me." My body reacts as if he'd said he'd like to just rip off my clothes and take me on the floor.

"Okay," I answer in a strangled whisper, suddenly needing to sag against the counter. "No cooking."

CHRISTY IS ALL DRESSED UP in a long, pretty skirt and filmy blouse, and Will looks preppy and handsome as always, blue blazer and Dockers.

"Bye, Snooky," my sister says, smothering Violet in kisses and a cloud of Eternity. "Mommy loves you! Yes she does! Mommy loves Violet! Aaaah…bwah!" She simulates the noise Violet makes when kissing someone.

"Okay, that's enough," I say, prying my niece out of Christy's arms. "Get out, you clearly need a strong drink. Bye, Will."

"Bye, Mags. Thanks, as always."

"Thank you, actually. Violet, honey, it's Auntie time!"

Violet grabs chunks of my hair and pulls with glee.

For the next hour, we play Farmyard Animals—at least, I do, crawling around on the floor, mooing, oinking, quacking—while Violet chortles and throws plastic toys for me to fetch.

"Mooo," I say, retrieving the yellow ring.

"Oooo," she echoes.

"You're a genius," I tell her. "Smart baby. Violet is a very smart baby."

"Banuck," she agrees.

As I hover over her crib, watching her sleep a little while later, I indulge, very briefly, in a domestic fantasy. *Just trying it on for size,* I tell myself, blushing. Me, watching the baby sleep. Malone, standing in the doorway. The baby has black hair like her daddy, gray eyes like me.

Then, embarrassed with my private stupidity, I go into the kitchen to see what Christy's left me to eat. She may not pay me to babysit, but she does feed me well. Ooh. Tuna casserole, our mutual favorite and something our mom refuses to cook, and chocolate chip cookies. Good sissy.

I'm watching TV when they come back, flushed and cheery. "My God, you guys," I comment, dragging my gaze away from Donald Trump's latest victim, "were you doing it in the car?"

"That's really uncanny," Will says. "The whole twin thing—creepy."

"I know," I tell him. "The fact that your pants are unzipped was just confirmation."

Will grins, zips and flies upstairs to look in on his precious while Christy flops down on the couch next to me.

"What did you do with Violet?" she asks.

"Oh, the usual. We lit matches and I gave her a few sips of vodka, which she really seemed to like, and then we went up on the widow's walk, and I let her stand on the railing. It was fun."

Christy hits me with a throw pillow. "So are you doing okay?" she asks. "About Colonel and all?"

I nod. "I'm okay. It's weird, though. I've never been without him, really. Not as an adult." My eyes grow misty, but I smile.

"Where were you the other day? I called you and even swung by, but Octavio said you took the day off."

I tell her about Malone, how he came over and slept on my bed like a good dog himself, how he took me to the festival, how incredibly nice he was the whole day.

"So you guys are…what? Dating? Back together?" she asks. She takes a cookie from the tin on the coffee table and bites into it. "These are great, aren't they?"

"Yes, they are. And I guess we're sort of…well… yeah. Dating. I guess so."

Christy cocks an eyebrow at me. "You're not sure?"

I sigh. "Well, it's weird. He's—he was great, he really was. But it's not like…"

"What?"

"Well, he's still kind of a stranger. When we were at the lumberjack thing, I asked him a couple of questions, you know, normal things, like if he's close with his daughter. What his first name is."

"You still don't know?" Christy interrupts.

"No, I don't. And he never really tells me anything. So we're together, but I don't know if we're just sleeping together or if we're actually going somewhere relationship-wise."

"Well, here's a great idea. Why don't you ask him?" my sister suggests.

I grimace. "Yeah," I muse, taking another cookie. It may be my fifth. "No."

"Why not, dummy? It shouldn't be a mystery. You have a right to know what he's thinking. I mean, what if he just wants a warm body once in a while and here you want marriage and children? I think you should ask."

I consider this. She has a point, of course, but then again, she's never confronted the challenge of engaging Malone in conversation, let alone *relationship* conversation. "Maybe."

I think about it as I walk home. The night is cool and misty, the damp air soft and gentle against my cheeks. Of course, my reluctance to talk to Malone stems from the fear that he does indeed just want a warm body. Then again, if that's the case, I shouldn't be wasting my time with him. As usual, Christy has a point. How irritating.

MY FATHER COMES IN for breakfast the next day, alone. He sits at a booth, which is fine, since the place is deserted this morning. Since six o'clock, I've had a grand total of four customers. I've paid my monthly bills, sent in my order to the food suppliers and cleaned the bathroom, and it's only nine o'clock. Judy left at eight, disgusted with the lack of patrons for her to ignore, and Georgie only comes in three times a week.

"Hey, Dad," I call from behind the counter. "What would you like today?"

"Maybe just some coffee when you have a chance, dear," he says. He looks out the window, his face somber. I come over and pour him a cup, then sit down.

"Is everything okay, Daddy? You look—"

"Your mother and I are getting divorced," he interrupts.

My mouth falls open, but no sound comes out, just a little wheeze. Dad shifts in his seat, then looks at the table, shaking his head. "I'm sorry, pumpkin."

"What—you—but—"

Dad sighs hugely. "I know. We've been married for thirty-three years now. Seems silly, doesn't it?"

My eyes fill, and I grab a wad of napkins out of the dispenser and blot. "What happened?" I whisper.

"Nothing. Nothing big, really. It's just—" He pauses, fiddling with the silverware. "It's not your mother's fault," he continues. "I just don't want to... I'm trying to say this gently, understand."

"You just don't want to live with Mom for the rest of your life," I supply.

"Right. I'm tired of hiding in the bomb shelter."

I sit up a little straighter. "Dad, look. I know Mom can be quite a...harridan sometimes. I mean, I certainly get tired of her nagging me all the time, but I thought..." My voice chokes off suddenly. "I thought you loved her," I finish in a hoarse whisper.

Dad's own eyes tear up. "I do. I did. But Maggie, the past few years...well, we haven't been happy. She hasn't been happy, and I'm just exhausted with trying to guess what mood she's in and why and how I can make it better."

"What does she think about all this?"

"She's furious." Dad's mouth tightens again, then wobbles. "She told me if that's what I want, then I'm even a bigger idiot than she thought and she'd be glad to get rid of me."

Sounds like Mom, all right.

Mom was never the kind of cookie-baking, Girl Scout leader mother depicted in most of our childhood books. She took care of us, certainly, fed us nutritious meals and sent us to bed on time. But there was always an edge to her, and while I never doubted her love, I often doubted that she liked me very much. Christy dealt with her better. She was the quieter, more studious, more helpful child, while I tended to be a little sneakier, disappearing when the kitchen needed cleaning up, drifting into the bathroom when the groceries had to be unpacked. And with Jonah, the classic little boy, always grubby, always making messes and losing things, Mom's thin patience had evaporated completely. Only after he moved out did Jonah become someone my mother really seemed to enjoy.

"We had to get married, you know," my father tells me, interrupting my bemused thoughts.

"Excuse me?"

"Your mother was pregnant with you girls when we got married." Dad, more composed now, takes a sip of his coffee.

"We're love children?" I blurt. "Christy and I are love children?"

My father gives a half smile. "Ayuh. You never figured it out?"

"No! Dad! One bombshell at a time!"

Octavio sticks his head out the door. "You still need me, boss?"

"No, no, Tavy. Thanks."

"I'm gonna run home before lunch, if that's okay," he says.

"Sure, sure. Fine." A moment later, the back door

closes, and Dad and I are completely alone. I look at my dad in a new light. "So. You knocked up that nice Lena Gray and had to marry her."

"Yup. You and Christy—two for the price of one."

"Did Mom want to get married?"

"Well, Maggie, that's what you did back then. None of this unwed mother stuff that goes on nowadays. You got a girl pregnant, you married her, and fast."

"So your anniversary is really…when?" Because my parents never really celebrated their special day (the reason now a little more clear), it was never a big event in our calendar year to begin with.

"We got married on March fifteenth. You and Christy came along six months later."

"The ides of March? You got married on the ides of March, Dad?" I start laughing. "No wonder you're getting divorced. 'Beware the ides of March, Caesar,'" I quote. "Shakespeare knew what he was talking about."

Dad graces me with a smile, but his eyes are sad. "Listen, sweetheart, your mother's going to need a little sympathy. Don't be too hard on her, all right?"

"Well, we're not really speaking at the moment," I tell him. "Not since I kicked her out of the diner the other day."

"Oh, that's right. Well, it would be nice if you could patch things up."

I roll my eyes. "Yeah. Sure. She only insulted my beloved dog on the day he died."

Dad sighs again. "I know, Maggie. But do it for me, won't you, dear?"

Of course I will, and Dad knows it. "Have you told Christy and Jonah?"

"I told Joe last night. I'm headed for Christy's now."

"Do you want me to tell her, Dad? You must be worn out."

His eyes shine with gratitude. "That would be great, honey. I'd appreciate that. You know you're my best girl, now, don't you?"

"Yes, and I know you say the same thing to Christy, you dog." I slide around to sit next to my father, wrapping my arms around his neck. "I love you, Dad."

"Thanks, baby," he whispers. "Sorry about all this."

"Where are you staying? I can't imagine you both in the same house, if Mom's on a tear."

"Well, my lawyer said not to leave home just yet—" His *lawyer!* He's already called a lawyer! "—so I'm still there. In the cellar, as usual."

He leaves a minute later. I watch him walk down the street, his shoulders slumped, eyes on the pavement. Poor Dad. He must feel completely desperate if he's resorted to this. And yet not just desperate—actually doing something about it.

I summon my sister to a late lunch at Joe's Diner and break the news as she eats. Christy isn't as stunned as I expect her to be. "I always wondered about that," she muses. "If they had to get married. It makes sense."

"You mean it explains why Mom's been in a bad mood since the day we were born?" I say, far less sympathetic than my sister. She really deserves her title of "the good twin."

"Well, yes, Maggie. I mean, in those days, there was a lot of shame over being pregnant before you were married. So suddenly she's twenty-two years old, and her life is mapped out for her. No choice in the matter now. She'd just finished college, remember? She wanted to be an editor in New York City, and instead she's pregnant and living in her hometown, knitting booties. For twins. The icing on the cake."

"She wanted to be an editor? I never heard that," I say. Christy breaks off a piece of grilled cheese and offers it to Violet, who opens her mouth as obediently as a baby bird.

"Yeah." Christy turns away from her baby to look at me. "Imagine, Maggie. The first girl in our family ever to go to college. Granddad would have been so proud, the whole town would have talked about it, little Lena, a college girl, look at that. And then bam. She's pregnant. Knocked up. No career, no New York, just mud season and black flies and two colicky babies."

"It does put things in a new light. You're right."

"All done, Violet?" Christy asks. "Are you all done?"

"Bwee," Violet says, squirming in the high chair. "Nahbo."

I gird my loins for battle and call my mom that afternoon, but the gods are merciful and I get the machine. "Hey, Mom, it's Maggie. I heard the news…um, sorry. Uh, I'll call you later, okay? Hope you're okay. Bye." A feeble message, but a message nonetheless.

I drop in on Mrs. K. for a visit and a chat, leaving my parents' situation out of it. Mrs. K.'s grand-niece is coming to get her for the weekend, and my tiny tenant is busy packing.

"Were you happily married, Mrs. K.?" I ask as her gnarled hands fold sweaters with surprising agility. Though she's only going for two days, she's got six complete outfits laid out on the bed. I sit on the comforter, handing her clothes as directed.

"Oh, *yes*," she replies. "We were. I'll take those pink argyles, dear."

"And what was your secret?" I smile, knowing how she loves to talk about Mr. K., who's been dead for more than twenty years.

"I think, dear, that our *secret* was lots of sex," she says matter-of-factly. "You can't be *too* unhappy if you're having lots of *sex.*"

"I see." I'm blushing. "Well. Good for you. That's great."

"I *miss* it, I must say," she says. "Of course, *now* it would probably *kill* me, but if you're going to die…"

"Mrs. K.!" I laugh. "You're so surprising."

"Well, now, people aren't really *so different,* Maggie," she tells me. "Dear, I need that *cardigan.* You and that scowling man, what's his name? McCoy?"

"Malone," I mumble, my face igniting.

"Yes, Malone. From the sounds of it, you'll be *very* happy." She laughs merrily. "You were quite *rosy* when you came home the other *day.*"

"Okay. Must run. Have a wonderful weekend." Mortified and secretly pleased to have impressed the old lady, I kiss her cheek and flee upstairs.

And speaking of secretly pleased, there's a part of me that can't help feeling a little…smug…about my parents' divorce. Though it's a shock, and not a good one, there's a certain sense of vindication floating around in my chest.

I always thought my father was too good for my mom. She never seemed to appreciate him, always picked on him, ordering him about like Napoleon sending his troops to Russia. And like Napoleon, she'd gone too far. I'm sorry for the embarrassment and discomfort, sorry that our family will never be the same, but it seems my mother had this coming.

I pull out one of my nicer sweaters and take a little time with some makeup. The volunteer appreciation dinner is guaranteed to be a fun event. Father Tim feeds us well, gives us plenty to drink. We usually out stay fairly late. Last time, Beth Seymour played the piano and we all sang. Later, several of us went into the church, supposedly for a midnight prayer, and ended up laughing so hard that Betty Zebrowski wet her pants. It's one of the better parties in town.

When I get to the rectory, everyone else is already there—Mrs. Plutarski, unfortunately, Louise Evans, Mabel Greenwood, Jacob Pelletier, Noah Grimley and Beth Seymour. Betty the pants-wetter is in the hospital for bladder suspension surgery.

"Maggie!" Father Tim barks as I enter. He leaps over to me and takes my hand warmly, holding on to it for a long moment. "How are you, dearie?" he asks. "I called you the other day, but you weren't home. I've been thinking of you and your lovely Colonel, as well."

"Thanks, Father Tim," I say, warmed by his consideration.

"I'm so glad you came. Now the party can really begin. A drink, Maggie? I've broken out the good stuff, and it's going faster than the devil in a roomful of Baptists."

Father Tim is in top form. He passes hors d'oeuvres, prying the tray out of Mrs. Plutarski's clenched hands as she tries to nail her part as "most helpful one here." Though I often compete for that role, tonight I'm content to be waited on. I chew contentedly on scallops wrapped in bacon and lobster cheese puffs and chat with Jacob, who reshingled the leaky part of St. Mary's roof last year.

"These are delicious, Father Tim." I gesture with my lobster puff as the priest refills my glass.

"I knew they were your favorite, Maggie," he says with a crooked grin. "I'd serve them at Mass if it'd get you coming back." I smile in response but don't answer. Jake wanders off to flirt with Louise Evans—apparently they had a thing in high school, some forty years past—and Father Tim's face grows serious.

"Maggie, I had a talk with your dear mother today," he says quietly.

"Oh, wow. That was fast. Yes." I take a deep breath. "How is she? I called her but she wasn't in."

"She's devastated, of course. And hoping your father will see the light. I've offered to do some counseling in the hope that we can make things better without having to resort to...well, you know." He pats my hand, then squeezes it. "It must be terrible for you."

"It's definitely a shock," I say carefully. "The thing is, Father Tim, my mother—well, she's not an easy person to live with. And she doesn't really try to see anyone else's point of view, if you know what I mean."

"That I do, Maggie, that I do. And yet we're talking about the sacrament of marriage. It's to be preserved at all costs. You don't just walk away from someone you love."

"Hmm," I say. "Yes, of course. But my father's been henpecked for years, Father Tim. You've seen that, haven't you? She really doesn't...well. Maybe now's not the time to talk about it," I say as Beth makes desperate eye contact with me. Noah Grimley has left the platter of shrimp cocktail and moved on to her, and as he's old enough to be her grandfather and missing his front teeth to boot, I must intervene. She did the same for me last fall.

"Maybe we can talk later," Father Tim suggests.

"Sure." Not that I'm dying to discuss my parents' marriage with anyone, to tell the truth. I walk over to Noah and ask about his new boat, a subject guaranteed to take any man's mind off sex, at least on the coast of Maine.

The party is wonderful. Father Tim entertains us, feeds us, pours drinks until we're all buzzed and laughing at stories of his Irish childhood, the pranks played by his six older brothers and sisters. And I can't help feeling special—it seems that he's going out of his way to acknowledge our friendship. "Well, of course, poor Maggie's heard this one already," he says at the beginning of a story, or "When Maggie and her daddy and I went to Machias last fall to pick up the statue from Our Lady of Fatima…" Edith Plutarski's face grows more and more sour, I note through the pleasant fog of wine. Definitely the sign of a happy night.

When we can eat no more, Father Tim walks us to the door. "Drive safely, Jacob," he calls to our token teetotaler. Jake'll be driving everyone who lives more than a few blocks from here, though Noah and I will walk back.

"I'll tag along with the two of you, if you don't mind," Father Tim offers. "I could do with a bit of air myself."

Noah wraps a few shrimp in a napkin and slides them into his pocket. Father Tim and I pretend not to notice. "You coming, Noah?" I ask as he surveys the rest of the leftovers.

"Ayuh," he grunts.

The night air is cold, feeling more like February than April, but it feels good after being in the stuffy rectory.

Noah's street is a block or two before mine, and Father Tim shakes his hand. "Thank you for coming, my good man," he says.

"No problem," Noah responds. "'Night, Maggie."

"Bye, Noah."

Father Tim pauses. "Well. I'll just see you the rest of the way home, shall I?"

"Sure," I answer. It's only a block. I can't help but notice that Father Tim looks…well, quite sad. My heart tugs.

"Is everything okay, Father Tim?" I ask as we walk.

"It's funny you bring that up," he says softly, his eyes scanning the heavens before returning to my face. As ever, the old attraction thrills through me as I look at his gentle eyes, his perfect bone structure. He doesn't say anything for a minute, and my heart starts thumping with nervousness. Or maybe it's guilt for still finding him so appealing. "Well. Difficult decisions lie ahead," he says obliquely, sounding more like a fortune cookie than a priest. He doesn't elaborate, and I don't ask him to.

It only takes a minute more to get to my little house. Father Tim turns to me. "I hope you know you're a special friend to me, Maggie," he murmurs. "A great friend."

Weird. "Sure." I swallow. "Right back at you." I glance up at my house to see if Mrs. K. is spying, then remember that she's out of town for the weekend.

"You have a way about you, Maggie," Tim says quietly. "I hope you know that. Even if things change, I hope…well." He looks at me intently, as if he's trying to telecommunicate something.

*If things change…*what the heck does that mean?

What's he trying to say? My face flushes. "That's nice. You're so nice. And—and—tonight. Was nice. Really nice. Thank you, Father Tim."

He doesn't move, just continues to look deeply into my eyes, then looks away, sighing. "Well. Good night now, Maggie."

"Good night! Thank you. Thanks, Father Tim! For everything. Bye, now!" I scurry the remaining distance to my porch, then race up the stairs, glad, perhaps for the first time, to put some distance between me and Father Tim.

CHAPTER TWENTY-TWO

"I HAVE A DATE with Malone," I tell my reflection the next afternoon. "Just have to go see Mom, get that over with, and then I have a date. With Malone."

It's a calming thought. Malone, after all, is not my angry mother. Nor is he a priest. No vows of chastity for Malone, that's for sure. "And thank goodness for that," I grin.

But something is definitely going on with Father Tim, and I'm not sure I want to spend a lot of thought on what it could be. When he didn't come into the diner this morning, I was surprised to find myself a bit relieved.

However, any sense of reprieve I might feel is cancelled out by the dread I have of seeing my mother. Still, I can't just ignore her, so I pedal my bike out to my parents' house, take a few cleansing breaths outside and go in. Dad is nowhere in sight, as usual, but Mom is sitting at the kitchen table.

"Hi, Mom," I say, bending down to kiss her cheek.

"Oh, Maggie. Hello," she answers. "How are you?"

"I'm fine," I say, pulling out a chair and sitting. "What about you? This must be very…" My voice trails off.

"Mmm. Yes, it is. Very." She stares at the table. "So. What's new? Did you get another dog yet?"

"Um, no. I think I'll wait a while. Mom, are you okay?"

She sighs and looks at the ceiling. "No, Maggie. I'm not. I'm the town laughingstock, dear. Divorce after all these years. Poor Mitchell Beaumont couldn't stand it another minute. That's what they're all saying, you know. Nice old Mitch, married to that bitch." She gives a grim smile to acknowledge her rhyme.

"Oh, jeezum, Mom, I don't think people are saying that," I blurt, though I myself have thought almost those same words verbatim. Many times.

"Well, you've always been naive," she says. "Want a drink?"

"Uh…no." I watch as she gets a bottle of vodka out of the freezer and pours herself a half a glass, then adds a shot of orange juice. It may be the first time I've ever seen her drink anything other than white zinfandel.

She takes a healthy swallow, pats down a stray lock of her curly hair, then sits back down with a thump. "So. What do you want me to say? Or would you like to tell me I'm a bad mother?"

I tilt my head, looking at her. She actually looks quite pretty today, for some reason. Then I see what it is; she's not wearing makeup. "You're not a bad mother, Mom."

"Well, thank you for saying that." She takes another slug of her pale orange drink.

"Mom," I blurt, "you were kind of rushed into marrying Dad, being a mother, all that. Maybe this is your chance to have some independence, start a new life, you know. That kind of thing."

"That's rich, Maggie," she says. "I'm fifty-five years old. I don't want a new life."

"You didn't want your old one, either," I point out cautiously. "You've been unhappy most of your life, haven't you?"

Surprisingly, she reaches out and takes my hand, frowning automatically at the roughness, my short fingernails, the cut on my left middle finger. "I want to tell you that's not true," she admits slowly. "I do love you kids. And your father."

"We know that, Mom," I tell her. "You don't have to apologize for anything."

"You're so generous, Maggie," she snaps, and only she could make it sound like such a put-down. "Oh, it makes me mad sometimes! You're just like my father, and your father, as well! Everything, anything for everyone and anyone! It drives me crazy, honey! You give away *everything* and never take anything for yourself, you with all the chances I never had! My God, honey, do you want to end up like me?"

My mouth hangs open, but Mom is on a roll. "Take a good look, Maggie! I was all set to have a life I'd dreamed of. Get out of Washington County, get out of Maine and live in a big city, have a career, really do something. I imagined myself climbing up the ladder at some publishing house, becoming like Jackie O or something, surrounded by books and creativity and excitement." Her fist slams down on the table, her voice rising. "And I ended up here, working in a stupid doctor's office instead! And now my goddamn husband is divorcing me and I'm terrified!"

My mother bursts into tears. I get up from my seat and kneel next to her, gingerly putting my arm around her shoulders.

"Mom," I say gently. "Listen. Calm down. It's going

to be okay. Daddy's not going to kick you into the street or anything. You'll be fine. And if you want to do something else, you can now. This is a second chance for you. You can move, you can get another job, do anything… Don't cry, Mom."

But she continues to sob. "You don't understand, Maggie," she chokes out. "It's too late. I'm too old. You can't teach an old dog young tricks. And before you know it, honey, you're going to be just like me."

So, OKAY, that didn't go too well, I think as I ride home. That was definitely not good.

I never thought of my mother as "poor Mom," but I can't seem to help it right now. Maybe Father Tim's right, maybe my parents should work it out. Then again, it seems like my dad has suffered enough. Besides, it's not like they'd be fighting for their old happy life. Maybe a divorce will give them both a new chance. Clean slate, all that crap. But I'm shaking a little. My mother was never afraid of anything before.

I decide to go to Malone's house, even though we had said seven at mine. I don't care. He'll have to deal with me showing up on his doorstep two hours early.

Malone's house is at the top of a hill, and I get off my bike and push it up the steep incline. When I'm a few doors away, I hear the nicest sound—someone's playing the piano. I pause and listen, but the wind is pretty strong, and I can't catch it all.

Afraid that he won't play if he knows I'm there, I push my bike into the neighbor's driveway, then walk into Malone's small yard, making my way around a couple of lobster traps that are stacked neatly near the side of the house. The living room window is open, and

I can hear quite well now. Smiling, I sit down on the ground, resting my back against the sun-warmed shingles. Malone continues to play, so I'm pretty sure I've remained undetected.

The song is lovely, a sweet, delicate melody. Occasionally, there's a change in key, so it goes from happy to sad, though the melody is still essentially the same. It sounds difficult, and once in a while, Malone stops and goes back to repeat a bit of the song. I even hear him swear once—"Shit," followed by the correct notes, then, "Gotcha." A car pulls up on the street, not far from Malone's, and I hope the driver doesn't see me. It would be embarrassing to be caught sitting here.

I don't get caught.

Instead, there's a knock on Malone's door. He stops playing. I'm about to get up when I hear a familiar voice.

"Malone? Oh, thank God you're home." It's Chantal. I freeze, midcrouch.

"What are you doing here?" Malone asks. Their voices are as clear as if I were in the same room.

"Damn it, Malone, you're not going to believe this." I think Chantal may be crying, and a strange sense of apprehension pins me to where I squat. "Do you have a sec? I need to talk."

"Sit down. What's the matter?" he asks. I hear the squeak of springs, a rustle.

"I'm pregnant."

The air is sucked out of my lungs. Chantal is pregnant? And she's telling—

"Oh, Christ," Malone says. "Oh, honey." Chantal bursts into tears.

The realization hits me slowly, their voices fading to a background undertone.

Chantal is pregnant. And Malone…

"How far along?" Malone asks, his voice coming back into reception.

"Just a couple weeks. I don't know what to do, Malone. This is the worst—"

My vision swims, my hearing fades, and my hands are clenched over my mouth. I've never fainted before, but this must be close. *A couple of weeks.*

A couple of weeks ago, Malone and I were sleeping together. And, apparently, he was also sleeping with Chantal.

I don't realize that I've left my spot under the window until I grip the cold handlebars of my bike. Without making a sound, I push it robotically down the road. When I reach Water Street, I climb on and ride to my sister's house.

It doesn't matter, I tell myself over and over, the wind biting my damp cheeks. *There was nothing real between us anyway.*

But it seems that there was, because I'm crying so hard I can barely see.

CHAPTER TWENTY-THREE

THERE'S A MESSAGE on my answering machine when I finally return to my apartment the next afternoon. I've been hiding at Christy's, and yes, I told her the whole story. She and Will fed me, let me put Violet to bed and opened a good bottle of wine. I slept in the guest room and went straight to the diner this morning.

The light on the answering machine blinks, waiting to tell me the big news. It takes me a minute to push the button.

"Hey, Maggie, it's Malone. Uh…thought we were getting together tonight. Call me later."

Really. He thought we were getting together. Not when another woman is carrying his child, that's for damn sure.

I flop down in a chair and hug a worn throw pillow to my stomach, my eyes hard. Chantal made no bones about the fact that she found Malone attractive. That she'd put the moves on him before. And she mentioned something about him having a crush on her once, long ago. Or more recently, as the evidence indicates. Yes, God forbid that Chantal doesn't get a man. Every damn male in town is required to adore her, aren't they? I clench my teeth hard, willing the lump in my throat to dissolve.

The edges of the throw pillow are frayed, the material thin from years of use. I really should make it a new cover, but why bother? In fact, as I look around my cramped little apartment, impatience rushes through me. Why do I have all this crap? Does anyone really need six TableTop pie tins? So what if they're collectibles? Suddenly, I hate collectibles. *Collectibles.* Why not just call them what they are? Old junk. Why own them? To collect cobwebs? If that's their purpose, they're doing an excellent job.

I jump up, grab some garbage bags and newspaper and start wrapping with a vengeance. I should have a yard sale. Or bring this crap to an antiques dealer. Suddenly, I want to have a spartan, clean living space. Just floor and futon, Japanese style. Or Swedish, maybe, with just a streamlined dresser for my clothes.

And clothes! I practically leap into the bedroom and rip open my bureau drawers. How many sweaters do I really need, anyway? About a third of them are my father's cardigans, which I've stolen over the years— maybe he'll want them back. And God, look at how many stained T-shirts I have. Working in a diner is no excuse. Surely I can afford clean shirts. When I dribble gravy or coffee on them and can't get the stain out, into the trash they shall go. Maybe I should have T-shirts made up for the diner. Yes. That's what I'll do. That will eliminate the question of what to wear every day. Just a black T-shirt with red writing. *Joe's Diner, established 1933, Gideon's Cove, ME.* Perfect. The summer nuisance will love them.

Ruthlessly, I stuff half a dozen shirts into a trash bag, vaguely noting logos of places I've been, sayings I thought were cute. Stupid cluttering crap. I barely

pause at the blue rat, stuffing it with far greater force
than necessary into the giant black trash bag. Good.
Bury it. Stupid cheap thing.

After Skip traded me in for a classier model, I moved
in here, renting the place from some summer people
who had bought it as an investment. When Gideon's
Cove failed to be the new Bar Harbor, they sold it to me
for an affordable price, and Dad and I overhauled the
place and found Mrs. K. as a tenant. It was so safe here,
so cozy and tiny. But now it seems crowded and stuffy,
just as my mind is crammed with memories of my
romantic failures.

Skip, of course, is at the head of the class. But there
were others, too, before Malone, before Father Tim. A
couple of years after Skip was Pete, a very nice guy
from a few towns over. We dated for a year, practically
living together at the end. When he asked me out for
dinner one night, I imagined that he was going to pop
the question. And I imagined myself saying yes. We
were very solid, very content, I thought. It wasn't a
huge romantic love, but I thought it would last.

Instead, Pete gently informed me that he was
moving. To California. And he would really miss me.

If he'd asked, I would have said, *No, no, I can't
possibly come with you. I love Maine. I don't want to
move. My life is here. My family.* Our breakup would
have been sad, regretful but required, because I honestly
wouldn't have left home for that guy. My heart was not
broken. Still, it would have been nice to turn him down.

I pull out a green sweater that still has a few golden
hairs on it. Colonel's hair. He must have rubbed his
head against me while I was wearing this. My eyes
fill—sudden, desperate longing for my dog flows over

me like a river. This sweater can stay, I decide, putting it in the "keep" pile. I blow my nose and continue purging.

After Pete was Dewitt, my boyfriend of four months. He asked me to put some distance between myself and my sister, successfully ending our romance with that one sentence. Unfortunately, he then told everyone that I had an "unnatural thing" going on with Christy and implied that I'd never find someone because I was fixated on my own sister. Asshole.

"Maggie?"

"Jesus! God! You shouldn't sneak up on people like that!" I squawk.

Malone leans against my door frame and smiles. I have to look away.

"Sorry," he says. "I knocked. Must not have heard me."

"Well. So. You're here. That's…" The animal magnetism he exudes shrouds my reasons for being mad. Oh, yeah. *Chantal.* Got it. "Okay, Malone, so what's up? What's new? Anything new?"

His smile fades. "Not really. Missed you last night."

"Did you. Hmm. Well. Something came up."

So he's not going to admit anything. You'd think even Malone would acknowledge something… *Hey, by the way, Chantal and I are having a baby. Wanna grab some dinner?* Fine. If he's not going to say anything, I'm sure as hell not going to admit I was lurking under his window the moment he learned of his impending fatherhood.

Swallowing bile, I feel so tired of having my relationships make me look like a fool. Skip, those other dweebs, Father Tim, and now Malone. I just can't take it. I won't be made an ass of again. I just can't. I finish stuffing the contents of my drawer into the trash bag, willing myself not to feel anything but anger. However, the image of Malone lying on my bed the night after Colonel died shoves its way into my head. How could he be so—

"Everything okay, Maggie?" he asks, a slight frown between his eyes.

"You know what? No. Everything is not okay, Malone. Here. Come in the living room, okay?" I shove my way past him into the mess I've made in the next room. "Sit down. Have a seat." I take a deep breath and sit on the other side of the coffee table, not wanting to be too close to him. He hasn't shaved today, and the memory of what it feels like to be kissed by Malone, that scraping sweetness, makes my knees wobble. Disgusted with myself, I force an image of him with Chantal. In bed with Chantal, kissing her with the same intensity that he kissed me. There. Wobbling over.

"What's wrong?" Malone asks quietly.

"You know, it's good that you came over, Malone. It's…look. You're here. So. The thing is, Malone, I—" My throat tightens inexplicably. "Malone, this isn't working for me. This thing you and I have going on. Whatever it is."

Though his expression doesn't change, his head jerks back a fraction, and for a tiny second, I feel bad for him. He's surprised. Didn't see it coming. Well, I know the feeling, don't I?

I keep talking, taking a grim pleasure in the fact at least that I'm not on the dumped end of this breakup stick. "You know. I mean, you're very…attractive, I guess…I mean, I think so, anyway. But aside from that...physical stuff...well, to tell you the truth, Malone, I'm looking for a little more."

He just stares at me, not frowning exactly, but almost—concerned. "Did something happen, Maggie?" he asks, and the kindness in his rough voice causes fresh fury to slap my heart like a rogue wave.

"I don't know, Malone," I snap. "Did it?"

His black brows come together. "What's going on?" he says, and now there's a note of irritation.

"You tell me." I stand in front of him, hands on my hips, daring him to admit what he's done.

"Are we fighting here?" he asks, scowling. "Because I don't remember us having anything to fight about."

Fine. He's being a coward. Fine. "I'll make it simple for you, Malone. You're really just not my type."

Score a direct hit—his mouth closes abruptly, his face is fierce and dark. "And just who is your type, Maggie? Father Tim, maybe?" he growls.

I cock my head. "Well, funny you should say that. Aside from the priest thing, yes, actually. He's a true friend to me. We talk, we have fun, we laugh together. We tell each other things. That's more of what I'm looking for. A friend and a lover. That's not so surprising, is it?"

"A friend? By that, do you mean someone to wait on hand and foot? Someone you can feed and clean up after?"

"It's called caring, Malone. When you care about someone, you do things for him. Hence the soup and pie I made for you the night you went for a swim in the forty-degree Atlantic! But you don't want that, do you?" My voice rises in anger. "So yes, I want someone who's not closed off from every human feeling, Malone.

That's what! Someone who can speak in full sentences. Someone who can actually answer a personal question when asked, someone who—"

"I get the point," Malone says, standing. "Fine. Take care."

He slams the door behind him, and I burst into tears once more.

CHAPTER TWENTY-FOUR

"BLESS ME, Father, for I have sinned," I say. "It's been twenty-two years since my last confession." Funny, how the words come racing right back. "Can we get to it, Father Tim? I really need to talk." So much so that I quick-stepped in front of Mrs. Jensen. I had tried calling Father Tim at the rectory, but he didn't return my call. He's been terribly busy lately.

"Well, Maggie, this *is* the sacrament of reconciliation. We probably shouldn't rush it. Though of course, I'm very glad to see you in church."

I take a ragged breath. "I'm sorry, Father Tim," I say roughly. "The thing is, I'm just so— I can't seem to—" My throat is gripped by all the misery of the past week. Colonel. My parents. Malone. Chantal. My own future stretches ahead of me, alone, childless, ankles swollen, no one to change my diapers in my dotage... Tears drip down my cheeks and I sniff wetly.

"What is it, Maggie?" Father Tim asks, his voice full of alarm and concern.

"My life is a joke," I manage. "I know what I want, but I just can't seem to get it, and I don't understand why everything is so hard and confusing."

Why do I miss Malone? Why have I analyzed every second we've ever spent in each other's company? Why does my mother's fear break my heart the way it does? Why can't people just meet and get married and be happy like Christy and Will? And worst of all, why does it feel like my last chance will die with Malone, even knowing what I know?

"I broke up with Malone," I blurt. "You were right. He's churlish."

"Ah, Maggie, I'm sorry. Sorry to be right." He leans forward so I can see his face through the filigreed screen of the confessional. "There are times when life tests us," he says gently. "Times that seem so lonely and bleak. It's how we handle these difficult situations that really proves who we are."

I swallow and wipe my eyes. "I've been so jealous of Christy lately," I admit in a whisper. "She has everything, Father Tim. Everything I want."

"And you're happy for her, as well, Maggie," he says. "You want those same things, there's no shame in admitting that."

"But it doesn't seem fair," I protest. "I don't want to end up alone, Father Tim. I get so scared sometimes that I'll be this weird aunt who'll be passed around like a virus. Like, 'It's your turn to feed Aunt Maggie'—'No, it was my turn last week! You do it!'"

Father Tim doesn't laugh, bless him. He doesn't say anything for a moment. "None of us wants to look into the future and see ourselves alone, Maggie," he nearly whispers. "No one wants that."

There it is again, that undercurrent of his own loneliness. Of sadness, maybe. Or am I reading into things? But there's something. I raise my hand to the screen that separates us, pressing against the pretty scrollwork of the metal, and suddenly...suddenly my old fantasy of being with him doesn't seem so ridiculous.

"Father Tim?" I whisper. Outside in the church proper, Mrs. Jensen coughs loudly.

"Maggie, you're such a wonderful person," he says, so softly I can barely hear him. "Don't be sad. Something's going to change, Maggie, and you won't be alone forever. Have faith."

I draw a shaky breath, dizzy at the thoughts that pour into my mind.

Mrs. Jensen hacks again, her cough bouncing off the stone walls of the church. Can't the old bag take some Robitussin? But the moment is over. Father Tim sits back. "Let's speak again soon," he says. "God bless you, Maggie."

FOR THE NEXT FEW DAYS, my thoughts keep me quiet, almost withdrawn. I go through the motions at Joe's, calling out diner slang for Stuart, hugging Georgie, joking with Rolly and Ben, passing out ballots. Father Tim doesn't come in, and the significance of his absence causes all kinds of ideas to flutter like birds against a window—unpleasant thoughts, really, that I don't want to dwell on. But fragments of words float through my mind... *Father Shea... You're special, Maggie... Something's going to change.*

And yet, while those thoughts are concerning, they're also just a reflex. When I look at the answering machine every afternoon when I come home, it's Malone I think of. *Did he call? Will he—* Then I stop myself. Malone has other problems to take care of. He won't be calling me. Besides, I don't even want him to call, do I? *Leave me out of it, Malone,* I command. He obeys.

Chantal leaves a message, a brief one, asking me to call her when I get a chance, no hurry, but I can hear the solemnity in her tone. There's a call I'm not eager to return. Slutty Chantal. Slutty Malone, too. Who needs 'em?

On Sunday, the Beaumont children are summoned for dinner as usual. Mom and Dad are painfully civil to each other, Dad carving the roast, Mom setting the side dishes on the table with terrible care. Jonah, Christy and I are very well-behaved and helpful, no jokes, no teasing. It's freakish and agonizing. Will is covering at the hospital, so there's no one to ease the tension, just us kids and Violet. Dinner takes an eternity, and even the baby's cheerful babble can't break the pall of gloom that hangs over the table. When Jonah actually volunteers to wash the dishes afterward, it's proof positive that something is dreadfully wrong.

"So what happens next?" he asks, his back to the rest of us as he runs the water. "Is one of you moving out?"

Mom and Dad's eyes meet across the table, perhaps for the first time today. Christy's eyes fill, and she lowers her nose to Violet's silky hair to hide the fact.

"Well, actually, yes," Mom says carefully. "Not just yet, but I'm thinking of moving to Bar Harbor."

"Wow!" I exclaim. "That's quite a change from—"

"You're moving?" Christy shrieks. "You can't move, Mom! Are you crazy? Are you out of your mind?" Jonah and I exchange a startled glance, but Christy keeps going. "No! You can't! It's—It's—Bar Harbor is so far!"

"Not really," Mom says. "It's just an—"

"It's an hour and a half, Mom!" Christy yells. "Don't you care about Violet? What about your only grandchild? And your children! Don't you want to see us more than once a month?"

"Christy," I begin, but she cuts me off.

"No, Maggie. It's selfish. You're being unbelievably selfish, Mom." She smacks her hand down on the table.

Our mother looks down at the tablecloth without comment. Dad is pulling his silent routine, and I feel a sudden tug of annoyance with him. Staying on the sidelines only gets you so far in life, and in a flash, I can see how hard it must have been for my mother— married to a man who never dissented, never voiced his unhappiness, just bobbed along with the tide until he was so miserable that he had to leave or drown.

"Is that what you want, Mom? To live in Bar Harbor?" I ask.

She sighs. "Well, in some ways, yes. I think it would be nice to be in a bigger place. Spread my horizons, expand my wings, so to speak. So Bar Harbor would be a step in the right direction."

"Then what?" Christy demands, shifting Violet. "Move to Paris? London?"

"Australia, I was thinking," Mom mutters, and I smile.

"Australia!" Christy yelps. It's almost funny to see— the former social worker acting like a spoiled twelve-year-old. Violet grabs a handful of tablecloth and stuffs it in her mouth.

Mom sighs. "I'm kidding, Christy. Okay? Just relax."

"My family is falling apart, Mom. I can't relax. And I can't believe you guys aren't going to even try to work on things! Get some counseling, for God's sake. Go see Father Tim! But moving is absolutely ridiculous."

"Jesus, Christy, shut up," Jonah says. "They're adults. They can make their own choices."

"What do you know about being an adult, Jonah?" my sister snaps. I haven't seen her so riled since Skip dumped me.

"He's right, Christy," I say quietly. "Mom and Dad have been married for a long time. If they want something different now, well, they're in a position to know. We're not. If Mom wants to live somewhere other than Gideon's Cove, she can. It's her life."

"Well, nothing's going to happen for at least a few weeks," my mother says. "Your father and I aren't getting divorced right away, just separated. And we'll see how things are after that."

"Dad's gonna be my sternman," Jonah informs us. Dad offers a tentative smile.

"What? Dad! Are you crazy?" Christy says. "A sternman? What do you know about lobstering?"

"That's neat, Dad," I say. "Christy, you need a drink. Mom, can we leave Violet here for an hour or so? Dewey's opens in ten minutes, and I think Christy and I should talk."

"Of course," my mother says, reaching for her grandchild.

"Enjoy," Christy snaps. "You won't be able to—"

"Shut up," I say, dragging her forcibly from the room.

We ride in silence to Dewey's, Christy driving with sharp movements, braking hard, jerking the steering wheel. She stomps into the bar in front of me, not making eye contact as we sit at a table in back. The bar is nearly deserted—it's four on a Sunday—and Dewey is still taking chairs down.

"Dewey, can we get a couple of…what do you want, Christy?" I ask.

"I don't care," she mutters.

"Scotch, I guess, Dewey."

"Sure thing, girls," he calls. He pours us our drinks and brings them over, then hustles off to fill the register.

"So what's your problem?" I ask my sister.

"Our parents are acting like idiots," she says.

"What happened to all that nice compassion you had last week? Poor Mom, getting knocked up, abandoning her dreams…" I take a sip of my drink and instantly remember the last time I had scotch—with Malone, the night Colonel died. I shove the thought aside.

Christy takes a sharp breath, and her eyes fill with tears. "I didn't know she would leave, Maggie! How can she—and Dad's going to become some stinky, weird old guy without her. A sternman! For crying out loud."

"But aren't you a little bit…I don't know, proud, in a way? That our parents are doing something new, that just because they're middle-aged doesn't mean their lives are carved in stone? I think it's kind of neat." Christy shoots me a death glare. "A little neat, anyway," I amend.

"No," she sulks. "It's not neat, Maggie. Mom is moving. Moving far." Her tears slip down her cheeks.

"I know you'll miss her," I say. "But she deserves a chance to do something different, Christy. She's not obligated to stay around and watch our lives anymore."

My sister stares out the window for another minute. "Oh, shit, you're right," she says, swallowing a mouthful of scotch. "You're right, you're right. I guess I just feel abandoned. And sorry for myself. I mean, I'll miss her, Maggie! And so will Violet. She loves Mom so much." Christy's face scrunches up in misery, and I reach across the table to squeeze her hand.

"Here now, what's this?" Dewey asks. "Maggie, why are you crying, hon?"

"I'm not," I say. "Christy is."

"Oh, dear, dear. No crying in my bar, sweetheart," Dewey says. "And the day I can tell you girls apart will be a banner day, let me tell you." He pats her head and walks back to the bar.

Christy gives me a watery smile. "Man, I was such a bitch back there, wasn't I?" she asks.

"Yes," I answer, smiling. "A right bitch. I'm so happy."

"Happy? Why?"

"Because it's high time I got to be the good twin," I say.

"You. You're so funny." She smiles genuinely now, and simultaneously, we reach out a foot under the table and nudge each other. "Hey, what happened with Malone?" she asks, her head swiveling to the door. My heart sinks like an anvil. But no, it's not Malone. Just Mickey Tatum, the fire chief.

"I broke up with him," I tell her. There's a tightness in my throat that the scotch doesn't alleviate.

"What did he say about Chantal?" Christy asks.

"Nothing. We didn't talk about it. He didn't say boo about her."

Christy sighs. "Sorry, Maggie."

"Yeah, well, other fish to fry, right? Other eggs to scramble. At least I cut bait before things got too…whatever." I don't fool Christy; she smiles sadly, seeing right through me. "I do have to tell you, though," I say, artfully changing the subject, "something's going on with Father Tim. Have you talked to him lately?"

"No. Why? What's up?"

Dewey comes over with a bag of potato chips. "For the beautiful weeping lady," he says, handing them to me.

"That's Christy," I correct, pointing across the table.

"Of course. For the beautiful weeping lady," he repeats.

"Thanks, Dewey," she says. "Just the ticket." She opens the bag and offers some to me, then takes a few herself. "So. Father Tim?" she prods.

"Well, I don't really know. But something's weird. He's been very…tender. And saying things that have sort of a double meaning."

"Like what?" Christy asks.

"I don't know. I can't remember exactly what he said—"

"That's a first," she interjects dryly.

"—but just sort of…well. Obviously I don't quite know." I can't bring myself to say the words aloud. Instead, I fidget in the hard wooden chair. "Do you want to go home and grovel in front of Mom and Dad now?"

Christy laughs. "Sure. You've been good twin long enough."

"That's you in a nutshell," I say, taking out a few bills and laying them on the table. "Always stealing my thunder."

Christy grovels, re-assumes her title and we all have apple crisp.

On the way home, I pedal my bike toward the harbor. It's a windy day, and a Sunday to boot, so most of the lobster boats are in, including the *Ugly Anne*. *Don't go down there, Maggie,* I warn myself. A large seagull glides down, landing a few feet away on one of the wooden support posts, the wind ruffling its feathers but not its composure. I envy that bird.

And if Malone was here? I ask myself. *What then? What would I say? How's Chantal? Are you happy that you'll be a father again?* That is, of course, if Chantal will actually go through with it….

I still can't reconcile the idea of Malone and Chantal together. For some reason, I thought—

"Oh, for God's sake, Maggie," I mutter aloud to myself. I mount my bike once more but remain where I am, one foot firmly on the ground, and continue to stare at the harbor. The wind carries the scent of pine and salt on it, stinging my cheeks, howling in my ears, but I still don't move. Malone's face is stuck in my mind, the harsh lines, craggy cheekbones, those tangled black lashes. The way he smiled at me, begrudgingly almost, as if he didn't really want to like me but just couldn't help himself. "Right, Maggie," I snort. "You're so irresistible that Malone got Chantal pregnant. Live with it."

"What say, theah, Maggie?"

My shriek causes the gull to startle off, echoing my sound. "Yikes! Billy! God, you scared me!"

Billy Bottoms takes the pipe from his mouth. "Sorry, dahlin'. Just comin' down to check somethin'. Thought you were talkin' to me."

"No, no. No. Not you. Just, you know, blathering to myself. Sorry. Have a nice day."

I need to do something, I think as I ride back home. I need to figure out a plan for the rest of my life. If my mother can make a big move, so can I. Last week, she was sitting at the kitchen table tying one on. This week, she's got a plan. I can do the same thing. I need to forget Malone and move on. Focus on other things. Take action.

Being at Dewey's has given me an idea. Not the most honorable idea, granted, but a pretty good idea nonetheless. An awful, horrible, wonderful idea.

CHAPTER TWENTY-FIVE

"MY CAR IS RUNNING a little rough," I lie to my sister on the phone a few days later. "Can I borrow yours?"

It's Monday. The diner is closed, the wind is blowing, and it's a great day to stay home and do nothing, but my idea has been lurking in the corner of my mind, and its patience wearing thin. Besides, I can't just sit around and think about Malone and Chantal all day.

Christy runs water in the background. "Sure. I'm not going anywhere. Can you believe how cold it is? Cripes, it feels like December out there, not April."

Maine has tricked us yet again, pretending to embrace spring while all the time getting ready to dump six inches of snow on us, mixing with the muddy ground in a sloppy, tired, icy goop. All four members of the town crew are out, wearily sanding the main roads, defiling the streets they cleaned just last week. I pull my hat down over my ears and wave to them as I slip and slide up Christy's hill. Then, as planned, I choose a particularly damp-looking splotch of gray snow, trip and land face down in it.

"Oh, jeezum, look at you!" My sister holds the door open, Violet balanced on her hip. "Come in here, you gawmy girl!"

"I slipped," I confess sheepishly.

"Well, go upstairs and change, dopey," she chides. "Do you want to stay for lunch?"

"Um, no, no, but thanks. Other plans. I, um…" God, I am the worst liar. "I'm going to the mall. After my errands."

"The mall?" Christy asks. "That's two hours away, hon."

"Right! I know. Maybe not the mall…. I need shoes. New shoes."

"Are you okay?" Christy gives me that knowing look, and I flee upstairs to raid her closet, as is the plan. I pull out some nice tweed pants and a silk sweater. A little scarf goes into my pocket. I glance at her bureau.

"Christy? Can I borrow some jewelry? I want to look a little nicer. I might, uh…meet a friend? For lunch. If I have time."

"Sure," she calls back. "Whatever you want."

By that, she probably doesn't mean her anniversary band, a circle of small diamonds that Will gave her to mark their first year together. But, I rationalize, she did say "whatever," so I take it, first using some of the hand cream she's got on her night table.

"Oh, you look so nice!" Christy comments. By nice, she means "like me," but I don't take offense. She has beautiful clothes, and the point of this little adventure is in fact to look like Christy. Violet, who sits on the kitchen floor banging a whisk on a pot, crawls over to me and drools on my—Christy's—boot.

"Thank you, baby," I say. "I'll be back around four, okay?" I grab the car keys from the counter.

"Take your time," she says. She smiles from her seat on the floor. "Violet, want to try this one?" She holds up a wooden spoon and demonstrates its banging ability. "Hey, Maggie, don't forget a coat. Yours is a mess." She gestures to her beautiful faux shearling coat, which hangs on a hook near the door.

"You're a great sister," I say, flushed with guilt. "Thanks a million."

"Have fun!" she calls.

Fun is not exactly what I have planned. I grab the diaper bag that my sister leaves in the garage, climb in the car, look in the rearview mirror and take out my ponytail. Then I brush my hair to a side part and tuck it behind my ears. The band goes on my left ring finger, the scarf around my neck, and *voila*—I'm Christy.

This very morning, I had called the rectory. "Mrs. Plutarski, hi, it's Christy Jones. How are you?"

"Hello, dear," Mrs. Plutarski said. "How's that beautiful baby?"

"She's wonderful," I answered sweetly. "Listen, I was wondering if Father Tim had a few minutes to spare for me today."

"Of course, honey," she cooed, and my jaw clenched. Mrs. Plutarski is such a pill to me. You'd think I routinely crapped on the altar, the way she treats me. When I ask to see Father Tim, she always takes great pains to tell me how busy he is. For Christy, though, he's wide open.

"How about one o'clock, Christy? I imagine you want to discuss your poor parents," she suggested, gossipmonger that she is.

"That's perfect." Violet takes her nap from noon to three, and the real Christy will be snug at home.

My heart is pounding as I pull Christy's Volvo into the rectory's small parking lot. I turn off the car and sit a minute. After being delayed for God knows how long, common sense finally makes an appearance.

Here I am dressed as my sister, about to trick a priest. *Nice, Maggie. Very noble.* For some reason, I had the notion that if Father Tim thought I was Christy, he'd tell me what was bothering him lately, why he kept dropping those hints about how special "Maggie" was. I roll my eyes in the rearview mirror. No. I don't think so. I'm not *that* much of a jerk. Whatever personal issues Father Tim is having, they're not my business. Maybe it was cabin fever, maybe I was just trying to distract myself from thoughts of Malone, but clearly, this is the stupidest idea I've ever had. Maybe the stupidest idea anyone's ever had.

Disgusted, I restart the car. I'll drive down to Machias and catch a movie, get a big bag of popcorn and some Swedish fish—

I scream as a knock comes on the car window.

"Father Tim! Oh! Wow!"

"Hello, there, Christy!" he beams. "Come in, dear girl, come in."

My stomach contracts with the agony of being caught. "Hi, Father Tim," I mutter.

Well, it looks like I'm going to have to go through with it, because I just can't think of anything else. Wobbling a bit in Christy's boots, which have a higher heel than I'm used to, I grab the diaper bag from the back seat—my prop, further evidence that I am my sister.

"Hello, dear," Mrs. Plutarski says from her position of power in the rectory office. "How nice to see you! Don't you look smart."

"Oh, Mrs. Plutarski, you are so sweet," I simper. "I

just love that color on you! Would you call that oatmeal or liver? It's wonderful!" *Don't blow it*, I warn myself savagely. *You got yourself into this mess, now just get out as fast as you can. If they figure out you're Maggie, you're dead.*

"Make yourself comfortable, Christy," Father Tim says, holding the door of his office for me. My toes curl in discomfort.

"Thank you for seeing me, Father Tim," I say, glancing around, trying not to make eye contact.

"You're welcome, my dear, you're welcome. How are Will and little Violet?"

"They're just great. Just great. Wonderful." *Okay, stop babbling. It's a dead giveaway.* I sit down, cross my ankles and try to have good posture. My gaze flits around the office. There's a note on his desk, and a prickle of warning goes through me at the sight of it. Though it's upside down to me, I can read Father Tim's writing... *Ask Bishop—*

"What can I do for you, Christy?" the priest asks. I look away from the note.

"Well, um, I guess you've heard about my, my, um, parents," I stammer.

"I have, yes." He smiles encouragingly. *Ask Bishop T. about—*

"And of course we're all...saddened. Quite saddened."

"It's a tragedy, thirty some-odd years of marriage," he murmurs. *Ask Bishop T. about the Father Shea situation.*

Holy moley! Jeezum! The Father Shea situation? The left-the-priesthood-for-a-pretty-woman-situation? Oh, my God! I gulp in a huge breath.

"Christy, ah, dear, don't cry, now. There's still hope, and if you turn to prayer, perhaps it will help your parents remember how sacred those vows were and still are."

How are your vows, Father Tim? Everything rock solid there? I realize that a response is required. "Mmm. Right. We're all taking it pretty hard. Uh, Maggie and me, I mean." I take a sharp breath at referring to myself in third person, then swallow. "And you know. Jonah, too."

"I've spoken with Maggie a bit. But how can I help you, Christy?"

"Oh, I suppose I was wondering…" *Yes, Maggie/ Christy. What exactly can you wonder about?* My mind drains of all intelligent thought. "How I can…um, support my parents? Other than pray?" I sound like an idiot because all I can think is *Father Shea, Father Shea, oh, shit, Father Shea.*

Father Tim glances out the window. "Well, as their daughter, Christy, you could remind them of all the good things their marriage has given them. You three children, of course, and their darlin' grandbaby. A life together, rich with family and happy memories, trials and tribulations, as well, of course…" His voice trails off, his eyes still focused outside. I get the strong impression he's phoning it in today. Lucky for me.

"You're right. Excellent advice." I swallow, then decide to risk it. "So, Father Tim, how are you? I mean, do you like it here? Being our parish priest and all? It's been, let's see now…a year?"

"Yes, yes, about that," Father Tim says, dragging his gaze back to me and forcing a smile.

"Well, the community is so lucky to have you, Father

Tim. You're a great priest. Very, um, holy. Devout, I mean." There. Said it, even if I sound like a jerk. "Will and the baby and I, we love church. I hope you won't leave."

His attention is suddenly laser-sharp. "Why? Have you heard something?" he blurts, leaning forward.

"Um…no. No, not really… No. Nothing."

Father Tim stares at me a minute, then sits back in his chair, relaxing. "Well," he says. "Change is inevitable, and we're none of us in control of our futures. That's in God's hands, as is everything."

Again with the clichés. "Well. Yes." I tuck some hair behind my ear. God, I feel guilty! Lying, tricking, deceiving a man of the cloth. I am surely damned. Sweat trickles down my neck.

"You have a wonderful family, Christy," Father Tim says, appropos of nothing.

"Thanks."

"I hope that you and Maggie…well. Never mind."

Desperate to somehow set Father Tim straight regarding my own feelings while not blowing my cover, I swallow convulsively. "You…you're a, um, a good friend to Maggie. It's nice for her to have a friend who's a priest. Very comforting. And she, you know, values your friendship."

"I'm counting on that," he says, smiling and rising. "She's very special."

Oh, my dear God. He's counting on that. I'm special. Shit! My pulse zings through my veins, my heart pounds. What does that mean? Why would he be counting on my friendship? And why is he so interested to know if I've—Christy's—heard something about him leaving?

"Well, okay, Father Tim, thank you so much for everything. I really should get back to the baby. Thanks. This was so helpful."

Father Tim's face is puzzled. "Glad to be of service, Christy," he says. He stands aside as I practically leap out of the room, nearly colliding with Mrs. Plutarski, who is too close to the door for any purpose other than eavesdropping.

"So nice to see you, Christy," she says, pretending to pick up a piece of paper already in her hand.

"It certainly is. Take care," I say distantly, grabbing my coat. I need some air. My head is buzzing and my hearing seems to be off, and I need to get outside and away from the rectory.

I burst into the slush, sliding and nearly falling on the sidewalk, then slip over to Christy's car, taking great gulps of air. Where did I put the keys? Where are the damn keys? I check the diaper bag and can't find them. *Father Shea!* How many compartments does this thing have? Diapers here, wipes there, changing pad, pacifier, teething ring, *Goodnight Moon,* a stuffed dog, a sterilized bottle in a sealed plastic bag, some emergency formula, but no goddamn keys.

And then, around the corner comes Malone.

"Shit!" I hiss. I can't believe the crap luck. Where are the fucking keys? Fifteen more feet and I'll have to talk to him.

"Maggie?" he says cautiously.

Without thinking, I turn and walk away from the Volvo and away from Malone as fast as I dare in the slushy mess on the sidewalk. Jerking open the door of the CVS pharmacy, I hustle inside, looking for a place to hide until he passes. I stop in front of the tobacco display, which hides me from the front door, and pretend to look at pipes. I'm sweating bullets.

"Hi, Mrs. Jones," calls a teenager from behind the counter. The Bates girl...what's her name? Susie? Katie? Bessie? Shit, I can't remember.

"Hello, honey!" I call a little too loudly.

The bell over the door rings, and Malone comes in. I scamper further down the aisle, then take a left. *Ha! Here, I'll go here.* I try to stop panting and run a hand through my hair. I'm shaking, but I should be safe. He wouldn't dare follow me here.

He dares. "Maggie?" His voice is low and grumbling and vaguely menacing.

I stretch my mouth into an approximation of a smile and turn to him. "Oh, hello, Malone. It's actually Christy. Don't worry, happens all the time." Shimmers of heat are rolling off my face. I snatch a box of tampons from the shelf and study it hard. *Extra absorbent for your heaviest days.* That should scare off any male.

Malone doesn't move. I shove the box back and grab some pads large enough to serve as dog beds.

"Why are you pretending to be Christy?" he growls.

I steal a glance at him. He's scowling, of course, and his hair is rumpled from the wind. He hasn't shaved today, and he's so ridiculously male that even here, even knowing what I know, my knees soften in a biological rush of attraction.

"Hi, Christy!" calls a red-haired woman I've never seen. She has a baby on her hip.

"Hello!" I call back, waving. "How's the baby?"

Malone folds his arms over his chest and narrows his eyes.

"A little fussy. Teething, I think. Your husband said I could try Motrin if it gets worse."

"Oh, yes. Motrin. That will do the trick. Mmm-hmm. Will knows these things. Definitely try the Motrin. Works for Violet." I shove the pads back on the shelf and go for the big guns—yeast infection treatments. I shake the box for emphasis, hearing the applicator rattle.

"Maggie," Malone rumbles. "What are you doing?"

"It's Christy, okay? You made a mistake. Even our parents mix us up. Now, I really need to concentrate because I have a raging yeast infection, okay? So goodbye."

He leans in close enough that I can feel the warmth of his body, and suddenly the box is shaking in my hands. *Do not look at him,* I warn myself. *Do not even turn your head.*

"I know who you are," Malone whispers. Then he turns and walks away. I hear the bell over the door tinkle, and he's gone.

"Don't be mad at me," I tell my sister as I hang up her coat.

"Did you dent the car?" she asks, taking a sip of tea. The baby monitor is on, the house warm and quiet, an oasis of calm.

"I pretended to be you," I admit, bracing myself.

"What? Maggie! Come on!" she exclaims.

"Hey, quiet now, you'll wake the baby," I say, grateful that there's a sleeping child to protect me from her wrath.

"Aren't we a little old to be switching?" Christy grumbles. "And what the hell for, anyway?"

"Is the water hot? I could use a cup," I say.

"Help yourself," Christy says, putting aside her crossword puzzle. "You got some 'splainin' to do."

"Yeah, okay. First of all, I'm sorry," I say. "I had just decided not to do it when Father Tim busted me. It was a bad idea. But you're not going to believe this." I spoon some sugar into my tea and sit down across from her. "I think Father Tim is leaving the priesthood."

"Oh, no!" My sister nearly falls out of her chair.

I tell her about my sophomoric routine and Father Tim's mysterious words, not to mention the *Father Shea situation.*

"So did he actually say anything concrete?" my sister asks, abandoning her irritation with me in the wake of the more shocking news.

"Well, no," I acknowledge. "But he's already said a couple of times that he's lonely…and then things like how special I am and that he's counting on me. And the Father Shea thing…. You have to admit, that sounds…you know."

"Promising?" Christy suggests.

"No! I was going to say scary, actually."

"Yeah," she agrees, tracing the grain of wood on the table. "Imagine the scandal, Maggie, if he left the priest-hood for you."

"I know."

"Do you love him, Mags?" She winces as she says it.

"No! Oh, shit, I don't know, Christy. I mean, sure, I love Father Tim. Who doesn't, right? And we really are great friends. I've always felt like there was some bond between us…."

"But?" she prompts.

"But…not that way. A crush is one thing, you know, but my God, no!" My sister nods. "Besides," I admit in a quieter voice, "I still have some…feelings. For Malone."

"Hmm."

"Not that that matters, right? Because of Chantal and all. I should just forget him. Malone was a fling, that's all. A pretty good fling, but there was nothing really… no real…."

Except there *was* something, and the truth brings tears to my eyes. He held my hand, took me to that hokey little lumberjack competition, comforted me, cheered me, made me feel like the most beautiful woman in the world, and I—

"I miss him," I acknowledge in a whisper.

Christy nods.

"He was at CVS," I say. "He knew I wasn't you."

Her eyebrows pop up. "Wow."

"I know."

We have fooled everyone at one point or another—our parents, our brother, our teachers, our closest friends. Only Will has never once confused us.

And now Malone.

CHAPTER TWENTY-SIX

"MAGGOT, you think you could run lunch down to Dad and me at the dock? We're overhauling the engine on the *Menace* and we're a mess."

"Sure, baby boy," I tell my brother. I've been at the diner since six this morning, and now, at nearly two, the place is empty. I could use the fresh air.

Today's special was lobster bisque, and there's just enough left over from the two giant vats I made this morning for Dad and Jonah. I throw together a couple of ham and cheese sandwiches on pumpernickel and fix two coffees the way my menfolk like them. A few coconut macaroons, plus one for me, and I bag everything up and set out to the dock.

The sun is blindingly bright today, and it's still cold enough that the snow has stayed on the ground. I walk carefully down the gangplank, clutching the boys' lunch to my chest, watching my feet so I don't take a header (wouldn't be the first time). I'm surprised to see my dad standing in a group of four or five men, who are apparently supervising Jonah—that is to say, they're slouching helpfully at the base of the gangplank, gossiping while a banging noise comes from my brother's boat.

"Hi, Dad," I call. "Hi, guys."

"Hello, sweetheart," Dad says, giving me a one-armed hug. "How's my girl? Need a hand? Isn't she pretty, boys? My little girl, all grown up."

I blink as the boys murmur assent. "Well. Thanks, Dad. Aren't you…jovial." I smile up at my dad. "Where do you want to eat?"

"Oh, I guess you can bring it to the captain, honey. Thanks."

"Your father nearly lost his finger today," Sam comments. The men guffaw as my father raises his hand and wiggles his fingers at me. "First thing you gotta learn, there, Mitch! Those mothers clamp down pretty goddamn hard!"

Apparently, this is hilarious, because the men all bark with laughter, Dad right along with them.

Bemused, I walk down the dock to the *Menace.* Seeing Dad out with the boys…it's different. "Jonah, lunch is here," I call as I step carefully onto the boat.

The door of the hold opens, and Malone comes out. My heart lurches, then sinks.

He's wearing his black peacoat and a scowl, wiping his hands on a rag. "Maggie," he grunts.

"Malone," I grunt back, instantly irritated. "Excuse me."

He doesn't step aside, just stares at me, looking both angry and…well, no, just angry.

"What? What do you want? Huh, Malone?" I snap.

"Hey, Mags, do you have enough for Malone, too?" Jonah sticks his head out of the hold. "He's giving us a hand." His head pops back in and he resumes banging.

"No, I don't have anything for you," I mutter, staring at Malone.

"You sure about that?" he asks, eyes narrowing.

"I—you—" My mouth works a minute before I force it closed. "Have a lovely day."

"Maggie," Malone says.

"What, Malone?" I ask, and I'm suddenly desperate for him to say something that would make everything the way it was, that would erase him and Chantal and whatever they did together, and the intensity of that longing makes my chest ache.

"Forget it," Malone says, and he turns his back on me.

"MAGGIE, I really need to see you." Chantal's voice is grim, and I wish I hadn't snatched up the phone. Of course, I'm at Joe's, and I don't exactly screen calls here. "I know you've been busy, but I have to talk to you."

I heave a sigh that could propel a sailboat to Deer Isle. "Yeah. Fine." I glance around the diner, which is sparkling clean at the moment. Six pies are in the oven for tomorrow, lunchtime is over, and despite my best efforts, I've run out of excuses. "Well, I'm free tonight."

And every night, now that I mention it. There has been no word from Father Tim, not even his usual calls for help on some committee. There's got to be a significance to this, I think. I've stopped going to Bible study, and aside from Mr. Barkham's funeral last week, I haven't seen Father Tim since I pretended to be my sister nearly two weeks ago.

"Can you come over?" Chantal asks. "Actually, this place is a dump. Can I come over to your place?"

"Sure. Come around eight." I certainly am not going to cook for her. She's been to the diner twice, but both times I leapt to the grill and asked Judy to wait on her, waving and pretending to be swamped with myriad duties. When she's asked to get together at night, I've put her off three times. I can't avoid her forever.

At least she doesn't know about Malone and me, so I don't have to suffer that particular embarrassment. Then again, he may well have told her. At any rate, they don't know that I know what I know. She can just tell me her big news and I'll pretend to be stunned. I practice gasping a few times in the mirror, but my face looks too sad.

When Chantal knocks on my door, an unwilling flare of sympathy goes off in my stony heart. Her face is gaunt and pale, circles smudging under her eyes. She looks thin, and I wonder if she's even still pregnant. I don't have to wonder for long.

"So. How have you been?" she asks, sitting on the couch. She grabs a throw pillow and hugs it protectively to her stomach.

"I'm fine. Would you like a glass of wine or anything?" I ask automatically.

"No. Sit down, Maggie, okay? We need to talk."

I sit stiffly in the club chair, rubbing a healing burn on my index finger. Chantal, as I have noted on many occasions, has lovely hands, plump and pretty with rounded nails that are always painted with clear polish. Malone may have said I don't have ugly hands, but compared with Chantal's…

"Maggie, I have something to tell you, and you're going to be shocked," Chantal says. I have always admired her bluntness.

"Okay," I say, forcing myself to look at her.

"I'm pregnant," she says in a low voice.

I don't gasp, but even though I knew what she was going to say, my stomach aches. "Really," I say.

Her face is tormented. "Yeah."

"Wow. So who's the father?" I ask cruelly. "Do you know?"

Her mouth drops open. "Um…yeah, I know."

"And what did he say?" My voice is hard, my posture painfully erect.

"Well, he's…he's not really in the picture. I'm gonna have the baby on my own."

Now I do gasp. "Really?"

This is a huge surprise—Chantal has made no secret of lusting after Malone. Images of Malone's daughter, the round-cheeked little girl in the photos at his house, flash through my head. The one time I saw him with her—if that really was his daughter, that is—he looked happy. He'd been smiling. I can't believe he wouldn't care.

Chantal toys with the fringe on the pillow, not meeting my eyes. "Yeah. So. Just me."

"But…I can't believe he doesn't…that he's not…" I swallow hard. "What did he say?"

Chantal's eyes shine with tears. "The truth is, Maggie, I'm not going to tell him. It was a one-night stand, and I really don't want to ruin his life by dumping this on him."

"Wait a minute, wait a minute," I blurt. "You didn't tell him? What about—" *Yes, and how does one confess that one was spying?* "I thought—I'd think—"

"Look. It was stupid. A bad mistake, and I'm paying for it, aren't I?"

My mouth is still hanging open. "Why do you think he wouldn't want a baby?" I manage to ask.

"Because I just know." Her tears spill over, and she sags back against the couch.

I sigh, running a hand through my hair. "Chantal…" I sit next to her and pat her leg. "Listen, I know who it is."

"Oh, my God, you do?" She sits bolt upright and looks at me in horror, a hand covering her mouth.

"Yeah. I overheard. At Malone's." A lump rises in my own throat. "And…I actually think he'd make a good father, to tell you the truth."

"Oh, Maggie, I'm so sorry!" she blurts, bursting into sobs. "You won't tell him, will you?" she pleads. "Don't tell him, Maggie, please."

"Well, honey, he already knows," I say, confused. "I mean, you told him."

"No. I just told you, I didn't. And I'm not going to." She seems to deflate in front of my eyes. "I already screwed up. I'm not going to wreck his life, too, and this would—"

"Okay, hang on one sec," I interrupt. "Who exactly are we talking about here?"

Chantal freezes. "Um…" She bites her lip. "Who are *you* talking about?"

I look at her a long moment, my heart thudding in my temples. "Malone."

Chantal's breath explodes out of her. "Malone? No. No, no. It's not Malone. I've never even slept with Malone."

My mouth drops open. I pull back to look at her more closely. "Well, you went to his house and told him you were pregnant."

"Um, right. Right. I did."

"But he's not the father?" I ask, my voice rising in confusion.

Now she won't look me in the eye. "He, you know…

Well, remember I told you how I picked him up that time, in high school? When he was in a fight? See, I guess I figured he…well, he owed me a shoulder to cry on. And he's the kind of guy who can keep his mouth shut, right? I didn't know who else to tell."

"Why not me?" Not that we have that kind of friendship…not that I've been all that close with Chantal…or that kind to her, to be honest.

She doesn't answer for a minute. "I'm telling you now," she finally says.

I slump back against the cushions. "So Malone's not…you didn't… Okay. Okay."

It's starting to dawn on me in a slow rise of panic that I've mentally accused Malone of something he didn't do. That I broke up with him over something that didn't happen. That for weeks now, I've been hating him, condemning him…that I said some rather hateful things to him to save my own stupid pride—"Who *is* the father, Chantal?" I ask through numb lips.

"Listen, Maggie, that doesn't matter, does it? I mean, the fact remains that I'm pregnant. I'm thirty-nine and a half, and I'm going to have a kid."

"Is it Chief Tatum?"

"No, no. Definitely not him." She looks away. "He's…um…can't have kids, didn't you know?"

I wince. No, I didn't know. Then it comes to me. "Oh, my God," I whisper, the blood draining to my feet. "Oh, Chantal, tell me it's not Father Tim…."

Her head jerks back in surprise. "Father Tim? Jesus, no! As if he would ever…come on, Maggie! I might be a little…flirty, but I wouldn't…you know…with a priest!"

Weak with relief (and yes, definitely shame), I

swallow a few times, then stand up. "I need some water. Want some water? How about some water?"

I get the water. Okay. So it's not Malone, thank God, and it's not Father Tim. Again, thank God. I gulp down a glass of tap water and bring another to Chantal.

"I'm sorry, Chantal," I tell her. "This is all…well, hell. I've been thinking it was Malone."

She takes the water gratefully. "It's okay," she says. "I can't believe you thought that. You know he's not interested in me. I actually thought he kind of liked *you,* though. Remember that night at Dewey's?"

A bitter laugh bursts out of my lips. "Right. Well, we…never mind. Listen, if you want to tell me who the father is, you could. You know I wouldn't tell anyone. I'm your friend, Chantal." Or I could be, if I put aside the jealousy I've always felt toward her.

Her eyes grow sad again. "No. It's just somebody… somebody from away. No one local." She forces a smile. "You know me. I like being on my own."

"It'll be different when you have a baby, though," I say. "And you never know, hon. The father might want to be involved."

"Maybe. Anyway. It's good to have you know." She squeezes my hand, and I squeeze back, caught between sympathy and a bit of shame.

"I'll help you out," I tell her. "I love kids. I'll cook for you and babysit and that kind of thing."

"Oh, Maggie," she whispers. "I don't deserve a friend like you."

"Sure you do! What a silly thing to say." I blush.

"Maybe you could come to the delivery. Coach me or whatever. Slip me painkillers."

"I'd love to," I say, hugging her. "It would be an honor."

She starts to cry again, and I smooth her beautiful hair. I've been a crappy friend, an untrue friend. I will make it up to Chantal.

Making it up to Malone will be a little harder.

CHAPTER TWENTY-SEVEN

THE LATE SPRING SNOW finally melts, leaving us in three fresh inches of mud. I slog to work, taking off my boots before going in through the back door and slipping on my cooking clogs. I throw together the batter for some muffins, then start breaking eggs for omelets and scrambles.

I know I need to see Malone, apologize and try to make things right. But it's going to be hard, and I need a little time to plan what I want to say. Can't be rambling all over the place as I usually do. Still, it's hard to find a nice way to say "I thought you were sleeping around on me, fathering children... Want to see a movie?"

"Hey, boss," Octavio says, coming in the back. "Nice day, don't you think?"

"I think it sucks, Tavy," I say. "I'm thinking of moving to Florida or something."

"I'm from Florida," he answers. "Don't go."

Stuart slides onto his stool at the counter. "Good morning, Maggie," he says. "Got any apple pie this morning?"

"Eve with a lid on it, coming up," I tell him, forcing a smile. "And one blonde with sand." I pour him his coffee and slide a creamer over.

"Cool," Stuart says, shaking out two sugar packets. "Eve with a lid. I like that."

"Mold with that?" I ask.

"Hmm…would that be cheese?" he guesses correctly.

"Yup. Side of cheddar."

"No, thanks, Maggie. No mold."

I settle down as I work. The diner, my shining little jewel, calms me. When Granddad owned it, I have to confess, it was much more a diner in the bad sense of the word. Fairly filthy, mediocre, greasy food, lots of prepared stuff that Granddad would just heat. Even if I don't win the best breakfast title, I know that Joe's is the heart of our town. Where would Rolly and Ben go? Who would throw Stuart his diner lingo? Where would Georgie work? Where would Judy pretend to work?

Speaking of Georgie, in he bursts, an ebullient ray of sunshine. "Hi, Maggie! Did you see the sunrise today? It was so pretty!" He hugs me tight. "I love you."

"I love you, too," I tell him. "Muffins are still warm if you want one, Georgie. Or two. And Tavy's waiting to scramble your eggs."

The regulars are in and out early, and only a couple of people still linger. I wipe down the counters and start the meat loaf for today's lunch special. Everyone loves meat loaf day, so I know we'll be busy.

The bell above the door tinkles and in comes Father Tim. I flush, remembering that horrid flash of a moment when I thought he was the father of Chantal's baby. "Hey, Father Tim!" I call out.

"Good morning, Maggie," he says. "How are you, Georgie?"

"Great, Father Tim!" Georgie announces. "I'm great!"

"How's everything?" I ask Father Tim. "I, um, haven't seen you for a while."

"Sorry, Maggie," he says. "I've been a bit swamped these days. Some difficult matters to attend to."

Difficult matters…like how to leave the priesthood? He slides into his booth and smiles up at me. I force a smile back. "I'm thinking it's the eggs benedict today, love."

Is it normal for a priest to call his friend "love"? Am I reading into too much here? What did the "counting on it" phrase mean, exactly?

"Maggie? Eggs benedict?" His smile is full of warmth.

"Right. Right, Father Tim. Coming up."

I FIND MYSELF pedaling up the hill to Malone's house on Thursday. The late afternoon wind gusts hard enough to make biking difficult, and I have to stand on the pedals to make it to the top. I still haven't figured out exactly what I'll say to Malone, but I can't put it off any more.

Because it's so windy, the lobster boats are all in today, bobbing wildly on their moorings. I stop and take in the view. The water is deep blue with sprays of foam dancing off the waves. White horses, my dad once called them. The sky is rich, a blue so pure you can almost taste it, thin cirrus clouds streaking across the horizon. The leaves on some of the earlier trees are out, and hyacinth and daffodils poke up here and there. The past few days have been sunny, and the mud has finally dried into earth. Tomorrow we may even hit fifty-five degrees, the weatherman says. People will be wearing shorts, teenagers will grease themselves up with baby oil and iodine and try to fry some

color into their skin. Maybe I'll take a hike up in the blueberry barrens. Maybe Malone will want to come with me.

I knock on his door, but there's no answer. However,
I hear a vague banging from the back, so I walk around
to the dooryard. Malone is wrestling some traps off his
pickup, and at first he doesn't see me. I take a minute
to study him.

It's hard to believe I ever called him unattractive,
because now he's the most appealing man I've ever seen.
Even compared to Father Tim. Long and lanky but with
the broad shoulders common to lobstermen, he moves
with efficient grace, hefting the pots onto the ground.
The lines of his face tell the story of Washington
County—severe, difficult and beautiful, too. His flannel
shirt flaps in the breeze, his workboots thunking against
the floor of the cab. Then he sees me and freezes,
midswing.

"Hi," I say.

He sets the trap down, then turns to unload the final
two or three. Not exactly the warm greeting that would
make this a little easier for me, but hey. He's got reason
to be mad at me; more than he knows, in fact.

"Got a minute?" I ask.

He picks up two traps, one in either hand, and walks
them to his cellar door, then returns to the pile of traps
and repeats the action. Apparently, he's not going to
stop.

"Um, Malone, well…listen, can you take a break
for a second? I really…just…I need to…" He tosses the
traps down with considerably more emphasis than the
last time and finally relents, leaning against the tailgate
of his truck, oozing impatience. I inch a little closer so
I won't have to yell to be heard. I'm nervous, I realize.

Of course, he's glaring and that doesn't do much to put a person at ease. Did he ever actually smile at me? It's hard to conjure at this moment.

"Thank you," I say, fiddling with the zipper of my jacket. "How are you? How've you been?"

He says nothing, just stares at me from those icy eyes.

"Well, okay, listen, Malone. Um, I'm here to apologize. Remember I said you weren't my type?" I wince even as I speak… *Of course he remembers, dummy, you were such a bitch, who could forget?* "Right. So anyway, here's the thing. I think we might have a laugh over this, actually."

Malone continues glowering, and he is, I must admit, excellent at it. A true skill.

I sigh. "Malone, look. I thought you were the father of Chantal's baby. That's why I broke up with you."

His eyes widen slightly, then narrow dangerously. My nervousness grows, and my mouth picks up velocity. "Yeah. I—I—I just misunderstood something. See, I was there, that night that Chantal told you she was pregnant. I was listening to you play the piano, and—" God, his scowl could make an Al Qaeda terrorist wet himself. "Okay, I guess I should've stayed and heard the whole thing, but I didn't. But she… I know that I was wrong. And I'm wicked sorry."

Malone considers me for another long moment. "You thought I slept with Chantal," he states, as if for clarification.

"Um, yes. Sorry." Adrenaline makes my feet prickle. I tuck some hair behind my ears and try not to look at that scowling face.

"Ever think about asking me?"

"Should have, but no." I realize I'm compulsively zipping and unzipping my jacket…zip, zap, zip, zap. "You can be…um, a little, uh, hard. Hard to talk to." Zip. Zap.

"That's great, Maggie. So you thought I was two-timing you, with Chantal, no less, and didn't bother saying anything about it. Great. Thanks for coming over." He picks up two traps and starts stacking them in the dooryard.

"Malone…"

"What?" he barks, and I jump.

"I thought…I kind of thought…"

"What? What did you think, Maggie?" He drops the pots with a crash and puts his gloved hands on his hips.

I wince. "Um…well, maybe you could…you know. Forgive me. Because I was thinking the wrong thing. That's why I broke—"

"No thanks, Maggie," he snarls. "I don't want the priest's leftovers."

Youch! Direct hit, like a blow to the head. My mouth drops open. "Leftovers?"

"Yeah," he says, coming over to me. I have to force myself not to look away. "You spend half your time drooling over that guy, dropping everything when he crooks his finger. You don't want to be with a real person. Think it's an accident you picked a priest to fall in love with?"

My head jerks back. "I'm not—"

"Don't bother. Any relationship you and I might've had was a joke, anyway. You were just killing time with me."

"I wasn't killing time!" I yelp. "You never—"

"You didn't want anyone to know that we were

together, did you, Maggie?" Malone asks. He jerks another trap off the truck and I jump out the way. "Think I didn't notice that?"

"Well, neither did you, Malone!" I snap, my face heating with anger. "It's not like you were falling over yourself to see me. You never came into the diner. You never came over for dinner or lunch or anything! We were *sleeping* together. We didn't do much more than that." His jaw clenches, and I continue. "What about that day you went overboard? I wanted to see how you were doing and you practically kicked me out of your house. That's not what happens in a real relationship, Malone."

Malone hurls the traps onto the pile and turns to face me, folding his arms across his chest. The anger shimmers off him in waves, and I feel my own rising to match it.

"See, the way I see it," I say tightly, "a relationship would involve, I don't know—talking? Communication? A little more than just sex, maybe? Now, okay, the thing when Colonel died, that was nice. But Malone, you barely speak to me! Not about your daughter, not about your family, nothing! I don't even know your first name!"

His whole face looks knotted and furious, but I don't care. Everything I'm saying is pathetically true, and if he won't talk, then I will. "Remember that piece of pie?" I snap. "I wanted to give you some pie for helping me out, but God forbid you should come in and eat it, right? God forbid that anyone is allowed to be nice to you, Malone, let alone—" *love you,* I'm about to say, but fortunately or not, he interrupts.

"Maggie—" he says through clenched teeth. His jaw

is iron, his neck stiff. "We're done here." And then he turns and walks away.

I'M SHAKING WITH RAGE the whole way home. Stupid Maggie, to think that Malone—Malone!—would forgive me. Ha! The wind snatches the words from my mouth as I mutter aloud. "Of course I thought you were the father! How many times does a woman burst in and say 'I'm pregnant' to a man who's not the father? Not many! So it wasn't such a stretch. You'd think you could cut me a little slack, Malone!"

Mrs. K. is lying in wait, an arthritic little panther, when I stomp up the porch steps. "Maggie, dear! I need a *favor*."

"Right," I sigh. "What is it?"

"Well, you don't *have* to help if you're in a mood, dear." She folds her arms and frowns disapprovingly.

"Mrs. K., whatever you need, I'm happy to help. I'm sorry. I've had a *really* shitty day."

"Would you like to tell me about it?" she asks.

I laugh grimly. "No. But thank you. I'd like to forget it, actually."

"We could watch a movie," she suggests, and there's a hopeful note in her voice.

"I'd love to," I say. "That would be just the ticket." I reach down and give her a careful hug. "Thank you, Mrs. K."

"Oh, how *sweet* you are! *The Fly* is on TNT tonight, and I've been dying to see it again!"

And so I fix us some dinner, cut the new bunion pad for her as directed and make popcorn. As we watch Jeff Goldblum vomit on and then consume a donut, Mrs. K. reaches over and squeezes my hand. "Things will get better, dear," she murmurs. "Don't worry."

"I love you," I tell her, and her cheeks flush with pleasure.

"I love you, *too,* honey," she says. *The Fly* goes into commercial break. "Now *tell* me, dear, when is that *handsome* man coming back? MacDuff?"

"Malone," I correct automatically. "We broke up."

"Oh, dear," she says. "Well. I'm *sure* you'll work things out."

"I don't think so, Mrs. K. He's a little too busy hating me to work anything out right now."

"Well, then, too *bad* for him, right, my dear? You'll meet someone *else* and he'll be sorry."

"Sure." I'm quite certain she's wrong.

CHAPTER TWENTY-EIGHT

THE NEXT DAY, Jonah drags himself into the diner. "My God, you look awful," I say. "Hung over?"

Jonah's groan of misery answers for him. "Just coffee today, Mags."

"Sure, baby boy." I take pity on him and set the cup gently on the counter. "What's new, buddy?"

"Oh, nothing. Hey, Maggot…" Jonah glances around. Only Judy is within range, pretending to read a book as she eavesdrops while Rolly gets himself more coffee.

"Judy," I say. "How about a ciggie break?"

She scowls. "Fine, fine. I always get kicked out when it's something juicy."

"At least you won't have to pretend to be working," Jonah offers.

"I'm not pretending anything, little boy." She cuffs him on the back of the head as she walks past. Jonah yelps, then winces.

"This is a bad hangover, isn't it? Such are the wages of sin, the Bible tells us," I say with mock seriousness.

"Save it," my brother mutters. "Maggie, are you seeing Malone?"

"Um, no. No." My face warms, and I grab a few ketchup bottles for refilling. "Why do you ask?"

"I don't know." Jonah sighs morosely. "I thought you guys were hanging out lately. Anyway, I heard something about him the other day." His voice trails to a mutter.

"Oh, really? What was that?" I ask, hoping for and failing to achieve a casual tone.

"He and Chantal are having a baby."

"No! No, they're not. What—where did you hear that?"

"Down at the dock," Jonah answers. He takes a listless sip of coffee, then shudders.

"Well, it's not really my business to talk about this, Joe, but…" Shit, what is the protocol on this? "See, actually, Chantal told me that the father is some out-of-towner. Not from here."

"Oh." Jonah stares into his coffee.

"Who told you it was Malone?" I can't help but ask. "I mean, does everyone know Chantal's…you know? Pregnant?"

"Yeah. Bunch of guys were talking at the co-op yesterday. Johnny French, Dad, Billy Bottoms, Sam…I don't know. But yeah. Word's out on Chantal."

"You guys gossip worse than a bunch of high-school girls."

Jonah forces a smile and presses his thumb against his eye socket.

"Want some aspirin, hon?" I ask.

"Sure," he says. I fetch the bottle and hand him two.

"Don't feel bad about Chantal," I say to my brother, remembering his long-standing crush on her. "Maybe the post office has your mail-order bride."

He gives a halfhearted laugh. "Thanks. Hey, you going to see Mom later?" he asks, standing.

I sigh. "Yeah. You?"

"Said goodbye yesterday. Can't believe she's really moving."

It is a little hard to believe—our mother, she of the Sunday dinners and good china, is moving out of the house she's lived in for thirty years. Both she and my dad are putting a good spin on things…new start, yadda yadda…but there's a sadness to both of them these days.

My dad's in the bomb shelter when I go over. He's crying as he screws in a perch on a tiny birdhouse.

"Hey, Daddy," I say, my throat growing tight at the sight of my father in tears.

"Oh, hi, Maggie," he says, surreptitiously wiping his eyes.

"You okay?"

"Well, I guess so. It's just a sad day, you know?" he says.

"You sure it's what you want, Dad? Are you having second thoughts?" I pick up a tiny scrap of wood shaving and toy with it.

Dad sighs hugely. "I think we need to try being apart," he says. "Being together hasn't made either of us real happy. Doesn't mean I don't love your mother, of course. I do."

"I know." I watch as he taps a shingle, no bigger than a postage stamp, onto the roof of the birdhouse. "That's a cute one," I say. "I like the tire swing. Do you think they'll use it?"

Dad smiles. "You never know."

Upstairs, my mom is folding some clothes into a suitcase. "Hi, Maggie," she says brightly.

"Hi, Mom. How are you?"

"Great. Fine." Her smile doesn't reach her eyes. "A door closes, a window breaks, you know."

"Right." I'm going to miss those screwed-up clichés. "Are you scared?"

"Mmm-hmm." She nods briskly and continues packing.

"Tell me about your job," I urge, sitting on the bed. It's hard not to cry, but I swallow and try to be excited for her.

"Well, it's nothing, really. I'll just be answering phones," she says.

"Still, you got a job at a magazine. That's great," I say.

"We'll see."

I look in the box of things she's packing, a surprisingly paltry amount. My mother is taking—for now, anyway—only some clothes, a few pictures of us kids and Violet and some books. She's leaving all the pots and pans, all the Hummel figures, the paintings, all the crap of a three-decade-long marriage, and starting fresh.

"I think you're really brave, Mom," I tell her.

She bursts into tears and sinks onto the bed next to me, covering her face with her hands.

"Oh, Maggie," she sobs. "I'm not. I'm terrified! I have no idea how I'm going to pull this off.... I have this awful image of myself, creeping back here in the dead of night because I just don't know how to live on my own."

"Mom, don't cry. It'll be okay. You can call me anytime, you know that, right? I'll come right down. It's not like you're going to the moon." I pat her back. "I'll help you pick out new towels and pillows and stuff like that. We can go to the outlets and have lunch. It'll be okay."

She looks at me hopefully. "You think so?"

I nod. "Absolutely. And if you do come back, it won't be creeping in the dead of night. It'll be because you want to, not because you have to."

She sighs, then blows her nose. "I hope you're right." She pauses. "You could come with me, Maggie. The apartment has two bedrooms." There's a touching note of hope in her voice, and I smile.

"Thank you, Mom. Thanks for asking. But I'm…I'm really happy here."

"Are you, honey?"

I think a minute. "Yes. I am, Mom. I know you wanted more for me, but I love what I do. Even if it's blue-collar, even if I've never really lived anywhere else."

"What about…marriage? Children?" she asks carefully. I can see she's trying not to have a fight.

"That would be nice. I do want those things," I acknowledge. "But it'll happen when it happens, I guess."

"I just don't want you to look back on your life twenty years from now, Maggie, and see all the things you could have done," Mom says, blowing her nose again.

"I think I'll look back and see all the things I did do, Mom," I say, a little starch creeping into my voice. "I'll see that I fed people and welcomed them, I helped them and kept them company…those are good things, Mom."

"They are, Maggie," she says, standing up to resume her packing. "But what about you, sweetheart? I want you to have someone to take care of you, too. You deserve that, you know. And if you can't find someone wonderful, someone like Will, then you need to take care of yourself."

I don't answer. It's hard to disagree with that. "Well," I say, forcing a smile. "You need to be thinking about your own life, Mom."

"You are my life, Maggie," she says matter-of-factly, not looking at me. "The child who needs me the most."

"WHAT CAN I GET YOU, girls?" Paul Dewey bellows a few days later. "Will the little mother be drinking tonight?"

My mouth drops open. "Dewey knows, too?"

"News travels fast," Chantal murmurs. "How about cranberry juice, Dewey, hon?"

"I'll have a Sam Adams, Paul," I call.

He brings our drinks over and sits with us, gazing lovingly at Chantal's breasts, which have grown noticeably in her delicate condition. "So, Chantal, sweetheart, who's the lucky guy?"

"Most guys in this town have been lucky at one time or another," I quip. Chantal chuckles, but Dewey turns a scowling face to me.

"That's no way to talk about a lady in her condition, Maggie. Shame on you."

"I'm so sorry, Chantal," I say. "Please forgive me for stating the truth."

She laughs, and I feel a rush of more affection than I've felt for her before. Chantal has never pretended to be anything other than what she is, and for that, I admire her.

"So, Chantal, you gonna come clean with old Dewey? Who knocked you up, girl?"

"None of your business, Paul," Chantal says coyly.

"Well, I heard a rumor," Dewey says.

"Oh, really? About little old me?" Chantal asks.

"Ayuh," Dewey says. "About you and a certain someone who hasn't been around much lately. Afraid to show his face, apparently."

Chantal and I exchange looks, her smile fading. "Really," she says. "Spill, Dewey."

Dewey does. "Malone. Is he the father?"

I choke on my beer, lurching forward in my seat as tears swamp my eyes and nose.

"No," Chantal says firmly. "It's not Malone. I never even slept with him, Dewey, and that's the truth."

"Well, that's not what I heard," Dewey drawls.

"And yet, wouldn't I be in a better position to know?" Chantal hisses, eyes narrowing, as I continue to splutter.

"Word on the street is that Malone won't own up to being the daddy. That he won't take a DNA test so he can avoid paying child support. Well, don't you worry, Chantal, honey. We'll make sure—"

"Dewey, this is the stupidest thing I've ever heard," I wheeze, still coughing. "If Chantal says it's not Malone, it's not Malone."

"And it's not Malone," she confirms.

"Sure, sure, darlin'. If you say so." Dewey hauls himself up and lumbers to the bar.

"Shit," Chantal mutters, patting my back. With her uncharacteristically straight answer, Chantal has cemented the idea that Malone is indeed the father of her baby. "Where did he hear that? Maggie, you didn't—"

"No!" I protest. "No, I didn't tell anyone anything." I consider for a moment. "Well, I told Christy what I thought, but she wouldn't tell anyone. I'm sure of that."

"Huh. Well, screw it. Someone else's name will come up in about five more minutes." She takes a sip of her juice and rubs her stomach unconsciously.

"Chantal," I ask. "Are you sure you shouldn't tell the father? Doesn't he have rights and stuff like that?"

Her face falls. "Maggie, it's not that simple. It would completely screw up his life. We only did it once, and I'm not going to saddle him with a kid."

"Is he married?" I whisper.

"No," she says. "But he's…look, I'm just not going to tell, okay? Oh, look. Malone just came in."

My physical reaction is immediate and dramatic. My face flushes lobster red, my legs go loose and watery, and my heart rate doubles. Malone sees us—it's hard to miss the only two females in the bar, especially when you're accused of impregnating one and have slept with the other—and gives a characteristically curt nod in our general direction. Then he sits at the bar and waits for Dewey to notice him.

Dewey ignores him.

"Can I get a beer?" Malone growls after a solid minute has passed.

"Not in my bar, you can't," Dewey answers.

"Dewey!" Chantal yelps. "Are you being an ass?" She pushes back from our table and sashays up to the bar. "Hi, Malone," she says.

"Hi," he grunts.

"Dewey, is there a problem here?" Chantal asks.

Malone stands up, glances at me and grabs his coat.

"No, no, no," Chantal says. "Stay, Malone. Dewey, what's your problem?"

"If a man can't acknowledge his responsibilities, honey, he can't expect people not to care," Dewey begins. "And I'm not the only one who thinks so. Heard you got some lines cut, Malone."

Oh, shit. A gear war against Malone. When a lobster

trap's lines are cut, the trap sits on the ocean floor and rots. Up here it's a shooting crime up here to tinker with someone's pots. But the men of Gideon's Cove feel very proprietary toward Chantal, who has given many of them a happy night or two, and if they think Malone is shirking his duties, they're bound to take action. Malone remains silent.

"I already told you, Malone's not the father!" Chantal barks. "I never slept with him, and it wasn't for lack of trying. *My* trying. Okay?"

"Don't worry about it, Chantal," Malone says. "See you."

Without any thought backing my movement, I'm up and across the bar in a heartbeat. "Hi, Malone," I say.

"Maggie." He gives me a quick once-over, then stares off over my shoulder. "Have a good night," he says.

"Malone, hang on." I put my hand on his arm to stop him, swallowing. Perhaps I should have thought before I acted, but apparently it's not my way. "People are saying you're the father of Chantal's baby," I announce pointlessly.

"Yeah, I picked up on that. Wonder where they got that idea."

It's hard to look him in the face, but I do. The scowl lines are in full force. "I didn't tell anyone what I thought, Malone. Well, except Christy. But she wouldn't say a word."

He just stares at me.

"That's probably why your lines got cut," I say stupidly.

"You think?" The contempt in his eyes stings.

"So what are you going to do, Malone?"

He shrugs. "Nothing. If Chantal doesn't want people to know who the father is, that's her business."

"Do you know?" I ask.

He looks at me and doesn't answer, choosing instead to pull on his coat. Chantal is still in a heated argument with Dewey. "Take care," he says, heading for the door.

"Malone?" I call, taking a step in his direction. He doesn't stop, doesn't even turn his head, just pushes open the door and heads out.

"Oh, great!" Chantal huffs. "He left! That's just great, Dewey. Come on, Maggie, let's get out of here. I'm very mad at you, Paul."

"Chantal, honey, I was just—" Dewey attempts, but Chantal is riding a wave of moral outrage, and out we go.

"Poor Malone," she murmurs as she takes out her keys. "Well, I'm kind of tired anyway, Maggie. See you Thursday?"

Her day for lunch at the diner. "Sure."

I go back to my lonely, too-empty apartment. It's looked strange since I purged my little collections; Dad's birdhouses and pictures of Violet are the only decorations I have left. Colonel dying has left a huge void, too. I click around the TV, too distracted to think about any one thing in particular.

At 2:00 a.m., I jolt awake. I *did* tell someone. By accident, of course—Billy Bottoms. That day at the dock, I was talking to myself. I didn't realize he heard me.

Shit.

Sleep is ruined for the night. I assure myself that Billy didn't hear me that day. And this is a tiny town.

Malone and Chantal have spoken at Dewey's any number of times, so there's no reason to think that this rumor is my fault. Chantal is generous with her affection, she flirts with Malone (as much as it's possible to flirt with Malone, anyway), so there you go. Billy didn't hear me. I'm sure.

I still can't get back to sleep.

CHAPTER TWENTY-NINE

A FEW DAYS LATER, I walk to St. Mary's in a gentle, steady, cozy rain. I miss Colonel so much it aches…the past few days have been so quiet, both at the diner and in my personal life, that I'm a little stir-crazy. The diner is closed for the day, the baking done. It's not my night for Meals on Wheels, and I've spent so much time at Christy's lately that she told me outright to give her a little space. Clearly, it's time for me to find another dog.

So. The high school had a dance in the church basement this past weekend, and I decide to go over and clean the kitchen, which always suffers during this type of event.

As I cross the street, I see Bishop Tranturo walking out of the rectory. Father Tim stands in the doorway, his arms crossed on his chest. He sees me and lifts his hand in a wave, then goes back in, closing the door behind him.

Bishop Tranturo has been around forever. He's not often seen in these parts, as we are a tiny parish, but I remember his round, jolly face from years past. When making his annual visit to confirm Gideon's Cove's Catholic teenagers, he usually stops by the diner for breakfast. In fact, he presided over my own confirmation.

I wonder what he's doing here. I wonder—

"Hi, Bishop," I call out, splashing across the street as he's about to get into his car.

"Hello, dear," he says. "I'm sorry, you are…?"

"Maggie. Maggie Beaumont."

"Oh, yes," he says, recognition lighting his cherubic face. "You're Maggie, from the diner. Of course. Nice to see you." He smiles and waits.

"So how are things?" I ask. "How's everything?"

"Just fine, dear. And you?"

"I'm fine. I'm…so. We love Father Tim around here. He's great. A great priest." My stomach cramps with anxiety.

Bishop Tranturo nods and looks over my shoulder.

"Is he leaving? Is that why you're here?" I blurt, glancing back at the rectory. "Is Father Tim…?"

The bishop sighs, his breath fogging in the cool air. "I think I'll let him tell you that himself, dear," he says. "Take care. God bless you, my child."

"Okay, yes. Thanks. And you, too," I say manically. "Drive safely. Bye."

I step back and let him get into his car. The rain is falling harder now, but I barely notice.

Father Tim is leaving the priesthood.

My heart pounds sickly in my chest and my legs feel weak and shaky. Lost in thought, I drift into the church and slide into the last pew.

It's empty in here, the smell of lemon oil and candles soothing and welcoming. The door clicks shut behind me, and I am alone in this haven of stillness. The rain patters against the small stained-glass windows, and below me, the furnace kicks on. The candles in the front flicker in the drafts. Only one light is on, shining gently on the cross that hangs over the altar.

I haven't been in St. Mary's for a while, too flustered by Father Tim to come here. And it's a shame, really, because it's lovely, truly a place to think, to open myself up and listen for a whisper of wisdom. I haven't done that in a long time. My embarrassment over Father Tim has distracted me from any true spirituality I might have had in the past year.

Father Tim. My mind is oddly blank as I sit there. Fragments of conversations slip through, but I'm unable to hold on to one. Father Tim has been lonely. He cares about me. I'm special to him. He's counting on that... and he asked me about Father Shea.

The question is, what if it's true? What if he's leaving the priesthood and wants to find someone? What if he thinks he wants to be with me? What then? It's not like I have other contenders...the pet psychic, the groin injury guy, the old men...and unforgiving, closed-off, angry Malone.

I rush outside and over to the rectory, bursting in on Mrs. Plutarski.

"Where is he?" I demand. "I know he's here."

"He's very busy," Mrs. P. answers. "What's got into you?"

"Father Tim?" I call, sticking my head into his office. He's not there. "Father Tim?" I shove my wet hair back from my face.

He comes into the common room, holding a cup of tea. "Ah, Maggie," he says warmly. "Just the person I wanted to see."

"Father Tim," I say, grabbing his arm. "I need to speak with you. It's an emergency."

Mrs. P. sighs dramatically. "Another death in the family, Maggie? Your goldfish this time?"

"Bite me," I tell her. Father Tim's eyes widen as I tow him through the common room, into the kitchen. I don't want Mrs. Plutarski to overhear us, and I know she'll try.

"Here now, Maggie, maybe you should slow down. In fact, I was hoping to see you—"

"Sit down," I tell him. He obeys, and I take a seat opposite him at the small table. "I just spoke to Bishop Tranturo. About, you know…you." My hands are shaking, the palms sweaty.

Father Tim's face grows somber. "Did you, now? I was hoping to tell you myself." He gives me a sad smile. "Maggie, you know I care—"

"Wait!" I bark. "Please wait. Don't say anything." I take a deep breath, then another, as Father Tim looks at me, concerned and expectant. "Okay…um, Father Tim," I say more gently. "Listen. You are a wonderful priest and the thing is, I understand that it's not always easy for you, but…" I swallow. He waits patiently. "Listen, Father Tim, you're a very nice, kind man. And of course I…you know. Care for you. But I think you're making a mistake. You know, about leaving. You can't just give this all up!"

Father Tim sighs and leans back in his chair. "I know, Maggie. It's been wonderful. I've loved being pastor here, as you know. But change is going to come, whether we like it or not."

I take another breath, my legs feeling weak and sick. "Does anyone else know about—about your, um, decision?"

"No, Maggie. I was planning to say something at

Mass." At *Mass!* My mouth falls open, but he continues. "Of course, the bishop knows, but that goes without saying."

"Okay, okay, wait. I need to say this." My hands are curled into fists. "We're friends, you and I, aren't we?"

"Of course, Maggie."

"And I think you have a lot of nice qualities." He blinks, ever patient. "Right. So. You know I had a killer crush on you." He smiles—is that a happy smile? Forgiving? Expectant?—and I force myself to go on. "But, Father Tim, I don't anymore. I just think you should know that. In case I was figuring into your decision in any way. Any way whatsoever."

The smile falters, flickers, then dies completely. "I'm not clear on what you're getting at, Maggie," he says slowly. "Why would you figure into it?"

"Because of the thing with Father Sh—um, what's that?"

He frowns, clearly puzzled. "Ah…well, why don't you say what's on your mind, Maggie?"

I bite my lip, wince, and go for it. "Um…I don't want you to leave the priesthood because of me."

Under other circumstances, Father Tim's reaction would be funny. He lurches back in his seat, then staggers to his feet, grabbing the chair and putting it between us. "Dear Lord, Maggie! I'm not leaving the priesthood!"

"Oh, thank God!" A hysterical laugh escapes my lips. "Oh, thank God! Great! This is great news!"

"How—why—where on earth did you get an idea like that?"

"I…um…ah…" *Breathe, Maggie, breathe. He's not leaving the priesthood.* "Well, Bishop Tranturo…he said you were leaving."

"I'm being transferred to another parish."

"Right. Oh, that is fantastic news." I heave a sigh of relief, my head spinning. Father Tim cocks his head. "Okay. That makes a lot more sense." I pause. "I guess I just thought that…well, you said a few things that I thought… I was afraid you had feelings for me, Father Tim."

His eyes narrow, and he keeps a good grip on the chair, and he keeps that chair solidly between us. "Maggie," he says, very, very carefully, "I think you're a lovely person, but no. No feelings of a romantic sort. At all. Ever. I'd hope we'd stay friends after I leave, but of course, nothing else."

"Well, that's great. Sure. I just could've sworn…" My heart rate is returning to normal, and I take a deep breath. "I mean, I'm sorry that the parish is losing you, but Father Tim, what about Father Shea? I mean, you…you seemed kind of interested in him, and there were these things you said about me and being friends and…" My voice trails off.

Father Tim closes his eyes in understanding. "Oh, dear. I'm so sorry if I ever led you to believe…oh, shite. No, Maggie, Michael Shea, formerly Father Shea, has been in hospice, and I had to ask the bishop if special arrangements might be required for his funeral, being that he was a priest at one time…nothing else, Maggie." He pauses tentatively. "I'm terribly sorry if I ever gave you any impression whatsoever that…well. I'm not sure what to say."

At this point, he could say he was pregnant and I wouldn't care. He's not leaving the priesthood, he's not in love with me, and I am simply limp with relief. No doubt other feelings are going to make themselves known sometime soon, but right now, all I feel is utter, beautiful reprieve.

"Let's not say anything, okay?" I offer. "In fact, if we could just pretend this conversation never took place…"

He offers me an uneasy smile. "That would probably be best," he agrees. "Though I'm glad to hear your crush on me is done."

I pause. "St. Mary's is really going to miss you."

"And I them. And now, Maggie, I have things I need to take care of…."

On trembling legs, I walk through the rectory. Alas, Mrs Plutarski's lips are white with disapproval, and I know her too well to believe she wasn't eavesdropping. She'll tell everyone. Once more, Gideon's Cove is going to have a good laugh over me, but right now, I simply don't care.

A bit numbly, I walk through the rain and find myself at the harbor. The boats are all out, as the demand for lobsters has already risen, though it's only May. I picture Malone out there, alone. Maloner the Loner.

I miss him irrationally.

CHAPTER THIRTY

ON MONDAY, my day off, I give Mrs. K.'s apartment a quick clean, leave her a chicken and spinach casserole and kiss her goodbye. Then I run back upstairs and survey my closet.

This errand has been a long time coming. I'm not sure what to wear. I'd be happy in a Joe's Diner T-shirt and jeans, but maybe something nicer would help at the critical moment. Plus, my mother will be happy to see me in something that's not stained, so I pull out some cream-colored pants that Christy bought me two Christ-mases ago and top it with a chocolaty silk shirt. I brush my hair and put it into a French twist, add some big gold hoops, a little lip gloss and mascara, a few dashes of blush. Then I hop into my car and head out of town.

It takes about an hour and a half to reach my desti-nation, and the drive is beautiful. The ponds gleam an electric blue under the cloudless sky, the leaves are that engaging shade of pale green. The sun beats through the windshield and I crack my window a little, turn up the radio and sing along.

I haven't heard from Father Tim since our last con-versation a week ago. He hasn't come into the diner, but the word is out that he's leaving. Most of Gideon's Cove is devastated. As for me, my feelings are still a bit mixed; I'll miss him because he was nice to have around, but I sure won't miss feeling so stupid when it came to him.

The directions I got off the Internet last night are fairly accurate, and I find the car dealership with no trouble, right next to McDonald's, as promised on Mapquest. I pull into the lot in my battered Subaru, a lump of coal among diamonds.

A rather pleasant thrill of anticipation and nervousness runs down my legs as I get out. I glance at my reflection in the car windows, then turn and go inside.

"May I help you?" asks a pretty woman behind the desk.

"I'd like to see Skip Parkinson, please," I say pleasantly.

"Of course." She presses a button on the phone. "Skip, please come to the front desk. Skip, front desk, please." Her voice is soothing and robotic.

I glance around the showroom while I wait, admiring the sleek lines and tasteful colors of the expensive cars. Cars are like racehorses to me—I enjoy looking at them and have little use for them. Given where I live and what I do, I require something far more pragmatic than a seventy-five thousand dollar big-boy toy.

"Hi, can I show you something today?" Skip's voice comes from behind me. I turn around.

"Hi, Skip," I say. He's wearing a beautiful charcoal suit, his blue shirt open at the neck, stylish as a European duke.

His mouth drops open with a quick intake of breath. "Maggie! Wow."

"Do you have a minute?" I tilt my head and smile.

It's so much more pleasant, being the surpriser, not the surprised.

"Um, sure. Sure. Uh, come on back to my office." He walks me to a soulless room in the back of the dealership, his windows overlooking the parking lot. A chrome-and-glass coffee table holds some expensive-looking sales brochures. There's a matching bookcase along one wall, a large desk covered with papers.

I sit in a leather chair and look around. Scattered on the walls and shelves are pictures of the Parkinsons—Annabelle, their children, even one of his snobby parents.

"So, Maggie, what a nice surprise," Skip says carefully, lowering himself into the chair opposite me. "Are you looking for a car?"

I chuckle. "No. No car, Skip. I'm just here to see you."

He tugs on his shirtsleeves and tries to look pleasantly interested, but a flush is creeping up from his collar. "Well. How nice."

I cross my legs and just look at him. Still a handsome devil. But his face is bland, a classic American face, well-proportioned features, brown eyes, the hint of gray in his tidy little beard. Only the lines around his eyes give him any distinction at all. I imagine being married to him, having him come home to our big, lovely house, handing him one of our kids. We might have a cocktail, and I'd feign interest as he told me about the irritating customer who went with the Audi instead of the Lexus SUV he can't seem to unload.

I'm glad we didn't end up together. That wasn't always true, but it is now. Suddenly, I realize I don't need anything from Skip.

"So, Maggie…" Skip says, pasting a fake smile on his lips. "What can I do for you?"

"Well, I guess I came for that apology you owe me, Skip," I answer. The smile falls off his face with a nearly audible thud. "But…well, I don't know. I thought it mattered. But it doesn't."

"Oh," he says. The flush has his face in its grip now. "Well."

"It was pretty bad, you know," I tell him. "You bringing Annabelle to town, not telling me that we broke up."

"That was a long time ago," he mutters.

"You're right. I guess I've sort of been cleaning house emotionally, you know? And it occurred to me that you never really…well. Like you said, it was a long time ago." I stand up. "Sorry I wasted your time."

Skip stands also. "That's it?" he says, a hopeful note in his voice.

I laugh a little. "Yeah. Kind of anticlimactic, isn't it?" I stick out my hand. "Take care. Your wife seems very nice."

His hand is softer than mine, smooth and pampered. "Thank you, Maggie," he says carefully. "Take care, yourself." He makes a movement to the door, but I wave him off.

"I'll see myself out. Goodbye, Skip."

When I've just reached the door, his voice stops me. "Maggie?"

I turn. "Yeah?"

"I am sorry." He looks a little forlorn, somehow. "I wish I'd done it better."

I pause, then give a nod. "Thanks for saying so."

I wave to the receptionist and walk out into the bright

sunshine. "Well, that was a waste of gas," I say to myself as I climb back in my car. But I'm laughing as I say it.

Around five, I find the building where my mother works and climb the stairs to the third floor. For a second, I just watch her from the doorway—she sits behind the reception counter, wearing a headset, talking animatedly. The wall behind her has *Mainah Magazine* painted in large green letters.

"Hi, Mom," I say when she clicks off from her conversation.

"Maggie!" she cries. We hug and kiss, and I breathe in her familiar perfume, realizing that I've missed her.

"Don't you look nice!" she says.

"You, too. I love your hair," I tell her. She really does look lovely…not younger, exactly, but very stylish in her bright green top and pretty scarf.

"Let me introduce you," Mom says, pulling me along. "Linda, this is my daughter, Maggie. Maggie, this is our editor, Linda Strong."

"Nice to meet you," I say, shaking her hand.

"Maggie owns a restaurant," my mother announces. "Cara, this is my daughter, Maggie."

"Hello, Maggie. We've heard a lot about you." Cara shakes my hands. "Where are you going for dinner, Lena?"

"Well, first I'm going to show her my apartment, then I thought we'd go to Havana."

The three women take a moment to discuss the various restaurant choices while I revel in the rare glow of my mom's pride. A restaurant owner. She's never called me that before. Formerly, I was a cook or I ran a diner, but today, I own a restaurant.

She loves hearing about my visit to Skip, loves

showing me her tiny apartment. Honestly, I can't remember a time when she's gone for so long without criticizing me.

"Do you miss Dad?" I ask as we eat dinner.

She thinks a minute. "Yes and no," she says. "It's quiet in the evenings. I'm so used to having him just be there, I suppose." Her voice trails off. "I don't really do anything on my own yet. But there are times when I think I've never been happier. I caught a mistake the other day, and Linda told me she didn't know I could proofread, and now she's asked me to look over everything before it goes out."

"That's great, Mom. It sounds like you really like it," I say, watching her flush with pleasure.

"I do. But there are also times when I cry, I'm so lonely," she adds.

"We miss you. All of us."

"I'll be home this weekend," she says. "To see the baby, and everyone else, of course." She pauses. "How are you, honey?"

"I'm okay," I say. "I...well. There are some things that are clearer to me these days, and I'm trying to kind of sort them out."

"Like what?" Mom asks.

"Oh, I don't know." I take another bite of fish, then decide to tell her. "I'm over my stupid crush on Father Tim."

"Finally." She smiles, not unkindly. "Are you seeing anyone, Maggie?"

I feel my back stiffen, preparing for battle. "No."

"I might have someone for you, dear," she says. "He works at—"

"No, thanks, Mom. I need a little break from dating,

actually," I interrupt. I take a breath. "I was seeing someone for a few weeks. Remember Malone?"

"Malone? The lobsterman?"

"Right. Well, we were kind of seeing each other, but then we had a fight." I take a gulp of water.

"Did you apologize?" Mom asks.

"Why do you assume it was my fault?" I snap, setting my glass down with a thunk and a slosh.

"Was it?" she says with a smile.

I grit my teeth, then give a rueful nod. "Well, yes, actually, it was. And I did apologize. But he's not the forgiving type."

"Well, when you're ready, then, you let me know and I'll give you this person's number. But you don't have— I mean, I hope…"

You don't have much time…I hope you won't wait too long…. I know what she wants to say. But to her credit, she stops herself. "Well. Good luck."

"I should probably get going," I say, glancing at my watch. "It's a long drive."

Mom's eyes fill with tears. "All right," she says, fiddling with her bracelet to hide the fact. "It was so wonderful seeing you, honey."

We walk together to where we parked. "Drive safely, now," she says. "Let the phone ring once so I know you made it home all right."

"Okay, Mom. Will do."

I kiss her cheek, hug her tight for a minute. It's still a bit of a shock that I'm taller than my mom. Even though that's been the case for more than fifteen years, I still expect to look up to her.

CHAPTER THIRTY-ONE

"I'M SO TIRED of being a joke, Christy," I tell my sister as we walk along the shore one afternoon. Violet sits in a backpack on my back, babbling happily.

"You're not a joke," Christy assures me. "You just drew the wrong conclusions, that's all. It could happen to anyone."

That's the nice thing about having an identical twin. Loyalty. I smile gratefully. Up ahead, a group of puffins scatters at our approach.

"Dird!" my niece yells. "Dird!"

Christy's mouth drops open in glee. "That's right, Violet! Bird!"

"Ah-do! Dird!"

"She's so smart," I tell my sister. Violet pulls my hair vigorously, jerking my head back.

"No, Violet," Christy says, unwrapping her daughter's pudgy fist. "No pulling."

The air is cool and damp, clouds blowing in from the east. Rain is in the forecast. Gulls cry above us and the waves slap at the shore.

"So what's wrong with Jonah these days?" Christy asks.

"I don't know," I admit. "He's been a real sad sack. Unlike him."

"Woman trouble?" Christy guesses.

"Maybe," I answer. "I saw him with some cute young thing a while back. They were kissing. He hasn't named names, though, so I really don't know."

"What about you?" Christy asks, bending down to pick up a piece of sea glass. She studies it for a moment, then slips it into her pocket. "What about your love life?"

I sigh. "I think I'm just gonna sit tight for a while," I say. "No more obsessing, no more dates. Someone will come along someday, maybe. And if not…"

"If not, then what?" she asks.

"If not, then I'm still okay," I tell her with a smile. "Can't have everything, unless your name is Christine Margaret Beaumont Jones."

It's true. It's taken a while, but I've been pretty…happy these days. The weight of Father Tim is off my back, as it were, my crush and wonderings finally gone for good. No more guilt over lusting after a priest, no more wasted hours imagining us together. I feel clean, somehow. Emptier, brighter. Like my apartment.

I smile at my twin, who looks beautiful today, her cheeks flushed with the damp breeze, her hair blowing in wisps around her face. "When are you going to tell me?" I ask her.

She stops dead, her mouth falling open, and I laugh and hug her. "Congratulations, Christy," I say, tears of happiness pricking my eyes.

"How did you know?" she asks.

"How did I miss it?" I ask back. "So how far along are you?"

She smiles hugely. "A month. It was a surprise, but we're thrilled."

"Of course you are. And so am I! Violet," I say, craning my neck to address my niece. "You're going to be a big sister!"

"Ah do!" she proclaims. "Go ba!"

When we get back to town, Christy and I part ways, and I watch her walk away. Melancholy pricks my heart. It's not that I'm jealous of her—I love her more than I love anyone. But she doesn't feel the same way about me. She has Violet and Will, and now a new little crittah on the way. And while that's as it should be, there's a small part of me that feels left behind. Once, *we* were all we needed, Christy and I. Just the two of us.

I see the *Ugly Anne* coming into the harbor. There are two figures on deck, a man and a woman. Jonah mentioned that Malone's daughter is going to be his sternman for the season. It must be nice for Malone, having his child with him all summer. Imagining that closeness, that biological link, causes a sting of jealousy to burn in my heart...and a prickle of shame, too. Because though Father Tim once said I made people feel wonderful, I'm quite sure I didn't get to do that for Malone. He did it for me, but I didn't reciprocate.

EARLY WEDNESDAY MORNING, I pack a suitcase and head out of town. Tonight is the Best Awards dinner from *Maine Living*, all the way down in Portland. Since my car isn't the most reliable vehicle in the world, Christy loans me the Volvo.

"Good luck! You'll win! You deserve it!" she calls from her driveway as I back down. "And you look fantastic!"

Last year, I had a great time at the dinner, meeting

other restaurant owners, picking up tips on publicity, advertising, media and the like. I had naively thought that Joe's might at least come in second, but we didn't. Of course, last year, I didn't realize the rules let us print out as many ballots as we wanted. The evil innkeepers (actually, they're quite nice) at Blackstone B&B were not so ignorant and won by hundreds of votes.

I don't know if it will mean a significant change if Joe's wins, but I know it would feel different. How thrilling to put "Best Breakfast in Washington County" in the window! *Maine Living* will feature the winner in an article with a color photo, which I can already picture: me, Octavio, Judy and Georgie—standing in front, the sun bouncing off Joe's chrome, the impatiens full and healthy.

And, I admit, as I pull onto the interstate, it would be nice to drop that nugget at the Blessing of the Fleet this coming weekend. Each year, the Blessing is a marker for our town. Who's divorced since last year? Whose kid got arrested for drug dealing? Anyone get married? Graduate from college? Buy a house? Have an affair? Bury a spouse? And each year for nearly a decade, I've remained the same. *No, still not married. Nope, no prospects. No kids. Not engaged. Not seeing anyone. Just at the diner, you know?*

But this year—hopefully—I could say, "Well, maybe you heard that Joe's Diner just won best breakfast in the county? No? Oh, well, it will be in *Maine Living* next month…" Each former classmate who returns to town would hear that Joe's Diner is moving up in the world. That Maggie Beaumont has a real accomplishment to her name.

"Who am I kidding?" I say out loud. "No one cares but me. And maybe Octavio." I turn on the radio.

It's a small event when compared with the Pope dying, say, or a U2 concert, but the Best Awards still attract a fair number of people. As a treat, I've booked myself in a nice room at the hotel where the awards are being held, a beautiful building on the water in Old Port. I check in, relishing the rarity of the act. The last time I was away for an overnight was last year, for this same event.

The room is small but elegant, and I indulge in a nap on the sleigh bed, enjoying the fine cotton sheets and down pillows. Afterward, I shower and dress carefully. Maybe I'll meet someone tonight, who knows? But the thought holds little appeal, oddly enough. God knows, I primped as carefully as a prom queen last year, hoping fervently that I would run into a good-looking, kind-hearted Washington County restaurateur or innkeeper. I didn't, but I sure as hell hoped.

Nope. This year is different. I'm not over Malone.

As I let his name enter my consciousness, loneliness wells up in my heart. It would be so much fun if we were together, if I had Malone's hand to hold tonight. I bet he'd look gorgeous in a suit. And if I didn't win, well, that would be okay. We'd still have a night in a city together. We could take a walk afterward, or order dessert in our room. We'd sleep past 6:00 a.m. and feel like we'd been away for a week.

"Too bad," I tell my reflection. "You blew it. Now get down to that ballroom and win that award."

I DON'T WIN. Blackstone Bed & Breakfast wins for the fifth straight year. I clap dutifully along with the others, congratulate the irritatingly nice couple and order a scotch. Later, when I'm safe in my room, I indulge in a quick cry. Then I call Octavio.

"We came in third," I tell him wetly.

"Hey, third's not bad," my cook says.

"Third sucks, Tavy," I sniffle. "There are only about three restaurants in the damn county!"

"Okay, now you're just feeling sorry for yourself, boss," Octavio says. "Third is pretty damn good when you live where we live. Okay? You should be proud of yourself."

"Right," I mutter.

"How much did we lose by?" he asks.

"Sixty-seven votes."

"Sixty-seven! That's great! Only sixty-seven! We'll definitely get it next year, boss."

I can't help but smile. "Thanks, big guy."

"See you Friday?" he asks. "We should have a good crowd this weekend."

"Yeah. See you then. I'll open." I hang up the phone and look out my window. Portland is so clean and bright and lively, but I'm suffering a bad case of homesickness at the moment. Poor Joe's. Such a cute little place. It deserves better than third. We *do* serve the best breakfast in Washington County, and next year, so help us God, we'll have the award to prove it.

This year, I'll do whatever it takes to get a restaurant reviewer to the diner. And a travel writer. I'll e-mail every day if I have to. Send letters. Or better yet, send scones or muffins. Bribe them with the quality of my goods. I can redo the menu, jazz up my lunch specials. Tavy's right. Sixty-seven more votes is not out of the question. My self-pity dries up with my tears. We didn't win, but that doesn't mean we're not the best.

I take the certificate I got from *Maine Living* and read it. "Congratulations to Joe's Diner, Gideon's Cove,

Maine. Second Runner Up, Best Breakfast in Washington County."

To hell with Washington County, I think, smiling wetly. Someday we'll get best breakfast in Maine.

CHAPTER THIRTY-TWO

THE BLESSING of the Fleet is held annually the third weekend of May. The boats fly their flags, the town decorates our three public buildings, local organizations sell hot dogs and lobster bisque on the green. The high school band plays, the chorus performs a few patriotic songs. Little Leaguers, the fire department, the board of selectmen and our three living veterans march in the five-minute parade. Then on Sunday, every boat in the harbor lines up and motors to Douglas Point, past the granite memorial for lost fishermen. They continue up to the dock, where the local clergy blesses them and prays for a safe and productive year.

Last year, Father Tim had been new in town, and I'd still been getting over the embarrassment of my mistake. In order to show what a good sport I was, I threw myself into the planning committee with a vengeance. I baked cookies for the first communion class to sell, donated my efforts to the Saturday night spaghetti supper at the church hall, helped decorate the podium on which Father Tim and the Congregational minister stood to sprinkle holy water on the passing boats. *I may be an idiot,* I was trying to convey after humiliating myself in front of the town, *but at least I'm a hardworking idiot.*

This year, I can admit that maybe Father Tim and I used each other a bit. He got a lot of work out of me this past year, and I, as I can now see quite clearly, got more than a guilty thrill concerning him. It's safe to be in love with someone you know you'll never have. Nothing is really risked when you know you can't lose. He was a distraction, an excuse, and a friend. No more, no less.

Saturday morning of Blessing Weekend dawns foggy and warmer than usual, and by 10:00 a.m., the sun is shining, the air is clear and it's a perfect spring day. May is the month of blackflies, but a strong breeze off the water keeps them away, and only the most determined bugs are able to draw blood through their tiny, painful bites. As Christy, Will and I walk down to the green, Violet in the carrier on Will's back, the smell of outdoor cooking—chowder and bacon, hot dogs and hamburgers and smoke—hits us in a thick, mouthwatering wave.

This weekend seems like a thank-you to the residents for not moving away to an easier place. Our sense of neighborhood and friendship is strong at the Blessing. People call greetings to each other, shake hands as if it's been weeks, not hours, since they last met. Couples hold hands, children dance with excitement. *When are the lobster boat races? Can we get a balloon? I'm hungry!* Everywhere, people smile and laugh. Music drifts in snatches on the breeze.

I wave to friends, customers, neighbors…there's virtually no one I don't know by name. Now and then, I catch a glimpse of Father Tim in his all-black priest clothes, but he is swamped with teary-eyed well-wishers.

Main Street is closed off to cars, and people stroll the block and a half of the "downtown," stopping to sample a cookie from the Girl Scouts, a muffin from the PTA. The chrome on Joe's Diner glistens from the cleaning I gave it yesterday. Octavio, Georgie and I hung out bunting while Judy smoked and squinted in approval. I feel a little thrill of pride looking at it, even though it's closed.

"Ow," Will says, reaching up to pry his hair from Violet's dimpled fist. "Let go, sweetie." He shifts the backpack as Violet knees him in the spine.

"Want me to take her, Will?" I offer. "You won't pull Auntie's hair, will you, pumpkin?"

"You sure?" Will asks gratefully.

"Sure," I say. "I'll take Violet and you two can stroll around alone for a while, what do you say?"

"I say thank you," Christy says, unsnapping the harness. "You're the best, Maggie." She holds the pack with Violet still in it as Will slides his arms out, then straps it on me.

"Agga," Violet says. "Agga bwee."

"She just said Aunt Maggie, clear as day," I say. "Did you hear? What an honor." Violet takes a fistful of my hair and tugs in affirmation, I'm quite sure.

Will and Christy laugh. "Meet you in an hour?" Will says. "We'll buy you lunch at the fire department."

"Sounds great," I say.

With Violet on my back, I don't feel so obviously single. We stroll around, stopping to admire the display of art projects from the first grade students, and I brace for the inevitable assessment that is an integral part of Blessing Weekend.

"Hey, Maggie!"

And here we go. It's an old high school classmate, Carleigh Carleton. She went to college in Vermont, as I recall. She also had a wicked crush on Skip.

"Hey, Carleigh," I say.

"Oh, my God, you had a baby?" she shrieks, her eyes popping. She never was that attractive.

"No, no, this is my niece, Violet," I tell her.

"Oh, sure. Christy's baby. That makes more sense!" Carleigh's smile is full of smugness and condescension. "I have three myself. Are you still working in your grandfather's diner?" What she means is, *Are you still stuck in the same job you've had since high school, since Skip dumped you? Haven't you gotten married yet, Maggie? Don't you know the statistics for a woman over thirty?*

"Yup," I say. "And what about you, Carleigh?" I pretend to listen as she tells me of her fabulous life, which is probably not nearly so fabulous in reality. But that's what Blessing Weekend is for, in a sense. Pretense. Leaving Carleigh, who has gained another fifteen or so pounds since last year, I note with deep satisfaction, I wander through the crafts tent on the green.

There are a few more Carleigh types, mostly women who nod sympathetically when I tell them yes, I'm still at the diner. *Poor Maggie,* they seem to be saying, *I may have married an abusive drunk, had to file a restraining order and gotten divorced before I was twenty-three, but at least I got married!*

I refuse to feel inferior. *Screw 'em,* I think. My life is just fine. I make a difference in this town. Violet knees me in the back, and I continue in a fog, absent-mindedly waving here and there. A familiar name jerks me out of my daze.

"…and that Malone person won't admit that it's his," the hideous Mrs. Plutarski stage-whispers to one of her wrinkled old cronies, Mrs. Lennon.

"Why not?" Mrs. Lennon asks.

"Because he doesn't want to be saddled with child support," Mrs. Plutarski says, as if she had actual information on the subject. "Well, that woman had it coming, if you ask me. All those years of—"

"Excuse me, what are you talking about?" I ask, shoving in between them, a tugboat between two tankers.

"Oh! Maggie. How are you, dear?" Mrs. Lennon asks sweetly. Mrs. P. assumes the lemon-sucking face she does so well.

"Child support? Admitting that something is his? Tsk, tsk, Mrs. Plutarski. Does Father Tim know you gossip like this?" I fold my arms, my moment of righteous indignation somewhat marred by Violet yanking my hair.

"This is a private conversation, Maggie," Mrs. Plutarski says coldly. "And I'd say you should be worried about what people are saying about *you* instead of butting into other people's conversations. Everyone knows that you thought Father Tim was going to leave the church for you." She smirks and cuts her eyes to Mrs. Lennon.

"You know what, Edith?" I say. "You're a nasty, gossiping, eavesdropping busybody, and no amount of ass-kissing of priests is going to change that. Mrs. Lennon, you have a nice weekend."

Enjoying Mrs. P's squawking rage, I walk away. "How was I?" I ask my niece. She doesn't answer. Glancing back, I see that she's fallen asleep. Her angelic face calms my seething anger, but my heart is still pounding, my face hot.

Poor Malone. He's done nothing wrong, but the town won't drop it. All day, I hear snatches of damning conversation—Chantal and Malone are the hot topic. During the trap-hauling race, when everyone crowds the dock to see which boat will make it in fastest, Christy and I stand with the firemen to cheer on Jonah and Dad. "Why do you think Malone's not here?" Fred Tendrey asks as he leans against a post. "Ashamed to show his face, I'd guess."

"Why should he be ashamed, Fred?" I ask. "He hasn't done anything wrong. He's not the one standing around looking down women's blouses. Maybe he doesn't want his daughter to hear a bunch of idiots gossiping about him, huh? Ever think of that?"

My protestations fall on deaf ears. Malone's boat *is* conspicuously absent from the festivities. Or maybe he never comes to the Blessing. I can't say I ever noticed before.

"She doesn't want Malone involved," I overhear Leslie MacGuire murmuring to her neighbor as they buy cups of chowder. "You know the rumors about his first wife. How she left in the middle of the night."

"Oh, that's right," the neighbor murmurs. My jaw clenches, but I say nothing. There's no point.

By four o'clock, I can't take any more.

"Guys, I'm heading out," I tell my sister and Will. "I've got a headache."

"You okay?" Christy asks, tilting her head.

"Yup. Just tired."

Though I have a ticket for the spaghetti supper and the rest of my family, including Mom, will be there, I walk away from town. Climbing the hill to my apartment, I glance back at the harbor. The lobster boats are done with racing for the day, bobbing on their moorings like cheerful seagulls, clean and freshly painted for the new season. The *Twin Menace* gleams, one of the newer boats, made more noticeable because the *Ugly Anne* is out. My heart squeezes almost painfully, imagining him off with his daughter. In another few weeks, it will be illegal to pull pots after four, but for now Malone is within the rules, if he's actually working, that is. And it doesn't seem as if he misses a chance to work very often.

Except for that one day when he took me to Linden Harbor.

I trudge down my street, spying Mrs. Kandinsky sleeping in her chair through the window. Peeking inside, I make sure her chest is still rising and falling with breath, then, assured that she's not dead, I go upstairs to my dark apartment.

THE NEXT MORNING, the smell of frying bacon and coffee welcomes me to my parents' house. Each year, we have a special breakfast before the actual Blessing of the Fleet. And we're all going to church, since it's Father Tim's last Mass. Jonah is slumped in a corner, pale and shaky, timidly nursing a cup of coffee. I lean over and kiss him loudly on the cheek.

"Is my wittle brother a wittle hung over?" I ask merrily, ruffling his hair. He moans and turns to the wall. "Hi, Mom."

"Oh, Maggie, is that what you're wearing?" she asks.

I look down at my outfit. Tan pants, red sweater, shoes that match each other. I raise an eyebrow at my mother, who sets the spatula down on the counter. "What I meant to say, honey, is why don't you wear a skirt once in a while? You have such gorgeous legs."

"That was better, Mom. Better."

"There's nothing gorgeous about Maggie," Jonah mumbles from the corner, apparently not in enough misery to resist bothering me. "Christy's the pretty one." I smack him on the head, savoring his yelp of pain, and pour myself some coffee.

"I can't wear a skirt today, Mom," I say, giving my mother a kiss, pleased to see her back in the family domicile. "I'm going out with Jonah for the blessing."

"Not if you don't stop yelling," Jonah mutters.

It's wicked fun to be on the water for the Blessing of the Fleet. Gideon's Cove looks like a postcard—the rocky shore, tall pines, the houses that dot the hills, the spire of St. Mary's, the gray wood of the dock. Last year, the whole family went on the *Twin Menace*; this year, because of Violet, Christy and Will opted to stay ashore, and our parents will keep them company.

Christy's face appears on the back porch. "Hello," she calls. She has also worn tan pants and a red top, but her outfit cost more, is made with better materials and generally looks better than mine. She hefts in Violet's car seat, a diaper bag that's bigger than my suitcase and a vibrating bouncy seat. Will follows her with a tiny bungy-jumping contraption that's made to dangle from a doorway and another bag.

"Where's Dad?" I ask.

"In the bomb shelter," Jonah answers. "Could you stop yelling, please?"

"Dad!" I yell cheerfully. "We're all here!" Jonah whimpers.

"Serves you right, Joe," Christy says. "Jell-O shots. For God's sake. We were at Dewey's last night, you know. Saw everything."

"Did I call you the pretty one?" Jonah says, rising specterlike from his chair. "I changed my mind. You're both hags."

Fifteen minutes later, we're all sitting around the dining room table, passing platters of pancakes, scrambled eggs, cranberry scones (my contribution) and bacon. Jonah has swallowed some Advil and looks less green, though he shudders as the eggs pass him. I plop a spoonful on his plate and enjoy the blanching that follows.

"So, Mom, Dad," Christy begins in what Joe and I call her social-worker voice, "how have things been since you've...been apart?" Her voice is carefully pleasant.

"Not bad," Dad says. "Delicious scones, Maggie. You sure can bake, honey."

Christy's eyes close briefly. "Great. Any decisions about what's next?"

"Scone, sweetie?" Will asks.

"No. Thank you. Mom? Anything to tell us?"

My mother takes a deep breath. "Well, we've been talking, of course." She looks at Dad at the other end of the table. Dad is looking out the window, apparently fascinated with the flock of springtime birds enjoying his handiwork. "Mitch? Would you like to tell the children what we're planning?"

Dad snaps to attention. "Oh. Sure. Sure. Okay. Well, we...we're...we're not getting divorced. For now."

Christy's face lights up. I take another piece of bacon and look at my mother. "But..." I prompt.

"Right, Maggie," Mom says. "But I'm going to stay in Bar Harbor. At least for the foreseeable future." She looks at me for assurance, and I smile. Christy's face falls.

"I'm sorry, honey," Mom says to her. "I know it's not what you want, but—"

"No, no. It's fine. It's okay." But Christy's eyes are spilling tears. "I'm sorry…." She starts crying in earnest, and Will puts his arm around her, pulling her face against his shoulder. "It's what you want that matters, Mom," she blubbers. "And you, too, Daddy."

Jonah shoots me a classic little brother smirk, and suddenly, we're laughing. "Poor little Christy, coming from a broken home," Jonah murmurs, and she starts laughing, too.

"Oh, shut up, Jonah," she says, wadding up her napkin and throwing it at him. "I can't help it if I care about our family. Unlike you, you freakish troglodyte."

En masse, we head for town, Jonah and me in his truck, our parents with Will, Christy and the baby in the Volvo wagon.

The waxy smell of candles mixes with the lingering scent of spaghetti as we walk into church. Since Father Tim won't be returning to St. Mary's after this, the place is as packed as if it's Christmas Eve. The full choir, all ten of them, is up in the loft, and Mr. Gordon is thumping out a tortuous, wheezing piece on the old organ. My family takes up a whole pew today. We call out quiet hellos, wave to our friends and neighbors and sit on the punishing walnut pews, prepared to offer up our suffering to the Lord.

The altar servers come somberly down the aisle, washed and brushed and looking like angels despite the hightop Keds that peek out from under their robes. Tanner Stevenson holds up the crucifix and Kendra Tan carefully swings the incense burner. Father Tim comes in last, resplendent in purple and gold, handsome as a movie star. He sings along with the entrance hymn, but his eyes meet mine, and he gives a little smile around the words to "Lift High the Cross."

For the first time in a very long time, I understand why people come to church. Not because they're forced to be here by their parents, not because the priest is so cute. I listen to the words and don't notice the brogue that pronounces them. For the first time in my adult life, I imagine that there might be something here for me. *Sorry I haven't been around. And sorry about lusting after one of Your guys,* I say silently to God. *No harm, no foul,* I imagine Him saying. It's much more comforting than *That will be a year in hell, young lady.*

At the sign of peace, Father Tim comes off the altar, moving slowly, a kind word for everyone, a blessing for the children. When he gets to the Beaumont clan, he leans in for a chaste hug. "I finally got you in church, Maggie," he says, and I'm touched to see tears in his eyes. "Right when I'm leaving, but here you are."

"We'll miss you, Father Tim," I whisper.

An hour later, Jonah and I are on the *Twin Menace,* the brisk breeze ruffling our hair. In honor of my presence, Jonah has placed a plastic chair on deck, where I now sit, sipping a cup of coffee.

"How's Dad working out?" I ask my brother as he stands at the wheel.

"Not bad," Joe answers. "He likes it. Loves hanging out with the guys. Better than building birdhouses, I guess."

"I think it's nice that you took him on," I say. Jonah looks older at the wheel. This is a side of him that I don't usually get to see. He looks manly, in control. Handsome, too.

"What are you smirking about?" he asks, raising his voice to be heard over the diesel engine.

"Oh, nothing. Just thinking how cute you are, Bunny-boy," I answer, using the nickname Christy and I unfortunately bestowed on him at his birth.

"Right," he says. He waves to Sam O'Neil, who is in front of the *Twin Menace* in the parade of boats.

"Best date you could get was your sistah?" Sam yells.

"At least my sister's pretty!" Jonah calls back. His smile is forced and drops off the minute Sam turns away.

The boats space out a bit more as we head for Douglas Point. The memorial is visible even from a distance, starkly beautiful against the backdrop of pines and stone. The mood becomes somber throughout our flotilla; no one cracks any jokes now. Jonah bows his head as we motor past. His eyes are wet when he looks up.

"Jonah?" I ask. "Is everything okay, buddy?"

"Oh, sure," he says, wiping his eyes on his sleeve. He adjusts course a bit, then shoots me a glance. "Not really," he admits.

"What is it, hon?" I ask. "You've been sort of glum lately."

His face crumples. "Oh, fuck it, Mags. I'm in love with Chantal and she won't give me the time of day."

My eyes pop. "You're what?"

"I know, I know. She's pregnant with some guy's kid

and…and…" It takes him a minute to get the words out. "It's just that I thought… I've always had a thing for her, Maggie. And now I think I'm in love with her."

Uh-oh. Oh, boy. Oh, shit on a shingle. "Jonah," I say carefully, "you didn't sleep with Chantal, did you?"

He swallows, looks at the deck of the boat, then nods. "I know you told her not to hook up with me, Mags. It was just one time. And afterward, she wouldn't return my calls or anything. I wanted to start seeing her, make it more than a one-nighter, you know? But she wasn't interested."

"You gotta be kidding me," I mutter, looking skyward.

It has to be. No wonder she wouldn't tell me. After all those threats, she actually went ahead and did it. With my brother. My *baby* brother. Whose diapers I changed.

The wind blows my hair across my face and makes whitecaps on the water. We're close enough to the town dock that I can see the crowds, catch slips of sound. There's the podium. There's our bear-shaped dad. Father Tim, still in his vestments, flicks holy water and makes the sign of the cross. Reverend Hollis from the Congregational church stands next to him, doing whatever Protestants do at these things.

I heave a sigh, then get up and go to stand next to my brother and rub his back. He chokes out a small sob. "Listen, sweetie," I say. "Did you ever ask Chantal if you were the father of her baby?"

"Yeah, of course I did," he says, wiping his eyes on his sleeve. "She said I wasn't. Said she was sure about it."

"I think she's lying."

Jonah's head snaps back. "What? Why? Do you know something?"

I sigh. "No. She said it was an out-of-towner, but…well, she just might be trying to protect you."

"Why? Why would she do that? Doesn't she—"

"Because, honey, you're twenty-six years old. And she's what, thirty-nine? She said a few things…." My voice trails off. "I bet it's you, Jonah. I think you need to ask her again."

My brother's face lights up in a sudden burst of joy. "Oh, my God, Maggot! Holy shit!" He claps his hands against his head. "Holy shit! Hold the wheel, will you, Mags?" He shoves me against the wheel, then goes aft.

"Jonah! Joe! Come on, you know I'm stupid around boats—"

"Chantal! Chantal!" Jonah bellows, cupping his hands around his mouth. In front of us, Sam's head jerks around.

"Jonah!" I bark. "The boat! I don't know what I'm doing here! We're gonna hit Sam!"

"Chantal!" Jonah yells again, his voice breaking. Heads start turning on the dock. "Chantal!"

Sure enough, we can make her out, her red hair as noticeable as a lighthouse beacon.

"Jonah," I warn, trying to figure out which lever will slow us down, "this is not the time—"

He ignores me. "The baby's mine, isn't it?" he bellows.

"Jesus, Jonah!" I yelp. "Mom's gonna kill you!"

People are pointing and talking, then shushing each other. "I love you, Chantal!" my idiot brother shouts. We're about thirty yards from the dock now, close enough that people definitely hear him. The crowd turns to look at Chantal, who is frozen like a moose about to be hit by a pickup truck.

"Chantal! The baby's mine, isn't it? I love you, I want to marry you!"

"Shut *up,* Jonah!" Chantal yells back.

Oh, to see my mother's face at this moment! I can't help it. I start laughing. I hear a splash, and sure enough, my brother has jumped overboard and is swimming to the dock. If the water is fifty degrees, I'd be surprised.

"Jonah! You fuckin' idiot!" yells Sam.

"Sam, I think I'm gonna hit you!" I call out.

"Steer out to sea, dumb-ass!" he barks.

"Okay, okay! No need for names." I obey, turning the wheel east. The *Twin Menace* cruises away from the parade. I decide to just turn the damn engine off and bob there. Safer than anything else I can think of. Besides, now I can watch.

The blessing has been put on hold as Jonah, always a good swimmer, works his way toward his lady love. He makes it to the dock and someone, Rolly, it looks like, pulls him up. I can't hear him, but I can see my brother clear as day. He pushes his way to Chantal, streaming water, and makes his case, his hands flying. I see her shaking her head, then putting her hand over her mouth. Jonah takes her in his arms and kisses her while my parents look on in stunned horror, and in spite of my reservations about Chantal, I find that my eyes are a bit wet.

Billy Bottoms pulls out of the parade and comes alongside the *Twin Menace* and jumps aboard as neatly as a mountain goat. His son, Young Billy, waves to me from the wheel of their boat.

"Hey theah, deah," Billy says. "Looks like your brothah's gonna be a fathah!"

"Looks like it," I agree, happily surrendering the controls to someone who won't get us killed.

The blessing resumes, albeit completely overshadowed by Jonah's proclamations, and Billy steers us past the dock, where Father Tim and Reverend Hollis dutifully bless us.

"Would you let me off here, Billy?" I ask.

"Sure enough, deah." Billy maneuvers the boat alongside the dock and I jump out. Christy is waiting for me.

"Holy. Mother. Of God!" she proclaims.

"Ayuh," I agree.

"Did you know?"

"Not until about five minutes ago," I say. "Where are they?"

Christy leads me up the ramp and through the crowd. My brother, a blanket draped around his shoulders, is drinking a cup of coffee, gripping Chantal's hand.

"Hello," I say.

"Hey, sis," Jonah says.

"Chantal," I grind out, "didn't I tell you Jonah was off limits?"

She grimaces. "Sorry, Maggie." She looks at the ground. "The damage is done."

"So it's his?" I ask.

"Yeah." She looks nervous, but her hand is in my brother's.

I take a big breath, then another, then take the coffee from my brother and have a long sip. "Well! Looks like I'm going to be an auntie again!"

What the hell. I give Chantal a big hug, because really, what else can I do? "Break his heart and I kill you," I whisper.

"Got it. Oh, Maggie, please forgive me," she whispers back. "He's just so…"

"Spare me the details, okay? He's my baby brother."

"She says she won't marry me, Maggie," Jonah says. "You need to work on her, okay?"

"Why would I do anything for you, idiot?" I ask Jonah, smacking his head. "You stranded me out there."

"And yet here you are." He smiles, his eyes filling with tears. "Thanks, Maggie. For figuring it out."

"You're welcome, dummy." I give him a hug, too. I guess it's not the worst thing in the world that could happen.

And then, aware that just about every single member of Gideon's Cove is standing around us, my vocal cords start doing their special thing.

"I hope you're all proud of yourselves," I announce. "For weeks now, you've been bad-mouthing Malone, spreading rumors, cutting his lines, all because you have nothing better to do than gossip. Shame on you! Malone did nothing except keep his mouth shut, which is more than I can say for anyone else here. Including me."

"It was a logical guess," Stuart speculates. "Malone never denied it."

"Malone shouldn't have to deny anything," I say hotly. "Besides, he wasn't even sleeping with Chantal. He was sleeping with me. So there."

Oops.

A speculative murmur goes up from the crowd. My mother frowns, my dad goes white, Christy grimaces, Jonah laughs.

CHAPTER THIRTY-THREE

WE SPEND the rest of the day as the chief entertainment. *Ah, the Beaumonts, always good for some laughs.* Jonah is beaming with pride. Chantal does a fair amount of eye rolling, but the pall that's been hanging over her is gone. She seems happy. I don't know if she'll stay with Jonah, but hey. Anything is possible.

"Another grandchild, Mom," I comment as the two of us sit at a picnic table.

Mom swats her arm; the blackflies are making themselves known. "Yes," she sighs. "And won't that be nice."

"Are you upset?" I ask tentatively. "I know Jonah's your favorite…."

"Oh, Maggie, don't be silly. Mothers don't have favorites. Someday you'll know that for yourself." She pats my arm. "I'm not upset. It's Jonah's life. I hope things work out for him, but it's really not my problem, is it?"

"I guess not," I murmur.

"I've reached a stage of life, Maggie, where I finally realized that your kids are going to do what they want. My job is done. You don't need me hovering, do you?"

"Well, I guess not, Mom. Not hovering. But still, we want you involved."

My mom smiles, then glances at her watch. "Well, I've got to get going," she says. "It's a long drive." She kisses my cheek, and I stand to hug her. "See you next week, all right, Maggie?"

We've decided to have lunch twice a month, just the two of us. "You bet, Mom. I'm looking forward to it."

"Me, too. Maybe you can get something done about those roots when you come."

Oddly reassured that she's still my insulting mother, I wave as she walks off.

Blessing Weekend is over. Families drift to their cars. Tables are folded, grills extinguished. Noah Grimsley is taking apart the podium. One of Octavio's kids runs past me, calling out a greeting, and then flits away, quick as a hummingbird.

"I've come to say goodbye, Maggie."

"Father Tim," I say. A lump rises in my throat.

"I'll be leaving first thing in the morning."

"Well. Do you have a replacement yet? For St. Mary's?"

"Father Daniels will be filling in until they find someone more permanent," he answers.

"Right." Father Daniels, now retired, is the priest who gave Christy and me our first communions.

"Take care of yourself, Maggie," he says, smiling though his eyes are bright with tears. "If you ever need anything…spiritual, that is…"

I laugh and pat his shoulder. "Take care, Father Tim."

WITH FATHER TIM GONE, the festivities over and everything cleaned up, I go to Joe's and make myself a cup of coffee. Sitting at the corner booth, I look out at the quiet street.

Father Tim's era is over, in my town and in my life; the new phase is waiting to begin. And suddenly I feel the overwhelming urge to see Malone. Before I know it, I'm walking, practically running to the dock. The tide is out and the ramp to the water is steep, but the lobster gods have heard me, because the *Ugly Anne* is pulled right up, not out, not at its mooring, but right there at the end of the dock, as if the fates want me to see Malone. As if it's meant to be. My feet pound against the weathered boards.

"Malone?" I call out, skidding to a stop. His boat is tied stern to dock, the bow furthest from me. A head pops out of the wheelhouse. Not Malone's head.

"Hi," she calls. The new sternman. His daughter.

Her resemblance to Malone is unmistakable—sharp cheekbones, thickly-lashed blue eyes, long and lanky. She's a beautiful, beautiful young woman. How old did Malone say she was? Seventeen?

Whatever force has propeled me this far suddenly falters. Maloner the Loner is lonely no more. Maybe he never was. After all, he's had a marriage, has a child, this lovely creature who's spending the summer with him. He already has his little family. He doesn't need me.

"I'm Emory," she says, picking her way gracefully around the coils of rope that litter the deck. She's wearing cutoff jeans and a tank top and yet she looks like she stepped out of a photo shoot. The lobstermen must be smitten.

I swallow. "Um…hi. Yeah. I'm Maggie."

"Looking for my dad?" she asks pleasantly. I don't answer. *What am I doing here?* I ask myself. If Malone wanted anything from me, he's had weeks to find me.

Emory raises her eyebrows. "Did you want to see Malone?" she repeats, and I feel even more like an idiot.

"Um, yeah. Actually, it's no big...deal. I'll come back—"

"Malone!" she calls. "Someone to see you, cap!"

Malone emerges from the storage area in the bow, wiping his hands on a grease-stained towel. "Aye-aye, skipper," he says, grinning. He snaps the towel at her as he walks past, and she giggles and leaps away.

God, he seems so *happy*. Malone of the scowls and lines has what he needs to be happy, and it ain't me. I briefly consider jumping into the water to escape. Worked for Jonah.

Malone catches sight of me, and the smile on his face falls like a stone. "Maggie."

I take a big breath and release it. "Yup. Hi."

He jumps off the stern onto the dock and puts his hands on his hips, and even though his daughter is watching, I can't help feeling the effect he has on me. My chest feels tight, my eyes hot and dry.

"You met Emory?" he asks.

"Oh, yes. Yup. Sure did. She's...she's...beautiful."

His face softens into a smile as he glances back at the subject of our conversation. I swallow against the lump in my throat. "Yeah," Malone agrees. "So. What's up?"

"Oh...it's—well..." Any plans I had have evaporated. To hide the fact that my hands are shaking, I stuff them in my pockets. "Um, well, guess what? It turns out that Jonah...you know, my brother, well, he's the father of Chantal's baby. And he just figured it out, and they're together, I guess. Sort of. So no one thinks it's you anymore."

His bottom lip is so full and soft-looking among the black razor stubble. Those irritating lashes drop for a moment as Malone looks at the dock.

"You knew, didn't you?" I ask. "About Jonah."

"Ayuh."

"You could've told me, Malone." My voice sounds soft and trembly.

He sighs. "Chantal didn't want me to. I thought you should know, but…well. Not my call." He frowns and looks back at his boat. He starts to say something, then apparently changes his mind.

I give in to my urge to flee. "You know what, Malone? I have to run. But you know, nice seeing you and all. Have a good night." I wave to Emory, who looks as graceful as a swan even as she stuffs a bait bag. "Bye. Nice meeting you." She smiles back, very sweetly, and tears burn in my eyes.

Turning to leave, I actually take a few steps before stopping. I came for a reason, after all. "Listen, Malone," I say, turning around. "Um, I just want you to know that… Listen. I accidentally helped spread that rumor about you and Chantal. I'm sorry for that, and I'm sorry I never gave you the benefit of the doubt. You deserved better."

I force myself not to look away. His face is unsmiling, not exactly scowling, but not happy, either, God knows. "I've been thinking about what you said, too," I continue, my voice unsteady. "About Father Tim and me, and you and me, and me killing time with you…" I'm babbling again. "Well, whatever. I guess I also wanted to say that…" I take a deep breath. "Malone, I never meant to make you feel…inferior. I think you're…well. Not inferior at all." I swallow. "Pretty superior, actually."

If he were to give me anything at that moment, I'd say more. If he smiled, if he took a step toward me, if he *said* something. But he doesn't, just looks at me. Finally, he gives a slight nod. "Thanks," he says quietly.

And that's it. I wait another second, then nod and, painfully aware of my every move, walk back down the dock.

Malone doesn't stop me. He doesn't forgive me, and he lets me go.

"What was that all about?" I hear Emory ask, but though I hear the rumble of his voice, I can't make out the words. I run up the gangplank because I don't want them to know that I'm crying.

OVER THE NEXT FEW DAYS, I feel a bit hollow. After all, I've lost four people in my daily life—Father Tim, my mom, Colonel and Malone. They were a big part of things, even if only for a while. Obviously, my mother falls into a different category, as She Who Gave Me Life, and though we're starting a better phase of our relationship, it's strange to have her gone.

Thank you for everything, God, I say morosely as I clean Mrs. K.'s apartment. *I'm glad I don't have cancer, I haven't amputated a limb, I'm not blind. I'm not an orphan, I have friends, health, home, all that crap.* Then I immediately chastise myself and apologize for calling it crap…but God knows what I mean. I'm not exactly a mystery wrapped in an enigma.

"I think I'm going to take a cooking class," I tell Mrs. K. when I've turned off the Electrolux.

"You're *already* a magnificent cook! Pooh!" she cries staunchly, thumping her cane for emphasis.

"Yes, well, thanks, Mrs. K. But I might like to learn

a bit more, you know? New sauces, new techniques, stuff like that. I'm trying to jazz up the menu at Joe's."

There's a master class being offered in Machias, twice a week for twelve weeks. I've already signed up. French Cooking with a Twist. It sounded fun.

"Well, as long as you *don't* change your *lemon* cake," Mrs. K. says. "Don't tamper with *perfection,* Maggie!"

Maybe at the class, I'll meet some new people. It would be nice to have someone else to pal around with. It's starting to dawn on me that getting out of Gideon's Cove once in a while isn't a bad idea. Chantal and I are still a little tentative with each other, but our friendship will survive her *shtupping* Jonah. After all, he may be my little brother, but he is also a grown-up. Theoretically, anyway.

Christy calls me later in the week. "Listen, I know the last time was a disaster," she says, failing to excite me about what comes next, "but Will knows this nice guy, a drug rep who came into the office last week. Can we give him your number?"

I sigh. I'm stretched out sideways on my bed, a pillow clutched to my side. It's no substitute for Colonel. I need to get another dog. "I don't think so, Christy," I say. "Not for a while. But I'll let you know, okay?"

"Is it Malone?" she asks. I had told her about my visit to the dock.

"Oh, Christy," I confess. "It was one of those things…I didn't realize how much he meant to me until it was too late. Dumb, huh? Stupid Maggie."

"You're not dumb," she chides. "It was a good learning experience. Think of it that way."

"You bet," I say with false bravado. "How are you feeling?"

Christy launches into a description of her fatigue and vomiting, then describes Violet's newest incisor in thrilling detail. I smile. "You still going out tomorrow?" I ask. "It's my day to babysit."

"Only if you want to," Christy says.

"I certainly do."

CHAPTER THIRTY-FOUR

On Sunday, I find myself back at St. Mary's. Christy, Will and Violet sit in the cry room, as Violet has discovered the church's impressive echo and enjoys piercing eardrums during Mass. Father Daniels is on the altar, his roly-poly figure barely contained in the vestments that once swirled gracefully around Father Tim. No danger in falling for Father Daniels, whose resemblance to Jabba the Hutt has been commented on many times.

My mind wanders as I sit there, a feeling of gentle peace engulfing me. The stained-glass windows, the flickering candles, the rock-hard pews and cracked kneelers seem familiar and dear to me. I'm glad I'm here. *This is my church,* I think. Father Tim was just a temp here, but the church belongs to me. Or it could, if I showed up once in a while.

Dear God, I pray as Father Daniels lifts the host high, *please look after my family. And Octavio and his gang and Georgie and Judy and Chantal and all the rest. And thanks for everything.* And this time, I'm sincere.

Mrs. Plutarski gives me the evil eye during the recession, but I don't care. I smile at my neighbors and wait for Christy and Will to fight their way out of the cry room.

"Nice Mass, wasn't it?" I ask.

"Was it?" Christy returns. "I couldn't hear a word. The Robinson twins were screaming the whole time."

We go outside and I stop dead in my tracks, causing Ruth Donahue to crash into me. "Sorry," I mutter.

Malone is leaning against the back of a bench, watching the door. Waiting, it seems, for me.

"Ooh, it's Malone," Christy murmurs. "What's he doing here? Hi, Malone!"

"Hi, Christy," he says. Then his eyes shift to me. "Maggie."

Adrenaline pricks at my joints, making my hands tingle almost painfully. "Hi, Malone," I say, and my voice squeaks. I clear my throat. "Hello."

His hands are cupped over his coat in a rather strange way, I notice, and the lines around his eyes crinkle as I come closer. Hope aches suddenly and sharply in my heart, and I swallow. He looks happy—for Malone, that is. Happy to see me.

Just then, Emory pops over to his side. "I'm starving," she announces in that perfectly confident way beautiful girls have. "Malone, can we get some breakfast? There's a cute little diner down the block." Her eyes light upon me. "Oh, hi. Maggie, right?" She tucks her arm through Malone's.

"Right. Hello," I say. I feel the blush creep up my neck, feeling very much like an outsider.

"Dad? What do you say? Breakfast?"

"Sure, Emory. Give me a second, okay?" Malone says.

An awkward silence falls over our little group. My heart is thudding. A crow calls in a nearby tree. Will clears his throat. "Hey, Maggie, we'll see you later," he says, towing my sister away.

"Right!" Christy says joyfully. "See you later." Her eyes are dancing.

Malone gives his daughter a pointed look. "Em, go find something to do for five minutes," he says.

"Sure, Malone," she says, trotting up the stairs of St. Mary's. We both watch her go, then, because there's no one left to look at, turn to face each other. My face prickles with heat. Malone swallows. It seems neither of us knows what to say.

Then, with one hand still cupping his stomach, Malone reaches into his coat and pulls out a very small puppy.

"For you," he says, handing the warm little bundle of fur to me. "It's a girl."

She's sound asleep, cuddled against my chest before I'm fully aware that I have her. Pale blond fur, silky ears, black nose. I can feel her little spine through her fur...clearly she needs a good meal. "Oh, Malone," I whisper, my eyes filling.

"Ten weeks old. Half yellow Lab. She's had her first shots."

"She's so beautiful. Aren't you, honey? Malone, thank you." I stroke her tiny little head and give Malone a watery smile.

He's not smiling back. He's practically glaring. My smile falters.

"It's Matthew," he growls.

I blink. "I thought you said she was a girl." He doesn't answer. "You want me to name the dog Matthew?"

"No, Maggie," he says, looking away. "That's *my* name."

The dog shifts in my hands and groans, a tiny, funny

sound. She wakes enough to chew on my thumb with her needle-sharp teeth, but I barely notice.

"It was my father's name, too," Malone says, still looking down the block. "My mom called me Little Malone when I was a kid, and then eventually she dropped the 'little.' Since my father knocked us around, I didn't really feel like using his first name anyway, so I just go by Malone."

His longest speech to me by far. Ever, maybe. "Oh," I manage.

His eyes snap back to me. "Maggie," he says, stepping closer. He takes a deep breath. "I've been thinking about what you said, too, about me and how I don't let people in. Talk. Whatever." He rolls his eyes, then swallows. "I'm not really the type, Maggie."

My shoulders drop a little. "Well, I guess not every—"

"But I'm willing to try."

My mouth pops open.

"Seems like I have a thing for you, Maggie," he says quietly, meeting my eyes with some difficulty.

My eyes are suddenly full of tears. "Well, that's great, Malone," I whisper, "because I know I have a thing for you."

Those slashing lines soften as he smiles. "Then why are you crying?" he asks.

"Oh, these are the good tears. Happy, lovey-dovey tears. You know. The kind when things go great and you didn't expect—"

Mercifully, Malone cuts off my words as he kisses me, right there in front of the church, on Main Street, clear as day for anyone to see, an intent, hard kiss that nearly makes me drop the puppy.

"Does this mean you guys are ready? I'm gonna faint soon." Emory is smiling at us from the door of St. Mary's.

"Sure," Malone calls. He puts his arm around my shoulders. "I hear Joe's has the best breakfast in Washington County," he says to me.

"You're right," I answer. My words are so ordinary, but happiness is rolling through me in big, warm waves. "The desserts are excellent, too."

"Good, because I think you still owe me a piece of pie."

He smiles and my heart swells. We walk down the street, the three of us—four, if you count my new puppy—and open the door to Joe's Diner.

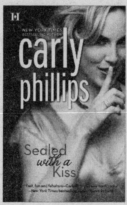

REQUEST YOUR FREE BOOKS!

2 FREE NOVELS
FROM THE ROMANCE/SUSPENSE
COLLECTION PLUS 2 FREE GIFTS!

YES! Please send me 2 FREE novels from the Romance/Suspense Collection and my 2 FREE gifts. After receiving them, if I don't wish to receive any more books, I can return the shipping statement marked "cancel." If I don't cancel, I will receive 4 brand-new novels every month and be billed just $5.49 per book in the U.S., or $5.99 per book in Canada, plus 25¢ shipping and handling per book plus applicable taxes, if any*. That's a savings of at least 20% off the cover price! I understand that accepting the 2 free books and gifts places me under no obligation to buy anything. I can always return a shipment and cancel at any time. Even if I never buy another book from the Reader Service, the two free books and gifts are mine to keep forever.

185 MDN EF5Y   385 MDN EF6C

Name _____ (PLEASE PRINT) _____

Address _____ Apt. #

City _____ State/Prov. _____ Zip/Postal Code

Signature (if under 18, a parent or guardian must sign)

Mail to **The Reader Service:**
IN U.S.A.: P.O. Box 1867, Buffalo, NY 14240-1867
IN CANADA: P.O. Box 609, Fort Erie, Ontario L2A 5X3

Not valid to current subscribers to the Romance Collection,
the Suspense Collection or the Romance/Suspense Collection.

Want to try two free books from another line?
Call 1-800-873-8635 or visit www.morefreebooks.com.

* Terms and prices subject to change without notice. NY residents add applicable sales tax. Canadian residents will be charged applicable provincial taxes and GST. This offer is limited to one order per household. All orders subject to approval. Credit or debit balances in a customer's account(s) may be offset by any other outstanding balance owed by or to the customer. Please allow 4 to 6 weeks for delivery.

Your Privacy: Harlequin is committed to protecting your privacy. Our Privacy Policy is available online at www.eHarlequin.com or upon request from the Reader Service. From time to time we make our lists of customers available to reputable firms who may have a product or service of interest to you. If you would prefer we not share your name and address, please check here. ☐

BOB07

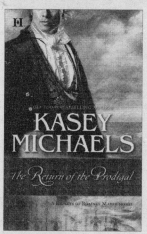

KRiSTAN HiGGiNS

77109	FOOLS RUSH IN	___ $5.99 U.S. ___ $6.99 CAN.
	(limited quantities available)	

TOTAL AMOUNT	$ _____
POSTAGE & HANDLING	$ _____
($1.00 FOR 1 BOOK, 50¢ for each additional)	
APPLICABLE TAXES*	$ _____
TOTAL PAYABLE	$ _____

(check or money order—please do not send cash)

To order, complete this form and send it, along with a check or money order for the total above, payable to HQN Books, to: **In the U.S.:** 3010 Walden Avenue, P.O. Box 9077, Buffalo, NY 14269-9077; **In Canada:** P.O. Box 636, Fort Erie, Ontario, L2A 5X3.

Name: _____
Address: _____ City: _____
State/Prov.: _____ Zip/Postal Code: _____
Account Number (if applicable): _____

075 CSAS

*New York residents remit applicable sales taxes.
*Canadian residents remit applicable GST and provincial taxes.

HQN™

We *are* romance™

www.HQNBooks.com

PHKH1007BL